W9-AGD-934

IT'S MY PARTY

Recent Titles by Cindy Blake from Severn House

GIRL TALK
I SAW YOU FIRST

IT'S MY PARTY

Cindy Blake

This first hardcover edition published in Great Britain 2003 by
SEVERN HOUSE PUBLISHERS LTD of
9–15 High Street, Sutton, Surrey SM1 1DF,
by arrangement with Simon & Schuster UK Ltd.
This first hardcover edition published in the USA 2004 by
SEVERN HOUSE PUBLISHERS INC of
595 Madison Avenue, New York, N.Y. 10022.

Copyright © 1999 by Cindy Blake.

British Library Cataloguing in Publication Data

Blake,   Cindy
    It's my party
    1.   Humorous stories
    2.   Love stories
    I.   Title
    813.5'4 [F]

    ISBN 0-7278-5953-6

Printed and bound in Great Britain by
MPG Books Ltd., Bodmin, Cornwall.

For Benjamin and Siena, the stars of any party, with all my love.

Thanks for chilling me out, holding my hand on take-off, and making me so incredibly proud.

Thanks, too, to my friend and fellow American abroad, Mr McGuire. It's a great name, Stryker. And a lot easier to pronounce than Edinburgh.

Chapter One

He looked out of place the minute he sat down at the table. He was too healthy and far too good looking. He certainly didn't belong in a casino, surrounded by men with grey faces, pot bellies and hooded, bleary eyes. As he put a huge stack of chips down in front of him, he smiled at the other players. No one smiled back. They were too busy coughing and smoking and oozing sweat off oily skin.

What's he doing here? Isabel wondered. Does he have a clue? Or will he lose all his money in five minutes and leave as abruptly and mysteriously as he arrived?

'Hi there,' he addressed the table, still smiling. 'I'm Ed.' Isabel involuntarily rolled her eyes. The men around her successfully hid their smiles. He might as well have said: 'Hi, I'm Ed, I'm the designated sucker tonight!' Introducing yourself at a poker table like this was equivalent to giving the Queen a friendly slap on the bottom. You didn't do it, not unless you were Australian or one of the Spice Girls.

This man was American, she could tell from his accent, so he almost qualified as an Australian, and if he could sing one note, he definitely qualified as a Spice Girl. But whoever he was, he should have known you kept quiet and played your hands and kept your head down when you first sat at a poker table. That was the whole point of the game – don't give anything away, not even your name. And definitely not your smile.

1

Isabel remembered seeing the same kind of disguised smirks on players' faces when she first arrived at the Empire Casino. Here we go, she knew they were all thinking. A woman on her own, out of her depth, probably just slumming for a night. Easy prey for the sharks. We'll be more than happy to take her money from her and send her home to Daddy or whoever is financing this whim. But she'd been very quiet and very careful and had shown within a short time that she knew exactly what she was doing. Now she was one of the sharks herself, eyeing up this newcomer's pile of chips and working out exactly how soon all of it would be hers.

'Who's Surfer Boy?' Micky, sitting on her left, nudged Isabel. 'Does he belong to you?'

Isabel shook her head.

'Yeah, so why are you staring at him like that, Iz? You never stare at me like that. Is it because he's handsome and I'm not? Are you a shallow woman? Are you going to break my poor, ailing heart and run off with Surfer Boy?'

'Micky – your heart is in perfect shape, you know that. It's in perfect shape because you've never used it.'

Micky laughed and began to whistle *Surfin' USA* between puffs on his cigar.

This is what I love, Isabel thought. Being one of the boys, part of this group of tough men who look as though they are all relatives of the Kray twins, trading insults and smart remarks. I should be out at wine bars or restaurants with friends, I should spend my Saturday nights at films or plays or parties. But I come here instead, to a place where nobody knows your last name or what you do for a living or anything except whether you're the type who raises with aces or check-bets with them.

What would my friends say if they knew? What would David say? There's no need to ask the question, actually. The answer is obvious. They'd be horrified. They'd all say I was a compulsive, addicted gambler, like my father. They'd say I need help. Shrinks would be called. People would worry and fuss and give me the number of Gamblers Anonymous. No. This is my secret. And it's going to stay a secret.

Isabel folded the cards she'd been dealt and looked at the man named Ed again. He wasn't nervous, she could see; he seemed self-confident and relaxed, unaware that he was the object of ridicule at the table. No, he doesn't have a clue, she thought as she watched him look at his cards. He isn't shielding them properly and the man to his right can see exactly what he's holding. She had seen it happen before – she'd seen players cheat by stealing glances at other players' cards, but then someone at the table had always said something, warned the victim to hide his hand, without actually accusing anyone of cheating and thereby creating a major incident. Major incidents slowed down play. Isabel had often heard the story of the time a man had had a heart attack at one of the blackjack tables in the Empire. People calmly stepped over his prostrate body and placed their bets.

Each time she'd heard this tale, Isabel had tried desperately not to envision the scene. She'd tried to laugh along with whoever was telling it, but she couldn't bring herself to. All she could see was the body of her father – not at the blackjack table in London, but at the roulette wheel in Las Vegas. That was where he'd keeled over and where he had died. She saw gamblers nonchalantly stepping over him, putting chips on numbers, ignoring everything except the action. Her father would have approved, she knew. He wouldn't want the play to stop because of him. On the contrary. He'd just be pissed off that he couldn't see which number came up on the wheel. Yet that didn't make the image less terrible for Isabel; it only made her ask herself yet again what was driving her to come to these clubs and sit at these tables and gamble like her crazy, doomed father.

Because I like it and I'm good at it, she answered herself. I'm not crazy and I'm not doomed. I have this under control. It's not a problem.

Now, though, no one was telling 'Surfer Boy' to hide his cards; they were playing on as if they hadn't noticed. Isabel knew she couldn't be the only one to have spotted the cheating, but there was a conspiracy of silence. Was it because Ed was a blond vision of health and fitness? Isabel wondered. Did the other men resent and envy him his good looks and easy manner? And what if she told him to be more careful? Would they then feel that she had somehow betrayed them, turned into a foolish girlie at the sight of a handsome face?

'Izzy – wakey wakey! It's up to you,' Micky said. She quickly pushed another hand of useless cards into the middle of the table and continued to watch the play in progress. The Cheater was a man she'd seen before, but only a few times. He was fat and loud and a lousy player; the kind of man she especially enjoyed beating. When he raised and Ed then called him, Isabel stood up and grabbed her bag.

'I'll be back in a minute,' she said to Micky, who nodded.

The club was particularly crowded that night and Isabel had to wend her way through throngs of roulette and craps players before getting to the stairs and then out of the foyer and onto the street. Use of mobile phones wasn't allowed in casinos for obvious reasons, so she walked around the corner before she pulled hers out and dialled.

'The card room, please,' she said when the receptionist answered. While she waited to be put through, she tried to decide whether to disguise her voice or not. Matthew, the card room manager, would answer, she knew, and he would recognize her immediately unless she put on some kind of accent. Although Matthew was discreet in normal circumstances, she also knew he was curious about her, sometimes too curious. Via Micky, who was Isabel's main link to the casino grapevine, she'd heard that Matthew had been asking if anyone knew what she did for a living or whether she was married and if so to whom.

'Card room,' Matthew announced in her ear.

'Hi there. Could you page Ed on Table Ten, please?' Isabel had raised the pitch of her voice and put on an American accent herself.

'Hold on.'

She waited as she heard the page for Ed and then waited another few minutes until Ed came on the line.

'Hello? Who's this?' he asked, clearly baffled.

'I'm the woman at the table with you. You aren't hiding your cards and the man on your right can see them. He's cheating.'

'He's what?' The voice was outraged and Isabel sighed.

'Look – don't make a fuss about it, all right? You're new here and this kind of thing happens. Just keep your cards hidden from now on and don't for God's sake tell anyone I made this call.' They think you're a wimp as it is, she almost added. If they knew a woman had bailed you out, they'd never let you live it down.

'Oh, I get it.' Ed said. 'It's like an initiation thing.'

'What?'

'It happens to everyone the first time they play here.'

'No. It happens to people who don't keep their cards to themselves,' Isabel retorted.

'Right. OK. Thanks. Thanks for telling me. I appreciate it.'

'Right.' Isabel hit the button to end the call and put the phone back in her bag. She hadn't meant to be quite so abrupt with him, but she couldn't help herself when he'd said 'it happens to everyone'. Undoubtedly he'd thought he could waltz in to the casino and make a killing without knowing the first thing about what he was doing; he had the demeanour of someone who was used to winning effortlessly in all aspects of life. How many women were waiting by telephones right now, hoping he'd ring and ask them out? Isabel dreaded to think.

By the time she'd returned to the card room, she almost regretted helping him. She could see, as she approached Table Ten, that he was now holding his cards in such a way he probably couldn't even see them himself. When she sat down in her seat, he lifted his head, looked across the table at her and nodded.

Isabel wanted to scream at his pathetic lack of subtlety; instead she turned her glance away quickly, her eyes ending up straight in the path of the Cheater's nasty stare. She stared right back, unflinching. When the Cheater finally gave up and focused on his cards, Micky touched her knee with his.

'Rescue Surfer Boy, did you?' he whispered.

'Not me,' she whispered back.

'Don't bluff a bluffer, Izzy.'

'I wouldn't dare,' she smiled.

The run of cards she had from that point on made her think some divine spirit was rewarding her for a good deed. She couldn't lose, and the rush of adrenaline built every time she picked up her hand.

'It's better than sex, isn't it, Iz?' Hermes, two seats away from her, asked after she'd raked in yet another pile of chips.

'How would you know, Hermes? You've never had it in your life,' Micky said.

'I've never had cards like that in my life, no,' Hermes replied with an exaggerated sigh. Everything about Hermes was exaggerated, Isabel thought. His tan was so deep he looked like a walking advertisement for a high-powered sunbed, his toupee didn't merely disguise a bald head, it swamped it in a towering mass of black curls, and just in case someone might forget he had been named after a Greek God, he wore a chunky gold necklace emblazoned with the name 'Hermes' in flowing letters. Isabel was fascinated by this necklace. Had he had it made for himself or had someone given it to him? A girlfriend? His mother? Did he ever remove it?

'Shut up and deal, will you?' Charlie, at the other end of the table, barked. 'You're like a couple of old women, you two. We all know neither of you have ever had sex and are never likely to, so let's get on with it. Let's give Izzy some more money. She's having a good time here. Deal her another pair of aces, Hermes. And watch the rest of us suffer.'

Hermes didn't deal her aces, but he did deal her an ace and a king, the next best hand. Isabel waited for her turn and raised the pot a hundred pounds. There was a collective sigh around the table and hands quickly tossed aside.

'I'll call that hundred,' Ed said, when his turn came. 'And raise. Two hundred.'

'You can't do that.' Charlie sat back in his chair with a frown. 'If you're going to raise, you have to raise first. You can't call and then raise.'

'I can't?'

Charlie put his hands over his eyes and shook his head. A small fan placed in front of him was supposed to blow the smoke away from his face, but Isabel always wondered why he bothered. The fan was useless in these basement rooms filled with men and women puffing away; all it did was circulate the smoke more. And Charlie looked as if he'd been on fifty cigarettes a day since birth anyway. His face had a Dickensian mortician's pallor, his teeth were a rotting pumpkin colour and he coughed like a tubercular patient. If he'd given up smoking, he'd come to the one place in the world where it wouldn't make the slightest difference.

'You can't call and raise,' he repeated, taking his hands away from his eyes and staring at Ed with disgust. 'You call. Or you raise. You don't do both.'

'OK.' Ed grinned. 'Whatever. I call.'

Isabel had been observing Ed's play and knew he was loose with his money and liked to bluff. Occasionally during the evening he'd try one of these bluffs and then look at her, after the bluff had failed and he'd lost the hand, with an insouciant expression. Look at me, I take risks was what Isabel decided he was trying to convey. I may have been a little stupid about not hiding my cards, but I'm not timid. I don't care whether I lose. I don't care whether you see me lose. I like to challenge people. And I always win in the end. In fact he hadn't lost a great deal, but enough to make a fair dent in his massive pile of chips.

Everyone else had dropped out of the pot, so it was just her and Ed. When the next three cards were dealt face up on the table, Isabel was careful not to move in any way or let so much as an eyelid flicker. There, in front of her, were two aces and a king, giving her a full house.

7

'Check,' she said immediately.

'Three hundred pounds.' Ed pushed the chips into the middle of the table.

Right, Isabel thought. I have to figure he has two kings in his hands, so he has a full house too. But mine beats his. He can't win. The worst that can happen is that he has an ace-king too and we split the pot. He's fallen into my check-raise trap and I'm going to squeeze him. If anyone thinks I was the one who told him about the cheating, they'll know I'm not so soft I won't take every chip he has left.

'Raise,' she said. 'Another three.'

Isabel watched as Ed picked up the chips in front of him. He turned them over and over in his hand, then looked up at her, with a cocky smile on his face.

'I raise too.' He glanced over at Charlie. 'I can do that, right?'

'You certainly can.' Charlie turned and winked at Isabel.

'Here—' Ed pushed his chips into the middle. 'That's all I have left. That's your three hundred and five hundred more.'

'Call.' Isabel picked out five hundred pounds' worth of chips and threw them into the pot.

'On their backs then,' Micky ordered.

'On their backs?' Ed stared at Micky.

'You're all in, mate. No more betting. Turn over your cards. Now we see what you have.'

'I can't get more money?'

'Jesus,' Charlie muttered. 'No. You play with what you have at the table. If you want to get more chips after this hand is finished, you can, and then you can come back and sit down again. But not now. You're all in. Turn over your cards.'

Ed revealed two kings and Isabel couldn't stop a tiny corner of her mouth from turning up. She showed her ace-king, folding her arms after she'd done so. Micky began to whistle *Sloop John B* and Hermes said: 'Where's your lottery ticket, Izzy? I bet you've won that tonight too.'

'Has she won?' Ed looked from Hermes to Charlie. 'I have a full house.'

'And so does she,' Charlie replied. 'Aces up – you have kings up.'

'There's no way I can win?'

'No,' Charlie smiled. It was the first time Isabel had seen Charlie look positively happy.

Hermes quickly dealt the next two cards. A five of hearts and a queen of spades came up.

'I guess that's the end of me.' Ed watched Isabel pull the chips toward her. 'There's no point getting more money when it's not my night. Thanks, everybody. I really enjoyed playing.'

'Come anytime,' Charlie said cheerfully. 'We'll be glad to see you again.'

'I will.' Ed nodded. 'I'll do that.' He stood up, took his jacket off the back of his chair and made his way round the table, towards the exit. As they were all watching him depart, he suddenly detoured from his path and came back. When he reached Isabel's seat, he stopped and leaned over her shoulder. 'You've won so much, you wouldn't mind coming to the bar for a drink with me, would you? I think you owe me after that pot you won. At least one glass of wine.'

'Thanks, but I don't think so,' Isabel said.

'Come on,' Ed smiled. 'I'll buy.'

'No, thank you.'

'What if I also did a backflip?' His smile turned into a grin. 'In the bar? Would that be enough to impress you?'

'The bar's not big enough.' Isabel looked straight at him, but her face was deliberately blank.

'You mean it's not big enough for both of us?'

'I mean it's not big enough to do a backflip in.' She wasn't going to budge or move one facial muscle. Having him come on to her here, in front of the table, was embarrassing. Even if she'd felt like saying yes, she wouldn't have. She was a poker player, not a woman looking for a date. The teasing she would get the next time she came in, if she did go to the bar with Ed, would be merciless.

'I bet you it is big enough.' Ed narrowed his eyes. 'Fifty pounds says it is.'

'I'll take you up on that,' Micky said quickly.

'Honestly, I don't want to have a drink. Or watch you perform acrobatics. I'm staying here.' Isabel returned her gaze to the cards on the table.

Ed tapped her on the shoulder and said: 'I bet *you* can't do a backflip.'

'You'd lose on that one, too.' Isabel turned to Hermes. 'Whose deal is it, anyway?'

'Whoa,' Ed addressed Micky. 'You know something? I bet she can. I bet she does a mean backflip.'

There was a different tone to his voice when he said this; Isabel could hear an affection in it which threw her off balance for a second. She almost turned round to look at him again, but then Micky began to hum *Help Me, Rhonda*, and Hermes barked: 'Your deal, Charlie.'

'I'll be back,' Ed said to no one in particular and then walked away from the table, putting his jacket on as he did so.

'Christ, Isabel,' Charlie remarked when Ed was out of earshot. 'You could have left a few pieces of him for the rest of us to pick up.'

'Sorry, Charlie.'

'I bet you are. I can see the remorse. It shines out of you.'

The cards turned against her then and Isabel spent another hour folding bad hands. When she had had enough, she left the table and went to the upstairs bar for a drink on her own, to celebrate a close to perfect night.

'Izzy—' Micky appeared at her side as she finished her glass of white wine. 'I want to ask you something.'

'Go ahead.' She hoped that he wasn't going to ask her again whether she'd been the one to tip Ed off; she didn't like lying to him, but she had an instinctive desire never to tell anyone the truth of that incident.

Micky sat on the stool beside hers and began to twirl from side to side.

'Yes, Micky?'

'Yeah. This is a serious question, Iz. I need a little time.' He stopped twirling and asked the bartender for a vodka and tonic. Isabel was silent as the bartender fixed it and then placed it in front of Micky.

'You brushed that wanker off good and proper,' he finally said after twirling the glass around as he had been twirling himself.

'I didn't want to have a drink with him.'

'No. Not even though—' he stopped and grabbed a handful of peanuts from the little tray beside him. 'Look, Iz, I may get a gig in Vegas.'

'That's fantastic, Micky.'

Six months before, when Micky had told her he made his living by boxing professionally, Isabel had needed her best poker face not to break into a smile of disbelief. He could have been in his late thirties, but was more likely past forty; his waistline was far from trim and he smoked cigars continually. Perhaps, she had thought, he was the Gazza of the boxing ring – a once-bright talent gone to seed. His nose was obviously the victim of a few punches, but Isabel had believed these had been delivered in pubs, not the gym. His claim to be boxing still, and making a living out of it, at first amused her and then worried her. If he was still fighting, it could only be as a punching bag for the real contenders. She hated to think of Micky being hurt.

'Yeah. A big fight. It's a big deal. Sky and all.' When Isabel looked blank, he said, 'You know. Sky television.'

'Fantastic. Really. I'm pleased for you.' She didn't want to ask him whom he was fighting or when this fight was supposed to take place. Certain that he was making it all up, she was loathe to press him for details and catch him out somehow.

'Yeah. So I was thinking. You know. We could get married and you could come to Vegas with me. We could get married in Vegas. You know. It would be fun.' He wasn't looking at her, but staring intently at the peanuts in his hand. 'I know you're younger and everything. And I'm not a prize the way some blokes are, but we get along great, Iz. It works. You're all small and dark-haired and thin and I'm big and fair and chunky. We balance each other out, you know? We'd make a good team.'

Isabel wasn't sure what to say. A proposal? Micky had never displayed anything but good-natured friendliness toward her. He had never tried to hit on her, never asked her out. Sometimes they'd have a drink together and talk poker, but for all she knew he could have a wife and five children tucked away in a house in the country. Did he really picture the two of them in a chapel in Las Vegas? Had he been working up to this moment for a long time? The thought made her feel so anxious on his behalf she kept silent in case she said something wounding.

'You know how married couples normally have nothing to talk about after a few years?' Micky looked up from his peanuts. 'We wouldn't have to worry about none of that. We just get a pack of cards out, right? And if we're out, if we're playing here, for example, one of us wins, we both win. You see?'

'I don't know, Micky.' She paused, trying to decide how best to answer him. She was desperate not to hurt his feelings, but the best option, to make a joke of it, might do just that. It was the first marriage proposal she'd ever received and she was flabbergasted. 'This is a little sudden, don't you think? I mean, we don't know each other very well.'

'Exactly.' He popped a few peanuts in his mouth. 'That's what I was thinking too. So I was thinking maybe we should take the car for a test drive, if you see what I mean. Maybe have sex a couple of thousand times before we get married, to see if it works.'

'Micky!' Isabel burst out laughing. 'You bastard.' She punched him on the arm.

'Hey—' Micky rubbed his arm. 'That's precious flesh you've just hurt. You can't blame a bloke for trying. I mean, most of the time I forget you're a woman, but sometimes I remember. Like tonight when Surfer Boy was trying to pull you. I felt like he was jumping the queue, you know.'

'Is that the line you always use on women? A marriage proposal?'

'Listen, you'd be surprised. It gets them thinking. You should have seen your face before.'

'What if I'd said yes, what if I'd accepted your proposal?'

'Yeah, Iz. Like that was in the cards. Don't bluff a bluffer, remember?' Micky reached for his glass, clinked it with hers and took a long drink.

'Do you realize that's the first time anyone has proposed to me? And it was a joke? My feelings are really hurt.' Isabel made a face and sniffed.

'Izzy, ninety-nine per cent of proposals *are* jokes, sometimes it just takes a long time to get to the punchline. And I can see how cut up you are. It's fucking painful. Anyway, you haven't answered my question.'

'What? The – how did you put it – test drive?'

'Yeah, the test drive.'

'It's such a compliment, being compared to a car.'

'There's worse things.'

'Micky—' Isabel shook her head.

'Oh, OK. Forget it. Forget I asked. But promise me something, Iz.'

'What?'

'Promise me if you ever decide to – you know – with one of us, promise me it won't be Hermes.'

Tilting her head and scratching it, Isabel waited for a long time before saying, 'I don't know, Micky. That's an awful lost to ask. You're going to owe me if I do promise.'

'You're having me on, right?'

Isabel shrugged.

'Come on. You're not serious. You can't fancy Hermes. You don't, do you?'

Isabel smiled. 'Gotcha,' she said. 'One all. We're even on the night.'

'You bitch.' Micky reached out and punched her lightly on the arm. 'You know something, we *would* make a good team. I'd propose again, but then I happen to know all the chapels in Vegas are booked up for the next fifty years.'

13

'What a shame,' Isabel sighed.

'Isn't it? Iz – I've been meaning to ask you something else. You can't really do a backflip, can you?'

Putting her elbow on the bar and resting her head against her hand, Isabel said: 'How much would you like to bet?'

Chapter Two

When Isabel went to work on Monday mornings, she often thought that if she'd set out to have a split personality, she couldn't have chosen a better way to cultivate one. The difference between the Empire Casino and her office on the Old Brompton Road was so stark she sometimes found herself holding her breath in order to re-program her thinking before she walked in. No one smoked at *Party Time*, the people working there dressed smartly, flowers were strategically placed on all available table tops; and, perhaps the most telling point of all, there were windows which actually let in light.

Instead of listening to tales of bad beats at poker hands and boxing matches in Las Vegas, Isabel heard, the moment she sat down in her office, what had happened at various parties given over the weekend. Had the food been perfect, had the music been perfect, had the event gone as well as she and David Barton, her partner, had planned it to go? After re-hashing and dissecting the parties already given, she'd then go into David's office to talk about what was coming up next on their schedule.

She liked having this time with Tamsin, her assistant, before seeing David; she needed it, because each time she saw David again after a weekend away, she had the same wrenching feeling of hopelessness. She would look at him, sitting in his old-fashioned wooden chair, dressed in one of his conservative suits and ties, always wearing a white shirt, and she would immediately think: he's mine, before immediately acknowledging he wasn't hers and probably never would be. She'd then have trouble focusing on what he was saying because she was busy berating herself for being one of those women she used to think were pathetically feeble, the type who swooned over an unobtainable man, the kind who spent her life daydreaming about the impossible.

'Get a grip,' she would lecture herself. 'Don't be silly. He's not a pop star and you're not thirteen years old. This is ridiculous. This isn't like you.' The problem was that at the same time as she was telling herself this, she was wondering whether in fact it *was* like her, exactly like her. She knew that Isabel Sands was not supposed to be an emotional mess, she was supposed to be the person who cleaned up other people's messes, but she also knew that she had a huge capacity for embracing irrational passions and believing the unbelievable.

When she was five years old, her father had pointed to a building on the Cromwell Road and said: 'That's where I started my ice cream business. That building is good luck. Make a wish on it.' Isabel had made a wish, the same wish she then made every single time she passed that building: 'I wish no one I love ever dies.'

When her father dropped dead in Las Vegas, she felt personally betrayed by that building. It hadn't kept up its end of the deal. But she also felt bereft. She missed having it, her own secret, special pile of bricks. So she transferred her allegiance. She picked another building, this one a newsagent's on the Kings Road where she had once found a ten-pound note lying on the floor, and now every time she passed it she made sure to give a quick wave and nod in its direction, not for immortality, but for luck.

Isabel would have liked to think of herself as a rational, sane 29-year-old woman who had a good career and a healthy emotional life, but how could she when she knew perfectly well she was the same 29-year-old woman who had a secret, heart-threatening passion for David Barton, who made secret wishes on buildings and who secretly went to a casino every weekend on her own to gamble?

Was gambling a rogue gene she'd inherited from her father? Was it in her blood? Why did she feel happier at a poker table than anywhere else in her life? She tried to tell herself it wasn't an addiction, that poker wasn't like roulette or blackjack because you weren't trying to beat the House, you were competing against other human beings. Playing poker wasn't the same as making impossible wishes and being ridiculously superstitious. It was a sport that required skill, psychology and the odd bit of luck. But if she wasn't addicted, why couldn't she *not* go on the occasional Saturday night? And why did she get such a rush of pleasure every time she went down those casino stairs?

Each Saturday morning she'd wake up resolved not to visit the Empire that evening, knowing full well she wouldn't be able to hold to it. She'd turn down any Saturday night invitations, skipping even important events like friends' birthdays. The fact that she generally won rather than lost money made her reason to herself that she was simply moonlighting, that poker was only another job. Yet she knew she was hooked. So how could she be surprised that she was equally hooked on another addiction – a married man? Sometimes she thought the only difference between her love for poker and her love for David Barton was the fact that she won playing poker and lost every time she saw David.

David was the worst hand she'd ever been dealt, but she couldn't bring herself to fold those cards any more than she could allow herself to pass the newsagent's without waving.

'He caged them, Isabel,' David said on this Monday morning, slapping the top of his desk with the palm of his hand while she accustomed herself yet again to the disturbing effect of seeing him after a weekend away. 'Stryker McCabe fattened up the pheasants like the witch fattened up Hansel, caged them, and then set them free when the guns were standing waiting for them. Can you imagine? The poor buggers were massacred in the thousands. They didn't stand a chance, even against some idiotic hairdressers from Los Angeles who have never shot a bird in their lives.'

'I thought they were stockbrokers from New York,' Isabel said, thinking: this is a deviation from the norm. Usually when I come in to see him, we discuss *our* parties, not a pheasant shoot organized by a competitive company. And I've never seen him so visibly irritated. David is not a desk-slapper, he doesn't even use his hands when he's talking. Why is he so upset?

'New York, Los Angeles, hairdressers, stockbrokers, what's the difference? The point is he *cheated*. Stryker McCabe and his company cheated. Those Americans came over to shoot game, not to fish in a bathtub. It's grotesque.'

Isabel nodded. It was grotesque, David was right. The problem was it was also grotesquely successful. If you organize a shooting party for a group of rich Americans, you want them to shoot plenty of pheasants so that they can go home with tales of their amazing prowess. You don't want to leave anything to chance. She looked behind David, to the wall of photographs decorating his office. They were all pictures of happy partygoers in various poses – holding glasses of champagne, dancing, in animated conversations – and they were all tangible proof of fun times and satisfied customers. The men at this shooting party would have their own photographs of themselves standing holding bunches of dead birds; if they didn't have these, *they* would feel cheated.

That's bizarre, she thought, remembering two nights before at the Empire. Cheating at poker is obviously wrong. But is it wrong when you're giving people exactly what they paid for? David thinks so. But then David would have called that man a cheater to his face; he wouldn't have sneaked round the corner and made a phone call.

'Did the Americans know the pheasants had been caged?' she asked.

'No. Of course not. They thought they were shooting in the time-honoured fashion, with beaters flushing the birds out of the woods. They didn't see the cages. All they saw was a bunch of unbelievably obese pheasants flying straight at them. And you know what else Stryker McCabe did? And by the way, I think he made up that name. I don't believe for a minute he was actually

christened Stryker. It's a cheat as well. Anyway, this party-
organizer extraordinaire, Mr Stryker McCabe, hired so-called
beaters to *pretend* they were doing their job – a group of angelic
twelve-year-old boys, who came in at drinks time dressed in rags
with grimy faces and sang *Food Glorious Food* in their best Oliver
Twist voices.'

'You're joking.' Isabel laughed.

'I am not. James told me; he had it from one of the gamekeepers.
Believe me, it's all the horrible truth. The Americans thought they
were poverty-stricken village boys and took up a collection for
them afterwards. Can you believe it? I mean, those boys are
probably at Eton, dressed in tails, as we speak. No doubt they used
the money to buy fags from the corner shop.'

'Or porno videos.'

'Probably both. *And* he hired actors to be waiters at dinner. He
made these actors watch *Remains of the Day* ten times and told
them to play Anthony Hopkins as they passed the potatoes. Could
someone please tell me the point of that little exercise?'

'I don't know,' Isabel sighed. 'I suppose McCabe thinks
Americans expect British servants to be just like Anthony
Hopkins.'

'I would have thought they'd expect waiters to be waiters. Full
stop.'

'It could have backfired on him. I mean, the waiters might have
suddenly switched Anthony Hopkins characters and turned into
Hannibal Lecter. That could have caused some trouble at
mealtimes.'

David laughed and Isabel felt inordinately pleased with herself.
She knew instinctively what to say to David; she knew how to
make him laugh and how to calm him down. His face didn't fit well
with fury; it was not part of his nature and she hated to see anger
creep into his pale brown eyes. Did anyone else notice how anger
affected him, how he'd hunch his shoulders and rub his right wrist
with his left thumb? Had anyone made as detailed a study of David
as she had? Isabel had catalogued every move of his, every twitch

and mannerism. I could write a thesis on him, she thought. Could his wife say the same? Now he was smiling ruefully, tapping the desk with the tips of his fingers.

'I know I shouldn't get so worked up. I can't bear the man, that's all. It's not that he and his company are competition. I don't mind that in the slightest. It's the underhanded way in which he competes.'

'We play by the rules and Stryker McCabe doesn't,' Isabel said. 'But he won't win, David. All these tricks of his might work in the short term, but not in the long run. People will catch on. They'll know he's a fraud.'

'You know what I hate most? The idea that these Americans weren't given the chance to fight fairly. Perhaps they could have shot the pheasants without all that extra help. McCabe is patronizing them when he rigs it in their favour. It's as if he were giving a party for children, not adults. He's deciding what *he* thinks is good for them. Oh—' David shook his head. 'I'm probably not making any sense whatsoever, am I?'

'No, you are,' Isabel quickly replied. 'You are making sense,' she then repeated, hoping this would make him realize how well she understood him. 'I know exactly what you're saying.'

'You do, don't you? Because you're like me, Isabel. You wouldn't stoop to using Stryker McCabe's methods either. I often think—' His voice didn't trail off, it disappeared entirely. Go on, she willed him silently. Tell me what you often think. Don't look out of the window like that, look at me.

'I used to wonder about you, you know.' His gaze was still averted, but his tone of voice was so intimate she could have sworn he had phenomenal peripheral vision and was watching her carefully.

'When you first approached me, I wasn't sure what your motives were, whether you were more interested in the potential profit of the business or the business itself. Now I know that we're on the same wavelength, but back then, back at the beginning I thought – well, I thought you might be a little bit of a spoiled brat. No offence. You know how I feel now.'

A spoiled brat. Isabel flinched. Had he really thought that of her? Was that his memory of their 'first' meeting? If so, it differed wildly from Isabel's, but then she knew he believed their first meeting had occurred eight months ago, when in fact they'd met fifteen years before on a day when David Barton had treated her as anything but a spoiled brat.

She'd been a bridesmaid at the wedding of a much older cousin whom she hardly knew. A fourteen-year-old bridesmaid decked out in a hideous Laura Ashley floral dress, feeling out of place and ridiculous. Isabel, a tomboy, a girl who could beat almost any boy her age in any running race, had been forced into this absurd dress, and had walked down the aisle of a huge church with what seemed like a million people watching. She'd tried her hardest not to make faces and to look dignified, but it wasn't easy. Her father had left her mother six months before and she didn't believe in all this wedding business, the 'happy ever after' vows the blissful couple made at the altar. All she wanted to do was make a run for home, put on some jeans and get away from the circus of flowers and smiles and photographs. But she knew that would only upset her mother, who had signed her up for this bridesmaid job, and she didn't want to do that, so she clutched the bouquet of pink roses she had to hold and kept smiling.

At the reception afterwards, she sat at one of the tables and tried to laugh along with the speeches. They were interminable and boring and unfunny. But it didn't end, as Isabel had hoped, when the last speech was over; it carried on mercilessly. The couple had hired a band. There was dancing. Her mother had come down with a bad cold at the last minute and wasn't there to look after her, she didn't know any of the other guests, and the people at her table had wandered off to socialize, leaving Isabel on her own, watching as men and women jived on the dance floor. She sat, feeling abandoned and foolish and lonely, studying the bride and groom as they danced to a slow song. He was holding her close; she was looking at him with adoration. Isabel began to cry and the second she began to cry she dived under the table to hide. For five minutes she was on her knees sobbing, unable to stop herself, not knowing what had sparked these terrible tears. When she controlled herself finally and surfaced, she grabbed a napkin, wiped her face and looked around anxiously to see if anyone else had noticed. No one had.

For the next ten minutes she sat chewing her knuckles and making remarks to herself about the idiocy of adults, who thought they looked fabulous on the dance floor when they actually looked like uncoordinated aliens. Somehow that cheered her up, and she was concentrating on an obviously drunk woman who looked as if she was going to fall on her face at any moment, when she heard a voice say: 'Wrong lighting. They've got the lighting all wrong.' She looked over to the man who had said this; he was sitting two chairs away from her at the otherwise empty table. She hadn't noticed his arrival, but then she'd been intent on the flailing, about-to-topple drunk.

'What's wrong with the lighting?' she asked, genuinely interested. It was the first comment she'd heard all day that wasn't about the joys of married love.

'Sorry,' he said, looking back at her. 'I didn't meant to say that out loud. But the lighting is too bright.'

'Right,' she nodded, looking around her at the lights. He *was* right. They were too bright.

'And the flowers on the tables – they have too much scent. They're overpowering.'

Isabel nodded again.

'I'm sorry.'

Why did he keep apologizing to *her*? Isabel wondered. He looked to be in his early or mid-twenties; it was hard for Isabel to tell exactly, but that was her guess. She waited for him to get up and leave her alone again, and was surprised when he didn't.

'I don't mean to be rude about the wedding,' he continued. 'But I've started working for a company that organizes parties and so I have a critical eye, I suppose.'

He was talking to her as if she counted, as if she were his age, and that made her suddenly self-conscious.

'These dresses—' she waved her hand at herself dismissively. 'They're the worst.'

'They're not good.' He smiled. 'But then I don't think I've ever seen a bridesmaid's dress that was good. Maybe brides don't want to be upstaged?'

'Shit. I hadn't thought of that.' Why had she said 'shit'? Now he'd give her a lecture about language and young girls and she'd have to hate him. She didn't want to hate him.

'Well, that's just a theory of mine. I could be wrong.'

'I think you're right. Definitely.' What else could she say to hold his interest? How could she keep this conversation going?

'What did you think of the canapés?' was the only question she could think of. 'Did you like them or not? I thought they were sort of messy. I mean, it was hard to eat them in one mouthful but you think you should, so you end up with a full mouth and look like a pig, you know?'

'Exactly.' He smiled again. 'That's exactly what I was thinking.'

'And this tent,' she said, gaining courage with every word. 'It's stuffy in here. It's so hot.'

'Not enough ventilation. Ventilation is crucial, especially in the summer.'

'Especially if you're going to have people dancing,' she added.

'You know something?' He narrowed his eyes as he looked at her. 'You're a very shrewd person. You'd be a terrific party organizer yourself.'

Isabel blushed.

'I'm David.' He held out his hand to shake hers. 'David Barton.'

'Isabel.' She shook it. 'Isabel Sands. That must be fun – organizing parties.'

David Barton shrugged. 'Yes,' he said. 'But it wasn't what I had planned to do with my life. I wanted to be a photographer, but I'm not good enough, not really. I have an eye for detail, but I can't translate it into photographs the way I should. Not to my

exactly why she hadn't done well on a test or why she was sulking in her room listening to music, instead of cleaning it up as her mother had told her to do. He was like a charm on an invisible bracelet; one she treasured and would never share. No one else knew about David Barton. She hadn't said a word about him to her mother or to her friends. They wouldn't have taken him as seriously as she did, she knew. They might even try to tarnish his image.

That image didn't stop her from dating boys or having relationships with men as she grew older, but she used him as a litmus test.

Whenever she met a man she fancied, she asked herself if he would bother to talk to a lonely fourteen-year-old girl at a wedding. And she'd only proceed with the relationship if the answer was 'yes'.

Unfortunately, the fact that they might talk to a fourteen-year-old girl didn't mean they'd know what to say to her, Isabel learned. Boys her age were vain and self-obsessed. Later on, men her age might seem perfect for a while, but they always let her down in the end. Not one of the men she'd had serious relationships with could talk to her the way he had – with those eyes staring straight at her, with that calm careful voice. Not one had taught her something she didn't know. And not one had ever made her blush.

After her father died, Isabel, then twenty-seven, inherited a large sum of money; not as much as people would have thought, given her father's public status as a tycoon, for he'd lost an incredible amount at casinos over the years before he lost his life there as well, but enough to make her sit back and try to decide how best to invest it. At the time of his heart attack she'd been working in the personnel department of Dickins & Jones, not a very exciting job, but one she knew she was good at; she had a talent for spotting quickly which people would work best in which positions. When she sat herself down to consider what to do with this extra income, she came up blank. The best idea she had was to put the money in the bank and carry on as she had been, with only

one difference. She'd buy herself a nice, small mews house. Otherwise her inheritance wouldn't change her life in the slightest.

When she went to work the day after the cheque had arrived
from the lawyers, she was pleased with herself. Why should this
extra money affect her? She was happy enough as she was. For the
past two months she'd been seeing a man she thought she might be
falling in love with, she enjoyed her work, she was in control of her
present and her future. Mentally patting herself on the back for
being so sensible about the inheritance, and making a note to ring
her bank manager at the first opportunity to discuss what sort of
account she should have, Isabel sat down at her desk and waited for
the first interviewee of the day to come in. The woman who walked
through her door was wearing a Laura Ashley dress.

'I always liked that story of the man who said "Eureka!" in the
bathtub,' her father had said to her once when he'd taken her out
to lunch at the Grosvenor House. 'You know – Archimedes.
Because that kind of thing happens in life. Inspiration hits you
from out of nowhere. It's as if a sign suddenly appears in front of you
– you just have to be able to see it. Some people refuse to see that
sign, they close their eyes. You know my famous ice cream
sandwich? I thought of that when I was eating a ham and cheese
sandwich one day. I had a sudden craving for ice cream and I
looked down at this ham and cheese and thought – I wish this were
vanilla ice cream in a chocolate sandwich. That was my sign. You
have to keep your eyes open, all the time, for those signs.'

Isabel found herself staring at the Laura Ashley dress, unable to
take her eyes off it. She had difficulty asking even the most simple
questions of this woman as she remembered her own bridesmaid's
dress, as she recalled the wedding, as she heard David Barton
saying, 'You'd be a terrific party organizer yourself.'

It was a sign, this dress. Fate or her father or a combination of
both was sending her this sign and she couldn't close her eyes.

That was what she should be doing, what she should use her
money for. She should go into the party business. It was all so
simple and so easy. Who had organized the Dickins & Jones

employees' Christmas parties to unanimous delight? Isabel. Who, when she went to any party, immediately thought of how she would have done things differently, how she could have improved the atmosphere? Isabel. Why hadn't she thought of it before? Because she'd been waiting for the sign, or the sign had been waiting for the right moment to appear.

Now that she had some capital, she could invest it in a party company. She was perfectly happy in her job, but she wasn't taking any risks and she wasn't using her talents to the utmost. Remember, you should never tread water, Isabel, you should swim, her father had said at the same lunch. It was the day before he'd left her mother for good, so she had decided afterwards that he wasn't talking about her life, he was talking about his own. Now she thought about it again and realized what he had said applied to her as well. She had been treading water. For the past three years at Dickins & Jones she'd been treading water. In poker terms, she would have been called a 'rock', someone who never takes risks, someone who sits and folds hand after hand, never daring to bet unless it was a sure thing. That wasn't the way she played poker and it shouldn't be the way she lived her life.

Isabel finally looked at the Laura Ashley woman's face instead of her dress. Her thoughts hadn't just wandered, they'd scampered away and she forced herself to remember what she was supposed to be doing. She concentrated on the interview for the next half an hour then hustled the woman out of the office and picked up the telephone. Within minutes, she'd learned from one of her party-animal friends that the best party-organizer in London was a company called *Party Time*. Within seconds of discovering that fact, she also found out that *Party Time* was run by a 39-year-old man named David Barton.

It all fell into place so quickly, Isabel had to ask herself why she'd never bothered to trace David Barton's movements before. He'd been such an instrumental figure in her life, but she hadn't ever enquired about him from anyone, she'd never looked him up in the directory, she had let him remain the stranger.

Because he was my secret, she answered herself. One of my precious secrets. I was afraid that if I saw him again he might be different. I couldn't bear that. So I wrapped him up and stored him as he was. Or else – she stopped, leaned forward in her chair and bit her knuckles. Or else I knew subconsciously that I had to wait. I had to wait to see him again until I was old enough. Old enough and self-confident enough to sit down at the table and ask him to dance.

During her lunch break, instead of phoning her bank manager, Isabel took a few deep breaths and then rang David Barton.

'I might be interested in investing in your company,' she said, after waiting what seemed like an eternity to be put through to him. 'My name is Isabel Sands. Can I come by and talk to you?'

'You *might* be interested or you *are* interested?' he'd asked in a very polite tone. 'There's a world of difference in a verb tense.'

Isabel Sands, she'd wanted to scream down the phone. Isabel Sands. Don't you remember?

'I *am* interested,' she replied instead.

'So it's not conditional?'

'Well, it *is* conditional. I mean, I need to talk to you before I decide anything. And I expect you'd like to talk to me as well. Wouldn't you?'

'I *might.*'

You'll remember me when you see me, she thought. You'll remember the girl who would be such a fantastic party-organizer. You've forgotten the name, but you'll remember the face.

David Barton then gave her a time to come to his office the next afternoon and Isabel, as he spoke, envisioned him sitting at that table in the marquee, staring without blinking.

All her carefully planned words for the moment of recognition came to nothing the next afternoon when she walked into his office. To her eyes, he hadn't changed one bit. She'd been fearful that he might have shrunk somehow over the years, that his physical presence would pale in comparison to her memory of it and her disappointment would have made her rage at herself for

29

taking him out of the well-wrapped and perfect box she'd put him in. But he was still as lean, as straight-backed, as dark-haired; his face hadn't seemed to age at all. Yet there was not even a hint of recognition in it. It was a little curious, a little wary, a little bemused. He was meeting a woman who wanted to invest in his company, Isabel reminded herself. And this woman was a stranger to him.

For her part, seeing him again was surreal, as if she had skipped fourteen years of her life and was back in that stuffy marquee, merely continuing the conversation. Isabel kept waiting for the moment when he leaned forward in his chair and said: 'Don't I know you?' but it never came.

He had been purely professional from the moment she arrived; shaking hands politely, offering her coffee or tea, and then quizzing her as to her intentions as if he were a prospective father-in-law and she the prospective suitor. Each time she thought she saw an opportunity to mention their first meeting, she hesitated and then lost the impulse.

If he has forgotten, she told herself, it means I'm not as memorable as I thought I was. I was simply a fourteen-year-old girl he chatted to and danced with for a few minutes. I wasn't special. And if I remind him, if I tell him it was his words which have me sitting here right now, he'll feel obliged in some way. He'll feel he has to take me on board. I don't want to put him in that position.

As soon as she explained to David Barton that she not only wanted to invest in *Party Time*, she wanted to work there as well, he frowned. Isabel realized that she'd never seen him frown and that the sight was painful to her. And at that moment she also realized that she had fallen in love with him when she was fourteen years old, had stayed faithful to his memory and was in love with him still. He wasn't a charm, he was real. She didn't love his image, she loved him.

'You can't buy yourself a job without any experience to back it up,' he'd said sharply.

'I've been going to parties since I was a baby,' she responded, amazed that she could carry on this conversation as if nothing had happened, as if her heart hadn't imploded. 'And I'm not talking about children's parties. I'm talking about real parties. Serious parties, if that's not an oxymoron.'

'Going to parties is not the same as giving them.' He'd looked at her with a new look – he wasn't appraising her any more, he was edging toward full-blown distrust.

'I also organized all the parties at Dickins & Jones, where I've been manager of the personnel department for the past three years. I—' Isabel hesitated, then decided to go ahead. 'I pay attention to details, details like lighting and ventilation, flowers, canapés.'

'Look, Miss Sands, that's good – details are important, I know. The point is, I'm not going to pretend I wouldn't love an influx of money. I've been running this business for four years now, on my own, and it has been ticking along nicely, but it could be better. I can't say it couldn't. Try and see this from my point of view, though. This is a company I've worked very hard building up, this is my life's work. You suddenly appear out of the blue. You want to invest *and* you want to work here. That's a huge heap of faith for me to take considering the fact that you've never worked in this business and we don't know each other, don't you think?'

'Yes,' she responded, 'it is.' He was staring at her with that same stare. She didn't blink either as she stared back.

'How about this?' David leaned forward, his elbows on the desk. 'Why don't you come and work here before you make an investment. If things go well for both of us, you invest. If it doesn't pan out, then you leave. It won't be messy then because we won't have to sort out any complicated financial arrangements. Does that make sense?'

'Would it make even more sense if I worked for a couple of months without pay? A test period, so to speak?'

'You'd do that?'

'Yes, I would.' Isabel nodded. 'It seems only fair. You're right, you don't know me, you don't know whether I'd be any good at the job. I'm sure I would be, but I have to prove myself.'

'Are you Geoffrey Sands' daughter?'

'Yes. Does that make a difference?'

David Barton put his head to the side, narrowed his eyes.

'I don't know,' he suddenly laughed. 'It might. But only because I loved those ice cream sandwiches. I used to be able to eat twelve, one after the other. Actually, it was fairly disgusting, now that I think about it. I haven't had one for years.'

'Why not?'

'My wife isn't a fan of ice cream.'

Isabel's left foot twitched.

'My father died a year ago,' she said.

'I know. I read about his heart attack. I'm sorry.'

'And yes, this is his inheritance money I'd be investing.'

'I figured.'

They were both silent then and Isabel found herself remembering yet again her dance with him, the way he had taken her hand in his and twirled her around.

'So—' he stood up, rubbed his hands together. 'It's a deal, then. You can come to work here and if all goes well, maybe we can celebrate with a feast of ice cream sandwiches and champagne. How does that sound?'

'Terrific,' Isabel replied, standing up as well. 'I'll give my notice in to Dickins & Jones tomorrow and I'll be in touch with you as soon as I know when I can start here.'

'You know, you're either a very brave woman or a very crazy one. Or both.' He came over to her side of the desk and shook her hand. 'You're leaving what sounds like a good job without any guarantees. Did you always want to be involved in the party business or is this a recent interest?'

'I've been interested in party organizing for a long time – since I was a teenager, in fact.'

'Ah,' David Barton tugged on his right earlobe. 'You have more of a history than I do, then. I didn't think much of parties when I was a teenager. I didn't start in this business until I was in my twenties, in fact.'

'I know.'

'What?' His eyebrows raised.

'I mean I guessed that you aren't the type of person who would have been a party animal in his teens,' Isabel replied, thinking that once again, she had been on the edge but couldn't bring herself to make that jump, that connection with him.

'Well, I would call that a shrewd guess of yours, but then I'm aware I don't look like a party animal as such. I look more like the designated driver who takes people home after parties; at least that's what I've been told on numerous occasions.'

'I probably don't look like a raver either.' She smiled.

'Oh, I don't know about that. Anyway, I look forward to hearing from you.'

The telephone on his desk rang then and Isabel said a quick goodbye.

That had been what David Barton believed was their first meeting, the meeting at which, he was now telling her, he'd thought she might be a 'spoiled brat'. That meeting had taken place eight months before this Monday morning. After two months working without pay for *Party Time*, she was on a salary and, one month later, Isabel put her money as well as her time into the business. She and David were now partners, sharing everything.

No, she corrected herself, we don't share everything. I've never told him that I adore him with a passion that frightens me, that he was the perfect person in my mind for all those years and that he became the perfect person in reality the moment I saw him again. And I've never told him about the wedding because I still believe one of these days he'll remember and when that day comes, everything will change.

'So you don't think I'm a spoiled brat any more?' she asked him, thinking: Oh, Isabel, why don't you just get out a fishing rod with a hook labelled 'compliments'?

'Isabel—' He shook his head. 'Please. But speaking of spoiled brats, spoiled fifty-something-year-old male brats, what about Paul Malcolm? When is our meeting with him scheduled?'

'Wednesday morning – at eleven.'

'Good. It's going to be huge, that party. We should work some more on possible themes. I like what we have already, but it wouldn't hurt to come up with some more ideas.'

'Right – but first, I forgot to tell you. Have you heard Stryker McCabe's nickname?'

'No.' David leaned forward in his chair. 'Tell me.'

'Stryker Mc*Babe*. You know, because of all those stunning young girls he's hired. That's another trick of his. He thinks male executives will give their business to *Your Fantasy Team* so they can liaise, so to speak, with the bimbos.'

'Stryker McBabe,' David laughed.

She'd made him laugh again. Everything was going to work out. It had to. She couldn't think of his wife, she wouldn't let herself.

'You could change your name, you know. Call yourself Isababe Sands,' he smiled. 'That would give us a competitive edge.'

Isabel managed not to preen visibly, but she couldn't stop herself from blushing.

Chapter Three

Stryker McCabe leaned back in his chair and crossed his hands behind his head.

'The guy has a thing about Trollope, OK? He sits in Texas and reads Trollope when he's not drilling for oil, and all he wants to do is go fox-hunting because there's a fox-hunting scene in every one of those novels, apparently. He wants twenty of his nearest and dearest Texan buddies to hunt down a fox in the perfect English countryside setting. All we have to do is set it up for him. Easy, right?' Stryker addressed this question to Belinda Hanley, who was sitting across the desk from him. But he didn't wait for her reply.

'First of all, we have to get him and his buddies invited by some member of some hunt, which I can do. I know one of the players, who happens to be a woman – a Lady, in fact. She has the title and she pours money into her hunt group or whatever it's called. I organized a party for her in New York she has never forgotten, so that's not a problem. I can convince her to invite Mr Texas and his group on her hunt.'

'Can these people from Texas ride?' Belinda asked, thinking: he could convince anyone to do anything. He could convince me to take off all my clothes right now. I wish he'd try.

'Christ if I know. Maybe they're used to hunting deer in helicopters with heat-seeking missiles as their ammunition – that *sounds* like a Texan oil man's style. But then your normal Texan wouldn't be reading Trollope, would he? So I guess they can ride, but I doubt whether they can jump over big ditches or those fence deals. We'll have to make sure there aren't any major obstacles in their path. And that the horses aren't too frisky. That might be a problem. But—' Stryker raised his forefinger in the air. 'That's not the *big* problem.'

'What is the big problem?'

'What do *you* think it is, Belinda?'

Stryker smiled at her and Belinda felt her facial muscles tense as her mind struggled to come up with the right answer. This might be an important test, and she didn't want to flunk it. What would the big problem be on a fox hunt? She had no clue. She'd never been on one. The only images she had came from television reporting of protestors. Belinda's face cleared and she beamed a smile back at Stryker.

'The anti-hunting lobby. They might picket or cause some sort of fuss.'

'Wrong answer. But a very good wrong answer, Belinda. An excellent wrong answer. Of course it's logical to think that protestors might be a problem, but if you think more, if you think a little bit laterally, you'll understand that protestors aren't a problem; in fact, they're a bonus. Men from Texas love show-downs. They'd like nothing better than to swear at a few long-haired, tree-hugging, animal-loving eco-nuts as they ride out onto the range, if you see what I mean. We *want* protestors. If there aren't any, we should ship some in.'

'I see.' Belinda tried not to frown. She had wanted so badly to get the right answer.

'Killing the fox. Now, *that's* the problem. I mean, we don't want them to spend all their money and come over here and then not get to smear fox blood all over their foreheads, do we?'

'Yuck.' She squirmed in her chair. 'It's so disgusting.'

'Of course it is. It's revolting. But that's not the point. The point is, we have to make sure these men get their fox. And how do we do that?'

Another question she couldn't answer. Belinda wished Stryker wouldn't keep putting her on the spot like this. It wasn't fair. She'd started working for *Your Fantasy Team* only six weeks ago. And this was the first time Stryker McCabe had called her into his office to discuss work. She didn't mind the fact that it was after office hours and she was staying late; on the contrary, she was chuffed to be asked. If he kept her late enough, it was just possible he might ask her out for a drink or dinner when they'd finished. But she couldn't begin to tell him the best way to kill a fox.

'Um. I'm not sure. Kill it beforehand and then put its body somewhere where they could find it?'

'Good thinking.' Stryker swung his legs up onto the desk. 'I like the way your mind works, Belinda. A pre-emptive strike would be great; unfortunately, though, it won't work. First of all, those guys want to be in on the kill, that's part of the rush. Secondly, hunt members are notoriously straightlaced. They wouldn't rig something like this. They have some perverse sense of honour, which, frankly, is beyond me, given that they hound these animals to death. So the premature murder of our fox is not the answer. We're stuck, aren't we? What do we do now?'

He raised his hands in the air in a gesture of dismay. Belinda stared at him and bit her upper lip.

'*Your Fantasy Team*'s Rule Number One, Belinda. Whenever there's a problem, we have to work out what the weak link is. Find the weak link and attack it.'

'The weak link?'

'Yes. In this case, the weak link in the fox-hunting chain. What do you think that is?'

Why had she taken this job? Belinda wondered, panicking as she looked at Stryker's expectant face. She had thought she was going to help organize parties. Normal parties with drinks and fabulous things to eat and bands and tents and flowers. Not fox hunts. At the interview, Stryker hadn't asked her questions like this, he'd simply chatted to her about her life, where she'd been to school, what her family was like. The fact that she hadn't worked in the

37

party business before didn't seem to bother him. None of the other girls he had hired had experience in the business either. They were around the same age as she, twenty-two or three, and all four of them had a crush on their boss. So far none of them had done a great deal of work – Stryker seemed to have everything organized and under control. Sophie, Danielle, Laura and she sat at desks in the huge reception area, answered phones, greeted clients, and traded girltalk and gossip. It had been the perfect job. Until now.

'The weak link in the fox-hunting chain?' she repeated. Someone on a television show had said once that if you don't know the answer to a question, you should ask it back.

'Yes. The weak link.'

He waited for her answer; she waited for some divine inspiration.

'The weak link?' She kept her eyes fixed on the floor as she threw the question back yet again. What if he did the same and asked her again? What if they kept repeating 'the weak link' to each other for the entire night?

'Yes. That's it.' He suddenly swept his legs off the desk and stood up. 'Exactly. The weak link is the terrier man. He's not rich, is he?'

'No, no.' Belinda looked up and shook her head vigorously. Had she said 'terrier man'? Had the words somehow magically come from her lips? How could that be? She'd never heard of a terrier man before. What *was* a terrier man? Whatever he was, he couldn't be rich. Or could he?

'Right again, Belinda. You're brilliant. He's not rich. If someone were to offer the terrier man let's say two thousand pounds to bag a couple of foxes and let them out right in the line of the approaching hunt, then the problem is not a problem any more. Sure, our Texans have to be able to kill the fox at the end, but the odds of failing are drastically reduced. A fox always runs downwind, so it's not as if these foxes are suddenly going to swing around and run off in the wrong direction, not if the terrier man does his job correctly, which is what he'd do for that amount of money, right?'

'Right.' Belinda nodded. 'Absolutely.' She still had no idea who this terrier person was or how he was supposed to 'bag' the foxes without smothering them to death or something equally horrendous, but at least Stryker seemed to think she understood.

'So we've done a great job here, haven't we?' Stryker paced back and forth behind his desk. 'We've solved the problem. Of course I'll need your help.'

Oh no, she thought, the panic attacking her again. He's going to ask me to find a terrier man and bribe him. How am I supposed to do that?

'I figure they'll want someone to speak at dinner after this wildly successful hunt. But who?'

'Who?' Belinda was beginning to get the hang of this now. That person on the television had known what he was talking about.

'Well, our man is a Trollope fan, as I said. So I think we either find some academic type who is an expert on Trollope. Or – and this is better, isn't it? – an actor who was in one of those BBC adaptations of a Trollope novel? What do you think?'

'Brilliant,' she sighed, feeling relieved and confused at the same time. Had she passed this test? Without answering one of his questions?

'Exactly. You've been fantastic, Belinda. A huge help. If you could check out those adaptations for me – find the most recent one and get me a list of the actors and actresses, then we're golden.'

'I can do that,' she replied with fervour.

'Great. Now—' He looked at his watch. 'I'm sorry to have kept you so late. I have to stay on for a while, but you should get going. Go out and enjoy yourself.'

'I don't mind staying if there's anything I can do to help.'

How old was Stryker? Sophie thought thirty-three, Danielle thirty-five, Laura thirty-four. Belinda herself had guessed thirty-one. In normal circumstances she wouldn't have fancied a man in his thirties, but Stryker was different. He wasn't only wonderfully handsome, he also had energy and enthusiasm and a way of making people feel special. If he'd asked her to, she would have *tried* to find the terrier man and hand him thousands of pounds, even if that meant she was doing something illegal. She could imagine that as a teenager he would have been the leader of whatever group at school was the 'in' one, the embodiment of what peer pressure was all about. If Stryker offered you a cigarette, you'd take up smoking. If he wanted more than a kiss, he'd get it.

As far as she could make out, he wasn't involved with any woman, not seriously anyway. Various females called the office, but the four girls compared notes constantly and found that there was no one name that came up more than others. Perhaps, as Laura had suggested, he'd left a tragic, broken relationship behind when he'd moved from New York to London. Why else would he have left America and come to Britain?

Belinda didn't want to leave, but she couldn't think of a good excuse to stay. She stood up reluctantly and began to make a move toward the door.

'Hey, Belinda—'

'Yes?' She stopped.

'When is your birthday? I'm sure I have it written down somewhere, but tell me again.'

'In April. 15 April.'

'Right.' Stryker took a pen, opened a diary and made a note. 'I always give birthday parties for people who work with me. It seems unfair for people in the party trade not to have parties themselves, doesn't it?'

'I guess so.'

'You think about what kind of party you'd like and let me know when we get closer to the time, OK?'

'Fine,' she smiled and swept her long blonde hair behind her ear. All her nerves had disappeared, and she was congratulating herself again for getting this fantastic job with this amazing, thoughtful, handsome man. One of these days he'd ask her out for a drink. Meanwhile she'd do some homework and find out as much about fox-hunting as possible. As Stryker had said, the fact that it was a revolting sport didn't matter. The point was to give people what they wanted. *Make the fantasy real* was his motto. *Give Stryker*

McCabe *whatever he wants* was now hers.

'I've been wondering,' she said, her hand on the doorknob. 'Why did you get into the party business in the first place?'

'My parents are both dentists, Belinda,' he replied.

She began to laugh, then covered her mouth with her hand.

'You see? Look at you. I tell you my parents are dentists and you immediately cover your mouth. When I tell people I organize parties for a living, they immediately smile. That's why I went into this business.'

'They're *both* dentists?'

'Yes. My mother drills and fixes cavities, my father puts braces on kids' teeth. I figured my legacy as their son is to give pleasure, not pain.'

'That's so sweet.'

'Thanks.' Stryker waved her out the door, went back to his desk and put his legs up again. 'Go have fun. Enjoy yourself. Drink lots of Coca-Cola and eat lots of chocolate. Keep those dentists in business. By the way – did you know—' He leaned forward and lowered his voice. 'Foxes lap up Coca-Cola by the gallon?'

'Pardon?' Belinda wrinkled her nose.

'Yup. They can't get enough of the stuff. Coca-Cola and caviare.'

'Where do they find it? I mean, how does a fox get caviare?'

'Beats me.' Stryker raised his hands in the air and shrugged.

Belinda's eyes travelled around the office for a few seconds then came to rest on Stryker.

'Maybe we could give some to the terrier man. Or hide some Coca-Cola and caviare in the right bush or something. You know? So the fox would go straight there?'

'Hey, that's a thought.' Stryker smiled. 'Have a nice night, Belinda.'

'Bye.' She gave him a little wave.

'Bye,' he waved back.

Watching Belinda exit his office, Stryker knocked his fist against his forehead.

I have to stop doing that, he told himself. I promised myself I'd stop making up absurd lies like that. It's not fair and it will land me in trouble again. Get your act together, Stryker. You're doing fine. Don't ruin it all now. Don't let Miss Fellowes back into your life. Miss Fellowes, the star performer in your recurring nightmare.

Looking at his legs resting on the desk, Stryker began to name all the bones in a human leg. He ticked them off one by one, then repeated the process on his arms. *Now* he could do it. He could name every fucking bone in the body. But now was twenty years too late. If he could have done the same aged thirteen, he wouldn't be sitting in his office thinking about Miss Fellowes yet again. He would have passed that test.

It wasn't even an exam, Stryker thought, rewinding the tape of his past and replaying the scene for what must have been the millionth time. That was the crazy part. It was only a test – a biology test. The questions were all on the bones in the body: femora, ulnae, all these odd names Stryker tried to, but couldn't, memorize. So he flunked it. That wasn't the end of the world. Other kids flunked as well, four others. The next week the five co-flunkees retook the test. This time Stryker studied especially hard, but he just couldn't get his head round all those bones. He flunked it again. The teacher, Miss Fellowes, set up another date the following week to sit another retake. Wednesday at four p.m. This time Stryker would be on his own; the other four had all passed second time round.

On that Wednesday afternoon, instead of going to the study hall and most probably flunking the test for the third time, Stryker went to the gym, to basketball practice – a voluntary activity. After it ended, he went straight home. He didn't think about getting caught by Miss Fellowes; he had decided that she wouldn't notice his absence, or that, if she did notice, she'd forgive him this understandable lapse, chalk up another 'F' and leave it at that. Bones in the body? What was the big deal?

The next morning, before Stryker had even reached his classroom, Miss Fellowes accosted him in the hallway. He noticed that bright red hair advancing on him first. That was what everyone always noticed about Miss Fellowes – her hair. It was a traffic-light red, blazing and frightening in its starchy mass. But that morning, her hair paled beside her face, the redness of which was enough to make Stryker think she might be having a heart attack. Her mouth, those thin lips and sharp teeth he was accustomed to seeing and which had always made him think of a dying rodent, suddenly covered the whole lower half of her face in a bulging, very much alive snarl.

'Where were you yesterday?' She spat it out. She didn't seem to want an answer, but he knew he had to give one.

'At basketball practice,' he said. He was shifting from foot to foot and he could feel himself begin to sweat. 'I had to be there,' he added quickly. 'I had to be at basketball practice. It was compulsory. Ask the coach. He said it was more important than a test retake. Ask him. He'll tell you.'

Miss Fellowes lit off down the hallway without saying another word. Stryker, watching her, felt sick to his stomach. What would happen now? Would the basketball coach back him up? Wasn't there a rumour that Miss Fellowes and Coach Hall were having a romance, though? If that was true, he was doomed. But no one would have a romance with Miss Fellowes, would they? It was impossible. Unbelievable. She couldn't be younger than forty-five. Coach Hall would cover for him, wouldn't he?

Twenty minutes later at Assembly, when school announcements were over and Miss Fellowes stood up, Stryker almost bolted from the Assembly Hall. Miss Fellowes had never addressed the entire school before. Why should she now?

'There is one person in this school,' she began, and Stryker knew this was it. He bit his lip to keep the tears from his eyes. 'One person who lies. Who has lied to me. I want you all to look at him now. Stryker McCabe – stand up.'

Stryker rose to his feet. He heard heads turn, he felt eyes upon him. He thought he was going to throw up. Or die. So he smiled.

'You have the gall to *smile*,' Miss Fellowes said, taking her time with each word. 'To smile? You're a liar. That's all I have to say. You're a liar.' She sat back down with the other teachers at the front of the Assembly Hall. Stryker, his legs shaking, sat down as well. He couldn't take the smile off his face; he could feel it stretched out there, unable to budge.

'Hey, Strike,' Jimmy Mulligan, the boy beside him, whispered. 'Ace. You don't give a shit, do you? I love it, man. The bitch gets on your case like that in front of everyone and you smile. I love it.'

And that was how the whole student population, Stryker learned subsequently, saw it. Stryker McCabe faces down the red-haired biology teacher, Miss Fellowes, the Bitch from Hell, and smiles. He doesn't care. Nothing bothers him. He's cool.

When the basketball coach threw him off the team that afternoon, saying: 'Mandatory? You know it wasn't mandatory practice, Stryker. You think I'd cover for you because you're a decent player? You think I'd lie for you to another teacher? Who do you think you are?' Stryker kept smiling. Boys gave him high fives, girls gave him winks. It was no problem for Stryker, after all. He didn't give a shit.

So what if all the teachers looked at him as if he were a convicted felon after that Assembly, and his grades went spiralling downwards? So what if the basketball coach was also the baseball coach and wouldn't let him try out for baseball in the spring? Did that matter to Stryker? No, man. Of course not. No way.

There was no contest. After that Assembly, Stryker McCabe was the most popular boy in his class by miles. He also became the most deceitful one. But Stryker's lies were lies with a difference. He began to lie purely for the sake of lying, telling such outrageous fibs only the most naive of people would believe him. He'd raise his hand in a history class and say: 'Did you know that when Abraham Lincoln gave the Gettysburg Address, he was on psychedelic drugs?', or he'd give his classmates little lectures on other cultures. Every single person living in Italy had pizza for breakfast, he'd inform them. If any Italian was found not eating pizza at breakfast, they would be arrested, thrown in jail and tortured.

When someone asked him the time, he'd check his watch and then answer five hours off. Even though almost all his classmates and teachers caught on quickly to this new-found habit of his, some still fell for a few of his wild stories and Stryker would get a rush of pleasure as he saw their dazed expressions. 'Bruce Willis wears a girdle' was one which had a whole clutch of girls in shock for at least a week.

The headmaster of his school met with his parents to discuss this 'problem' of Stryker's and he was dutifully sent to a child psychologist. In an articulate and thoughtful manner, Stryker explained that he made up these lies to entertain people, that he knew the difference between truth and fiction, that he would try very hard to stick to the truth from then on. He never mentioned Miss Fellowes. He was, he said, smiling, just having some harmless fun.

After that meeting, Stryker picked and chose carefully. At the right moment, with the right person, he'd tell a whopper and watch for the reaction he loved to see, but he kept it to a limit; he paced himself. Sometimes he'd get lax and let himself go in a class with a particularly idiotic or annoying teacher, but generally speaking he managed to rein himself in.

As he advanced in his teenage years, he concentrated on the perks he received for having become so phenomenally popular, one of which was parties. He was invited to every party a classmate had and he began to give parties himself. By the time he was eighteen, he knew he had a knack for organizing these bashes; he knew who to invite with whom, what music was the best to get people up and dancing, how to create an atmosphere of fun. Stryker McCabe, Mr Cool, Mr Don't Give a Shit, Mr Teller of Crazy, Hysterical Lies, was also, by the end of high school, a living legend. No one could throw a party like Stryker. No one even came close. He was it. He was the Party Man.

'You're gonna be famous, dude,' Jimmy Mulligan told him on the last day of school. 'After you've finished at whatever that dipshit college you're going to is called, you're going to take

Manhattan by the balls. You're going to be the best party person in the world, I know it. Remember to invite me to a couple of those, will you?'

A few minutes after Jimmy had given him a farewell bear hug, Miss Fellowes walked up to Stryker McCabe.

'I still don't know those bones, Miss Fellowes,' Stryker said, grinning. He could afford to be generous. He'd forgiven her. If she hadn't caught him lying that day he might never have been so popular, he might never have realized the talent he had, the talent to throw the best parties in the world. He could have ended up being a boring stockbroker.

'You don't know anything, Stryker.' She reached out, put her hand on his shoulder and squeezed it. Hard. 'You're as shallow as glass. And you're still a liar. I've been watching you, you know. All these years. You think they're funny, don't you? Those ridiculous lies you tell. But they're not funny. And you're sick.'

Stryker kept smiling. He knew if he stopped he'd either burst into tears or strangle her.

'It was only a *test*, Miss Fellowes.' He could feel his smile being dragged off his face by a force he couldn't control. 'I was thirteen years old and you humiliated me in front of the whole school.'

'A humiliation which you deserved,' she replied. She shook her red head and walked off. Stryker turned his back, set off in the opposite direction and told himself he'd never have to see the woman again. He was starting a new life. Miss Fellowes was gone for good.

At four o'clock the next morning he woke up sweating, the voice of Miss Fellowes ricocheting around his brain. She had been standing in the Assembly again, standing and pointing a finger at him. 'You're still a liar,' she said, this time in a whisper. He had looked around the room for help, but all the teachers and students were whispering as well. He tried to put his hands up to his face to cover it, but they wouldn't move. Paralysed by shame, he stood and listened as the whispering turned to shouts of 'liar'.

He forgot about the nightmare by the afternoon of the next day and he forgot about Miss Fellowes the moment he left his home town of Warwick, Rhode Island, and went to a small community college in upstate New York. As soon as he graduated, Stryker moved to Manhattan and began to work in the party industry. Within five years, by the time he was twenty-seven, he had started his own company, *Life's a Party*. Life for Stryker *was* a party; he was prospering, he was footloose and fancy free, he was the happiest of campers.

'And then I blew it,' Stryker said out loud, looking around his empty office, and shaking his head. 'I'm such a stupid fucker, I blew it. I told one of my goddamn lies to the wrong person. Why? Was I looking to self-destruct? Sure I told my silly lies during college days. And yes, I kept telling them afterwards, but never to anyone important. Only to people I thought might be amused. If someone was gullible enough to believe me, I'd tell them the truth eventually. So why did I tell my biggest, most important client – my client who had more clout in Manhattan than the Statue of Liberty – why did I tell him that you can find out if a man is impotent by the way he walks? That it's a well-known medical fact that if his toes point out when he walks, he's either in trouble on the sexual front or he's going to be. Why say that? Because I thought he'd know I was kidding? Shouldn't I have learned you can't assume anything about anyone, much less bet on the fact that they have a sense of humour?

I should have known he'd go to a goddamn specialist and spend thousands of bucks to be told this was a bunch of bull. I should have guessed he'd go ballistic and fire me and then badmouth me all over town. Why the hell didn't I check out how he walked before I said that? And why keep telling those dumb stories anyway? It's all Miss Fellowes' fault. I never lied before I had that run-in with her. I was a normal kid before that fucking bones test.

Stryker stood up, and raised his hands in the air.

'So – ladies and gentlemen of the jury. That's my speech. There you have it. Stryker McCabe hightails it out of Manhattan. He flies over to London to start afresh. The night before he leaves he has another nightmare about Miss Fellowes, the Bitch from Biology. And what does he do when he gets there? Wait for it? – you'll love this. He tells his sweet, not so bright, but very beautiful assistant, who has a strange habit of repeating the last few words of whatever he says – he tells her that foxes love Coca-Cola and caviare. And this sweet young thing believes him.

'I ask you: has Mr McCabe learned his lesson?'

Stryker snorted. He went over to the door, picked his coat off the hook and walked out of the office. But not before pointing an imaginary gun to his temple and pulling the trigger.

Chapter Four

At six-thirty David poked his head into her office.

'Isabel? Even party planners go home at a decent hour. It's late, you should stop working.'

'I've just finished.'

'Good.' He stepped inside. 'Actually, I was wondering – would you like to join me for a drink? My brother Peter is in town and I thought you might like to meet him – or are you busy?'

Busy? I broke off my relationship months ago because of you. I wait here every afternoon hoping you'll ask me out for a drink. I try never to leave the office until you've left. On the five occasions you've invited me for an after-work drink, I've leaped at the invitation. Busy? I don't think so.

'No, as it happens, I'm not. And I'd like to meet your brother.'

I'd like to meet anyone in your family except, of course, your wife. I'd like to meet your family and dazzle them with my charm. I'd like to dazzle you with my charm, show you how I can be a funny, fun woman away from the office. I'd like you to have such a fantastic time at drinks that you'll stay on and have dinner. At which point I'd like your brother Peter to disappear.

David was standing beside her, holding her coat out, when Isabel collected herself and dismissed her wild thoughts.

'Are you going to be warm enough in this?' he asked as he helped her on with it.

'I'll be fine, thanks,' she replied.

Why am I such a sucker for your manners? Why am I so pitifully impressed by the fact that you help me on with my coat and open doors for me and always walk on the outside of the pavement? There I was smirking at Ed for being such a sucker at the poker table on Saturday. I beat him in the sucker stakes hands down.

They locked up and left the office together. As soon as they were outside, David stopped and stood still, a stricken look on his face.

'Are you all right?' she asked, wondering if he had changed his mind and was going to tell her he couldn't bring her along to drinks after all.

'I just remembered something. Something I can't believe I forgot.'

Is it now? Is now the moment? Outside on a cold, windy evening? Have you suddenly remembered the wedding? Why now? Why here? I had hoped it would happen, that your memory cells would finally click in, somewhere else, somewhere private.

'We were supposed to celebrate, remember? I told you we would have champagne and ice cream sandwiches if everything worked out, if you joined *Party Time*. And we've never done that. We've never celebrated. I'm so sorry, Isabel. We should have celebrated months ago. What an idiot I am.'

'It's all right, honestly. It doesn't matter.'

Of course I was hurt when we didn't celebrate. I couldn't believe that you'd forgotten, that when we signed the contract you didn't make some sort of fuss over it all. I'd remembered the champagne and ice cream sandwiches, but that was yet another thing I didn't want to remind you about – I wanted you to remember for yourself. I even began to think you have selective amnesia; your memory works perfectly for the most part, but you forget everything important to do with me.

'I'll make it up to you,' he said, putting his hand on the small of her back and guiding her to the left. 'I promise. We'll celebrate soon.'

With some women, it's the neck. With others it's their hair. With me, it's the small of my back. Touch me there and I'm a basket case. You bastard. You have no idea what you're doing to me. Or do you?

'Peter's a pilot. He flies for LIAT in the Caribbean. He's a real character. You'll love him, I'm sure.'

'I'm sure.'

'Sam, my other brother, is in Canada. He works for a newspaper in Toronto. He's not as much of an extrovert as Peter, but then it's hard to imagine anyone being as much of an extrovert as Peter. You'll see when you meet him. He loves to talk. Here we are—' David held the door of the pub open for her and ushered her inside. 'Peter should be here somewhere.' Isabel took a quick glance around the room and saw a tanned man sitting at a table with sunglasses perched on top of his head, and a leather jacket hanging over his chair.

'Is that him?' She motioned toward the man, but he was already waving at David.

'Yes, that's him. That's Peter. He thinks he's still in Antigua, even though it's February in Fulham. He'd addicted to the beach life.'

Surfer Boy, Isabel thought. But this man didn't have the blond hair or blue-eyed Californian looks of Ed. When they reached his table, he stood up to greet them, hugging David, then shaking hands with Isabel.

'Peter, this is my partner Isabel Sands. Isabel, this is my brother, Peter.' David pulled out a chair for Isabel. 'What can I get you to drink, Isabel? The usual?'

The usual? Isabel smiled at him and nodded. He must have registered on those five occasions that I ordered white wine, she thought. All we talked about then was the business, the weather, the news, but at least he noticed what I was drinking.

'I'm sure you'll keep her entertained while I go to the bar,' David said to Peter. 'But don't tell her any embarrassing stories of my youth, all right? I'm trying to keep up an image, you know. I don't want you to shatter it in two minutes.'

'Would I do that to you?' Peter feigned shock. 'Would I sabotage my brother's reputation with a story – a story, say, of his humiliation in a certain school Christmas play?'

'Peter—' David reached over and squeezed his brother's neck. 'Don't go there. Or I'll retaliate. And I have a huge arsenal, a stockpile of weaponry with which to retaliate. Remember that time when you were ten years old and—'

'OK – OK. Enough said. Go get the drinks, David. Isabel looks thirsty. I'll be good. I promise.'

David smiled at Isabel and walked to the bar. She felt herself bask in that smile for a second before turning to concentrate on Peter.

'David tells me you're a pilot.'

'I am indeed.' He spread his hands out like aeroplane wings and made engine noises. 'I'd love to tell you tales of near misses and saving thousands of passengers with my supernatural skill, but that would be dishonest of me. The only problem my passengers have is finding their luggage at the end of the trip. That's the bitch about flying. Forget bombs or wind shear or clear air turbulence – luggage. Luggage sucks.'

Isabel laughed.

'Do you know what a pain in the ass vanity cases are? I mean why? Why do women tote those things around? They don't fit under the seat, but no one wants to check them in the hold, either. Now why is that? Fear of being separated from a cleansing cream?'

She laughed again. Peter had David's dark hair and brown eyes, but his face differed; he had a careless, detached air, the expression of someone who was determined to be amused by life. The sun had hardened the skin around his eyes and mouth, but he looked like a little boy who loved to entertain, a child who couldn't wait to stage a puppet show.

'It didn't surprise me when David told me you'd invested in *Party Time*,' Peter continued. 'I met your father once.'

David arrived back with two glasses of white wine and sat down in the chair on Isabel's right.

'Has he been good?' he asked. 'Or has he betrayed me?'

'I've been wonderful,' Peter said, sitting up straight. 'I've even made her laugh. And, aside from telling her every detail of your tragic performance in the Christmas play, I haven't mentioned your name. In fact, I was just telling Isabel that I met her father once. When I was flying the chopper in New York.' Strangely, Peter didn't look at David as he was explaining this to him; he kept his eyes fixed on Isabel. 'Great man. Amazing man.'

'Thank you.'

'And so young-looking. He must have been fifty when I met him and he looked all of twenty-five, if that.'

'Mmm,' Isabel nodded, thinking: not again. How many times do I have to hear this? Yes, he looked young; yes, all my friends at school thought he was my brother when they first met him; yes, he married a series of women half his age after he divorced my mother; yes, I have five half-sisters and one half-brother whom I've met only once – at his funeral. Tell me something I don't know. Tell me he mentioned my name once during the flight.

'He had so much energy. Honestly, just having him on board made the experience into a party. Is that what it's like?' Peter finally shifted his gaze from Isabel to David. 'Having Isabel in the office? Is it one big party?'

'It's fun,' David replied. 'She has that energy, definitely. She keeps me on my toes. We have a lot of fun.'

You've never told me that. You've never said anything remotely resembling that. Somehow Peter's presence has loosened you up. I don't have to fish for compliments, they're landing on my lap. I hope Peter stays here. I hope we can sit like this for hours and hours while Peter asks you questions about me and you say lovely things.

Right, Isabel. Dream on. He's being nice, that's all. What did you think, that he'd trash you in front of his brother? Give it up. Saying that you're fun is slightly different from saying he's in love with you.

'My God, what a breakthrough.' Peter threw his hands up in the air. 'David, the original young old fogey saying the word "fun". What have you done to him, Isabel? How have you wrought this magic?'

'Peter – I'm not *that* bad.' David grimaced. 'I'm not an old fogey. I run a party company, remember?' He turned to Isabel. 'Tell him I'm a barrel of laughs, Isabel. Tell him I do the tango every lunchtime and let off fireworks every afternoon.'

'He *is* a fantastic dancer.' Isabel didn't dare look at David as she said this.

'Isabel. Poor Isabel. You're imagining things.' Peter shook his head sadly.

'She is not. She knows just by looking at me that I have incredible rhythm. You're jealous, Peter. This is a pathetic instance of sibling rivalry. You'd kill to have my natural talent on the dance floor. Have you forgotten when I gave you dancing lessons? How I taught you to jive?'

'Please—' Peter shuddered. 'I've managed to repress that particular painful scene of my childhood.'

'You taught him how to dance?' Isabel couldn't manage to repress her own jealousy. How many people had David taught to jive? Was she one of millions? Was that why she was so forgettable?

'I tried to teach him. The apposite word in that sentence being "tried". He—' David was stopped by the ringing of a mobile phone. He reached into his jacket pocket, frowning. 'I'm sorry. I thought I'd turned this awful contraption off.' He flipped it open and put it to his ear.

His wife, Isabel thought.

'His wife,' Peter whispered to her. 'Keeps him on a short leash, doesn't she?'

'Right.' David was saying. 'Yes. Of course. All right. I'll be there. I'm having a drink. No. It's all right. I'll be there. I'll leave now.'

Peter was making motions with his hand, signalling a tugging on an imaginary leash.

'I'm sorry.' David closed the phone and put it back in his pocket. 'It seems I have to leave now.'

'Excellent!' Peter clapped his hands. 'Now I have Isabel to myself. Think of the stories I can tell. The real truth. The unexpurgated version.'

'I can give you a lift home,' David turned to Isabel.

'Don't be silly. She hasn't finished her wine yet. Besides, *I'm* the pilot, David. It's my job to take people to their destinations. I'll escort her home.'

'I'd like to stay, thanks,' Isabel said.

'I win!' Peter threw his arm around Isabel's shoulder. 'I get to keep you!'

'I apologize for my brother, Isabel.'

'Go. Leave.' Peter shooed David away. 'She'll be safe with me. I won't sell her to the gypsies, I promise.'

David shook his head and pinched the bridge of his nose.

'I'll see you tomorrow then,' he stated, putting his hand on Peter's shoulder. 'And don't listen to anything he says, Isabel. Not one word. He's thoroughly untrustworthy. He's a shark.'

'Me? A shark? I'm a pussycat, you know that. And Isabel knows it too, I'm sure. I bet you're a gambler like your father, Isabel. Which means you know how to tell the sharks from the pussycats.'

'Yes, of course. Didn't I tell you? Isabel goes to the track every afternoon.' David laughed. 'You've been in the sun too long, Peter. It has affected what was already a very dodgy brain. Goodbye, you two,' he patted Peter's shoulder. 'I'm sorry I couldn't stay.'

'Bye,' Isabel said, careful not to watch him as he departed. She felt another absurd pang of jealousy. David had patted Peter's shoulder. He hadn't touched her.

'Gorgonzola time,' Peter said after David had gone out the door.

'Are you hungry?' Isabel reached out for the menu on the table.

'No, no. I meant it's Gorgonzola time for David. You know – Jenny. His wife. She has two sisters, both of whom work in the City like she does, both of whom are as high-powered and as ambitious as she is. All three of them are Gorgons. So I call Jenny "Gorgonzola".'

'Oh.' Isabel kept her face blank.

'You've met her, haven't you?'

'No.' Isabel shook her head and took a sip of wine. 'I haven't.'

I try to pretend she doesn't exist. Whenever he mentions her,

55

I'm very polite, but I don't prolong the conversation. I don't ask about her. I don't want to know.

'You haven't had the pleasure? God. Lucky you.'

'I don't – I don't think—' Isabel faltered and then came to a stop. Clearly Peter was not too fond of Jenny. Part of her wanted to hear why and part of her knew her motives for wanting to hear why were shameful.

'Oh, don't worry, Isabel. I'm not saying anything I wouldn't say to Gorgonzola's face. She knows how I feel about her. We used to be an item ourselves, as it happens.' Peter pulled out a packet of Bensons from his pocket, tapped one out and lit it. 'Sorry,' he said as he exhaled. 'I should have asked. Do you mind?'

'No, not at all. I'm the only person I know who's never smoked but who likes passive smoking.'

'If you sit beside me long enough, you might just get a passive tan too,' Peter smiled. 'Now you're being very discreet, aren't you? You want to know whether Jenny broke my heart by dumping me for my older brother, but you're too polite to ask. So I'll tell you. It wasn't like that. She and David didn't get together until a couple of years after we split up. Ours was – what would you call it? Puppy love. No, correction. Pussycat love.' Peter chuckled. 'We both grew out of it very, very quickly. Now poor David is shackled to her for the long haul.'

'I'm sure that's not such a terrible prospect,' Isabel protested feebly.

'Are you?'

His amused expression was disconcerting her, as was the fact that he hadn't take his eyes off her for more than a few seconds since she'd met him. It wasn't that he was looking at her with any sexual suggestiveness; he was simply studying her very closely.

'I'll get us another round,' he said. 'Be back in a tick.' He stood up and went to the bar.

Peter and David's wife? Had that created tension between the brothers? They seemed relaxed and playful with each other, but perhaps there *was* a sibling rivalry, a huge one. Isabel recalled Peter saying 'I won' in that gleeful tone of his when she had decided to stay with him. Perhaps she shouldn't be sitting here now. She should make her excuses and leave. Yet she didn't want to – she wanted to find out more. She felt as she did whenever she slowed down in her car to look at an accident. You shouldn't be doing this, she would say to herself. This is ghoulish. Don't look. But her foot didn't press on the accelerator. She didn't speed away. She observed the splintered glass and the wrecks of cars. She looked out for bodies.

'So—' Peter put a glass of wine down in front of her and returned to his seat. 'Now that you're my newest best friend – by the way, you are my newest best friend, aren't you?'

'Peter—' Isabel sighed. 'You're mad.'

'Ah, but you say it with evident affection. You love me. Good. Anyway, the point is now I can tell you what I've been hoping for from the moment I heard about you. I've been hoping that you'd be the one to solve the problem.'

'What problem?'

'The Gorgonzola problem. And now, meeting you, I'm sure you can – if you haven't already, that is. The way I see it is this: David falls in love with you, divorces Jenny and the pair of you party together into the sunset.'

'You're completely mad,' Isabel stated, her heart beating so fast she felt as if her wine had been spiked with amphetamines.

'And you're completely, madly in love with my brother.'

'That's not true.' Isabel controlled her facial muscles, but she could feel her foot twitch under the table. That was the one movement she couldn't control, what poker players call 'the tell'. Some players, when they were bluffing, played with their rings, some rubbed their earlobes. There were all sorts of physical give-aways that signalled when a person was nervous. She was lucky that hers was, for the most part, invisible.

'Fine.' Peter waved his hand in the air dismissively. 'Whatever you say. Look – I'm perfectly aware I shouldn't, technically, be having this conversation with you. We've just met, blah blah blah.

The point is, I'm worried. You don't understand, Isabel. You don't know our mother. Who is the most controlling person on this planet, as far as I can make out. Though Jenny runs a close second. I broke away. I escaped. So did Sam. He moved to Canada, you see. The two of us are at a distance. But David's caught. He's not only here, in my mother's orbit, but he has also married her clone. It's such a waste. David used to be – well, in the old days, he was my hero. And now I feel sorry for him. I want him to break out. I thought you might be able to help him, that's all. You may not gamble like your father, but you have his expansive personality, I can see.'

'Expansive?' Isabel was startled by his remark. It was the last word she would ever have used to describe herself.

'You know, you don't have to talk as much as I do to be expansive.' He smiled at her and touched her forearm.

'I don't think I'm much like my father,' Isabel said very slowly. 'But then I didn't see him after he left home. He went back to live in America. He'd call occasionally, but that was it.'

'Did you miss him terribly?'

'I—' Isabel felt her stomach tighten. 'I'm sorry, Peter. I'm not used to talking about myself to strangers.'

'Ouch.' Peter took the sunglasses off his head and put them on the table. 'That hurt. Not only am I not your newest best friend, I'm a stranger. And a busybody too. Well, I've told you about my life, but then I tell everyone about my life. Go into any bar in the West Indies. Any customer or bartender you meet will know about my mother, my brothers, my childhood. I tell everyone.'

'Why?' Isabel was riveted. So used to keeping secrets herself, she found it hard to imagine why someone would broadcast the details of his life to anyone who would listen.

'Why not?' he said, then paused. 'I don't know. I suppose my own life strikes me as fascinating, so I think people should hear about it.'

'Do you recap your childhood to passengers in the planes you fly?'

'No,' he laughed. 'But now that you've given me that idea, I just might. "Ladies and gentlemen, our cruising altitude is twenty-two thousand feet. I've turned the seat belt sign off. Now let me tell you about the time I was at a friend's house and my mother came to pick me up and I asked if I could stay five more minutes to watch the end of my favourite television show and she said: "I spent nine months of my life waiting for you to get the hell out of my stomach, why should I spend one more minute of my life waiting for your benefit?" '

'She said that?' Isabel sat back, shocked.

'She did indeed. I have to say, I'm glad Jenny and David don't have children. I can hear Gorgonzola delivering the same kind of sweet, maternal remarks.'

'That's so cruel.'

'Oh, it's nothing in comparison to a lot of things she did. You wouldn't believe how she used to treat David. Especially when he was going through his "I'm going to be a photographer" phase. He'd show her one of his photos – and they were quite good, actually, he had talent – anyway, he'd show our mother a photograph and she'd turn it around and around in her hands and never say a word. Not one word. No praise, no encouragement, not even constructive criticism. She'd look at it and hand it back. End of story.'

'What about your father?'

'Oh, he died when we were young. I was five, David seven, Sam ten.'

'I'm sorry.'

'So am I. Anyway, drink up and I'll get you another.'

'I can't.' Isabel realized she couldn't digest any more information or any more stories. She'd found out so much so quickly she needed to go home and think about it all, on her own. 'I have to get going now, I'm afraid. It's late.'

'No it isn't.' Picking up his sunglasses from the table, Peter placed them back on his head. 'You've had enough of me, that's all. Completely understandable. It happens often in my life. I'm left talking to the air. Perhaps that's why I'm a pilot. But let me see you to your abode, wherever that may be.'

'I'm fine on my own. It's only a couple of minutes' walk from here.'

'Don't be silly. I told you – my job is to take people to their destinations. And you don't even have any luggage.'

Isabel laughed.

'You see, you *do* love me. You can't laugh at someone's jokes unless you're a little in love with them, or at least very much in like. Haven't you noticed that?'

'I hadn't thought about it,' Isabel said. 'But I think you might be right. If you don't like someone, you never think what they say is funny.'

'See? So we're back to being best friends. And so quickly. What a relief. Now—' He stood up and put on his leather jacket. 'Time for me to escort you. Let me help you on with your coat.'

However terrible David and Peter's mother had been, she'd definitely taught them both manners, Isabel thought. Peter also walked on the outside of the pavement, but at no point did he put his hand on the small of her back. She was surprised that he didn't talk, but accompanied her in a relaxed silence.

'Here we are,' she said when they reached her house. 'Number Ten Roland Way.'

At that instant the door opened.

'Hey—' Lily, her housemate, rushed out, keys in her hand. 'Hi, Iz. Sorry, I have to run. I have a hot date and I'm seriously late.' She gave Peter a quick look and wave, then ran across the mews to her car, jumped in, started it up and took off.

'Whew.' Peter stared after her. 'That must be a *scalding* date.'

'I guess so. That was Lily – she shares the house with me. She's also my best friend. My *old* best friend.' Isabel smiled.

'Ah, my competition.' Peter returned her smile.

'Thanks for walking me home.'

'My pleasure,' he bowed.

'Peter. You know, it's very dark outside. Do you really need those sunglasses on your head?'

'Isabel. You might think there is no chance of brilliant sunshine blinding us at – what is it?' He checked his watch. 'Seven-thirty on a February night. But I live in hope. What can I say?'

'Well, *I* hope I see you again soon.'

'I'm sure you will. I'm here for another week, staying with David and Gorgonzola.' He gave her a kiss on both cheeks. 'And you are like your father, whether you know it or not.' With those words, he put his hands in the pockets of his jacket and sauntered off down the mews.

Two hours later, as Isabel sat with a glass of wine, watching television, Lily came in, threw her coat on the sofa and herself next to it.

'What happened to your hot date?' Isabel asked, turning off the tube.

'It turned cold. Icy. The guy is a sleazoid. Halfway through dinner, he told me how much he likes my ass. I told him he *was* an ass and left. Besides—' She sighed. 'He doesn't play tennis.'

'You have to get over this tennis obsession, Lily. You don't play yourself. So why do you need to find a man who does?'

'Don't ask me, Iz. It's just one of those things. I've always had it. Since I was a kid, I've known I couldn't take any man seriously who didn't have an overhead smash in his repertoire.'

'I guess that narrows down the field.'

'I know.' Lily made a face. 'And the field is narrow enough as it is. Where are these men? I feel as if I were playing a game of sardines. All these men are hiding under beds or up in attics or in closets. I'm the last person left, wandering around trying to find them and no one is even giving me a hint. Speaking of closets, who was the cute gay guy?'

'What cute gay guy?'

'The one you were with when I left.' She picked up the bottle of wine on the table in front of the sofa and studied the label. 'Ah. Pinot Grigio. Fun and fruity, just like the man I saw you with.'

'That was David's brother, Peter. And he's not gay.'

'I've been looking for a leather jacket like that for centuries. Do

61

you think I could buy it off him? Is he impoverished? Of course he's gay, Iz.'

'He's *not* gay. He couldn't be. He told me he'd had a relationship with David's wife – before David did.'

'So? You think gay men never have sex with women? There's a gay rule book that forbids it? Maybe he had a relationship with her before he came out.' Lily pulled off her boots, put her feet up on the sofa and began to massage her ankles. 'He's gay, Isabel. Trust me. And you were grilling him about your beloved David's wife? That's not like you. That's something *I* would do. If I were stupid enough to fall in love with a married man, that is. Which I'm not. Or at least I haven't been lately.'

'Can we keep off the topic of David for two seconds? Is that possible?'

'Hey, *you're* the one who had his brother in tow. Not me.' Lily stopped massaging her feet for a second and stared at them in disgust. 'My feet are killing me. I had to stand up all day, modelling a madras shirt, no less. I bet Kate Moss doesn't have to model madras. Why hasn't anyone recognized my supermodel status? Why am I stuck doing catalogue work? I thought that job at Dickins & Jones was boring – this is worse. The photographer kept telling me madras is back. Which doesn't make any sense to me. I look at madras and think of Bermuda shorts. Would anyone wear them except on the island of Bermuda itself? Where would you go wearing a madras shirt? Madras? Would *you* be caught dead in madras? What were you doing with his brother anyway?'

Isabel was used to Lily's method of talking, the way she switched subjects in midstream with no warning and no apparent logic. She'd even learned to understand Lily's thought process, which was no easy task. Often, when other people were around, she found herself translating, explaining what Lily meant and exactly what she was trying to say. Isabel thought some of the confusion might stem from the fact that Lily had spent two years working and travelling in America and had picked up the American way of speaking with a vengeance.

Although she was born and grew up in England and had been back in London for four years, Lily made a point of watching every American television show on offer and using American slang and colloquialisms alongside English slang and colloquialisms, all of which made for a schizophrenic kind of speech pattern. Isabel wondered whether she understood her so well because she was half-American herself. She'd only been to the States once, to her father's funeral, but she could remember exactly how her father spoke when she was a child. Sometimes just listening to Lily made her feel nostalgic for him, and a wave of grief would roll over her, then slowly subside.

'I was with Peter because he walked me home. David introduced me to him when we were having a drink after work.'

'*Another* drink with David.'

'Don't start, Lily.'

'I wouldn't start if you stopped. Iz. Remember Jack? Do you remember how much of a hard time you gave me about him? I'm just returning the favour.'

Jack was a married man Lily had had a short and disastrous affair with the year before. In fact, Jack was the reason Lily was living with Isabel now. She'd announced to her previous flatmate that she was moving out, thinking she and Jack were on the verge of living together. Jack had assured her this was the case and that he was going to get a divorce. He'd even told her he'd found a place for them to live. As it turned out, he'd lied on all counts and Lily had been both devastated and homeless.

Isabel lived through the Jack fiasco with Lily and rescued her by suggesting she come and take the second bedroom in the mews house. Having Lily as a lodger was wonderful in most ways, but at times like this Isabel found herself wishing she lived alone.

'I'm not having an affair with David, so there is no similarity between me and him and you and Jack. I asked you before, Lily. Couldn't we let this subject drop?'

'All right,' Lily tossed her head. 'Okey-dokey. Did I tell you? I bought a brill moisturizer on my lunch break today.' She draped herself over the back of the sofa and retrieved a carrier bag. 'Guess where I got it.'

'Dickins & Jones.'

'The one and only,' Lily laughed. 'Going back into that place gave me the shivers, but after a few minutes, I loved it. Some of the same old people are there. Can you believe it?'

The first time Isabel met Lily, three years before, had been when Lily came into Dickins & Jones looking for a job.

'I'd like to work in something to do with make-up,' she'd said. 'Or toys. If you sell them. If you don't, you should, because toys are like make-up in a way. Do you have a food department? Because I know a lot about olives.'

Looking at this tall, open-faced, striking woman with curly auburn hair and constantly shifting expressions, Isabel had thought: 'She's special. She's a force of nature. It's fun just to be in her vicinity.' Against her better judgement, she gave Lily a job in the cosmetics department. Although Lily had a knack for selling, she was also a chaotic employee, as Isabel had suspected. She'd round up co-workers for lunch breaks which far exceeded the time limit allotted, she would start chatting with other salesgirls and advise them to quit; occasionally she'd do Celine Dion impersonations at the counter in a very loud, off-tune voice. Just as she was about to be sacked, a male customer buying scent for his wife announced to Lily that she'd be perfect as a model in the Lands' End clothing catalogue he was working on. Lily started a new career, but she maintained her friendship with Isabel. Whenever they were both depressed, they'd start talking about the old times at work and end up in hysterical, uncontrollable laughter.

'Let me guess.' Isabel thought for a moment. 'Is Helene still there?'

'Yup. I think she'll die there and be embalmed by Elizabeth Arden. Speaking of death, you haven't answered my question.'

This time even Isabel couldn't follow Lily's thought pattern.

'What question?'

'My question about madras. Would you be caught dead in it? Tell me the truth, even if it hurts.'

'No. I promise you, I'd never wear madras.'

'Good.' Lily began to examine the bottle of moisturiser she'd pulled out. 'That's a relief. It says here I should put this on twice a day. It has copper in it. Does that mean it will stop me from getting wrinkles *and* arthritis?'

It took a few seconds for Isabel to make the connection, but eventually she did, remembering that people with arthritis often wore copper bracelets.

'Definitely,' she said. 'Are you *sure* Peter is gay?'

'Remember, Iz, one of my brothers is gay. I know gay.'

Isabel nodded. She couldn't dispute evidence like that. Peter was gay. Why hadn't she picked up on it? Probably because she was too busy listening to his stories about 'Gorgonzola'. Did David know? Yes, he must. Peter wasn't capable of keeping a secret like that, Isabel thought. And she was sure he wouldn't want to anyway.

'So how *was* the man whose name I'm not supposed to mention? Was he the perfect gentleman as always, pulling out your chair, helping you on with your coat? I know *you* think that's cool, but *I* think all it means is that David should get a job in a restaurant. He'd be perfect as a maître d'. You really should introduce me to him soon. I know a lot of good opportunities for him.'

'Lily—'

'Sorry.' She put up her hands. 'Forget I said anything. The only thing I've ever learned in life is that people fall in love with unbelievably strange types. You know, the photographer today told me he has a thing for those Two Fat Ladies. What's that all about? Their cooking?'

'I'm not in love with David.' Knowing that if she admitted her feelings for David to Lily she'd get a lecture which would last a week at the least, Isabel had continuously denied being in love with him.

'Have some more wine, Iz. I don't know if you're trying to fool yourself or me, but it doesn't wash. We both know what the situation is; you're trying to avoid my superior clarity on the subject of married men, my wisdom gained from painful experience. One of these days, you'll break down and tell me how crazy in love you are and I'll tell you how crazy you are. However, if you'd be nice enough to get me a glass so I don't have to move these fucking feet, and pour me some of that wine too, I'll play the game and keep my mouth shut for now. Deal?'

'Deal.'

Chapter Five

'I appreciate you coming to me, Mrs Malcolm.' Stryker leaned forward in his chair and flashed a smile. 'But I'm not sure I understand. This is your anniversary party, yes?'

'Yes.' Julia Malcolm didn't return his smile. 'Our fifth anniversary.'

She couldn't have been more than twenty-five, not with that face and body. Which meant she'd hit paydirt very early in life. Well, more power to her, Stryker thought.

'So, presumably, you're giving this party together. I'm confused as to why you don't want me to tell your husband you've come here – I mean, that's fine. I won't say a word, but it's a strange request.'

'I made a mistake, Mr McCabe. When we first thought of giving this party, I suggested to Paul that he hire a company called *Party Time*. He's been in contact with them, discussing it all. Now I think that's an error, I think he should hire you. If I tell him I've changed my mind, he'll think I'm indecisive. I don't like being thought of as indecisive. I'm *not* an indecisive person.'

'I see,' Stryker nodded. What the hell difference did it make if she changed her mind about a party organizer? He couldn't figure it out, but then it didn't really matter why she wanted to keep this visit a secret. She was offering him the chance to land a mega party. He had heard plenty about the British entrepreneur Paul Malcolm. A man who gathered a huge amount of publicity and even more money. Giving a Malcolm party would be a coup. And a nice change from figuring out how men could kill more effectively in their pursuit of blood sports.

'I think your company is much more imaginative, much more original than *Party Time*.' Julia Malcolm's elbows were resting on the chair arms and she steepled her fingers in a prayer position. Stryker was interested to see that, although she wore a wedding ring, she had no engagement ring to go with it, no big diamond or ruby or sapphire rock to show off. 'I want a party no one will forget. So does Paul. It will be a very big party, Mr McCabe. A lot of important people will be there.'

'Can I ask you how you heard about *Your Fantasy Team* in the first place?'

'From Fiona Gregory. You remember Fiona, don't you?'

Stryker flinched, but covered it by stretching his smile even wider.

'Of course I remember Fiona,' he said.

I always remember my mistakes. And she was one of them. I broke my rule for her. Stryker McCabe's Rule Number Two – never sleep with a client. Well, I slept with Fiona, in the Pierre Hotel in New York. Bad move, Stryker. She then expected me to take ten per cent off the bill for the party she was giving. And had a shit fit when I wouldn't. So why is she recommending me now?

'She said you gave great—' Julia Malcolm paused, looked down at her lap, tugged her very short skirt down an inch. 'Parties.' She looked up again, with a coy little grin.

'I do give good parties,' Stryker replied, his smile gone. 'And of course I'd be interested in giving this anniversary party for you and your husband. However, if he's already hired *Party Time*, on your recommendation, I don't see how I can make a play for it.'

'Oh, I wouldn't worry about that.' Julia crossed her legs. Stryker noticed the pink high-top sneakers again. Were women supposed to wear sneakers, or, as the Brits called them, trainers, with black tights and a leopard skin skirt? He'd been struck by the neon pink when she'd first walked in. Maybe she wanted to draw attention to her legs. Actually, that was a pretty good idea. The legs were worth looking at. But then so was the rest of her.

'Paul hasn't signed a contract with *Party Time* yet. I think what you should do is get together some promotional material and fax it to him, along with some ideas. Paul loves themes, you know. If you come up with the right theme for the party, he'll be thrilled. And that's where I come in. I can help you. I can tell you what he'd like.'

'What you'd both like,' Stryker suggested. He couldn't get a feeling for this woman at all. She had married Paul Malcolm, a rich, successful man who was at least twenty-five years her senior, but she didn't appear to him to be the typical 'Trophy' wife. Her short black hair had a disconcerting streak of white running through it; her clothes were more punk than designer, her eyes were so narrow it was difficult to see what colour they were. Yet she was beautiful, definitely. Unusually beautiful and voluptuous. When she'd first walked into his office, he'd felt a hefty tug of desire. Now, though, he mentally backed off. He thought if he could see those eyes properly, he would have viewed a lot of calculation and even more arrogance.

'Exactly. What we'd both like.' She ran her hand through her hair, touching, strangely enough, only the white streak. 'You haven't been in this country very long, have you, Mr McCabe?'

'It's Stryker. No. A few months, that's all.'

'Well, you'll find, the longer you're here, that Englishmen love to dress up. What they especially love to do is dress up like women.'

'Oh.' Stryker knew he should take this statement in his stride, but he wasn't sure how blasé to be. 'I guess that's—'

'Fun.' Julia cut in.

'Right.' Stryker nodded, relieved that she'd finished the sentence for him.

'My husband likes dressing up in women's clothing. However, I don't think he'd want to broadcast that fact.'

'No, I guess not.'

This is getting weirder by the second, Stryker thought. What does she want me to do, suggest a Transvestite Ball?

'If you can come up with a party theme which would cater to this penchant of his, then you'll be off to a good start.'

Penchant?

'Nothing too obvious, of course. But I'm sure you can be subtle when you want to be. People have their extra-curricular activities, you know. There's nothing wrong with that, is there? A little fun on the side? You wouldn't object to that yourself, would you?' She had a lilt in her voice, a teasing come-on.

The woman was a player and she wanted to play with him, clearly. Maybe he'd done something that night with Fiona which had earned him a reputation. Stryker McCabe, party man, sex god. If so, he couldn't remember what the hell it was. As far as he could recall, sex with Fiona had been fairly routine. So how was he supposed to handle this? He wasn't about to leap in bed with Mrs Paul Malcolm – no way. She was not only a potential client, she was also kind of scary. Maybe it was the white streak in her hair. Or maybe it was the fact that she was married to a guy who liked to wear women's clothes and she didn't seem to have a problem with it. Or any problem telling other people about it, for that matter. Whatever the case, he knew he couldn't afford to turn her down in any way which would offend her. This party was a big one, a big one he wanted to hook. He'd have to tread carefully.

'Extra-curricular activities are great,' he said. 'As long as they don't interfere with work. On occasion, I've forgotten that principle. But nowadays—'

'Oh, please.' Julia Malcolm interrupted him again. Her eyes were wide enough now to let him see she thought he was a fool. But he still couldn't make out their colour. 'I'm not trying to pull you, Mr McCabe. I don't expect the same kind of service as Fiona received.' She smiled. A smile which included a large helping of disdain. 'This is strictly business. I want *Your Fantasy Team* to organize this party. I won't be asking for any discounts. Not that I'm the one who will be paying you anyway.'

'Right.' Stryker felt himself blushing. He had been a fool. He'd walked into this trap somehow. She may not have been hitting on him, but she was sending out signals. As soon as he made it clear he'd received them, she'd effectively slapped him in the face. English women. Were they all this tricky?

'So—' She picked up her purse, pulled out a card. 'Here is my card. Our home fax number is on the bottom. If you fax any relevant material you have on *Your Fantasy Team*, plus some clever ideas for a theme for our party along the lines we've discussed, I think I can guarantee that Paul will choose you.' She stood up, flicked the card onto his desk. 'You should do all this by tonight at the latest. From what I understand, Paul is thinking of signing a contract with *Party Time* tomorrow. Now—' She hooked her bag onto her shoulder. Its leopard skin print matched her skirt. But her jacket was denim, denim with a few rips. 'We didn't have this conversation, am I correct?'

What was she? A member of the Watergate break-in squad?

'No.' He successfully hid a burgeoning smile. 'We didn't have this conversation. You weren't here. I've never heard of you. I've never met you. They can torture me for weeks, for months and I won't divulge—'

'Goodbye, Mr McCabe,' she said, turning around and walking out.

'Oh.' He watched her disappear. 'Fine. Fantastic to meet you. Great talking to you. Can't wait to do it again.'

'So what do you think?' David was pacing, hands in his pockets. 'Which idea is best?'

'*The Godfather* theme, definitely,' Isabel said. 'It would appeal to all Malcolm's instincts. Power. Control. The man behind the scenes pulling all the strings. Plus we can have fantastic Italian food and great music. *And* everyone can dress like gangsters and their molls. That gives plenty of scope for the men and the women to have some fun. The Mafia still has a cachet, you know. People still love all those Mafia, Wiseguy films. It works. It's a brilliant idea, David.'

'It's not bad.' He shrugged, went back to his chair and sat down. 'We can put it to him tomorrow morning.'

71

'There's just one problem I can see. Only one.'

'What's that?'

'Well, it's an anniversary party. *The Godfather* isn't exactly a romantic theme. Sexy, yes. Romantic – no.'

'I don't think that's a problem.'

'You don't think his wife might want something a little more – well, tender? I've never met her, but most women would, I suspect.'

'I don't know.' David turned his head away, gazed out of the window. 'You have a point, Isabel. But she's young, from what I gather. From what I've read about her, anyway. She's about twenty-five or so, I think. She might be less interested in romance than most women.'

'Because she's young?' Isabel asked, thinking – no, young women, young girls, are *more* romantic. Unless, as common gossip had it, Julia Malcolm had married Paul Malcolm for one reason only.

'I don't know. Perhaps you're right. I don't know anything about her. Maybe we should pitch two ideas to him – *The Godfather* and something else – something romantic, as you put it. Then let them decide.'

'We could suggest something around a wedding theme,' Isabel said cautiously.

'What? All the guest come as brides and grooms?'

'It's a possibility. Brides or grooms or vicars or – or anyone or anything to do with a wedding. Some people might want to dress up as the cake.'

'That would be good.' David laughed, then drummed his finger-tips against his lips, a gesture Isabel had found herself copying more and more often.

'Or bridesmaids, of course. Some women might want to be bridesmaids.'

'It's not a bad idea, Isabel. Not bad at all.'

'Although I've always thought bridesmaids have to wear such ugly dresses.'

'Well, I doubt many people would come as bridesmaids. The women will want to come as the bride, but they can then choose

72

unusual wedding dresses, a wedding dress their mothers would never let them wear. Leather, spandex, you name it.'

Clenching her teeth and her fists, Isabel sat in the chair across from David and told herself yet again that she couldn't keep dropping hints like this. When he didn't pick up on them, she felt humiliated, frustrated and depressed, all at the same time. He didn't remember. That was obvious. She should have known by now; however much she referred to their first meeting, in whatever context, he was oblivious.

'I'll go back to my office and start working on it. I'll make some notes. It might work best if I present the wedding theme to him and you present *The Godfather*.'

'Fine. We haven't come up with locations yet, though. For either of these ideas.' David glanced at his watch. 'I'm going out to lunch in a few minutes, but I should have *The Godfather* theme, location and all, sorted by the end of the afternoon. Why don't you come back in around five and we'll see if we've covered everything?'

'Fine,' Isabel replied. Where are you going to lunch? And who are you going with?

'Oh – before you go, Isabel. Peter told me what a wonderful time he had with you yesterday evening. I think he's fallen in love.'

'Don't be silly.' Isabel smiled.

'No – honestly. You've made a conquest.'

'Peter's lovely. But he's hardly in love with me. He likes to exaggerate.'

'That's true.' David nodded.

Feeling oddly deflated by David's agreement, Isabel stood up to leave.

'Is this a business lunch you're having?'

'No. It's with Peter, actually.'

'Ah.' But this time I'm not included. I shouldn't feel hurt, I should understand. He's your brother, you need time alone with him.

'Well, say hello to him for me, and have fun.'

'There's that word again – fun. The fun Peter insists I never have,' David laughed. 'You must wonder what you've got yourself into. Working with such a stuffed shirt.'

'Never,' Isabel said with embarrassing fervour. 'I've never regretted coming here – not for one second.'

David stood up as well and approached her. When he was a foot away, he stopped, leaned against the front of his desk and crossed his arms.

'You're a precious person, Isabel Sands, you know that? Precious in the best sense of the word.'

'Thank you.' She held his gaze. She held her breath. And waited.

'Right.' He looked at his watch again. 'I'm going to be late. Old fogeys are always on time. It's one of our more endearing qualities. Or more irritating, depending on your point of view. See you later.' He touched her shoulder as he walked past her, out of his office.

Oh, fabulous. Say something like that and walk out. Leave me standing here in a daze. There are times when I love you so much I hate you with a passion.

The woman sitting across from him this time wasn't wearing pink high-top sneakers or anything in leopard print. She had on a dark blue wool skirt which came down to her knees, a frilly white blouse with a high collar, and a blue velvet Alice band. Her shoes were unremarkable. Her face even more so. It had a plumpness to it, a round vacant look which reminded Stryker of a lemon chiffon pie. Why lemon chiffon, he couldn't figure out. But there it was -- a lemon chiffon pie. Sitting in front of him. With that ridiculous headband.

Does she think it will keep her brains from falling out? Stryker asked himself. If so, she was sadly mistaken. As far as he could work out, any brain matter she might have possessed had migrated long ago, to a part of her body where it would never be seen again.

'It's been *yonks*,' she was saying. 'Absolute yonks since I've given one of these parties. Thomas is ten years older than Guy. We

74

hadn't planned on having Guy, not really. It wasn't something we had thought about. He simply came along. I must have forgotten to take . . . well, you know – and there he was suddenly. What a surprise that was!'

Stryker nodded, waiting for her to cut to the chase. He knew he might be in for a long wait.

'And now suddenly tomorrow is Guy's third birthday and there is not one, not *one* entertainer to be had. I've tried them all. Rung every number in the Yellow Pages, even. It's my fault, I suppose. You have to book these things far in advance. It's almost as tiresome as putting them down for schools. We had *such* problems getting Thomas into Colet Court – you wouldn't believe the amount of work that went into that – a full-time job, let me tell you. If anyone says to me that motherhood is not a job, well, I tell them to just try to get their children into the right schools. Then come back and tell me all about it. Anyway, you're my last chance, Mr McCabe. You must be able to help. I've heard how amazing you are. Brilliant. I know you can find me an entertainer. Or one of those clowns. Or one of those balloon-blowers, the sort who make little animals out of balloons, you know that clever trick they have. Children adore those little animals, don't they?'

'I guess so. But I don't organize children's parties, Mrs Sampson. I'm very sorry, but I don't have any idea where I could—'

'Of course you do. Fiona told me how clever you are. You must know someone.'

'Fiona?' Stryker put his hand to his forehead and covered his eyes.

'Yes, of course. Fiona Gregory. She's the one who recommended you to me. She said you are remarkably talented. We were having lunch at the Hurlingham and I told her what a fix I was in and she told me to come to your office straight away and you'd sort me out. And that's precisely what I did. I got into my little Range Rover and drove over here – parking is impossible around here, did you know that? I drove round and round for decades before I finally found a meter. And then – could I find the right coins? Why do they insist on one pound and twenty-p pieces? It's absurd, don't you think?'

'They're making new meters now. Ones which take twenty-pound notes.'

'That's ridiculous! Twenty pounds?'

'Mmm. Twenty pounds for ten minutes.'

'But that's just absurd. No one would pay that amount.'

Stop it, stop it right now, Stryker. This one's too easy to be fun, anyway.

'Back to your birthday problem. I wish I could help you, Mrs Sampson.'

'Polly.'

'Polly. Do you remember that movie, *Parenthood*? Steve Martin was the father and when the entertainer didn't show up for his son's birthday party, he entertained the children himself.'

'You can't be serious?' Polly looked at him. The lemon chiffon pie was aghast. 'Giles? At a children's party? He couldn't blow up a piece of bubblegum, much less a balloon.'

'Well, that leaves Giles out, I guess.'

'I guess.' Polly snorted. 'Poor Guy. And he was so excited. He's invited everyone in his class, you know. If no one entertains, he'll be the only child who hasn't had somebody perform. Can you imagine?' Polly paused. 'The shame of it. It will break his little heart.'

Picking up the telephone, Stryker buzzed Belinda.

'Belinda? Mrs Sampson – Polly – is in a desperate state here. She needs an entertainer for her child's third birthday party tomorrow. Any ideas?' He doubted Belinda would be able to help, but he had a sickening feeling that if he didn't deliver what she wanted, the only way he'd get Polly Sampson out of his office now would be to physically remove her.

'An entertainer?' Belinda asked.

'An entertainer.'

'You want an entertainer?' Belinda repeated.

'That's what I said, Belinda. Do I need to say it again?'

'No.'

Stryker waited.

'Can you help, Belinda? Do you know anyone?'

'Um.'

'Do any of the others know anyone? Would you ask them? I'll hold.'

Stryker smiled as pleasantly as he could at Polly Sampson as he waited for a reply.

'Sorry, Stryker.' It was Laura's voice on the line. 'None of us know any entertainers for children. You could try the Yellow Pages.'

'Gee, thanks,' Stryker said.

'No problem.' Laura's voice was breezy. Stryker put down the phone.

'What time is this party?'

'Four o'clock tomorrow afternoon. If I don't cancel it. Poor little Guy.'

'All right. Listen, I'll do it. As it happens, I can blow up balloons into animal shapes. But that's all I do. Understood? I can't do magic tricks or anything else. Just balloons.'

'Would you wear a costume?'

Stryker put his head in his hands, covering his face. He counted to ten, very slowly. This is what you get for breaking your own rule, McCabe. The curse of Fiona Gregory, coming right back at you. Suck it up, you idiot.

He took his hands away from his face, aimed his gaze at Polly Sampson's headband and narrowed his eyes.

'What kind of costume are we talking about?'

Isabel watched as David went through the notes she'd made on the Wedding Party theme. He nodded his head a few times as he read, he drummed his fingertips against his lips, once or twice he pursed his lips and squinted.

'Excellent,' he said, after he'd turned over the last page. 'I like it. It's a good alternative to *The Godfather*.'

'We can decorate the venue as a church,' she added. 'I thought of actually having it *in* a church, but I think it would be difficult to find the right one, and also it might be a little bit imposing.'

'You're right,' he nodded again. 'What time is our meeting with Malcolm tomorrow morning?'

'Ten.'

'Looks like we've got this sewn up, Isabel.'

'I hope so.'

'Oh, don't worry. I *know* so.'

David's eyes were glassy and Isabel wondered whether he'd had a lot to drink at lunch; she couldn't imagine it as she'd never seen him drunk or even tipsy. Had Peter prodded him into having an extra bottle of wine? Wanting to ask him about his lunch, but worried that she would appear too intrusive, Isabel kept silent.

David left his desk and wandered over to the window overlooking the Old Brompton Road. He stood there, staring out, his hands in his pockets. For a few minutes she watched him, waiting for him to say something, but as he remained mute she decided she should leave him alone. Just as she made a move to get up, he turned around.

'I have some big decisions to make, Isabel,' he said quietly. 'Some very big decisions.'

'Decisions about work?'

'No. I wish that were the case. Decisions about my life.'

'Oh.' What did that mean? Did it mean what she thought it did? What other big decisions were there in life besides work? Marriage. Love. Who you wanted to be with for the rest of your life. What had Peter said to him? He couldn't have told him she was madly in love with him, could he?

'Hello there, party animals!' Peter called out, walking into the office. 'I was wandering the streets and decided I needed a rest. So of course I came here. Isabel, you look stunning.' He came over to her, gave her a hug and kissed her. 'Love the ice blue. I have a shirt in the same colour myself.'

'Thank you, Peter. It's nice to see you again.'

He had interrupted what might have been the most crucial conversation of her life, but in a way she was relieved. She would prefer talking to David about these 'decisions' in a more private place, not in his office. Since he had now broached the subject with her, she was sure he'd carry on, sometime soon, perhaps even after work, and after work was only a half-hour or so away.

'Should we pitch our Paul Malcolm party ideas to Peter and see what he thinks?' David asked, moving away from the window and toward his desk.

'Why not?' Isabel smiled at Peter as he pulled up a chair from the corner of the office and came to sit beside her.

'I can't wait.' He rubbed his hands together. 'Party time! Party on down! Tell me about the atmosphere, the food, the drinks, the music, the sex.'

'The sex?' Isabel raised her eyebrows at him.

'I told you yesterday, Isabel. I live in hope.'

'Shall I go first?' David asked. She nodded at him and he presented *The Godfather* theme, describing it to Peter in detail, turning into a salesman as he spoke.

'Fabulous,' Peter applauded when David finished. 'Bravo. I adore it. Could I come as Frank Sinatra?'

'Hang on a minute – it's my turn now,' Isabel said. 'This is a wedding party, Peter.' She noticed that Peter shot a quick look at David, but she couldn't read what the look was meant to convey. 'A wedding party to celebrate an anniversary . . .' She explained the theme, how it would work with decorations and food and dress. This time, when the speech was finished, Peter not only applauded, he stood up as he did so.

'Brilliant. I love the confetti and rice coming down from the ceiling at the end. It's a nice touch for the happy couple. Although I think the rice should be wild rice, just to keep things upbeat.'

Isabel laughed.

'She adores me,' Peter said to David. 'She laughs at all my jokes so I adore her too. *We're* the happy couple. Do you think you could do me a tiny favour and have a sex change operation, Isabel? That's not a lot to ask, is it? Not when you're in love.'

That answered Isabel's unvoiced question. David did know Peter was gay.

'Well, it seems your idea might be the winner, Isabel,' David commented, with no touch of competitive rancour in his voice. 'We'll see what Malcolm says tomorrow, but my guess is he'll go for the wedding party.'

'What about Mrs Malcolm?' Peter queried. 'I saw a photo of her in *Hello* while I was having a cappuccino at a cafe this morning. She's a piece of work, isn't she? Stunning in a sort of ratbag way. I mean, she must have millions to spend on clothes and she wears the most bizarre assortment of – of items. I could have sworn, when I first looked, that her necklace had dead animals hanging from it, but when I inspected it more closely I could see they were freakish-looking feathers mixed in with clumps of mud.'

'Mud?' Isabel asked.

'It looked like mud to me. Mud with little tiny stones which looked like the eyes of dead animals.'

'I have to see this photograph.'

'*Everyone* should see this photograph. How she wears that stuff and manages to look seriously beautiful at the same time, I don't know. Anyway, she certainly doesn't look the type to wear white as she cuts the cake with her aged hubby.'

'She won't mind,' David said.

'No? Why not?'

'From what I know, which is next to nothing, she doesn't really care about clothes. Whichever theme they choose, she'll show up in whatever she chooses to show up in.'

'Bully for her.' Peter nudged Isabel. 'We admire people who don't care about clothes, don't we? Because we know we care far too much.'

'That's true,' Isabel smiled. 'Is she going to be at this meeting tomorrow, by the way?'

'I have no idea.' David looked at his watch and stood up. 'We should get going, Peter. Jenny expects us back for drinks.'

'Is it that late?' Peter stood up as well and slapped his cheek lightly. 'I have to make a telephone call before the end of business hours. Would you mind if I use your office, Isabel? This call is a little private.'

'A scalding date?' Isabel asked.

'God, I hope so. You don't know how much I hope so. Where *is* your office, anyway?'

'Out the door here and the second door on your right. Dial nine to get an outside line. Good luck, Peter.' She crossed her fingers and smiled.

'Won't be long, David, I promise. Five minutes at the most. More likely two seconds. We can't keep Jenny waiting, I know.' Peter waved the crossed fingers of both his hands at Isabel and went out.

When the telephone rang, Stryker answered immediately with the words: '*Your Fantasy Team*, Stryker McCabe speaking.'

'Stryker. It's Peter here. Peter Barton.'

'Peter.' Stryker tried to put a face to the name. Peter Barton. An English guy named Peter Barton. Nothing clicked. 'Hey, good to hear from you. How's it going?'

'Fine. Everything's fine. Except the weather, of course. I can't get used to the cold, even though I grew up in it. When I left Antigua on Thursday night it was eighty-five degrees. When we landed in Gatwick and the captain told us the temperature, I almost stormed the cockpit and flew back to the sun. Anyway, I'm here for a week and I thought I'd give you a ring, see if you'd like to meet up.'

Aha, Stryker thought. *That* Peter. The pilot he'd met when he was doing a recce of a hotel in Antigua for a party a group of musicians was throwing. Peter and he had somehow started talking to each other in the bar of the hotel and ended up, as Stryker remembered, getting completely hammered on some lethal cocktail called Antigua Smile.

81

'How did you find me, Peter? I mean, how did you know I'd moved here? I haven't seen you in – what is it?'

'Eight months. The world's a bizarre place, Stryker. I'm speaking to you from the enemy camp.'

'Sorry, you've lost me. Is there some pissed-off old girlfriend of mine living in London? Are you at her house now? Who is she? How's she looking? Should I see her again? Oh shit – please don't tell me you're at Fiona's.'

'Fiona? No. When I said enemy, I meant enemy. I'm at my brother's office.'

'You and your brother are enemies? Which are you? Cain or Abel?'

'No, no, that's not it at all. Don't you remember what I told you in Antigua?'

'Peter, we were drunk, as I recall. That's all I remember – the fact that I can't remember.'

'Well, I told you that my brother David works as a party-organizer too. In London. And I'm in his office right now. No. Actually I'm in his partner's office.'

'David Barton? You're David Barton's brother?'

'I am.'

'Oh.' Stryker frowned at the phone. Should he feel guilty about stealing the Malcolm party from Barton? No. Why should he? No contract had been signed yet. It was fair game.

'That doesn't make a difference, does it? I'm not involved in *Party Time* at all. I have nothing to do with it.'

'Hey, Peter—' Stryker said, at a loss as to what to think. Was Peter Barton calling him to get information out of him? Had David heard through the grapevine that Julia Malcolm had come to his office?

'You're a smart man if you have nothing to do with party organizing. It can turn you off parties for ever. You can spend your time daydreaming about becoming a hermit, never seeing another glass of champagne, never, ever, seeing another band, another menu, another fucking tent.'

'It's that bad?' Peter laughed.

'No. Not really. I like to exaggerate.'

'So do I.' After a few seconds of silence, Peter continued: 'What do you say? Would you like to meet up?'

'Sure.' Why not? Peter must have a reason for wanting to see him again. He'd like to know what that reason was.

'How about tonight?'

'Sorry. I'm busy tonight.'

'Tomorrow night?'

'Could we do lunch instead of dinner? I'm out every night this week.'

'Every night?'

The man is insistent, Stryker thought. But I don't want to be rude. And if he's after me for information, he'll be too late to get any that can help his brother. I'll have signed the deal with Paul Malcolm by tomorrow morning.

'How about lunch tomorrow, Peter? Does that work for you?'

'Absolutely.'

'Where would you like to go?'

'There's a nice restaurant I used to go to before I left London for good. It's off Sloane Square and it's called Sambucca. Does that sound all right?'

'It sounds great. I'll book it. One o'clock?'

'One o'clock. And Stryker, I want to say how pleased I am that you're in London. I look forward to meeting up with you again.'

'Same here,' Stryker replied.

'Do you remember what I look like?'

'Of course.' *Did* he remember? No, he didn't. But he probably would as soon as he saw Peter again.

'That's nice. I certainly remember what you look like.'

'See you tomorrow then.'

'Have fun whatever you're doing tonight.'

'I will. Goodbye, Peter.'

Stryker put the telephone down and turned back to his computer screen.

Paul and Julia Malcolm's Fifth Anniversary Party

Theme: *Some Like It Hot*

This theme allows for guests to dress in a variety of ways. It can either be taken as a reference to hot weather – i.e. beach/tropical clothes or to the film *Some Like It Hot*, starring Jack Lemmon, Tony Curtis and Marilyn Monroe.

How explicit do I have to be? Stryker wondered as he read. Do I have to tell Paul Malcolm that Curtis and Lemmon dress up as women throughout the movie or does he know already? He must know, if he has a 'penchant' for that type of thing. Julia Malcolm told me to be subtle. I won't put the cross-dressing reference in. If he doesn't know *Some Like It Hot*, he'll ask what the movie is about when I see him. *If* I see him.

I've got to get my skates on, finish this, fax all the publicity. And get out of the office by eight o'clock. Plus, at some point tonight I need to practise blowing up balloons.

Christ, Stryker, you've really landed yourself in it this time. Three-year-old kids? They'll murder you.

Chapter Six

Isabel was making last-minute notes on the Wedding Party, working late into the night as Lily slept upstairs, done in after another day spent modelling madras. When the doorbell rang, she leapt from her chair at the kitchen table and swore as she saw coffee spill over the last page of her proposal.

'Isabel, Isabel. Wherefore art thou, Isabel?' a voice boomed, a voice she immediately recognized as Peter Barton's. Running to the door and opening it, she pulled him in by the hand and whispered: 'Shh. You'll wake up Lily. It's late, Peter. What are you doing here?'

'Do you know that doesn't mean what everybody thinks it means?' he asked, looking around the front room and then heading for the sofa. He was wearing a white suit and still had the sunglasses on top of his head.

'When Juliet says: "Romeo, Romeo, wherefore art thou, Romeo?" she's not asking *where* he is, but *why* he is. Why, of all the men in the world does he have to be *Romeo*, the one man she isn't allowed to love. Why couldn't he be Joe Bloggs instead of the person her family hates? "Wherefore" meant "why" in those days.' Peter threw himself on the sofa. 'I'm not drunk, by the way, Isabel. I wish I were, but I'm not.'

'I'm glad to see you, you know that, Peter, but why did you come? Is something wrong or is this just a friendly drop-by?'

'I've come for two reasons.' Peter held up two fingers. 'One is to further the cause of true love.' He curled one finger into his palm. 'The other is because I'm scared shitless.' He did the same with the second finger, made a fist, then opened his palm wide as if he had just performed a magic trick.

Isabel went and sat beside him. She could sense that he *was* frightened and she wondered what could have happened.

'True love should come first. So I'll tell you straight off: David and Gorgonzola are not the world's happiest couple. In fact, I would say that their marriage is doomed. Which is a wonderful prospect as far as I'm concerned, but maybe not so wonderful as far as my brother is.'

Isabel didn't know what to say. She thought she must look as terrified as Peter did. Was it possible? Or was Peter exaggerating?

'Let me tell you what happened, as I can see you're speechless. As you know, David and I went out to lunch together. And at this lunch he told me he was miserably unhappy with Jenny, that he thought she was as unhappy as he was, that sooner or later they'd have to bring things to a head, but he wasn't sure when. "Is there a right time to ask for a divorce?" he asked me. "Of course there isn't any 'right' time," I replied. "So," I said, "It's probably best to dive in and do it as soon as possible." I was very circumspect, Isabel. I didn't trash Gorgonzola. I didn't order a bottle of champagne to celebrate, though I certainly wanted to. I sat back and listened.'

'Has he been unhappy for a long time?' Isabel asked.

'It would seem so. He said he married her to please our mother, as if I didn't know that already. He said she doesn't love him. He said he doesn't love her. He did *not* say that he loves someone else, but then he wouldn't. He'd keep that to himself. If, say, he had fallen desperately in love with his female partner, he would want to keep her out of it, if you see what I mean. Until the deed was done, the divorce papers signed. Then he'd be a free man and could come to this new relationship without any baggage. That's the way David works. I think it's quite sweet, actually.'

'What happened tonight? Did they have a row? Is that why you're scared?'

'They did indeed have a row – although that's not why I'm scared. I'll tell you about that anon. Now I will tell you about the row. As I'm sure you recall, we were due at a drinks party at David and Jenny's house. Lots of her City cronies there, all of them ineffably boring. So boring I acted more camply than I ever have in my life. Which did not endear me to Gorgonzola, I have to say. By the way, did you know I was gay straight off, as soon as you met me?'

'Not when I met you. Lily told me she thought you were. Her brother is gay.'

'So she has the antenna to pick up on it. That makes sense. Anyway, no one would have needed antennae at that party, I'll tell you. I was a walking neon advert for gay lib tonight. In fact, I think at one point Jenny came very close to assaulting me, but she had no weapon to hand, poor thing.

'Howsoever – back to the narrative – after the party had ended, David and I were chatting in the kitchen and were having a disagreement. David and I don't fight, we disagree. And in walks Gorgonzola, who promptly goes ballistic. She could have powered the Concorde with the sheer force of her fury. Apparently David hadn't said the right thing to one of the City honchos there. In other words, he hadn't kissed this idiot's ass enough. David, for the first time in his life, as far as I know, entered the fray. He began to yell. I've *never* heard him raise his voice. So I slunk off and hid in the sitting room. A few minutes later the door slammed, David had stalked out. Jenny, in full rampage mode, came into the room, saw me and flew at me. She said, and I quote: "If you insist on prancing around like Lily Savage on cocaine, go do it on the stage, not in my house."'

'I went up to my room like a schoolboy and waited to hear if David came back in, but by eleven-thirty I was tired of waiting and came here – to see you.'

'Do you think David is all right?'

'He'll be fine.' Peter retrieved a cigarette and lighter from his

87

pocket. 'This was the opening salvo, so to speak. It will be messy with Jenny, I'm sure. She'll probably take him to the cleaners, even though she makes loads of money herself. Jenny is like that, she's greedy. Even in bed. Oh God.' Peter closed his eyes and grimaced. 'Why did I have to remind myself of that? Anyway, as long as *Party Time* keeps on the way it's been going, David will be all right financially, I suspect. I *hope*.'

Isabel's thoughts were reeling, her stomach was churning. If David was waiting to be free until he made any sort of romantic approach to her, then his restrained manner with her over these months made perfect sense. It was even possible that he not only remembered their first meeting, he felt exactly the same way she did about it, and was waiting until the right moment to bring it up. And if Jenny was as difficult as Peter was making her out to be, Isabel wouldn't have to feel racked with guilt over their marriage failing.

'It's going to work out for you, Isabel. You two will be blissfully happy, I know.'

She couldn't trust herself to say anything, not yet. What if Jenny and David were making up right now? That was possible, too, wasn't it? She couldn't put all her cards on the table. Soon she might be able to, but not yet.

'So what are you frightened of, Peter? I don't understand. Are you frightened of Jenny? She can't do anything to you, can she?'

'No.' Peter shook his head, lit his cigarette and inhaled. 'I'm not frightened of Gorgonzola. I'm frightened of a man. A man named Stryker McCabe.'

'Stryker McCabe?' Isabel felt her head jerk back. 'What has Stryker McCabe got to do with anything?'

'Do you think I could have a glass of wine?'

'Of course, I'm sorry. I should have offered you some before.' Isabel got up and went into the kitchen, in a state of confusion mixed with joy. She felt like jumping up and down, but she was so dazzled by Peter's mention of Stryker McCabe she couldn't concentrate on her own vision of possible happiness.

'All right,' she announced as she went back in and put two glasses of white wine and an ashtray on the table. 'What the hell does Stryker McCabe have to do with anything, and why are you scared of him?'

'Have you seen him?'

'No.'

Peter took a gulp of his wine.

'Well, if you haven't see him, it might be harder to explain, but I'll try. Do you believe in love at first sight?'

'Yes,' she replied after a second's hesitation. 'Yes, I do.'

'So do I. Because I've experienced it. I was sitting in a hotel bar in Antigua and a man walked in the room and I looked at him and thought: this is it. This is the person who is going to change my entire life. This is someone I want to be with for my entire life. This is what everyone has been talking about, what people write songs and books about. *Now, finally*, I understand.'

'Stryker?'

'Stryker.' Peter nodded. 'I was sitting on a stool at the bar and I thought to myself: all right, Peter, an earthquake has just hit and maybe you're the only person to feel the shock waves and maybe you're not. But this is what's going to happen. You're going to make a pact with yourself now. If that man comes and sits beside you here you'll never be the same again. You'll be in love with him for ever. If he doesn't come and sit beside you, you will forget him and forget the earthquake and get up and get out of this bar as quickly as humanly possible.'

'He sat beside you.' Isabel's voice was a whisper.

'He sat beside me.' Peter leaned back against the sofa and closed his eyes. 'He sat beside me and I *practised* saying hello under my breath for two minutes, getting the nerve up to say it out loud. But he beat me to the punch.' Peter smiled. 'He asked me if he could have a cigarette. He told me he'd given up smoking a week before and if I was nice enough to give him one, could I please be nice enough not to give him another if he asked for another later.'

89

'And?' Isabel prompted after a long pause. Peter finally opened his eyes.

'Sorry. I was replaying that scene in my mind. If you knew how often I'd replayed that scene . . . ' He turned to face Isabel and she saw a self-mocking look in his eyes. 'I'm a hopeless case. Anyway, we spent the evening at the bar and had a lot to drink and at least two packets of cigarettes each.'

'What happened at the end of the evening?'

'He left. He said, 'Great to meet you, Peter' and left. Simple as that. No pat on the back, no handshake, no little wave of farewell. Nothing.'

'I have to ask you something, Peter. Is Stryker—'

'No, he isn't gay. Would God want to make life easier? Oh, I could pretend, I *have* pretended that he's in the closet, desperately waiting for me to open the door for him. But no.'

'You're sure.'

Peter slumped, put his half-smoked cigarette out.

'I'm sure.'

'So why—' Isabel put her hand on his forearm, 'are you frightened of him now?'

'Because I'm seeing him tomorrow. When he walked out of that bar, Isabel, he didn't leave me. He took up permanent residence in my heart. You don't know how much will-power and self-control it took not to fly to New York and see him. I kept telling myself that this would fade, that my feelings would subside over time; a period of recuperation after the earthquake and all will be well. Time heals. Blah blah blah. Well, time didn't fucking heal anything. And one day I took the plunge and called his office in New York. God knows what I would have said to him if he'd been there. "Hi, Stryker, how's the weather? Seen any good films lately?" Shit.' Peter put his head in his hands.

'He wasn't in New York. Some kind person told me he'd moved to London. To *London.* I couldn't believe it. I thought, for a few, brief shining moments, that he'd been thinking about me as much as I'd been thinking about him, that he'd moved here deliberately with me in mind, knowing I came back to visit fairly often. I'm not a well man, Isabel. The line between sanity and madness is growing thinner by the second.'

Isabel hadn't taken a sip of her wine. She was gripped by this story, amazed that, of all the people in the world, Peter should have fallen for Stryker McCabe, the man who cheated at parties. Stryker McBabe, the person she and David had been laughing about only the day before.

'Hang on a second. Was that Stryker you called from my office?'

'Yes. I rang him this afternoon and I'm seeing him for lunch tomorrow. What will I say, Isabel? How can I survive this lunch? I have to make sure I stay sober and don't blurt my heart out. He doesn't know I'm gay. I was ridiculously careful that night not to say anything that might make him think so.'

'Why? Why not tell him?'

'Please. He would have fled as fast as those muscular legs of his would carry him. If he knew I was gay, he'd be looking for it.'

'Looking for what?'

'The yearning. The same look you try to hide when you're with David. You know how fellow Masons can identify each other with their secret handshakes? Well, it's the same with people who are yearning, we have a certain look. A straight man, when he's with a man he knows is gay, checks it out, makes sure there is nothing of that kind going on, even if he does it subconsciously, you know? If he sees yearning, he doesn't feel safe. Women do it on dates, too. They need to know whether this man they're with is a pathetic specimen of desperate love, someone who will call them twenty times a day, someone who might stalk them if things go wrong. So they look for the sign – the yearning eyes. I didn't have to worry that night because Stryker wasn't looking for it. He thought I was a bloke getting drunk and smoking cigarettes with him, not a victim of an earthquake.'

'I have that look when I'm with David?'

'Oh, Isabel, yes. You're not bad at hiding it, for the most part. But yes. Of course.'

'Do you think – do you think he sees it?' Isabel reached for her glass of wine.

'Hard to say with David, but I'd guess so. Don't get upset, though. The way I see it, David's yearning too. There *is* something different about him, definitely, and I'm sure it's love.'

'But does he have that look when he's with me?' Isabel felt as if she were consulting a specialist in diseases of the heart.

'Yes, he has a sort of yearning, a sort of far-away yearning. Yours is up close.'

Far away? What did that mean? Was that good or bad?

'Don't look so anxious, Isabel. You're fine. As I said, you two will be blissfully happy. It's me we have to worry about. Your future brother-in-law. You have to help me, you know. I'm doing my best for you, coming here and filling you in on David and Gorgonzola. Can't you come to lunch tomorrow? Sit at the next-door table and knock me unconscious with a blunt instrument if I start babbling?'

'I'm still not sure I understand. You know he's straight. What do you *want* from this lunch?'

'I want to see him. That's all. I suppose I'm like a tourist who wants to sit gazing at the Taj Mahal. I know I won't own the place, but at least I can look at it. I have to look at it. Gaze into his eyes, all that rot. Obviously I'd like him to gaze back into mine with adoration, but I know there's not much chance of that happening.'

Isabel realized she'd had versions of this conversation many times before, but on all those occasions she'd been talking with a female. What do I say if he rings? How can I be nonchalant when my heart is beating in heavy-metal time? Why did I have too much to drink and tell him how I felt? All these questions and all this angst were familiar to her. Hearing them from a man was odd, but it was also comforting.

Maybe men and women weren't that different, after all, she thought. Perhaps both sexes were equally subject to obsession, self-doubt and dreams of the perfect romance. Perhaps even Stryker McCabe was smitten with someone as well, was sitting somewhere right now, pining over an unrequited love. On further reflection, she doubted it. Men like McCabe didn't allow themselves to lose control. They were always the objects of the desire, not the ones desiring. Poor Peter. He'd said he knew there wasn't "much chance" of Stryker returning his adoration. And that was the tip-off. He'd left the window a tiny bit open by not saying it was impossible. He needed all the help he could get.

'You'll have to approach him as a friend. But that's so difficult.' Isabel sipped her wine and thought. 'It might be best not to see him at all.'

'No, I have to see him. I have to.'

They were both silent for a moment. There's nothing I can say or do, she said to herself. He's intent on seeing him, he'll most likely get hurt, but I can't stop him. After all, I know how he feels. You're standing on a railway track and the train is coming at you at full speed and you can't move. You can't save yourself. You're committed. You're in love.

'What did you and David disagree about?' she asked finally, trying to steer the conversation away from Stryker.

'Stryker McCabe. The answer to every question is Stryker McCabe. I mentioned to David that I'd met him and liked him. I was very casual about it, testing the waters so to speak, and David said: "He's a con man, Peter. You'll be lucky if you never meet him again. I hope *I* never meet the man." Then I asked how he could judge someone whom he'd never met and he said: "You should show more judgement yourself when you *do* meet people" and I don't know where we would have gone from there because in came Jenny and the rest is history.'

'I hope he's all right.'

'I told you to stop worrying, Isabel.'

'I can't help it.'

'No.' He patted her on the knee. 'I know. You can't. We're in the same boat, except your boat is about to take sail and mine is sinking. Christ, even if all my prayers were answered and Stryker suddenly changed his sexual preference and rushed into my arms, I'd be faced with a Romeo and Juliet situation, given the fact that my older brother seems to have taken an inexplicable loathing to my – what shall I call him? My fantasy man, how's that?'

'Appropriate. His company is called *Your Fantasy Team*.'

'Exactly. You don't dislike him, do you?'

'I don't know him.'

'But you don't like what you've heard about him.'

'His methods are different from ours, let's just say that.'

'Ah,' Peter smiled. 'The tactful tone. You *do* dislike him. But you wouldn't if you met him, Isabel. I'm sure of that. Neither would David.'

'I'm sure you're right.' Isabel returned his smile. 'If my newest best friend adores him, I know he must be . . . be . . .'

'Amazing is the word you're searching for.'

'That's it. Amazing.'

'Can I stay here tonight, Isabel? I can't face going back and possibly seeing the hatchet face of Jenny at the door. Would it be too much of an imposition?'

'Of course not. You can sleep on the sofa. I'll get you a sheet, a blanket and some pillows.'

'You're a life saver, you know that?'

As Isabel moved to get up and fetch the bedclothes, Peter put his hand out to stop her.

'You haven't confessed to me yet. You haven't told me how you fell in love with David, how long you've been in love with him, whether it happened at first sight, any of the crucial details I'd love to hear, I *need* to hear.'

'Another time, Peter. I promise I'll tell you, but another time.'

'Why? Why not now?'

'Because it's too soon.' She paused and crossed her fingers. 'It would be bad luck. And anyway I have to get to sleep. We have a big meeting with Paul Malcolm tomorrow.'

'Tomorrow.' Peter dragged his hand down his face. 'Tomorrow. Help. What the fuck am I going to wear?'

Looking at his creation, a balloon which resembled a particularly disgusting sausage, Stryker sighed and then popped it. What was he doing, blowing up balloons at one o'clock in the morning? How crazy was he? And what had ever made him think he could do this gig in the first place? He hadn't blown balloons into animal shapes for twenty years. Trying to do it again wasn't like getting back on a bicycle, it was hellishly difficult. Especially after years of smoking cigarettes. His lungs hurt and his heart was pumping. Was there any way to get out of this party? No. He was caught. He'd promised. He was screwed.

When the telephone rang he felt relief – he was spared from blowing up another of those monsters; and then panic – had something awful happened to one or both of his parents? Was it bad news?

'Hello,' he said cautiously. 'Stryker McCabe speaking.'

'Mr McCabe, it's Julia Malcolm. I rang to tell you you did a good job. The *Tatler* piece on your company was excellent. *And* the *Some Like It Hot* theme caught Paul's imagination.'

'He's seen the movie?'

'Of course. He was puzzled as to how you got our home fax number, but I told him you're obviously a clever and resourceful man. That raises your stock. My husband admires resourceful people. He's one himself.'

'So I've heard. Tell me something, can he blow up balloons?'

'Excuse me?'

'Never mind. Inside joke.'

'We're discussing business, Mr McCabe, not jokes.'

'Yes. Of course.'

What's that tone in her voice? Stryker asked himself. Is it fatigue? Irritation? No, it's authority. She's twenty-five years old and she's chock full of authority. No joking around for Julia Malcolm. She's a serious person, even if she does wear laughable clothes.

'So what is my next move?' he asked. 'Do I call him tomorrow – no *this* morning?'

'He'll ring you. Be at your office by eight and he'll ring you then

95

and set up a meeting. My husband works quite quickly, so I would think you'd be seeing him shortly after he rings.'

Hey, I have nothing else to do, lady. I don't have a company to run or anything. I'm thrilled to be called at one o'clock in the morning – at home. I can't wait to get that call at eight a.m. and run over to see Paul Malcolm. It's not as if I'm a serious person, after all. I give parties, right? That's a joke in your husband's book, isn't it?

'Fine,' Stryker said. 'I'll be at my office by eight.'

'Good.'

Julia Malcolm hung up

Nice talking to you, Stryker said to the air as he picked up another balloon.

Chapter Seven

Isabel heard the chatter as soon as she came downstairs the next morning.

'Come off it,' Lily was saying. 'You can't wear it in the West Indies. It's too hot. The leather would melt. And I've heard that story before, so I win. My story beats yours.'

'I love this jacket. This jacket means a great deal to me. And I've heard your story before, too, so you *don't* win,' was Peter's reply.

Isabel finished her descent and saw them both sitting on the sofa, the leather jacket between them. Lily was stroking it; Peter had a proprietorial hand on its collar.

'So you two have met properly,' she said.

'Good morning, Iz.' Lily stood up. She was dressed in a pair of plaid cotton pyjamas, her hair was tied back in a pony tail and she appeared to have a slathering of the new copper-based moisturiser on her face.

'Yes, we have met properly. We've been up for hours, actually. I was awake early and so was he. When I came down I thought I was dreaming. There was my perfect leather jacket on the sofa. Then, just as I was going toward it, to get my hands on it, I heard a growl from behind me, and there was Peter, with a mug of coffee in his hand. He scared me rigid. Naturally, we began to tell each other ghost stories. The best one wins the jacket. There's a pot of fresh coffee in the kitchen, by the way.'

'Thanks.' Isabel went and poured herself a cup, then rejoined them, sitting on the arm of the sofa. Any irritation she occasionally felt toward Lily for harping on about her relationship with David vanished. Living with someone who said: 'Naturally we began to tell each other ghost stories' was worth occasional nagging.

'Anyway, beat this, Peter. I heard this one when I was in the States,' Lily said as she continued to stroke the jacket. 'This is a true story, by the way. A girl I met in a sauna told me it happened to a friend of hers. This friend, I think she was eighteen or so? She went on her own to her parent's beach house for the weekend, but she wasn't entirely alone, she brought her dog with her. In the middle of the night, she wakes up, hearing the dog sort of whimpering. It must have been a loud whimper to wake her up, but anyway, she gets up and goes to the stairs. She doesn't turn on any of the lights because she doesn't think anything is really wrong. She just wants to make sure her dog is all right, so she calls out his name. Next thing she knows, the dog is licking her hand and she pats him on the head and goes back to bed and falls asleep. Right? Are you with me so far?'

'She's alone in the house and she doesn't turn on the lights?' Isabel asked.

Both Lily and Peter glared at her and Isabel, taking the cue, kept her mouth shut.

'The next morning she goes downstairs and the first thing she sees is the dog's head. The severed head of her wonderful dog is lying at the foot of the stairs in a pool of blood. Beside it there's a note. And the note says—' Lily paused, inhaled, and exhaled dramatically. '"People can lick hands, too." Can you believe it? People can lick hands, too.'

'People can lick hands, too.' Peter grimaced. 'That is *gruesome*, Lily. That is the most gruesome story I've ever heard. I can't believe you told that story at – what is it? Nine o'clock in the morning? How am I supposed to function today? People can lick hands too. Oh God, that's awful.'

'Do I win?'

'You win.' Peter sighed, picked up the jacket and deposited it on Lily's lap.

'It is awful, isn't it?' Lily laughed, hugging the jacket to her. 'But I bet it took your mind off lunch for a millisecond.'

I should have known, Isabel said to herself. I should have known Peter would tell Lily about Stryker within two seconds of meeting her again.

'Peter and I are going out shopping later,' Lily announced. 'We have to find something he can wear for this big lunch. I said that white suit is ridiculous in winter, even with that to-maim-for tan. And I have the day off from madras, thank God. What do you think would appeal to Stryker? The casual look? The designer look? The dishevelled look?'

'I've never met Stryker, remember?' Isabel was worried. Was Lily giving Peter false hope? 'I doubt he'll be too interested in what Peter wears. By the way, does he know you're David's brother, Peter? I forgot to ask you that last night.'

'Yes, I told him. I informed him that I was speaking to him from the enemy camp.'

'Oh.' Isabel turned her face away and felt her heart tighten. Had Stryker agreed to this lunch in order to pump Peter for information about *Party Time*? From what she'd heard about him, the answer was probably 'yes'. What a nasty piece of work. What a slimy, loathsome man. Despite Peter's belief that he'd hidden his sexuality, Isabel guessed that Stryker had, indeed, picked up on it. He probably knew Peter had a crush on him and was going to use that knowledge for all it was worth. Having lunch with Peter was equivalent to fattening up yet another pheasant for the cage. It wouldn't help to warn Peter about Stryker's motives, though. He was too far gone to listen to reason on the subject of Mr McCabe.

She doubted, however, that Peter knew anything of consequence about the workings of *Party Time*. It wasn't as if they had state secrets locked away, or the formula for Coca-Cola. And the biggest party looming on the horizon, Paul Malcolm's, was theirs already. There was nothing Stryker could do to steal that away now; the contract would be signed in a few hours. Still, she didn't like the idea of Peter talking to Stryker about David. Would he tell him about their childhood? About their mother? Gorgonzola? His marital problems? Isabel heard herself sigh as she realized Peter had most likely already told Stryker various details about David, facts that were probably written down and filed under 'My Competition' in Stryker McCabe's bimbo-heavy office. All that she could hope now was that Peter would be discreet about David's current emotional life.

'Isabel?' Peter snapped his fingers. 'Come back to us, Isabel. I can tell you're nervous about this lunch, not as nervous as I am, but nervous nonetheless, and I can guess why. No, I won't let any secrets slip. Not any. I have an agenda for this lunch, you know. I am going to be casual, cool, nonchalant, brilliant, funny, witty, charming and sober.'

'Easy peasy,' Lily said, putting her hand on his shoulder. 'Piece of cake. Tell him the "people can lick hands" story. I bet he'll love that one.'

'You think so?' Peter raised his eyebrows.

'Yes, but leave it till *after* you've eaten.'

'Good advice.' Peter nodded.

'You two are impossible,' Isabel smiled. 'And I'm jealous now. Has Lily taken my place, Peter? Is she your newest best friend?'

'You and Lily can fight over me,' Peter replied. 'I like that idea. Could I be very presumptuous and ask if I can sleep on your sofa for the rest of the week? I'm flying out on Saturday, and I promise I won't make a mess. I couldn't face seeing Gorgonzola again, and I think I should give those two space at the moment.'

'Gorgonzola?' Lily asked.

'Of course you can stay,' Isabel said.

'Are you allergic to cheese?' Lily blinked and stared at Peter.

'It's a long story, Lily. I'll tell you while we're shopping.'

'How do you know if you've been robbed by a gay man?' Lily stood up and put on the jacket.

'The house is tidier than when you left it, there are fresh flowers in the vases and all your furniture has been rearranged.' Peter sighed. 'That's an old one, Lily.'

'I know, but it's one of my favourites. Doesn't this look fabulous on me?' She twirled around and then curtsied.

'It looked better on Peter,' Isabel said. 'But then I have to say that to keep up my ranking in the new best friend stakes. Anyway, I should get going.' She stood up as well. 'Have fun shopping. And good luck with Stryker, Peter. I hope it goes as well as it can. I hope – oh, I don't know what I hope. I suppose I hope when you see him this time there won't be any earthquake. You'll get over him.'

'I don't think so.' Peter frowned.

'He's that gorgeous?' Lily asked.

'He's a Greek God.'

Isabel thought of Hermes and smiled.

Fifteen minutes later, when Isabel walked into her office, she was shocked to see David there, pacing up and down, rubbing his wrist so hard she thought he might be in danger of doing something harmful to his pulse. He had what Lily referred to as the 'dishevelled' look; his suit was creased, his curly brown hair uncombed. Had he been up all night, she wondered? Where had he slept?

'There's been a disaster, Isabel,' he announced, still pacing. 'A total disaster.'

What? Had he gone home and had an even bigger row with Jenny? Were they going to get a divorce right away? Had she kicked him out of the house? Isabel struggled harder than she could ever remember doing to keep any emotion from registering on her face. He was in pain, obviously. The fact that his pain might turn out to be her pleasure was not something she could think about now.

'What's happened?' she asked, staying very still.

'I'm so furious, I'm at a loss. I don't normally get angry, you know that. I like to think I can control my emotions, for the most part. But this is too much.'

101

'What's happened, David?' she repeated.

'Stryker McCabe has struck again.'

Isabel stepped back, feeling suddenly that she was in the middle of a strange dream. She'd prepared herself, she'd been ready, more than ready, to listen to David talking about his fight with Jenny. She'd even, in those few seconds, decided to tell him she already knew the story, had heard it from Peter. If she and David were going to be together, she couldn't lie to him, not even once. As soon as she was certain he felt the same way about her, she'd tell him about her poker playing, she'd tell all the secrets she'd been keeping for years.

The prospect of that moment, when she could finally reveal all of herself to a person she trusted, had been heady. Those two words – Stryker McCabe – had turned everything upside down in an unreal, almost hallucinatory somersault. Isabel didn't speak. She couldn't.

'Do I ring Paul Malcolm? Do I tell him a verbal agreement should be honoured? Do I have to remind him there is such a thing as a gentleman?'

He's talking to himself, Isabel thought. I might as well not be in the room. But what is he talking about?

'David—' Isabel finally took off her coat, hung it on the back of her chair and went to sit down at her desk. 'I'm sorry. I don't understand what you're saying. Could you explain, please? What has Paul Malcolm – or Stryker McCabe – oh God.' She brought her fist to her mouth and chewed on her knuckle. 'He's stolen Malcolm's party from us, hasn't he?'

David grabbed a piece of paper from his pocket, strode over to her and put it in front of her.

'Look at that and tell me I shouldn't be apoplectic,' he said, taking a step back and shoving his hands so far down in his pockets she thought they'd go straight through the material.

I don't want to look, she thought. It's like the end of a poker hand, when the person you're playing against throws his winning cards down on the table and says: 'Read 'em and weep'. She glanced up at David, saw the impatience in his eyes and made herself read the fax.

Dear David and Isabel
I am sorry to inform you that I will not be requiring the services of *Party Time*. As it happens, I received an advance copy of *Tatler* and saw an intriguing article on a new party company called *Your Fantasy Team*. I have decided that YFT's spirit matches exactly what I am looking for re my fifth anniversary celebration.
With best wishes for the future,
Yours sincerely,

Paul Malcolm.

'He can't.' Isabel continued to stare at the fax. 'We're meeting with him *this morning*.'

'He can and he has. We haven't signed a contract.' David approached her desk again and took the fax. '"As it happens, I received an advanced copy of *Tatler*." Listen to that. As it happens. As it happens, Stryker McCabe *sent* him an advance copy. He must have heard that Malcolm was giving this anniversary party and was going to hire us. It's disgusting, underhanded behaviour on his part. Now, why doesn't that surprise me?'

'We should pretend we didn't get the fax,' Isabel said, her mind snapping out of its paralysis and whirring into action. 'Go to his office for the meeting, pitch our ideas. If he listens to us—'

'He won't even *see* us, Isabel. He's made his decision. He'd kick us out on the spot and I, for one, am not keen on being humiliated like that.'

'I'll ring him. I'll ring him straight away. I know I can convince him. Please let me try, David.'

David sat down on the canvas chair across from Isabel and stretched his legs out, drumming his fingers against his lips as he stared at his black wingtip shoes.

'I suppose it wouldn't hurt,' he said. 'Yes. Go ahead. Ring him.'

Isabel flipped open her directory, found Malcolm's number and picked up the phone.

'If you get through, ask him if his wife knows he's changed his mind.'

'Why?'

'Well, we keep forgetting it's her party as well. She might not be as intrigued by *Your Fantasy Team* as he is. After all, we have the reputation. McCabe's a newcomer. She might not want to take the risk of using someone relatively unknown. It's worth mentioning, anyway.'

'You're right. That's clever,' Isabel nodded. They worked well together, she and David. They could bounce ideas off each other easily, and take each other's suggestions without any feelings of insecurity. She punched in Paul Malcolm's number and then told his secretary who she was. A few seconds later the secretary came back on the line and told her he was in a meeting.

'I'll wait,' she said. 'I'll wait and keep waiting until I talk to him. No matter how long it takes.'

During the ten minutes Isabel was kept on hold, she and David discussed which idea she should pitch to Malcolm – *The Godfather* theme or the Wedding Party one. Neither could decide which one would be better, and when she finally heard Malcolm's voice saying, 'Hello, Isabel', in a distinctly disgruntled tone, she cradled the phone against her ear, put both hands up in the air and waved them, signalling to David that she needed a final decision.

'Go with your instincts,' he said quickly. 'You choose.'

'Hello, Paul,' she said brightly. Obviously, being formal with him in her previous dealings and addressing him as Mr Malcolm hadn't helped. If he liked Americans so much, he must like being on a first-name basis.

'Have you had my fax?' he asked.

'Yes, I have, but—'

'Then there's no need for a conversation. I'm sorry, Isabel, but I have made up my mind on this.'

'Paul, please. All I need is a minute of your time. Whatever you may have read about Stryker McCabe and his company, you should be wary. I'm not saying he's not good, but he's not a patch on us. A: he doesn't understand English. I mean—' Isabel caught her mistake and grimaced at David. 'Of course he understands English, but he's not *English*. He's American. He doesn't know London. He's not sophisticated. B: he doesn't have the contacts in the business we do. But I'm not going to take your time pointing out his weaknesses, I want to tell you *our* strength. We came up with an incredible theme for your party, Paul. You'll love it. It's a wedding party, which is why it's so appropriate for your anniversary. Guests come dressed as brides and grooms, but—' Isabel hesitated for a second only. She knew one second was all she could afford. 'It's a wedding party with a difference. An Italian wedding, like the one at the beginning of *The Godfather* film.'

'Yes!' David whispered, making a fist.

'Stop right there, Isabel. A: you're too late. I've already signed with *Your Fantasy Team*. B: although your idea is fine, I prefer Stryker McCabe's. It's as simple as that. Now, I'll keep you two in mind—'

'Sorry to interrupt, Paul, but can I ask you what Stryker McCabe's idea for a theme is?'

'You can ask. I don't intend to answer.'

'Does your wife approve of this change of plans?'

'What the hell business is that of yours?'

'I'm sorry. I thought she'd love the wedding party concept, that's all.'

'She's perfectly happy with what we have. She's ecstatic, actually.'

'If we could pitch our idea to you face-to-face, I'm sure you'd see how well it would work for you both. You'd be doing yourself a disservice if you didn't listen. That's all I'm asking. Let us make an appointment to come and see you.'

'Isabel.' Paul Malcolm then made a noise which sounded as if he were tired of swatting flies away. 'One more time. I've signed with Stryker. I rang your office at eight forty-five this morning to tell you both, but no one was in, so I faxed. The early bird catches the worm, or in this case, the early bird catches the client. Stryker was in *his* office at eight. He came to see me at eight-twenty. These Americans are keen, aren't they?'

Fuck off and die violently, Isabel felt like shouting. Instead, she said: 'Well, if anything goes wrong, you know who to ring, don't you?' She had assumed a chirpy, no-problem voice. Paul Malcolm might come back; she didn't want to alienate him. There was always a chance Stryker might muck up somehow.

'Yes, I know who to ring. By the way, have you met Stryker McCabe?'

'No. No, I haven't.'

'You should, you know. He has the most phenomenal amount of energy. And he's a good-looking man as well. I think you'd like him, Isabel. He has a sort of charm, a charisma. I don't often think that about other men. I like to reserve those adjectives for myself,' Paul chuckled, and Isabel faked a chuckle to accompany his, thinking: Why don't you meet up with Stryker and Peter for lunch and you and Peter can fight over him. That would be fun, wouldn't it, Paul?

'In fact, I'll send you that *Tatler* piece on him now. I'll fax it. You can see why I was so taken with his way of thinking.'

'That's a terrific idea. Thank you, Paul. But I'd like to say, I think you'll come back to *Party Time* soon. Perhaps sooner than you think.'

'We'll see about that. I have to run. Goodbye, Isabel.' Paul hung up before Isabel could return his farewell.

'Sorry,' she said to David. 'No sell.'

'I gathered. What was the "terrific idea?"'

'He's going to fax us the *Tatler* article on *Your Fantasy Team*. Isn't that sweet of him? He thinks Stryker McCabe is charismatic. Charming.'

'I see.' David had a way of half-closing his eyes when he was disappointed which made Isabel want to find a hot towel and press it to his forehead.

'Excuse me.' Nella, David's secretary, knocked as she said this, then came in to Isabel's office and handed David a sheaf of papers. 'This fax just arrived from Paul Malcolm's office.'

'Thank you, Nella,' David said quietly, studying the first page. 'It's an article on our competition.'

'I know,' Nella said in a contrite voice. 'I'm afraid I sneaked a look. Stryker McCabe and *Your Fantasy Team*. There's a photo of him, too. I've been wondering what he looked like.'

'And does he—' David narrowed his eyes, 'look charismatic to you?'

Nella blushed, a sight which surprised Isabel. She realized that she had an ageist assumption that people over forty didn't blush any more. Nella was in her mid-forties, but for the brief time her face had reddened, she looked twenty years younger. Nella can show up for lunch with Stryker too, she thought. At this rate, they could start a new game show hosted by Chris Tarrant. All the contestants declare undying love for Stryker and the audience votes for the person they think is most desperate about him. The winner gets an all-expenses-paid holiday with the world's most charismatic man.

'He's all right,' Nella said brusquely. 'Nothing special.' She left then, and David concentrated on the article, talking to Isabel intermittently as he read.

'A lot about New York, the parties he gave there, blah, blah, blah, how he gives individual attention to each client – as if we don't . . . how he sees London as a challenge . . . and oh, this is good – he has taken up Irish citizenship. That's how he got round immigration. His grandparents are Irish. Isn't that convenient? No reason as to why he left New York . . . more about how parties should be fantasies come true, how much he relies on his clients to inspire him. What a load of—' David stopped, looked from the fax to Isabel.

'So we've lost Paul Malcolm. It's not the end of the world. Let's not give Stryker McCabe any more attention than he deserves. We should keep going, forget this, put it behind us. And get back to work. How's the Palmer party looking?'

This is like dancing, Isabel said to herself. I take his lead and follow it. He wants to move on from this débâcle and I have to help him do just that.

'Fine. The Palmer party is going to be magical.'

'Exactly.' David rose from his chair. 'We do a fantastic job, Isabel. We're the best and we'll stay the best. You know, that was brilliant. The way you combined *The Godfather* and Wedding Party themes. It's his loss.'

'Well, you know that old saying. Revenge is a dish best tasted cold.'

David approached her and kissed her on the top of her head.

'You're a star, you know. I don't know what I'd do without you,' he said, then threw the fax in the wastepaper basket and walked out.

Isabel stared at a photograph on her wall. It was a picture of Fred Astaire and Ginger Rogers, dancing together in *Top Hat*.

It's beginning, she thought. We've taken the first step. The real dance, the emotional waltz, is beginning.

A few seconds later, she reached in and retrieved the fax from the bin.

Let's see what Mr Charisma looks like, she said out loud.

Across the top of the first page a photograph showed a man leaning against a desk, champagne glass in hand. Isabel stared, read the caption: 'Striking a Party Pose – Stryker McCabe comes to London'. Her eyes zeroed in on his face and stayed there.

'Hi there, I'm Ed,' she heard the voice say.

The voice that came out of the mouth of the man who was looking up at her with that same sucker's grin.

Chapter Eight

Stryker walked into the restaurant hoping to hide the fact that he had no idea what the person whom he was meeting looked like. But just as the maître d' approached, he saw a man waving from a corner table, a man he instantly recognized as the pilot from the bar in Antigua. Dressed in black trousers and jacket with a white shirt, Peter Barton looked as naturally tanned as anyone Stryker could remember seeing. The sunglasses on top of his head seemed a little out of place on a cloudridden winter's day, but Stryker was used to seeing men who sported sunglasses constantly. It occurred to him that Freud might have had some fun figuring out the symbolic meaning of shades, but then Freud would have gone apeshit about a man whose parents were both dentists.

'Hi there,' he smiled, as he shook Peter's outstretched hand. 'Terrific to see you again, Peter. You're looking great.'

'Thank you.' Peter pumped his arm, stopped, then pumped it again, before releasing his grip. 'You're looking great, too, Stryker. London must suit you. Sit down, please—' Peter gestured to the chair opposite his. 'I hope you don't mind. I've ordered us both a glass of champagne.'

'Are we celebrating something?'

'No. I mean, not exactly. It's just I thought champagne might be . . . you know . . .'

'A good idea?' Stryker continued to smile as he took his seat. 'It is. In fact, as it happens, *I'm* celebrating something, so it's nice to have someone join me. Although I doubt you'll be too pleased when you hear what it is I'm celebrating.'

'Are you getting married?'

'No way.' Stryker laughed. 'God. What made you think such a scary thought?'

'I don't know.' Peter picked up his napkin, then put it down on his lap again. 'Actually, I do know. It's probably because I heard this amazing, scary story this morning. It's a ghost story—' The waiter came with the glasses of champagne and two menus. Stryker was about to look at what was on offer, but Peter put his menu down on the table top and kept talking.

'The person who told me this story swears it's true and I believe her. Anyway, this girl, I think she's eighteen or nineteen years old, and she goes to stay in her parents' house on the beach with her dog and she wakes up in the middle of the night—'

'People can lick hands, too, right?' Stryker grinned. 'I love that one. It's a classic. But I wouldn't count on it being true.'

'Oh. Right. I thought maybe you hadn't heard it. Oh well.' Peter reached out for his champagne. 'Cheers, then.'

'Cheers,' Stryker nodded and took a sip. The first time he'd heard that story, he'd been fourteen years old. Some girl sitting beside him on the school bus had related it and the last line had scared the hell out of him. He could picture the dog's severed head, even the handwriting on the scrawled note penned by a madman.

'Are you all right, Stryker?' she'd asked loudly. 'You look terrified.' Kids all around the bus turned to stare at the startling prospect of a frightened Stryker McCabe. He'd responded by picking up her hand and licking it. She screamed and the entire busload of fourteen-year-olds had ended up laughing hysterically. Stryker could remember licking the girl's hand, how weirdly perverse he'd felt when his tongue touched her skin, but he couldn't for the life of him remember her name.

'The fact is, Peter, I've just signed a contract for a huge party. But I know *Party Time* was angling for it too. So if you celebrate with me, you might feel it's at your brother's expense.'

'What party is this?'

'Paul Malcolm's. The entrepreneur. It's his fifth wedding anniversary.'

'But David and Isabel are doing that party. I know they are. We were discussing it yesterday.'

'I'm afraid yesterday's gone. I heard about it through the grapevine and sent Paul a little information about me, about *Your Fantasy Team*. He called me early this morning and presto – what is it they say here? Bill's your uncle?'

'Bob. It's Bob.'

Peter Barton looked incredibly nervous, Stryker thought. *Had he been sent here by his brother to spy?* To find out information on *Your Fantasy Team*? Would they spend lunchtime covertly quizzing each other about the party business?

'Bob, right. What a bizarre expression that is. Anyway, I could say I'm sorry for your brother, but that wouldn't be very honest of me. And I'm sure his company is doing well enough without that particular party. *Party Time* has a good reputation.'

'Yes, yes it does. David and Isabel are very good at their work.'

'It's Isabel Sands, right? That's her name?'

'Yes.'

'Well, I'm very good at my work, too. And I think a healthy competition is good. Gets everyone competing fired up.'

'I suppose so.'

Peter lapsed into silence and Stryker wondered what was going on in this man's mind. Now that he had seen him again, he remembered more of that evening in Antigua. Peter had talked. And talked. And talked. The stories he had told had been entertaining, Stryker recalled, although at the end of the night they'd become a little morose. There had been some truly horrible tale of his mother, but Stryker couldn't bring it to mind now. At the time, he'd sat back in shock. And smoked another cigarette.

'You don't have a cigarette on you, do you, Peter?' he finally asked, unable to think of another conversation re-starter.

'Yes, yes I do.' The relief on Peter's face was so evident Stryker felt as if he'd given him a longed-for Christmas present.

'I've stopped again, except for the occasional one. But I spent all night blowing up fucking balloons and I need a treat.'

'Balloons?' Peter asked, giving Stryker a Benson and Hedges and lighting it for him with what Stryker noticed was a shaking hand.

'You won't believe this. I have a gig as an entertainer at a children's birthday party this afternoon. Don't ask me how I got myself into that one, it's too long a story. Anyway, all I can do is blow up balloons into animal shapes, but I'm pretty shitty at it, to tell you the truth. This party is going to be a disaster. All these kids looking at me like I'm a—' Stryker stopped.

'A what?'

'Never mind.' Stryker inhaled and shrugged.

'I think that's wonderful, doing that, for whatever reason. Our birthday parties, my brothers' and mine, were all parties my mother gave for herself. All her friends and their children, none of our friends. Sometimes I think that's why David went into the party business. You know people who give other people nicknames all the time? I think secretly they want to be given a nickname themselves. And I believe David wants to be given a party, you know. A real party.'

'Maybe all of us in the business do.'

'What sort of party would you like for yourself?'

'Ah.' Stryker finished the champagne in his glass. 'I don't think I know the answer to that.'

'Stryker—' Peter took a deep drag of the cigarette he was smoking, then stubbed it out. 'You deserve a party.' He looked away then, but not before Stryker caught something in his eyes, something which made him close his own eyes for a few seconds. When he opened them, he saw that Peter was studying the menu.

'What do you think?' he asked. 'Would you like some pasta? The spaghetti marinara used to be excellent here. And maybe a bottle of Pinot Grigio to go with it? I had some last night and it was very good.'

112

'Sounds great to me. That's a relief.' Stryker leaned back in his chair. 'I always hate trying to decide what to order. I keep changing my mind.'

'Do you change your mind about things often?'

Stryker waited to reply until he'd signalled the waiter and they'd given their orders.

'Some things, yes. I asked a woman to marry me once. Two seconds later, after she'd said "yes", unfortunately, I changed my mind.'

'Did she take it badly?'

'She wasn't thrilled.'

'I suppose it's possible to fall in and out of love quite quickly.' Peter picked up his fork and began to scratch the tablecloth with it.

'It is. In fact, I fell in love at first sight the other night. That's never happened to me before, and I'm still trying to recover. I saw this woman and it was as if . . . as if . . .'

'An earthquake had struck?'

'Exactly,' Stryker nodded. 'I'll probably never see her again, but I can't get her out of my mind. I saw her in a casino of all places. She beat me in a big poker hand and I tried to get her to have a drink with me, but she wouldn't.'

'It might have been worse if she had. You might be even more desperate now.'

Peter was now making patterns with his fork on the white cloth. What he most definitely wasn't doing was making eye contact with Stryker.

'More desperate?' Stryker said softly. 'God, I hope not. This is bad enough. Now I go to that same casino every night, hoping she'll come back. I'm getting to be a fairly good poker player, but I haven't seen any sign of her. I want to ask the other players about her, but I think they'd think I was even more of an idiot than they think I am now. You wouldn't believe some of the people at this place. There's a man named Hermes, the toupee he wears is out of this world. I don't think I've seen anything like it since Liberace.'

'I love casinos. But I'm a hopeless gambler. I lose everything. Very rapidly.'

Peter looked up from the table then, but quickly turned his eyes back down.

'You should come with me, Peter. Help me to hunt for my elusive prey, the mystery woman. You don't have to gamble when you're there.'

'I don't think so.' Peter frowned at his fork. 'I don't think I'd be able to help you.'

The waiter arrived with the bottle of wine.

'Well, it's probably a waste of time, anyway. She won't show up again. Although all the guys there seemed to know her, so I would guess she's a regular. It's bizarre, you know. Obsession. For all I know she's unattainable. Happily married with three kids. But that doesn't seem to make a difference to my feelings.' Stryker paused. 'Maybe if I *did* get to sit down with her, on our own, I wouldn't feel the same way. Maybe if I saw her again, I'd get over it. What do you think?'

'Depends what she's like when you see her again.' Peter picked out another cigarette from his packet and stared at it as if it were a diamond ring. 'She might be just as lovely, just as charming. And just as unattainable.'

'In which case I'd have to give up and bite the bullet, wouldn't I?'

'Bullets aren't easy to digest.' Peter jammed the Benson into his mouth, lit it and finally met Stryker's eyes with his.

Stryker held his gaze steadily while he said: 'No. But if you take a bullet one little sliver at a time, very gradually, it might be a little easier to swallow. When you know you're in a hopeless situation and you have no choice.'

'You think it's a hopeless situation?' Peter continued to stare at him. His eyes were now so full of sadness, Stryker hesitated. For an instant.

'Yes, Peter, I *know* it's hopeless.'

'Well.' Peter turned away then and focused on the waiter, who had arrived with the plates of spaghetti marinara. 'All I can say is that it's impossible for some people to give up. Some people live in hope. There's nothing anyone can say or do to change that. They have these hopes and they suffer because of them.'

'Ah,' Stryker said, picking up his own fork. 'I think people can recover. I think they can find other hopes, hopes and dreams that can become real.'

'I don't think so.' Peter sighed and pulled up a thread of spaghetti with his fork, which promptly fell back onto the plate. 'Things happen, Earthquakes. And you *don't* recover.'

'Hey.' Stryker speared a clam. 'Want to bet on that?'

For the first time she could recall, Isabel left work without saying goodbye to David. She sneaked out of the office at five, having managed to avoid him all day. If she saw him, she knew, she'd have an irresistible urge to tell him she'd met Stryker McCabe. Which meant she'd also have to tell him about her Saturday nights at the Empire. When she had that particular conversation, she didn't want it to be mixed up with business as well. He knew how her father had died and she knew he'd overreact to the idea of her gambling as well. With all the troubles he was having at the moment, she didn't want to add another worry. Also, if she had any sort of personal conversation with him, she'd have to tell him Peter was staying at her house. The idea of then having a discussion about the fight with Jenny, about his marriage and his feelings, an idea which had seemed inevitable and right when she'd walked into her office that morning, now seemed precipitate. For the moment, patience was required, and Isabel was an expert at being patient. She had spent thirteen years waiting for her father to visit her or to ask her to visit him. The fact that he hadn't done either didn't mean she wasn't a master of the art of waiting.

When she walked in her front door at five-fifteen she was not surprised to find Lily and Peter together again on the sofa. Peter sat with his back toward Lily as she rubbed his neck and shoulders.

'It will be OK, Peter,' Lily was saying in a soothing voice. 'I promise you, it wasn't as bad as you thought it was. It can't have been that bad. I'm sure it wasn't. Hello, Izzie. Come and tell Peter he hasn't made a total ass of himself.'

'Peter?' Isabel crossed the room and kneeled on the floor in front of him. 'Oh no. What happened?'

'He doesn't know,' Lily answered as she kneaded his neck. 'That's the problem, as far as I can make out. I got back a few minutes ago myself. He doesn't have a clue what happened.'

'What does that mean? Did Stryker stand you up, Peter?'

'No.' Peter sighed. 'He was there all right.'

'So? I don't understand.'

'We had this conversation. He told me he'd fallen in love with a woman at first sight. Except I don't know if that's true. I think he may have made it all up.'

'Why would he do that?' Isabel shrugged herself out of her coat and settled down, hugging her knees to her chest.

'I think he may have seen the yearning.'

'The earning?' Lily asked, moving her hands to Peter's scalp. 'What's that? Did you pull out your bank statements?'

'The *yearning*, Lily.' Peter sighed again. 'The yearning in my eyes. I'm not sure, that's the problem. *He* closed *his* eyes, just for a second, and then he started to talk about this woman, this woman he's obsessed with. But he may have invented her, you see. That's what I'm not sure of. He might have made her up to let me know he wasn't gay and would never be, but also to let me know he understood my position, how I felt about *him*'.

'Wow. Way too complicated for me, Peter. I mean, I'm not even on the first page here. I'm as lost as you can get on this one.' Lily gave Isabel a cock-eyed look. 'Are you following, Iz?'

'I think so. Are you saying it was like a coded conversation, Peter?'

'Exactly. At least that's what I think. He didn't want to shout "get away from me, you faggot" and run out of the restaurant screaming, so he very subtly brought this woman into the conversation, saying he has no hope of being with her, which I think

116

translated as: "Peter, you have no hope of being with me".'

'On the other hand, she could be real, couldn't she?' Lily asked.

'Possibly.'

'What did he say about her?'

'I do not want to talk about her.' Peter took out a cigarette. 'I do not want to talk about her.' He lit it. 'Whoever she is, if she is, I do not want to talk about her.'

'I think we got the picture, babe.' Lily reached around Peter, took the cigarette from him, took a puff and then returned it.

'Peter.' Isabel put her hand on his knee. 'It doesn't sound like you made a fool out of yourself. You knew already he isn't gay, so if he talked about a woman that shouldn't have surprised you too much.'

'I was *shaking*, Isabel.' Peter waved the cigarette in the air. 'I calmed down a little bit as the lunch went on, but when I lit his cigarette for him I was trembling so much I thought I'd end up missing the cigarette entirely and setting his hair on fire. He must have thought I'd just been let out of a mental institution. Plus, I ordered spaghetti. Can you believe it? Can you imagine what it was like trying to get it onto my fork and then from my fork to my mouth, especially as I had no appetite whatsoever and thought I might be sick at any second?'

'You should never, ever eat pasta on a first date.' Lily gripped Peter's head between her hands and shook it from side to side.

'Lily—' Isabel fired a quick glance at her. 'This wasn't a date.'

'Did I tell you he'd already heard the "people can lick hands" story?'

'You told me the second I walked in,' Lily nodded. 'Sorry about that. I didn't know it was a classic, promise. Anyway, I still say it's true.'

'After the coded – or uncoded – bit of the conversation, we talked about all sorts of things. My being a pilot, his time in Manhattan. He's entertaining at a children's party this afternoon, blowing up balloons into animal shapes. Can you believe that? I think he's the most wonderful person in this universe. Or any other universe, come to think about it.'

117

'Yes, but did he say he wants to see you again? That's the crucial bit.'

Lily stopped massaging and went to sit beside Isabel on the floor in front of Peter.

'He said to give him a ring when I felt like it.'

'Oh great,' Lily laughed. 'So when did you ring? As soon as you saw a phone box?'

'I have an infinitesimal amount of pride.' Peter sat up straight. 'I'm going to wait until tomorrow morning.'

'You know, I once rang a boy I fancied. I was ten years old and I rang him at six-thirty in the morning on a Saturday. His father answered the phone. He said: "What the hell are you doing calling at six-thirty on a Saturday morning?" I said I couldn't wait. Needless to say, the relationship did not flourish.' Lily shook her head. 'It was a shame. He was seriously cute. He even had a little bald spot. A ten-year-old boy with a bald spot – it was so sweet. I wonder if I should track him down and try again.'

'Did Stryker say he has much of a social life in London?' Isabel asked, attempting to keep her tone neutral.

'If you call going to a casino every night a social life, yes.'

'Every night?'

'That's what he said. Every night. He's—'

'What's he do that for?' Lily cut in.

'I'd guess he goes to gamble, Lil,' Isabel answered. 'That's the logical reason.' She looked up at Peter. 'So nothing has changed. You feel the same way?'

'I feel even more the same way.'

'Oh.' Isabel frowned.

'He told me he got the Malcolm party, Isabel. I'm sorry about that.'

'What, *the* Malcolm party?' Lily turned to Isabel. 'He stole that from you? What a bastard.'

'He's not,' Peter protested, standing up and beginning to pace. Isabel noticed that, like David, he paced with his hands in his pockets. 'It's business, that's all. He can't help it if he's good at it.

You'd love him if you met him, Lily, I know you would. And so would you, Isabel. He's—'

'Charismatic?' Isabel put in.

'No. I mean, yes. But it's not that. He's nice. Genuine. Warm. He's a good listener. He *cares*.'

Isabel was trying to do two things at once; first of all, listen to and comfort Peter, secondly work out how she could implement the crazy scheme she'd been forming throughout the day. The fact that Stryker McCabe went to the Empire every night meant the far-fetched plan she had hatched was not so far-fetched any more; it had a chance of working. She didn't even have to wait for the weekend now, she could go to the Empire this evening and meet up with him; she could start to put the plot she'd been formulating all afternoon into action. But could she leave Peter when he was in such a bad state?

'Are you doing anything tonight, Lily?' she asked. 'I have to go out. I don't want to leave Peter alone, but there's something I have to do.'

'Does that something involve a *gentleman* who, like this love of Stryker's, is also possibly more a figment of your imagination than a real person with a high availability factor?'

'No, it does not.'

'I'll be fine,' Peter sighed. 'You can both leave. I'm not a cripple. I'm an idiot, yet. A desperately besotted idiot. But I'll survive.'

'Good,' Lily smiled. 'I'll put Gloria Gaynor on and then make us some spaghetti and give you lessons on how to twirl it as you wait for the next however many hours to pass until you can ring him. I'd say five in the morning is the earliest.'

'You're brutal, Lily.'

'No, I've been there, Peter. And the only way out is to laugh with friends who have been there too. Who have visited that country called Unrequited Passion. Trust me.'

'I must be certifiable.' Peter smiled at her. 'Because I do. I do trust you.'

Two hours later Isabel descended the stairs into the Empire Casino.

119

Instead of heading for the poker tables, she skirted the room, discreetly eyeing who was playing that night. The first person she recognized was 'Ed'. He was on Table Twelve and Micky was sitting beside him. All the other chairs were occupied, one of them by Hermes, but there was no sign of Charlie. Keeping herself hidden from their sight, she approached Matthew and asked to be put on the list for Table Twelve.

'Hey, what are you doing here on a weeknight, Izzy?' Matthew asked, combing his gelled black hair with his fingers.

'Yeah, I dunno, I just sort of felt like it,' she answered, surprised at herself for slipping into a bad imitation of Micky's way of talking.

Matthew gave her an odd look and said: 'There's a seat at Eleven now if you want one. Omaha. High low.'

'No thanks, I'll stick with Hold 'em. Table Twelve. I'll wait.'

'It won't be long, I'd say. George has almost tapped out, as far as I can see.'

'OK, page me when there's a free seat, please.' She smiled at Matthew and retreated, deciding to stand behind a group at a blackjack table. No one would notice her there and she could safely observe what was happening at Table Twelve from a distance.

She watched. 'Ed' was keeping his cards well hidden, Micky was clearly making Micky comments and Hermes was fingering his necklace, then riffling his chips. It would have all been normal enough except for one thing. Micky kept turning to 'Ed' after saying something, with a look which Isabel, even from fifteen feet away, recognized as a desire for approbation. 'Ed' would then say something back and Micky would laugh. Not only did Micky laugh, but Hermes joined in as well. These three were having a whale of a time, Isabel could see as each hand was dealt. They were a regular little comedy act. The fury she felt seeing this made her want to stamp her feet and cry foul. Stryker McCabe had not only stolen Paul Malcolm's business from her, he'd not only reduced Peter to a wreck, he'd co-opted *her* friends, her secret friends. She had spent ages trying to get these people to accept her as an equal, to respect her, and Stryker had managed to worm his way into their affection in four days, or rather four evenings.

'Izzy – Table Twelve.'

Having concentrated so hard on this upsetting Micky/ Hermes/ Stryker alliance, she'd missed seeing someone else get up from the table and leave. For a second after she heard the page, she hesitated. She wasn't sure any longer that she wanted to go ahead with this plan of hers. She wasn't sure she wanted to stay here and witness the male bonding, hear the laughter, watch the pleasure slide across Micky's face as Stryker, otherwise known as Ed, showered him with his 'charisma'. Micky was hers. He'd flirted with her four nights ago. The least he could have done was stay faithful for a few days. Still, her name had now been called, and she could see Micky looking around the room for her. Keeping her head high and a contrived smile on her face, Isabel detached herself from the group of blackjack players she'd been hiding behind and approached Table Twelve.

'Iz, what the hell are you doing here on a Wednesday night?' Micky greeted her.

'I was a little short of cash, so I thought I'd come by the bank here and make my withdrawal.'

No one laughed. Why didn't anyone laugh? That was funny, Isabel said to herself. All right, maybe it wasn't hysterical, but they would have laughed before. Before Stryker.

'Hi there.' Stryker glanced at her as she sat down at the opposite end of the table from him. 'I was hoping to get a chance to win some of my money back from you one of these days.'

'Well, now you have it,' Hermes stated. 'But you know already, Iz is no easy target.'

'You mean not like I was on Saturday?' Stryker grinned. 'Is that what you're trying to say, Hermes?'

'Heaven forbid,' Hermes grinned back.

This is sickening, Isabel thought. I don't know if I can stand this.

'You know what the saying is, don't you, Ed?' Micky nudged him. 'If you can't spot the sucker at the table within the first ten seconds, it's you.'

'You could have told me that on Saturday, you know. Instead of watching me make an ass out of myself.'

'Yeah, right. I'm going to tell you you're the sucker like I'm going to tell you to fold when I have the nuts on the flop?'

'OK.' He shrugged. 'I take your point, Mick.'

Oh, this is fantastic, Isabel thought, straightening stiffly in her chair. He's calling him 'Mick' now. And someone has obviously taught him the poker language. Suddenly he knows what 'having the nuts on the flop' means. I have to calm down. I have to sit patiently and do what I came to do. I can't get up and walk away. There's too much at stake.

'So, Iz—' Micky said as he dealt the next hand. 'What's with the blouse?' He didn't look at her as he said this, he kept his eyes on the cards he was distributing, but Isabel could hear the rebuke in his voice and she felt herself coming dangerously close to blushing. From the moment she'd first come to the Empire, she had dressed conservatively. She wasn't going to be one of those women who tried to distract male players from their game by wearing short skirts and revealing tops; she was above that kind of ploy, she didn't need that sort of help. Instead she'd worn unflattering, loose clothes, eschewing both make-up and jewellery. Izzie was one of the boys at the Empire; when she saw other women players flashing their feminine assets, she would give them a disparaging, superior glance and then get back down to the business of playing. But this night she'd dressed up, not too ostentatiously, yet sexily nonetheless, wearing tight black velvet trousers and a white see-through blouse. Underneath the blouse was a flesh-coloured lacy top. It was what Lily called her 'on the pull' outfit and Isabel hadn't worn it for ages. She should have known that Micky would make a comment. She should have planned what to say. Instead she sat silently, willing the blush to stop before it became embarrassingly evident.

'Don't give her a hard time just because she's decided to look like a girl for once in her life, Micky,' Hermes said. 'Deal the cards.'

Micky hummed *I Wish They All Could Be California Girls* as he dealt and Isabel looked at the cards she'd been given – a pair of jacks. When her turn came to play, she folded them. Jacks might easily have won her the pot but she hadn't come here to win. She'd come here to lose, to lose to Stryker McCabe. If she played cleverly enough, she could lose to him without appearing to be doing it on purpose. That was the beginning move in the long-term scheme she had hatched and she was determined to carry it off: lose to Stryker, get him on his own for a drink, then challenge him to a one-on-one game. If he was as much of an egotist as she thought he was, he wouldn't be able to resist playing against her and he'd think he'd have a good chance of winning.

Of course he wouldn't win. He couldn't beat her; he wasn't skilled enough. But the stake they'd be playing for wouldn't be money, it would be Paul Malcolm's party.

At eight-thirty the next morning, Stryker McCabe would be on the phone to Paul, telling him he couldn't organize the party after all. By nine, Paul would be on the phone to Isabel, asking *Party Time* to take over again.

The plan wasn't foolproof, but it was inspired. It was, Isabel knew, a scheme her father would have loved. If there was any kind of after-life, and if he were watching her right now, he'd have a huge, dazzling smile on his face.

But losing on purpose was not as easy as she had anticipated. Isabel, as she played, remembered a scene in a Fred Astaire/Ginger Rogers film she loved. Fred, desperate to see Ginger, goes to her place of work, a dance studio. He pays to have a lesson with her and then dances horribly, falling all over the place, so that she will have to continue teaching him. Apparently it was one of the more difficult scenes Astaire had to perform in his films, as dancing badly ran against all his natural instincts. The same was true for Isabel. Folding winning hands was almost physically painful and she needed all her control to bet against Stryker when she knew she couldn't win. At the same time, she had to be very careful not to lose too much or play too badly. Hermes would have asked her what the hell was wrong with her; Micky would figure that *something* suspicious was afoot, all sorts of questions would have been asked afterwards.

The mental energy required to keep the right balance of losing hands to Stryker without seeming to lose them on purpose had drained her after two-and-a-half hours. That, and listening to Micky and Hermes treating Stryker as their long-lost brother. After she'd lost a small pot to Stryker yet again, Isabel grabbed the few chips she had left and rose from her chair.

'I think I'd like that drink now, Ed,' she said. 'The one I turned down on Saturday. If you're still on for it.'

'Absolutely,' he replied. 'Good idea. And I'll pay for it, since I've been lucky enough to win back the money I lost to you on Saturday.'

'I wouldn't call you lucky.' Micky said. His eyes narrowed and they were focusing on Isabel. She turned her face away from him.

'Are you coming back, Ed?' Hermes asked in a surprisingly gruff tone. 'Or are you gone for good?'

'I'll be back tomorrow night.'

'Good. Because, you see, Micky and I might have been thinking you've only been coming here to see Izzy again. And if that were the case our feelings would be hurt.'

'Hey, Hermes, I wouldn't hurt your feelings, would I?'

'I hope not, Ed.' Hermes began to shuffle the deck. 'For your sake, I hope not.'

'I'll see you guys tomorrow.' Stryker stood up, put on his jacket, picked up his chips and joined Isabel. 'Time to cash out.'

'Was he serious?' he whispered to Isabel as they headed for the cashier's desk. 'I mean, was that a threat? What did he mean "I hope not, for your sake"? Is he in the Mafia or something?'

Isabel laughed.

'Don't just laugh. Tell me. Is he a mob enforcer?'

'With that wig?'

'Right.' Stryker laughed as well as he handed his chips in and waited for the cash. 'Right. Stupid of me. Sorry. I don't know these guys, that's all. I mean they could be Mob men or they could be astronauts, for all I know. Except Micky told me last night he's a boxer. That can't be true, can it? He'd get murdered in any ring, wouldn't he?'

Now they were heading for the bar and Isabel was smiling, thinking how well her plan was progressing, how easy it had been to get him alone. If he had turned down her invitation for a drink, she would have been foiled, but he hadn't. He'd taken the bait. All she had to do now was reel him in and land him.

'Whatever Micky does, I'm sure he can take care of himself,' she said, as they sat down at a table. 'So. We haven't introduced ourselves properly. What's your last name, Ed?'

'McCabe.'

'Ed McCabe. That's a nice, simple name. What would you like to drink? I think I'll have a vodka and tonic.'

'Sounds good. I'll join you.' Stryker waved the waiter over and gave him their orders, then turned back to Isabel. 'Actually, I'm Edward Stryker McCabe. That's my full name, and before you ask, Stryker was my mother's maiden name. That's what I'm called most of the time – Stryker – but when I came in here on Saturday, I thought Ed would be better. Easier. People sometimes look at me as if I've made Stryker up when I say it.'

'Really?' Isabel sat back a little and regarded him. What was it about him that had sent Peter into a tailspin? She couldn't see it. He was handsome, but he wasn't what she would have called devastating. And why had he chosen to use his middle name if he knew it sounded fake? That was an immediate point against him, not that Isabel didn't have plenty of negative points as it was.

'Well, you know, Stryker does sound a little like some B-movie actor's name. But you haven't told me yours, Izzy. Your last name.'

'Sands,' she answered. 'Isabel Sands.'

'Shit.'

Ha, she thought. Got you. Your turn to be surprised. Your turn to be wrong-footed.

'Excuse me?'

'Sorry.' Stryker shook his head. 'I didn't mean to say that. But you're not the Isabel Sands who works for *Party Time*, are you?'

'I am.'

The waiter came with their vodka and tonics. Isabel deliberately kept her gaze on him, rather than on Stryker. When she finally did meet his eyes, he was staring at her as if he'd just discovered the theory of relativity.

'You knew who I was all along, didn't you?' he asked her. 'Wait a minute – no . . .' He paused, took a sip of his drink. 'You didn't know on Saturday. But then you found out somehow. You found out I'm the man who runs *Your Fantasy Team*. I'm your competition. And you came here tonight, when you don't usually come here, to see me again. Why?'

Things were going much faster than she'd thought they would. He'd made a lot of quick and true assumptions in a short time. She could be coy and pretend she didn't know who he was and hadn't come here to see him, but she suspected he wouldn't believe her protestations. He was more clever than she had anticipated, but all that meant was that she had to cut to the chase more quickly than she'd planned.

'I came here because I have a proposition for you.'

'Oh yeah?' Stryker leant back and crossed his arms. 'Tell me about it.'

'You stoke the Paul Malcolm party from us—'

'I did not—'

'And I want it back.'

'Dream on.'

'I'll play you for it.'

'What?'

'I'll play you for it. Poker. Head to head poker. If you win you get to keep the Malcolm party, obviously, *and* I'll give you the next two big parties that come *Party Time*'s way. I'll manoeuvre it somehow, make sure they go to you instead of us. If you lose, you call Paul tomorrow morning and say you have to back out of the contract. I'm sure you can think of some reasonable excuse.'

'Give me a break.' Stryker unfolded his arms and laughed. 'You're nuts. *And* you're desperate.'

'You don't think you can beat me?'

'Oh please, Isabel.' He tapped his right hand against his forehead. 'How dumb do you think I am? I mean, what's the deal here? You come in tonight and you lose a few hands to me, right? So I'll think you're not as good as everyone says you are. So I'll put my neck on the line in some macho display and go head to head with you, as you put it, and lose my biggest contract. You honestly thought I'd fall for that?'

'You don't think you can beat me?' she repeated, thinking: he's a *lot* cleverer than I thought he'd be. But he'll still fall for it. If I play my hand right, he'll still fall for it.

'So how are the two lovebirds?'

Micky suddenly appeared before them, chair in hand. He wedged it in between their two seats and sat down heavily.

'You planning your wedding? Or an Olympic backflip tag team?'

'I've challenged him to a head to head match, Micky. And he won't take me on,' Isabel said.

'Scaredy cat.' Micky landed a soft punch on Stryker's shoulder. 'I've wanted to go head to head with Iz for years, Ed. What's the problem?'

'Oh, great. Is this part of the set-up, Iz? Get Mick to come along at the right moment and up the macho stakes? You're a piece of work. You really are.'

'What the fuck is going on here?' Micky looked from Stryker to Isabel and back again. 'Jesus, you look like you're in the ring together. What have I missed?'

'Ed's name is Stryker, Micky. It's his middle name, but the one he uses normally.'

'What? As in striker on a football team?'

'It's spelt with a "y" ' Stryker sighed.

'Yeah, so what does that have to do with anything?'

'Not a lot,' Stryker sighed again. 'I have something Isabel wants. So she wants to beat me in a poker game and get it.'

'Get it *back*. That's the accurate way of putting it,' Isabel said.

'You steal her watch on Saturday, Stryker with a "y"? Are you a klepto? Should I check my pockets? Come on – what's going on? What does he have that you want, Iz? What's going on with you two? Do you know each other? Is there a history here?'

'It's a long story, Micky, I—'

'It turns out we're competitors, business competitors,' Stryker interrupted her. 'In case she hasn't told you, Iz organizes parties, that's what she does for a living, and that's what I do for a living too. I just got the contract for a party she wants.'

'Mmm.' Micky looked once more from Isabel to Stryker and back again. 'Parties. What a fucking stupid thing to do for a living. Jesus, Iz. I thought you were in television or something. Something that required a few brain cells. No wonder you never told me. What a disappointment.'

'Thanks, Micky.' Surprised at how hurt she was by his comments, Isabel reached for her vodka and tonic.

Stryker held his hand to the side of his mouth and whispered, 'He likes us, really.'

'So, you hire those bullshit clowns?' Micky asked, turning to Stryker. 'You blow up balloons and shit?'

'You don't know how right you are.'

'Fuck me. And—' he turned back to Isabel. 'You want to play him head to head so *you* can hire the bullshit clowns?'

'Micky—' Isabel put her elbow on the table and her head in her hand. 'That's not exactly—'

'Which is why you've been playing like a drain and losing hands and why you're suddenly wearing that fuck-me blouse? To get Stryker with a "y" here thinking he can beat you? Shame on you, Iz. That is what I would call truly unbecoming behaviour.'

'Micky!' Isabel felt as if she'd been punched in the stomach, punched so hard she had had the wind knocked out of her. Micky wasn't only betraying her, he was humiliating her, and he was sounding like someone out of the Old Testament as he was doing it.

'Still—' Micky pursed his lips, reached into his pocket for a cigar. 'I have to say, I'd like to see it. You two one-on-one. 'Cause I'm not so sure he wouldn't give you a run for your money or your balloons or whatever, Iz. I'm not at all sure he wouldn't.'

'Do you mean that?' Stryker asked.

Isabel inhaled and held her breath. A double bluff. That was what Micky was up to. He wasn't turning on her, he was helping her. He was giving Stryker the incentive to take her on. My God, she thought. He would have been an incredible double agent. John Le Carré could have written volumes about Micky. He is a genius. He is a hero. I adore him.

'Yeah, I mean it. The reason I say it is that you two play very different. Meaning you're both good in different ways. Different styles. I'd like to see it, that's all.'

'Well,' Stryker put his palms up. 'What the hell.'

'Does that mean you're gonna take her on, "Y"?'

Stryker smiled. His smile was so good-natured, Isabel flinched for a second. Remember it's only charisma, she told herself. It's Stryker McBabe being Stryker McBabe. It isn't real. Don't get sucked in. You have to beat him, not join him.

'Sure I'll take her on.'

'Great. Let's do it at my place. It's not far from here. How about it, Iz? How's that sound? I have some beer, some wine, some chips. Neutral territory. I'll deal for you. Everything on the up and up. Everything fair and square.'

'Fine by me.' Isabel quickly touched Micky's forearm. 'Thanks.'

'So let's do it.' Micky stood up and rubbed his hands. 'But Iz, you're going to have to do something about that blouse. I've got a sweatshirt you can borrow. It's clean. Otherwise, forget it. Right?'

'Right.'

Isabel smiled. Stryker put a ten-pound note on the table.

And Micky began to hum *Little Deuce Coupe*.

129

Chapter Nine

Isabel looked at her cards: a ten and ace of diamonds. It was Stryker's turn to bet and he pushed a small amount of chips into the middle of the table. This was a bad move on his part; if he had a reasonable hand he should have tried to scare her out with a big bet, but it was one of the few times since they'd sat down to play that he'd made a mistake.

They'd been in Micky's flat off the Edgware Road for three hours now and Isabel was feeling panic creeping up on her, stealing into her heart and making her muscles tense, her fists clench. Stryker was beating her; not by much, but he was winning nevertheless. Now, maybe, she could relax a little. This hesitant bet of his signalled a chink in his play, a chink which would widen into a chasm given more time. She had to wait him out, that was all.

Yes, he'd done better than she'd expected, much better, but he'd also had some luck. Given time, he would self-destruct and she would win. She had to. There was no choice in the matter. If she didn't win, she would be forced to give Stryker McCabe contracts for two parties, and how could she possibly manage that?

Don't panic, she told herself. Panic is unnecessary and distracting.

Isabel responded to Stryker's bet by raising a large amount, and exhaled in satisfaction as she watched him fold. He then stood up and excused himself while Micky pushed the chips she'd won into her stack.

'Nice, Iz,' Micky commented when Stryker was out of earshot. 'Good bet.'

'He's much better than I thought he'd be,' she replied, pushing up the sleeves of Micky's navy-blue sweatshirt which had the words 'So Few Women, So Much Time' written across the chest. 'I never thought we'd be playing this long.'

'I told you he was good.' Micky shuffled the cards. 'You shouldn't be surprised.'

But it's been a night of surprises, Isabel said to herself, looking around the room. One of the bigger shocks of her evening had been walking into this flat of Micky's, which was not only tidy but aesthetically pleasing. The walls were magnolia, the floor was of polished wood and the furniture, though minimal, was comfortable. She had envisioned a white shag carpet with cigar ash flecked through it and a general atmosphere of men-behaving-badly disarray. Micky was obviously proud of his place, and when he ushered them in he went immediately to straighten a framed black and white photograph of Mohammad Ali which was hanging slightly askew on the far wall.

'Attention to detail,' he stated as he did so. 'God is in the details. God or whoever's in charge of this show.'

As Micky pulled out a folding card table from a closet, retrieved a green baize cloth, some poker chips and then set about finding snacks, drinks and a sweatshirt for her, Isabel and Stryker stood awkwardly, not speaking, not even looking at each other. Like two finalists at Wimbledon before going on to the Centre Court, Isabel had thought, we're gladiators preparing for battle. There's no time for chit-chat or pleasantries. All we want is to get down to the action to see who wins.

The subsequent three hours of play were remarkable for their seriousness. No jokes, no trading remarks, nothing but poker. Micky hadn't cracked a smile or teased them. He'd shuffled and dealt, shuffled and dealt. The one time Isabel had gone to Micky's loo for a break, she'd come back to find Stryker and Micky sitting silently at the fold-out table, both smoking, both with their legs stretched out.

When Stryker returned to the table, Isabel noticed a weariness in his eyes. I've got him on the ropes now, she thought. He's fading. He's not used to the sustained concentration a game like this requires. He's losing it.

'Back to business,' he announced, rubbing his hands and sitting down.

'Back to business,' Micky echoed, letting Stryker cut the deck, then dealing the cards yet again.

The next three hands made Isabel's heart warm with a thrill of impending victory. Stryker was betting with hopeless hands and losing.

He was, as poker players labelled it, 'on tilt', his brain shutting down like a pinball machine that's been pushed too hard. She was level with him and gaining fast; the tide of the evening had turned in her direction and she had to restrain herself from giving Micky a quick look of collusion, a look which would say, 'It's all over now. Finally. He's down for the count.'

Instead, she concentrated on her cards, the nine and ten of spades. She could hit a straight or a flush with those cards, they were playable, definitely, especially as Stryker seemed to have lost his grip. It was his turn to start the betting and he wagered a pathetically small amount, making the same mistake he'd made before going to the loo. He was playing with nothing, she knew. Hoping she'd fold, hoping to steal her ante without even showing his hand. It was a sad attempt at a bluff, and Isabel responded with total confidence. With one authoritative sweep of her hand, she shoved all her chips into the middle of the table, sat back, and waited for him to fold.

Stryker stared at the chips. He looked at his cards again. He reached back with his right hand and rubbed his neck. What he didn't do was fold. Isabel kept her eyes on his face, watching for a sign. What was he thinking about? Was he really considering matching her bet? Had she made a huge mistake? No. He was taunting her, that was all. Making her sweat. Pretending he was considering his cards.

Go ahead, she thought. Take all the time in the world. You're going to fold in the end. And I'm not going to give you the satisfaction of seeing my nerves. Go on, Stryker McCabe, look at me. Try to catch me out, I dare you. You won't see one emotion on this face.

He picked up a few chips, jiggled them in his hand, put them down again. And then he lifted his eyes to Isabel's. She couldn't make out what was going through his brain, but she kept her own expression neutral. Her foot was bobbing up and down under the table, but her face was showing disinterest, she knew, disinterest verging on boredom.

'OK,' he finally said, switching his gaze to Micky. 'How much is in the pot exactly?'

Isabel wanted to scream. He was drawing this out beyond the point he should have, beyond reason. He wanted to know how much was in the pot before folding? She'd witnessed other players playing this psychological trick before, but she would never do it herself. It was a waste of time, a silly ploy.

Micky did a quick calculation of the chips in the middle of the table, then Stryker's remaining ones.

'She's setting you all in, Y. You match the bet and you lose the hand, that's it. End of story.'

'Right,' he nodded. He took another glance at his cards.

As if you don't know what you're holding? Isabel said to herself. Get a life.

She watched as he put both hands on his chips and began to move them forward into the middle of the table. She watched and thought: No. You can't. Pull them back. You can't call me. Isabel stared. He didn't pull back. He left them there, with hers. She felt as if a cold winter wind had suddenly come screaming through the flat, making her shiver in her sweatshirt. This was the hand, the hand that would decide her fate. And she was holding the nine and ten of spades. Isabel wanted to rewind the tape. Why hadn't she simply raised him a little? Why jump the gun and push the whole bloody lot in? What had she been thinking? How could she have been so stupid?

'So,' Micky said, straightening in his chair. 'It's showdown time. Here we go. On their backs.'

Stryker turned over a pair of sixes. Isabel felt dizzy seeing them. A pair. He had a pair. She turned away and focused on the photograph of Mohammad Ali, trying to get her balance back.

'Izzy – on their backs,' Micky said quietly.

He had a pair. She didn't. The odds were he'd win. She was stuffed. She was screwed. She'd ruined everything with one bad bet. Blinking, she kept struggling to get a clear sense of Ali's face, not this swirl of dots she was seeing. It doesn't matter, she thought. There must be some way around this disaster. Two small parties. I can send two tiny parties Stryker McCabe's way. No one will ever have to know what's happened here. But what if Stryker tells? He could blab to everyone in the business about this bet. Why didn't I think before I made it? David will find out then. And he'll lose all respect for me. He'll think I'm mad, he'll—

'Iz—' Micky put his hand on her forearm. 'Let's see your cards, yeah?'

Reaching out and turning over her nine and ten, Isabel felt fury. Fury at having been caught in a bad bet like this, fury at having been outwitted by Stryker McCabe.

'You don't stop, do you?' she muttered, glaring at Stryker. 'You take everything. You *conquer*. And you don't care who gets hurt.'

'Isabel—' Stryker leaned forward, put his hand out as if to touch hers, then drew back.

'Iz—' Micky interrupted. 'The hand isn't over yet. And as I remember, this whole thing was your idea in the first place. This isn't the way to behave.'

Micky was doing it again, chiding her, as he had done earlier in the evening, at the Empire. Isabel blushed and kept quiet as Micky threw away the top card of the deck and dealt the next three face up. A nine of hearts, a ten of clubs and a six of diamonds.

She closed her eyes. She heard herself say, 'Fuck, fuck, fuck,' and as soon as she realized she'd said this out loud, she wanted to disappear for ever. Seeing the nine and ten had given her a millisecond of hope. Her two pair would beat Stryker's sixes. But now he had *three* sixes. All the blood had drained from her body into her face. She could feel the heat of her blush, the fiery shame of being a terrible loser, yet she was still shivering. More than anything she wanted to leave that flat. Get out without having to congratulate Stryker, without apologizing to Micky for bad behaviour, just *run*. But she couldn't. Two more cards had to be dealt, one of which might save her. A nine or a ten. She needed one or the other for a full house.

Isabel opened her eyes and saw Micky throw away another card from the top of the pile and then deal one face up. The queen of hearts. For an instant she imagined herself sliding under the table and weeping, as she had at the wedding. Except this time she would be noticed. And David wouldn't arrive to rescue her. Isabel couldn't look at Stryker, she couldn't look at Micky dealing the last card, she was paralysed by self-loathing and disappointment. Once again, she turned her head to the far wall and stared at Mohammad Ali.

I can't remember. Was he ever beaten? Did he ever lose a fight? If he did, how did he handle it? Was he as shabby, as shameful, as I am?

'Shit!' she heard Micky say. 'Fucking hell. The river, no less. The river can drown you.'

The river. That's what the final card was known as – the river. Isabel knew what had happened. A nine had come up. On the river. She'd won.

'Tough beat, Y,' Micky said. And Isabel slowly rotated, allowed herself to look at the miracle on the table in front of her, stared at the nine of diamonds lying there nonchalantly.

'Congratulations, Isabel.' Stryker's hand was stretched out across the table. Isabel shook it, but couldn't look him in the eye. She would not have been able to shake his hand if she lost, she knew it.

She felt his strong grip envelop hers and she did her best to give as strong a shake back. 'I'll call Paul Malcolm early tomorrow morning, OK?' he continued, after he'd let go.

'Stryker,' she said, struggling to pull herself together. 'I'm sorry about what I said before. I'm tired. I'm not myself tonight. I'm sorry.'

'Hey,' he smiled.

The man is smiling, Isabel thought. This is adding insult to injury. He's not only a good loser, he's a generous loser. And I'm a prat.

'It's late. I understand. Don't worry about it.' He picked up a can of Coca-Cola he'd had resting on the floor and took a swig. 'It's not exactly fun to lose, but it's a hell of a lot better than my afternoon was.'

'What, Y? You get knifed this afternoon?' Micky stood up, stretched.

They're acting so normally, as if nothing special has happened. How can they? This is momentous. I don't understand why Stryker isn't more upset. I don't understand what's going on here. I'm in shock and they're joking around.

'I didn't get knifed, but I did get attacked. By a bunch of three-year-old kids. I was entertaining at this children's party, blowing up balloons into animal shapes. Only my animals didn't look like any animal anyone has ever seen in the wild or in captivity. They looked more like blobs from outer space. So the kids got their own back by squirting ketchup and mustard all over me, and climbing all over me, and basically taking turns kneeing me in the groin.'

'Ouch.' Micky laughed. 'Do you want some whisky?'

'Love some.'

Micky went off to the kitchen at the back of the flat and Isabel made a beeline for the loo. She needed some cold water on her face and time to take in what had happened. She'd made an idiot of herself, definitely. Micky hadn't even offered her a drink. But she'd won. That last nine had given her Paul Malcolm's party. She would have liked to explain why it was so important to her, how much it would mean to David, especially in this time of total stress, yet she knew she wouldn't be able to explain properly. The only way to excuse her bad sportsmanship would be to admit her feelings. 'I love David Barton. I'd do anything for him. I *had* to win, don't you see? Not for me, but for him. That's why I was so angry, that's why I lashed out at Stryker. I needed to win for David.'

Would they understand? Speculation was useless. Isabel knew she wouldn't say anything. She'd just do the best she could to behave well now. Try hard to be friendly to Stryker and win Micky's affection back.

Wiping her face, Isabel looked at her reflection and grimaced. Win Micky's affection back? Go back to the good old days when we were mates? He and Stryker are like Butch Cassidy and the Sundance Kid, they're joined at the hip now. How can I go back to the Empire on Saturday and face them? I don't want to see Stryker again, not if I can help it. And I don't want to go to the Empire. It isn't my private place any more. Stryker has invaded it, exposed my secret. I could go someplace else, another casino, but perhaps this is a sign. Tonight was my big win, the one that counts. I should quit while I'm ahead. And then when I tell David about my poker playing I can talk about it in the past tense. I can say it's over. I've stopped. It will be sad to lose Micky, Hermes, Charlie, all of them. But it has to be that way. This is the end.

When she returned, Isabel saw that Stryker and Micky had moved from the front room, where they'd been playing, into the sitting room on the left. They were sitting side by side on Micky's big, dark blue sofa, their legs resting on the pine coffee table in front of it. Peter would die to be Micky right now, she thought. Stryker's new best friend, his cohort, his brother-in-arms.

'Yeah, Iz – I've put a glass of whisky there for you too—' Micky motioned to the table beside the armchair across from the sofa. 'Go on,' he said, turning to Stryker.

'Yeah, so they made me play this game. Pass the package or something.'

'Parcel,' Isabel said, sitting down and picking up her glass. Stryker, she noticed, had begun his sentence with 'yeah', the way Micky almost always began his. Which couple were they? Butch

Cassidy and the Sundance Kid or Don Quixote and Sancho Panza? Or a combination of both?

'To tell you the truth, it was kind of fun. I even found myself thinking a good party for adults would be one with a children's party theme, you know? So adults could revert to childhood for a night. Throw food at each other and play stupid games.'

'It's been done to death.'

The second she said this, Isabel knew she had sounded like a wet blanket, a *freezing* wet blanket. She was digging herself a deeper hole every time she opened her mouth. 'I mean, it's a fantastic idea, that's why it's been done so often.'

'So—' Stryker threw his arm over the back of the sofa. 'What are you going to do for Malcolm's party now that you've got it. What theme have you got in mind?'

If she didn't answer him, she'd appear, if it was possible, even more ungracious than she had all evening. She didn't want to respond, but if she kept to her plan of not going to the Empire again, this would most likely be the last time she'd see Micky. The thought that he'd remember her as a bitch made her decide to go ahead and tell Stryker. He couldn't steal the idea now, anyway. Even if he was a supreme bastard and reneged on his deal to pull out of the Malcolm party, he wouldn't be able to use the Wedding theme. Paul Malcolm already knew that was *Party Time*'s suggestion.

'We had decided on a Wedding theme, as it's an anniversary party. An Italian wedding, like the one at the beginning of *The Godfather*.'

'*The Godfather?*' Micky chuckled. 'Excellent. Are you going to hire a few hit men for the occasion? Or what? Have a dead horse's head sitting in the middle of the buffet table?'

Isabel tried to laugh along with him. She was looking at Stryker's expression; it was non-committal.

'You don't think that's good?' she asked him.

'It sounds all right,' he replied.

'All right?'

'OK, fine. It sounds fine.'

'What was your idea, Stryker? I'm sure it was *brilliant*.'

'It's irrelevant now, isn't it, Isabel, whatever it was?'

'Hang on, you two. It's like you're back at the table playing poker again. Chill out, Iz.' Micky pulled a cigar out of his shirt pocket. 'I say we should play some more – but this time I get to take part. Because I'm thinking maybe *I* could win a party. How about that? I give great parties. Great themes. Like once I had a paper bag night. So everyone wears a paper bag over their heads, you know. With a number on it, and you talk to each other by using the number on the bag and no one knows who anyone else is and we all get so shit-faced we don't care. How's that for a piss-up?'

Stryker grinned and Isabel laughed.

'Or once I gave a keyring party. You know those? Where you throw your keys into a pile and you pick someone else's keys up and swap partners like they do in the suburbs? Except, with my party, we didn't swap partners or wives or nothing, we swapped cars. For a day, you get to drive someone else's car.'

'What kind of car did you end up with, Mick? A Rolls-Royce?'

'A bloody Bentley, Y. Turbo Mulsanne. You thought I'd say a Rabbit or a Lada or something, didn't you? No. I got the Bentley. Best day of my life, until I got stuck in one of those frigging car parks with sharp corners and couldn't fucking control the thing and ended up scratching the shit out of it.'

'Not a good test drive?' Isabel smiled at Micky.

'Yeah, Iz, you know something? You're cute when you smile. You reconsidering my offer?'

'Sorry, no.' Isabel stood up. This was the time to leave, she knew, and the right note to leave on. 'I'd love to play some more, but I'm shattered. And I've got a lot of work to do tomorrow.'

'How about you, Y, you up for some more Hold 'em?'

'Sure,' Stryker shrugged. 'All I have to do tomorrow is cancel a contract.'

'Stryker, I'm sorry—'

'Isabel, I told you, don't worry. That was a joke. Look, let me show you there are no hard feelings. Let me walk you to a taxi.'

'You don't have to, really.'

'I want to. It's three o'clock in the morning, remember? I don't think you should go out taxi-hunting on your own and Micky has to get the chips set up again.'

'All right,' she nodded. 'Thank you.'

'Here are the keys to get back in—' Micky took them out of his pocket and threw them to Stryker. 'Don't go off with my car, though.'

'Do you still have the Bentley?'

Micky rolled his eyes.

Isabel went over to him, gave him a big hug and a kiss on both cheeks.

'Thanks, Micky. For everything.'

'Yeah, no problem. See you Saturday, Iz. Meanwhile, remember I'm available as a hitman for that party of yours.'

'I will remember.' Isabel put on her coat and headed for the door, Stryker following behind her. She turned and waved at Micky a last time before leaving, but he didn't see her. He was up on his feet, engrossed in shadow boxing with the wall, singing, *When I Grow Up To Be A Man.*

She and Stryker walked to the lift without speaking and, when it arrived, stepped in in silence.

'You know, if you jump up and down in an elevator while it's going down, you can make it travel ten seconds faster per floor.'

Isabel, facing the front, didn't turn around to look at Stryker when he said this.

'If you *scream* while you jump up and down, it travels twelve point two seconds faster,' she stated.

'True. But you have to scream in German.'

'Because?'

'Because German words are heavier.'

'Heavier than Russian?'

'By a millionth of a . . . a . . .'

'Millilitre of sound?'

'Exactly.'

140

She could sense his smile at her back, that grin of his.

The door opened then and she stepped out, waited for him, and proceeded, again in silence, through the lobby and out onto the pavement.

'Oh, damn,' she said. 'I've still got Micky's sweatshirt on.'

'He won't mind.'

'No, I should give it back.' She hesitated, thinking how unbearably silly that blouse of hers would look to Stryker now, now that he knew why she'd worn it in the first place.

'Listen, it's freezing. Give it to him on Saturday. You're coming to the Empire on Saturday, right?'

Isabel gave a semi-nod and was relieved to see a taxi ten yards away from them. Stryker hailed it, Isabel gave the driver her address and said a hasty 'Good night, Stryker' as she was climbing in.

'Listen, Iz. When you think about the Malcolm party, think cross-dressing, OK?' He gave her a little wave and shut the door.

'Cross-dressing? What—'

But the taxi had taken off down the street and Isabel was thrown back in her seat.

I'll post Micky the sweatshirt. And if I'm very lucky I'll never have to see Stryker McCabe again, she thought, settling back. But I don't have to think about Micky or Stryker any more. The point is, I've done it. I've done the impossible. I can't wait to see David's face when Paul Malcolm rings us tomorrow. We can celebrate. We can get some champagne, maybe even some ice cream sandwiches. We can party. I won't tell him about the game, not yet. This game is my very last secret.

I won!

I won, I won, I won!

So why, she asked herself, as she stared out the window at ghostly figures walking along Edgware Road, why do I suddenly feel as if I'd lost?

'Yeah, so you want to cry a little before we play, Y? Get that terrible loss out of your system? What's that word? Emote?'

Micky was back on the sofa, a bottle of whisky at his feet, his cigar lying smouldering in the ashtray by his side. Stryker wondered where his television set was, and why he had a computer, sitting on a desk at the far corner of the room. He couldn't picture Micky at a keyboard, but then he couldn't picture Micky in a boxing ring, either.

'I'm fine, Mick. Don't worry about me. It was only a party.'

'Oh sure.' Micky nodded. 'Absofuckinglutely. Only I was under the impression parties are your business.'

'One lost party isn't going to kill me.' Stryker sat down in the armchair Isabel had vacated.

'No? Not even if it's Paul Malcolm's party, right?'

'Right.'

'You know—' Micky picked up his cigar and studied the tip. 'People say that fights get thrown all the time. Boxers take dives for money. But I've been fighting for – what – twenty-something years now, and I ain't ever seen that happen. Not once.'

'Really?'

'Yeah. So I'm thinking, well, it's interesting. To see someone throw a match. Watch his face when he takes that dive, see how he reacts, what he looks like when he gives it away.'

'That would be interesting.' Stryker nodded.

'It *was* interesting.'

Refiring his cigar with an 'I Love Las Vegas' lighter, Micky took a few puffs and watched the smoke waft towards the ceiling.

'I thought you just said you'd never seen it happen.'

'Not in the ring, Y. But at the table here, tonight. I watched you take that dive.'

'Mick, come off it. I had a pair, remember. A pair. Even a low pair, in a head to head game is a great hand.'

'I watched as you went on tilt.' Micky put his feet up on the table in front and crossed one ankle over the other. 'It reminded me of this book I was reading a while back. I read a lot, you know. Which might surprise some people, but it's true. Anyway, there's this sentence in this book where someone does something and it's *not inadvertent*. That's the words the writer used. *Not inadvertent*. I took some time to work that out, you know, what it meant. But that was you tonight, when you went on tilt. That was *not inadvertent*.

'Then I watched as you decided whether or not to go all in when Iz made that bet. You're taking your time all right. You're figuring it out. You're guessing she has a better pair, aren't you? Or an ace-king at the very least. Your sixes won't stand up. I saw your face when you matched her bet. I saw what it looks like to take a dive. Then I saw what it looks like when that dive gets screwed up. You should have seen yourself, Y, when she turned over the nine/ten. I thought you were going to have a fucking fit.'

'I—'

'And I'm wondering. Why? Why suddenly toss it all away? You'd been doing good up till you went on that not inadvertent tilt. You were ahead. And then you go to the toilet and you come back and fall down flat. Boom. Lifeless corpse in the ring. You take the dive and then suddenly you're scared out of your skin that those sixes are going to give you mouth-to-mouth, pick you up off the canvas, and not only pick you up, make you the champ. Why's that, Y? Why were you so set on losing? You tell me. I'm not giving you another drink until you do.'

Stryker sat without responding for a few seconds, then held out his empty glass. Micky took his legs off the table, poured a shot and sat with his elbows on his knees, his narrowed eyes intent on Stryker.

'Maybe—' Stryker took a big sip out of his glass. 'Maybe I started to notice something. Maybe I saw how nervous she was, how her hands were clenched so tightly all the time, how frightened her eyes looked. Maybe I thought this game meant something more to her, more than the party, the money it would bring in to her company, whatever. There was more to it, Mick. I don't know what, but she was *terrified* of losing. Maybe I thought she needed it more than I did. No one should be so scared. I know what it feels like to be that frightened. It's as simple as that.'

143

'So you were sweating bullets when she showed the nine/ten.'
Micky nodded.

'You better believe it. You're right. I thought she had a high pair,
I was convinced of it. Why else make such a big bet? I was
expecting her to raise me a little, then I would have folded. But
when she bet like that, I assumed she had something huge. I
couldn't believe that nine/ten. I was praying for that third nine or
ten for her. Praying.'

'Me too.'

'You wanted her to win as well? You didn't fix the deal, did you?'

'Y, if I could have fixed the cards I would have dealt out three
nines on the flop and given her four of a kind, put her out of her
misery straight off.'

'Why did *you* want her to win?'

'Listen, I've known Iz for a long time now. Not known like we're
the best of pals or anything, but known enough to like the woman,
to respect her. She's one of a kind, a good-looking bird who can
handle herself at a table, who is fun to play with, muck around
with, you know. She's one of the boys. Or at least she was until
tonight. From the moment she walked in to the Empire I thought:
who the fuck is this? It ain't Izzy. It's like she's had a facelift or
something. Except it was her whole personality. Like she'd been
invaded by some alien. I saw how nervous she was too. That wasn't
Izzy. And I wanted Izzy back. To get her back I reckoned she'd have
to win. Simple as that.'

'Simple as that.' Stryker took another belt of his whisky.

'But I didn't count on you being some kind of saint, Y. Throwing
the game and all.'

'Yeah, well, you can see my halo, can't you?' Stryker motioned
to the top of his head. 'Or is it so bright it's blinding you?'

'Fucking hell.' Micky pointed his finger at Stryker. 'I get it now.
Of fucking course. You're fucking in love with her.'

'I adore it when you speak in such a romantic fashion, Mick.'
Stryker smiled.

'But the way it's looking to me, she'd not only kick you out of bed, she'd step on your face when she got out herself. Poor Y. Sacrifice will get you nowhere, you know.'

'What's going on here, Mick? I thought we were going to play poker, not talk about who is going to kick who out of bed.'

'*Whom*. Get your grammar right. And we *are* going to play poker, right now. Enough of this love shit.' Micky got up and began to move towards the card table in the front room. Stryker stayed sitting in the armchair, turning his glass of whisky around in his hand.

'You coming, Y?'

'What happens?' Stryker asked in a musing tune, staring at his glass. 'What do you do when you're boxing and you go into the ring and you meet your perfect match?'

'You meet your perfect match?' Micky turned back to face Stryker and folded his arms across his chest. 'You start a fire.'

They were dancing. Isabel could see them through the window before she opened the door. Peter and Lily were doing some strange step she'd never seen before, but they seemed to have it well choreographed, going back and forth across the front room in time to a song Isabel couldn't hear. When she went in, she identified it as *I'm So Excited* by the Pointer Sisters. Isabel saw that they'd moved the sofa back against the wall to give themselves more room.

'Iz!' Lily stopped, mid-dip. 'What do you think of our new dance routine?'

'It looks fabulous.' Isabel smiled, took off her coat, and went over to sit on the displaced sofa. 'What is it?'

'It's called the Peter Lily,' Peter said, panting slightly. 'We made it up. It's a radical dance for the Conservatives.'

Lily went to the stereo system and turned down the sound. 'It's a variation on the salsa. Not that I know how to salsa. But it feels Spanish, anyway. We were planning to dance till dawn, so if someone asked either of us how our night was, we could say: "I danced till dawn". But we may have to abandon that project. I'm fading.'

Isabel saw three wine bottles on the table at the back of the room, and a huge bowl.

'How was the spaghetti-twirling lesson?' she asked.

'Peter's a pro now,' Lily said. 'A star. So—' She rejoined Peter and put her arm around his waist. 'How was your evening?'

'Fine. I went to my aunt's.'

'What did I tell you?' Lily looked up at Peter. 'The ancient aunt again. The same one she goes to visit every Saturday night. The one who lives in Berkshire, the one who never telephones here. Marris. Mrs Columbo.'

'Who?' Peter reached for his cigarettes in the pocket of his shirt.

'You know, Marris, Niles' wife on *Frasier*, the woman he always talks about but who never actually appears on screen. Same as Detective Columbo's wife. He goes on and on about her as he solves murders, but we never see her.' Lily left Peter's side and went to sit beside Isabel. 'Why don't you tell us the truth, Iz? I'm seriously bored with this aunt business.'

'I *do* have an aunt in Berkshire.'

'Sure. Right. Whatever.' Lily sighed. 'I like her sweatshirt, Iz. "So Few Women. So Much Time". Just the kind of fashion item an aged aunt would purchase on a trip out to the shops in Berkshire.'

'She likes to dress casually.'

'Which is why you went out in your on-the-pull outfit. And why you reek of cigar smoke. I can see you two now, in those smoky nightclubs in Berkshire, dancing away in your sweats, taking a tab of E every couple of hours. Your aunt is some hot babe, darling. And you're a shitty liar, always have been.' Lily hiccuped. 'Damn. Where's the vinegar? It's the only way to cure hiccups. Drinking vinegar.' She rose and weaved toward the kitchen.

'I'm exhausted. I'm fading too.' Isabel stood up and walked to the staircase. 'And I have to get up early tomorrow. Are you all right, Peter? Are you sure the sofa is comfortable enough?'

'It's perfect,' he said. 'Tell me again what time I can ring him, Lily?' he shouted. 'I've forgotten what you said last.'

'Nine-thirty is the earliest,' Lily replied, coming out of the kitchen with a vinegar bottle in her hand and taking a swig.

'Will someone make sure I'm up by then?'

'I will, promise. See—' She waved the bottle in the air. 'It works. Do you think it's true?'

'What?' Isabel paused before ascending the stairs.

'Do you think it's true that people who dance well together are great in bed together too?'

'Um—' Peter coughed nervously. 'I don't know about that.'

'Oh, relax, Peter, I'm not going to try to convert you. I wonder if Stryker's a good dancer.'

'I'm sure he is.'

'But what if he wasn't? A good dancer or a good anything else? I mean, what if you did manage to get Stryker in bed and he was hopeless? Would that change everything? Would it make you feel differently about him?'

'Lily, you ask the most bizarre questions.' Peter coughed again.

'What do you think, Iz?'

I think David's a wonderful dancer.

'I think I'm going to bed and that you should, too.'

'You sound like my mother,' Lily groaned. 'All right, OK, you win. I'll go to bed.'

I won, Isabel said to herself as she climbed each step. I won. I shouldn't have won, but I did. I was lucky. And maybe my luck will last.

Chapter Ten

Isabel was in her office by eight-thirty the next morning, waiting. She had a large cup of coffee sitting in front of her on the desk, which she would reach out and sip every thirty seconds or so.

Now, she thought. Stryker is ringing Paul Malcolm's office now. Their conversation won't last long. Paul will hang up, annoyed at Stryker for pulling out and then he'll dial this number. It should be ringing now.

She went through these same mental steps hundreds of times as she waited, wondering why it was taking Malcolm so long. Had Stryker changed his mind? She couldn't hold him to the bet, she knew. Perhaps that was why he'd been so unconcerned by his loss. He was going to cheat. He had no intention of giving them the party. He was a con man. A liar. A cad. A bounder . . .

When the phone rang, Isabel took a few seconds to stop listing Stryker McCabe's failings. By the time she picked it up, it had rung three times. Good, she thought. Don't let Paul Malcolm think you're too eager, answering the phone on the first ring. And remember, you have to be surprised. Shocked. No, not shocked, that's too much – surprised.

'Hello.'

'Isabel? It's Paul Malcolm here.'

'Paul! What can I do for you?'

'You can throw me a party,' he chuckled. 'I've changed my mind.

Decided I want *Party Time*. I slept on it last night and thought you were right about McCabe. He doesn't have the connections you do. He's not English.'

Don't rub it in, Isabel. Be cool.

'Well, I have to say, I'm pleased you feel that way, Paul. Should we reschedule our meeting?'

'Good idea. But, Isabel. One thing. You know that theme of yours, the what was it? Something to do with the Mafia?'

'A Wedding theme, Paul, based on the wedding in *The Godfather*.'

'I don't like it.'

'But you said—'

'Yes, I said it was all right, but that was when I thought I wouldn't be using your company. Frankly, it strikes me as boring.'

'You don't think it's romantic?'

'Oh, to hell with romance. I want something *fun*. Something original. I want you to understand – without the perfect theme, well, I'm considering cancelling this party altogether. Or doing it off my own bat. Tell you what. Why don't you and David come over to the house this evening for a drink? That gives you plenty of time to come up with the perfect idea. And you can meet Julia, my wife. It *is* half her party, after all. Even if the expense is wholly mine.' He chuckled again. His chuckle was forced, insincere. She hated the sound of it. But she didn't have to like her clients; all she had to do was deliver the goods for them.

'Great, Paul. We'll be there. What time?'

'Six-thirty.'

'Fine. You know, I think—'

'Have to run. Goodbye.'

Isabel heard the dialling tone, replaced the receiver and stared at it. A perfect theme? She'd already thought of a perfect theme, but he'd discarded it. Now she had to start all over again. Well, that shouldn't be too difficult. The hard part, getting the contract back, was over. Thinking up another theme should be easy in comparison.

'You're in early.' David's face appeared behind the opening door. 'Work, work, work?'

'I have some news to tell you.'

'Good news?'

'Good news.' Isabel was savouring the moment, wanting to draw it out as long as possible.

'Should I receive this good news sitting or standing?'

'Sitting. Definitely.'

David came in, sat down on the chair and made a show out of getting comfortably positioned.

'I'm ready now. Stun me. Surprise me.'

Something is going wrong, Isabel thought, looking at his legs crossed at the knee. This isn't the way I expected it to happen. There's something unnatural about the way he's sitting. He looks as if he wished he could be somewhere else. As soon as I tell him the news, though, he'll be glad he's here.

'Paul Malcolm rang earlier. He wants us back.' She watched his face. She waited for the smile. The joy.

'Really?'

Why didn't he sound surprised? He was as blasé about getting this contract back as Stryker had been about losing it the night before.

'Yes, really.'

'Well, that's wonderful.'

'You don't sound very excited.'

'Don't I?'

'No.'

'Well, I am.' He slapped the arms of the chair and stood up. 'Fantastic news, Isabel. Good way to start the day.'

Good way to start the day?

'Aren't you going to ask what happened to Stryker McCabe?'

'I'm afraid I don't care what happened to Stryker McCabe. I should get to my office, start making some calls. There's a lot of work to be done today.'

'David? Hang on. Aren't you excited? I thought you'd be thrilled.'

'Do you want me to jump up and down and clap my hands and shriek with joy.'

'Yes, absolutely. Go wild, leap on the desk, shout, scream.'

He didn't laugh. He got up from his chair, looking at her as if he were disappointed in her frivolous nature.

'Sorry, Isabel, I'm not in the mood for histrionics. I'm pleased we have the contract back, though. That is good news.' Turning, he headed for the door.

'Wait, David. Before you leave, I need to tell you something. Paul wants us to go round to his house for drinks tonight. I said we would. His wife will be there, apparently.'

'Oh.' He stopped in the doorway.

'Yes. And also, he doesn't like the Wedding theme. He says he will cancel the party if we don't come up with the quote perfect unquote theme.'

'So we'll come up with the perfect theme. Why don't you come in to my office in a couple of hours? Tell me what new ideas you have and I'll tell you mine.'

He took a step out the door. She was desperate to stop him again but couldn't think of a reason.

'David?'

'Yes, Isabel?'

The way he said her name made her think of her childhood; whenever her mother was irritated or disappointed with her, she'd call her 'Isabel' in an identical tone of impatience.

'Sorry, but I wanted to ask. Are you all right?'

'I'm fine.' He smiled, finally, but it was an odd sort of smile, one she'd never seen before. Slightly askew and somehow excluding her from its presence.

'Never better, in fact.'

'Oh.' She planned on asking him why he had never been better, but he was gone before she could get it out.

Wait a minute, she thought, on the verge of running after him. Let me tell you. I did something remarkable last night. I won a poker game. I won our party back. Tell me how wonderful I am, kiss

151

me, make passionate love to me on any available piece of office furniture. Don't leave me sitting here on my own.

She looked down to see her fingers grasping the edge of her desk. Get a grip? I have *a grip*, she said to herself. Why can't I seem to get a life?

'Peter, wake up! It's him! Wake up for Chrissakes!'

Peter opened his eyes and saw Lily hovering above him. She had a mad, excited look, the look of someone about to take a parachute jump for the first time.

'Stryker McCabe is on the phone. *He's* rung *you*. Wake up!'

'Stryker?'

'Stryker.'

Peter leapt from the sofa.

'Where's the phone? Where's the damn phone?'

'In the kitchen. On the wall. Here—' She grabbed his hand and led him into the kitchen.

'I need coffee, Lily. Oh shit. What time is it?'

'Nine-fifteen.' Lily put her finger to her lips when they entered the tiny kitchen, took the receiver from the counter, covered the mouthpiece with her hand. 'Here. There's a cup of coffee there by the sink. Black. You can have a quick hit now, before you say hello.'

'You're not bullshitting me?' Peter mustered enough energy to glare at her. 'It's actually Stryker? I'll kill you if you're having me on.'

'I'm not. It's him. If he hasn't hung up already because of waiting so long.'

'Right.' Peter took a deep breath, closed his eyes. 'Right.' He opened them and took the phone.

'Hello?'

'Peter. It's Stryker McCabe.'

'Stryker. Hello.'

'I hope I haven't woken you up.'

'No. Of course not.'

'I looked up your brother's number and called his house. Some woman there gave me this number for you.'

'I'm staying at a friend's house.'

'Listen, I want to ask a favour. I need to talk to you. Can you come around here, my office? I'm off the King's Road. We could meet at Picasso's – it's a coffee place. Do you know it?'

'Yes, I do.'

'Can you come right away?'

'Absolutely. I'm not far away.'

'Great. I really appreciate this, Peter. I need your help, and I think you'll *want* to help.'

'Any way I can be of service,' Peter said.

'Thanks. See you in around fifteen minutes?'

'Fine. Goodbye, Stryker.'

'Any way I can be of service?' Lily walked into the kitchen. 'You're such an easy lay, Peter.'

'He needs to talk to me. He wants my help. I have to be there in fifteen minutes. Christ. I don't have any clothes. I was going to sneak in and get some while Gorgonzola was out today. Look at this shirt – I've not only slept in it, it has spaghetti sauce all over it. I can't wear it.'

'You can have the jacket back. Just for this once.'

'But I need some sort of shirt.'

'Hang on.' Lily disappeared up the stairs, then rushed back with the sweatshirt Isabel had worn the night before.

'Lily—' Peter shook his head. 'So Few Women, So Much Time? I couldn't possibly wear that.'

'Do you have a choice? Nothing else Izzy or I have will fit you.'

'Could I wear that jacket without the sweatshirt?'

'You want him to think you're a Chippendale?'

'All right, all right. I don't have a choice. I won't take off the jacket. He doesn't have to see the sweatshirt. What do you think he wants? He said he needed my help. Help for what?' Peter went into the sitting room, picked up his trousers from the back of the sofa and climbed into them.

153

'Don't ask me.' Lily threw her hands up in the air. 'What do I know? At least *you* have a date. I don't think I've ever had a date at nine-thirty in the morning. Those boxer shorts are very attractive, by the way. I wouldn't mind a pair like that myself. Except once, on a ski slope. I did have a morning rendezvous. In Aspen, Colorado. This incredible ski instructor—'

'Later, Lily.' Peter threw on the sweatshirt. 'Where's my jacket?'

'My jacket is upstairs in *my* wardrobe.'

'Can you fetch it? I have to comb my hair and brush my teeth.'

'Spray something on that sweatshirt while you're at it. It still reeks of cigars. What the hell *was* Izzy doing last night, I wonder? Sometimes I think she's a high-priced call girl, you know. Why else all the lies about the stupid aunt?'

'You think a rich client is going to give her *this*?' Peter pointed at the sweatshirt. 'Come on, Lil. Get moving. I'm going to be late.'

'He's late, he's late, for a very important date,' Lily sang as she took the stairs two at a time. When she reached the top, she stopped and called down to Peter. 'Maybe Stryker's going to come out. But it's a weird time to choose to come out, isn't it? Nine-thirty in the morning?'

'Any time is a good time,' Peter replied. 'Any time at all.'

Stryker ordered two double espressos and considered having a croissant, but decided on a cigarette instead. He was too tired and too wired to eat. By the time Peter arrived, he'd finished one double espresso and was starting on the next. The caffeine was hitting him like a sledgehammer to the heart.

'Peter,' he said, standing up to greet him. 'Thanks. Thanks for getting here so quickly.'

'No problem.' Peter sat down, and so did Stryker.

'The heating in this place has gone berserk. It's like a sauna in here. Don't you want to take off that jacket?'

'No. I'm fine. Really.'

'I'm glad *someone*'s fine. I'm a wreck. I've been up all night, playing poker. My brain is in meltdown. Want a coffee?'

'Yes, please. You look fantastic, Stryker, sleep or no sleep.'

'I'm tired. I don't know if I'm hungover or still drunk. I'm in the same clothes I wore all night. I look like shit, Peter.'

Stryker signalled a waitress and Peter ordered a cappuccino.

'You want a cigarette?'

'I've got one, thanks.' Peter pulled a packet of Bensons and a lighter out of his jacket. Stryker caught a quick glance of the sweatshirt he was wearing and felt a strange stab somewhere in the vicinity of his ribs.

'What's that you're wearing?'

'This. Oh, it's nothing. A silly sweatshirt.'

'But what does it say?'

'Nothing.'

Stryker leaned over and pushed Peter's jacket open.

'Where'd you get that?'

'I borrowed it from the friend I'm staying with.'

Peter is staying with Isabel? Some other woman answered the phone. Who's she? And why is Peter staying with Isabel? Was I wrong yesterday? Did I misread his signals? Are he and Isabel . . . Hold on. Calm down. Concentrate. Isabel is David's partner, and Peter is David's brother, so Isabel could easily be a friend of Peter's. And Peter could easily be staying with her as a friend only . . . and the knee bone is connected to the thigh bone and the thigh bone's connected to . . . Stop it, Stryker. Pull yourself together. It's caffeine you're overdosing on, not speed.

'Is this an old friend of yours?' he asked after the waitress had delivered the cappuccino.

'It's Isabel Sands, actually.' Peter puffed nervously. 'I don't normally wear women's clothing, although this isn't hers. Oh God, why is this so confusing? What I mean is that *she* must have borrowed it from a man. Or else her aunt.'

'Her aunt? Her aunt has a sweatshirt saying "So Few Women, So Much Time"?'

Stryker kept his gaze firmly fixed on the sweatshirt.

'She may have invented an aunt. She may be a high-priced call

155

girl on the side. At least that's what Lily says, but Lily's mad. Oh dear. This isn't getting any better, is it? Of course Isabel isn't a call girl. My mind's a little fogged too. I had a late night as well. Stryker, you said you needed some help. Tell me how I can help you.'

How late a night?

'Isabel didn't tell you where she got it? Who she borrowed it from?'

'No. Can we switch the subject? It's embarrassing enough to be seen in this thing. I would prefer not to have a discussion on its provenance.'

Ah, so she's keeping it a secret, her win. She's not telling anyone about me. Or Micky. Why? And is Peter gay or is he straight? Was I wrong about him before? What was that old commercial for hair dye? 'Is she a natural blonde or not? Only her hairdresser knows for sure.'

'Well.' Stryker sat back, picked up his second double espresso and downed it in one go. 'That's what I wanted to talk to you about, in fact – clothes.'

'Clothes?'

'To be specific, cross-dressing.'

'Cross-dressing?'

Stryker tried to light his next cigarette, but his hand was shaking so much the match went out before he could manage it.

'Here, let me,' Peter offered, flicking his lighter on. 'Stryker, I'm sure this is very difficult for you. I understand, believe me. And I would love to help. I know a lot of men who are into cross-dressing. I don't happen to be one myself, but, well, things can change. I'm open to it. We could go on a shopping expedition, we could—'

Oh shit. Stryker put his head in his hands. Now I know for sure.

'No, no, Peter. I'm so sorry. You've misunderstood me. I'm so tired I'm not talking straight. But I *am* straight. And I'm not a cross-dresser.'

'You have a friend who is?' Peter smiled. 'A close friend you don't want to name? I understand.'

'Oh God.' He could feel his shoulders slump, his body collapse.

It took all the energy he had left to sit up straight and look Peter in the eye.

'No. Let me try to explain. Clearly. This morning, for reasons which are too complicated to go into, I cancelled my contract for Paul Malcolm's party. Mr Malcolm was not too pleased. In fact, he was furious. Now, I know he will have called your brother's company and re-hired them for this anniversary party of his.' Stryker paused, puffed on his cigarette. He was getting a second wind, he could feel it. 'Are you with me so far?'

'Yes, but I don't understand—'

'Sorry to interrupt, but you will understand, I *hope*, by the time I've finished. Paul Malcolm was particularly displeased because he loved my idea for his party, and he didn't love your brother's idea. He said his wife didn't like your brother's theme and was dead set against giving *Party Time* the business. His wife went out of town yesterday. She's back this evening, apparently. Anyway, he said that unless *Party Time* comes up with a theme he is passionate about, he'll cancel the party altogether. Or give it himself, without a party-organizer's help. Using my idea, given that I've been so unprofessional. I told him he couldn't do that, that I'd give a party with that theme before his anniversary, so it would be old hat by then. Again, he was not pleased. The guy's an asshole.

'In any event, the point is, Peter, unless your brother can come up with a better theme than I have, he won't get the party. And he *should* get the party. He *has* to get the party.'

Peter blinked.

'That's what you wanted my help with?'

'Yes.'

'I see. You didn't, you're not—' He stopped, turned his face away from Stryker, blinking furiously. Then he picked up his cappuccino and took a small sip. 'No, actually, I *don't* see. I don't understand at all. Why did you say you wanted to talk to me about cross-dressing? And why do you want David to get this party so badly?'

'I think he needs it more than I do.'

'What? You think *Party Time* is in trouble?'

157

'Let's just say I've heard rumours.' Stryker felt as if he were back at the poker table, bluffing with a very bad hand.

'That can't be the case. *Party Time* is doing well, I'm sure. David might have some financial difficulties if he goes ahead with his divorce, but I'm sure he has a handle on it. Isabel would know if he didn't. They're the perfect partnership.'

'They are?'

'Yes. In every sense of the word.'

'In every sense of which word? Perfect or partnership?'

'Partnership. At least that seems to be the case. What I mean is, they have a romantic partnership as well as a business one.'

Stryker bit on his cigarette so hard he almost broke off the filter.

So Isabel and David Barton . . .? Great. That's just great. Plus David Barton is on the verge of getting a divorce in order to, presumably, further this in every sense of the word perfect partnership? Fantastic. They can live happily ever after. Meanwhile here I am, the sap who has just bitten the hand of Paul Malcolm, who was intent on feeding me. And for what? So I can be the guy with the halo. What am I going to do? Play the harp while Isabel and David Barton walk down the aisle?

'I need more coffee,' Stryker announced, signalling the waitress.

Peter picked up the spoon from beside him, put it down, picked it up. Stryker ordered a third espresso then leaned forward, his elbow on the table, his chin resting on his palm.

'I'm sorry, Peter,' he said.

'About what?' Peter began to stir his cappuccino around and around in his cup, his eyes fixed on the liquid.

'I led you on, back there. I didn't mean to. I think I know how you feel.

'I don't think you do,' Peter whispered, still stirring.

'Peter, I know you have feelings for me, all right? I have no idea why you do, but you do. And as it happens, I have feelings for someone who doesn't have them for me, remember? We're in the same boat. That's what I was trying to tell you at lunch yesterday. I thought you understood.'

'You were telling the truth about that woman at the casino?'

'I was.'

'Have you seen her again?'

'Yes, last night.'

'And it's hopeless?'

'It's looking more and more hopeless by the second.'

'Oh.'

'So I *do* understand.'

'Do you?' Peter tilted his head, ran his hand through his hair. 'Do you understand I fell in love with you the minute you walked into the bar in Antigua?'

'Well, I figured it had to be love at first sight. I mean, if you get to know me, I doubt you'd be enamoured.'

'Don't tell me you snore and you don't put the top back on the toothpaste.' Peter sighed. 'I don't care. I *do not* care.'

They didn't speak as the espresso arrived and Stryker tried to think what to say next, how to talk to Peter without sounding dismissive or patronizing. Peter Barton was a nice man, a good-looking man with a good sense of humour and, Stryker could sense, a huge heart. Why couldn't Peter have fallen for a gay man? At least that would have been easier. But then, why had Stryker himself fallen for Isabel? He'd had plenty of relationships in his life, but he'd never been at such a loss in a woman's presence before. When she'd walked into the Empire the previous night, he'd had a crazy desire to stand up and applaud. And when she'd been sitting at the poker table at Micky's he'd wanted more than anything to take those clenched fists of hers and uncurl them. I want to put her at her ease, he thought. In bed, at work, everywhere. I want her to relax and I want to excite her. How nuts am I?

'Peter?' He started up the conversation again, in a dreamy voice. 'What do you think it is? This kind of . . . feeling? Where do you think it comes from? What I mean is, how can it hit you so hard at first sight?'

'I can't analyse it, Stryker. Believe me, I've tried. But I can't.'

'I was thinking about it at six o'clock this morning. The only thing I could come up with was that when I looked at her, when I first really looked at her, I thought: this is the woman I'd like to be if I'd been born female. Off the wall, huh?'

'I don't know.' Peter shook his head back and forth as if juggling thoughts. 'It's an interesting idea. But that hardly applies to me and you, does it? I can't even imagine myself as a straight man.'

'Do you find women attractive, ever?'

'Do you know how many straight men ask gay men that question?' Peter sighed.

'Do you? Tell me the truth.'

'Yes, I find women attractive, aesthetically speaking. I adore Isabel, for example. And I think she's stunning.'

'But you wouldn't want to—'

'No.' Peter said quickly. 'No. I've only had one experience with a woman. That was enough, let me tell you. I know my own sexual preference.'

'And I know mine.'

'Oh. We're going to have the "let's be friends" conversation now, are we?'

'That's up to you. Do you want to be friends?'

I can't believe I'm having this conversation with a man, Stryker thought. Although, surprisingly enough, it's easier having it with a man than a woman.

'I don't know.' Peter ground out his cigarette, groped for another one and lit it. 'I suppose, since it is now officially hopeless, I should give up and renounce you, never see you again. But I have a slight problem with that.'

'Which is?'

'I can't do it.'

'Can you do "friends"?'

'Do I have to? Are you *absolutely* sure?'

'Peter . . .'

'All right. I'll try friends. I can't guarantee anything, but I'll try.'

'You want to begin trying now?'

'This is depressing, Stryker.' Peter frowned, then suddenly

stopped frowning and laughed. 'All right. Now. Why not? You be Chandler, I'll be Joey, how's that?'

'Great.' Stryker laughed as well and leaned forward. 'Here's the deal. Bear with me. We're going back to the beginning, back to cross-dressing. Paul Malcolm likes to wear women's clothes. This is a fact I happen to know and your brother doesn't. Paul doesn't want his predilection to become common knowledge, OK? So my theme for his party, which was *Some Like It Hot*, appealed to him. If your brother wants the Malcolm party, he should come up with another cross-dressing theme. I thought you'd be able to help, give him some advice, think of something better than *Some Like It Hot*, without telling him you'd talked to me.'

'Paul Malcolm likes wearing women's clothes?' Peter's eyebrows arched. 'The world becomes less boring all the time.'

'Can you think of a good theme?'

'Stryker – this is insane. Why are you doing this? Why are you so keen on helping David? It doesn't make sense.'

'I know it doesn't.'

'So why?'

Stryker tilted his head back and looked up at the ceiling. He bit his lip. He squinted. He rubbed the back of his neck. And then he returned his gaze to Peter.

'Because I want to prove something,' he smiled.

'Prove what?'

'That I may lie sometimes, I may take shortcuts, I may even do some things which some people would consider cheating. But I am not as shallow as glass.'

When Isabel walked into David's office at noon, he was standing at the far wall with his back to her. She thought she saw him combing his hair with his hand in the reflection of one of the glass-framed photographs, but she decided she must have imagined it.

'Oh, hello,' he said, turning around to face her. 'How is the theme hunt going, then?'

'I have a few ideas.'

161

'So do I. I'll start first, shall I?' He motioned to the chair, then went to sit behind his desk. Once again, he crossed his leg over his knee and smiled that odd smile. 'Before I begin, I should tell you we're going to be joined by Peter. He rang and said he was on his way over a few minutes ago and I told him about this new theme business.'

'Good,' she said. 'David, *I* should tell *you*. Peter's staying with me. Sleeping on my sofa.'

'He's told me, actually. That's very nice of you, Isabel, to put him up. It's a little difficult at home at the moment.'

'I gathered.'

This is worse than gawping at an accident. I'm overjoyed that David is having problems at home. I was *hoping* he'd have problems at home. Big, huge, irreconcilable problems, leading inexorably to a divorce. This is worse than rubbernecking. It's ambulance chasing, hoping the ambulance ends up delivering the victim dead on arrival.

'Anyway, it's all sorting itself out. Still, I think it's probably best if Peter stays with you. He and my wife have something of a history.'

How is it sorting itself out? I need to know.

'I gathered that as well.'

'Peter.' David smiled again. This time it was his normal, natural smile and Isabel felt a surge of relief. 'I warned you, Peter loves to talk.'

'I don't mind at all. I love hearing him talk.'

'He could never keep a secret, either. Once, when we were younger, I quite liked a girl who lived not far from us. She came over for tea one day and Peter, then aged twelve, opened the door for her and said: 'David fancies you rotten, he wants to get into your knickers.'' David laughed. 'That was the end of that budding romance.'

Who was she? What did she look like? Why am I asking myself these stupid questions? The question I need the answer to is: what is going on at home? Please, please tell me.

'Anyway, back to work. I was thinking of a black and white ball. Everyone dressed in black and white, black and white decorations, black and white flowers, possibly even food in black and white.'

'David.' Isabel controlled the look of disbelief she knew was about to suffuse her face. 'I think that's been done, hasn't it? Truman Capote gave that famous black and white ball in New York.'

'Yes, of course.' She could see him stiffen slightly. 'But that was years ago.'

'That's true.' Isabel forced herself to nod.

'Or we could suggest a children's party. You know, with entertainers, children's games, children's food, back to kindergarten days.'

The same idea she'd so witheringly dismissed when Stryker proposed it. Isabel sat still, struggling with a response. He was on tilt, clearly. What had happened at home yesterday? Had they had such a major row he'd lost his mind? Was that why he'd been so unfazed by the news of getting the Malcolm party back? Could she ask him, could she tell him these ideas were useless and ask him what had happened to make him lose all his business sense?

No, not when he's sitting like that. When he uncrosses that leg, when he sits the way he usually sits, I'll ask him. That will be my sign.

'It's a thought,' she said slowly. 'I was wondering whether a funfair would be good. We could set up a carnival, complete with rides and gypsy fortune tellers—'

'No way. Forget it. Deeply boring.'

She couldn't have heard him correctly. He couldn't have spoken like that to her. But he had, hadn't he? Who was this man sitting opposite her? Not David. Definitely not David.

'Howdy, partners!' Peter was standing in the doorway, wearing his leather jacket and carrying a Paul Smith bag. 'Here, Iz, this is yours.' He came into the room and tossed it to her, then went to pull up another chair. Inside the bag she could see Micky's sweatshirt. What was he doing with it?

'David tells me you're back in the loop with Paul Malcolm's party.' He winked at Isabel. 'Except you have to come up with a new theme. Which is why I'm here. I'm here to give all my expertise on party giving. And all for free. Fill me in on themes so far.'

'David and I have had a few ideas. One, a black and white ball. Two, a children's party. Three, a funfair—' Isabel paused. She was still trying to recover from David's rebuff, trying to think of excuses for his behaviour. He was tired. He was upset. His marriage was falling apart. She was the person he felt safest with, so he could let out his frustrations on her. That must be it. It had to be.

'And here's another one,' she continued, feeling slightly better. 'Noah's Ark. Everyone comes as animals. Couples can come in pairs, others can come randomly and then possibly match up, if you see what I mean. We could rent out the Ark building on the Talgarth Road for the party. We might even be able to manage a fake flood.'

'Mmmhmmm.' Peter nodded.

'You're not impressed?' David asked.

'I like Noah's Ark the best of those. The black and white ball will invite possibly unflattering comparisons with Truman Capote's, the children's party is tedious to my mind. The funfair isn't bad, but I always think someone will end up suing at a party like that. Get whiplash on a dodgem ride.'

'Noah's Ark.' David turned his head and stared out of the window. Now, finally, he uncrossed his legs. 'I suppose it has a certain cachet.'

'The problem with Noah's Ark is the people who come on their own,' Peter said. 'You can't guarantee a match. There might be only one hedgehog, for example, or one skunk, unless you coordinate it all beforehand, which means that you'd have to tell people which animal to dress up as. I think people don't like to be told *specifically* what to wear. They want some choice in the matter.'

'That's true,' Isabel agreed.

'What about the Russian Revolution?' David asked, continuing to gaze out the window.

Isabel and Peter exchanged a glance, and Peter spoke.

'Sorry, David. That sucks, not to put too fine a point on it. You have five hundred people dressed as serfs? Or five hundred Lenins? Those are pretty much the only choices available on that one.'

'Well.' David turned back to them. 'I haven't told you my best idea. James Bond. 007.'

'Uh huh.' Peter made a sceptical face.

'It's good from all angles – clothes, decoration, etcetera.'

'David, you've seen Paul Malcolm. *I've* seen photos of Paul Malcolm. A less likely James Bond has never been born.'

'Well, feel free, Peter. Run down every idea either of us has,' David snapped. 'You tell us what to do, why don't you?'

Peter stood up. He put his hands in his pockets and strolled around the perimeter of the office, taking in every photograph on the walls. When he'd finished, he went and leaned against the window.

'Stryker McCabe named his company *Your Fantasy Team* for a reason,' he stated. 'Parties are all about fantasies come true. Parties with themes give people a chance to live out certain fantasies, to be creative with themselves, to *change* themselves for one night. You dress up and you become a different person. You can be Robin Hood, you can be Maid Marian, you can be Prince Charming, you can be Cinderella. It's a chance to . . . to explore.'

Isabel was gripped. Peter had a mesmerizing voice when he was being serious and thoughtful. Suddenly she could imagine him flying a plane, in charge of other people's safety; she could hear him assuring passengers that the upcoming turbulence was nothing to worry about.

'So you take that concept, the concept of fantasy, and you play with it. Yes, you can let men be James Bond, or you can let all the partygoers be children, or you can tell them to be animals. All these choices can kick-start fantasies.' He paused. He looked at Isabel.

'Who would you be Izzy? Who would you be if you were born a man?'

'Sorry?'

'What man would you like to have been born as?'

'I don't know.' Isabel drummed her fingers against her lips. 'Let me think for a second? Any man?'

'Any man. Dead or alive.'

'This is going to sound silly.' She sneaked a quick, embarrassed look at David. 'I know I should choose someone like Mahatma Gandhi, someone important in history. But I might as well tell the truth. I'd like to have been Fred Astaire.'

'And you? David? What woman would you like to be?'

'I should say Ginger Rogers, shouldn't I? But I have to tell the truth as well, don't I?'

'That would be preferable,' Peter smiled.

'Marlene Dietrich.'

'Marlene Dietrich?'

'Yes, Isabel. She was sexy, she was intelligent, she was talented. And mysterious. I always thought she had an air of mystery.'

An air of mystery, Isabel thought. Am I mysterious? Am I like Marlene Dietrich in any way, shape or form? She was a seductress. Could I ever call myself that? No. And I can't act and I can't sing and the only movie star I've ever been compared to was Joanne Woodward, Paul Newman's wife. And that's because she played a card shark in a film once. Hermes said I reminded him of her when I beat him out of a big pot. Does this mean David thinks of himself as sexy, intelligent, talented and mysterious? Does he want to be all those things? Or does he want the woman he loves to be all those things? Maybe I should go out and buy myself a hat with a veil.

'It's interesting, isn't it? The choice we make says a lot about us,' Peter commented. 'And that's exactly why I think that should be the theme of Paul Malcolm's party: come as the person of the opposite sex you would most like to be. A sort of gender-bending party.'

'Who would you be?' Isabel asked him.

'Ah, that's easy. Amelia Earhart.'

'So everyone would come in drag, so to speak. They'd be cross—

' Isabel stopped. She sat back. She stared at Peter.

'I'm sorry, Peter, I don't like it,' David stated. 'It's all right in terms of costumes, but the theme doesn't run far enough. It doesn't cover food, decoration, flowers, venue—'

'We can work on that, I'm sure there's a way,' Peter said. 'And the same goes for some of the other themes you've suggested. Exactly what kind of food would you serve at a James Bond party? Yes, you serve martinis, but you'll run into trouble after that.'

'He has a point,' Isabel put in.

'I may choose Marlene Dietrich, but I hardly want to *dress up* as Marlene Dietrich. I'd look a fool. I doubt very much that Paul Malcolm would want to go to his anniversary party in women's clothes.'

'Paul Malcolm will like it, David. Trust me. We're in Britain, remember. Where ninety-nine per cent of the male population can't wait to get into a dress. Or so a friend of mine said to me recently. All I'm asking is that you include it in your list of themes you present to him. That's all.'

'What makes you so sure Paul will like it?' Isabel asked.

'I'm psychic.' Peter shrugged.

Was this a coincidence? The cross-dressing idea? Or had Peter been talking with Stryker McCabe? No. Why would Stryker talk to Peter about Malcolm's party? Unless . . . unless he wanted it back and knew, somehow, that Malcolm would loathe and despise the idea of cross-dressing. Was Peter helping Stryker reclaim the party by suggesting the worst possible theme? No, Peter wouldn't do that to David. Perhaps it *was* simply a coincidence.

'Well, that's my contribution, people.' Peter stood up. 'I don't see how it can hurt to include it. I have to be off now. I'm meeting Lily for lunch.'

'I'd love to join you,' Isabel said. She knew, if she could get Peter alone for two seconds, she'd find out whether he'd been talking to Stryker.

'Sorry, Iz. This is a girltalk lunch.'

'But I'm a—'

Peter had kissed her on the top of the head and was out the door before she could say another word.

'What do you think we should do?' she asked David. 'Do you think we should pitch all these ideas? Should we include Peter's?'

'Isabel.' David stood up as well. 'I wouldn't worry about it. It will be all right on the night, I guarantee. I have to go as well, I'm afraid. See you later.'

David exited almost as rapidly as Peter and Isabel was left alone in his office, abandoned and bewildered. She had too many questions and no answers. Coming into work this morning, she'd felt so excited; now she was deflated and depressed. Looking at the Paul Smith bag lying on the floor beside her, she asked herself once again: what was Peter doing with the sweatshirt? Why go into her room, get it and bring it here? What was going on?

And where had David rushed off to? Why hadn't he stayed to talk to her? To apologize for being rude about her idea? Nothing made sense today. Nothing.

A hat with a veil. Fishnet stockings. A German accent. A husky voice. An air of mystery. Could she acquire all these by the time David got back and be his perfect female? Absolutely. And he'd come back, take one look at her and burst out laughing. She had to stick with Joanne Woodward. If Joanne was good enough for Paul Newman, she should be good enough for David Barton. The only problem was that Stryker McCabe looked a lot more like Paul Newman than David did. Who would Stryker choose to be as a woman? One of Charlie's Angels, she guessed. Probably Farah Fawcett Majors. Or a Baywatch Babe. The thought of Stryker in a woman's swimsuit made her smile. He could form a new girl band called the BeachGirls. Micky would love the idea.

What was she doing thinking about Stryker and Micky? They were both gone from her life now. She was a reformed person, with no bad habits. The Empire had toppled; she was no longer queen of the casino.

Will Hermes miss me? she wondered. Charlie? The others? Maybe for a while, but not long. There will doubtless be another woman to take my place at the table.

I hate her, Isabel thought. Whoever she is, I hate her. And I could beat her if I went back, I know.

Isabel, Isabel, she knocked her fist on her forehead. Stop it right now. Why are you so competitive? You're manufacturing some poor woman who doesn't exist to compete with, to beat. Slow down. Or you'll drop down dead before you see which number comes up on the wheel.

Chapter Eleven

The floor was composed of large Italian tiles, the tiles a spotless white with a pale blue edging. There were two huge, pale blue rough silk sofas which looked as if they could each seat seven people, four armchairs big enough to camp out in, bookshelves fitted with beautifully bound volumes and a maid to serve champagne and hors d'oeuvres. In the far corner, beside the French windows, stood two trees, one lemon, one lime. Isabel could make out the lemons and limes had been fastened on with wires, but they'd been done cleverly; she doubted many people would spot the fraud. What was odd, however, was that there were no paintings. The royal blue walls of the Malcolms' drawing room were blank.

This is a summer house, she thought. Even though there are fires in the two fireplaces, it's a house for hot days. They'd passed the dining room on the way to the drawing room and Isabel had taken a quick peek. It was a conservatory designed to appear as if it were in the open air. The dining room table had a huge canvas umbrella over it, the kind you expect to see in restaurants in Italy. Why didn't he like *The Godfather* idea? Isabel asked herself. This could be a palazzo on the Costa Smeralda. All that's missing is the Mediterranean.

David was sitting a few feet from her on one of the sofas, a glass of champagne in his hand. Paul Malcolm kept shifting around in his armchair, unable, it seemed, to get comfortable. So far David had tried out three different themes on him. Much to Isabel's consternation, he'd presented the Black and White Ball, the Children's Party and James Bond. All three had received a negative response.

'David,' Paul Malcolm laughed. 'Look at me. I'm five foot nine, I weigh ten stone and I wear glasses. James Bond? Are you having me on? It would be more appropriate to have a Woody Allen theme.'

Isabel was beginning to feel the same panic she'd felt at the poker table the night before, when Stryker was winning. What was David up to? Why was he being so unprofessional?

In the taxi, on the way to Belgravia, he had kept telling her to stop fretting.

'I'll handle this meeting,' he said. 'Sit back, relax. I'll take care of things.'

This instruction had infuriated her. David and she were partners. Why the hell should she sit back and relax? What wasn't he listening to her any more? And why hadn't he come back from lunch or wherever it was he'd gone until a few minutes before they were due to set off to Malcolm's house? She'd paced round the office, she'd rung him constantly on his mobile but had no reply; she had begun to think he'd been in a terrible accident when he'd waltzed into the office, saying, 'Ready? It's time to get going. Time to close the deal with Paul.' Speechless and angry, Isabel had grabbed her coat.

'Here, let me help you,' he'd said. But she had brushed him off, heading for the stairs on her own.

Each time, during the cab ride, when she'd tried to explain her doubts, telling him they hadn't prepared enough, that they should postpone this meeting, he'd told her to 'relax'. As they'd pulled up outside Malcolm's house, Isabel had turned to him and said: 'Is there something I'm missing, David? Do you not want this party, for some reason you're not telling me?'

'Everything will be fine, Isabel,' he'd said, patting her on the shoulder. 'I know you think I'm acting strangely, but don't worry.

The party is ours. I'm in a good mood, that's all. Thinking back on it, I'm not sure you've ever seen me in a good mood.'

'Yes, I have,' she said brusquely. But then they were at the door and a butler who actually did look like James Bond was opening it for them.

After Paul Malcolm's dismissal of his last idea, David looked, for the first time since they'd arrived, a little worried.

'We thought Mrs Malcolm would be here,' he said.

'We're meeting her for dinner at Mark's Club,' Paul Malcolm said. 'At least that was the plan. I assumed we'd be celebrating together. She's flying in from Paris. However, I have yet to hear a theme which excites me.'

'My mother lives in Paris,' Isabel put in, playing for time, hoping David could regroup and get his act together. 'With my stepfather. He's French. She's been there for ten years now. I always think I should visit more often, especially these days, with the tunnel.'

She was finding it difficult to look at Malcolm. The lower half of his body refused to stay still; he wiggled and wriggled in a disconcerting manner. And he was wearing a hairpiece, she was sure. Not as obvious a one as Hermes', but a hairpiece nonetheless.

Clearly, he was used to having people at his beck and call. He hadn't mentioned a dinner celebration on the phone; he'd simply assumed they'd join him if he so desired.

'That's nice, Isabel,' he said in a thoroughly bored tone. 'I've found that the Eurostar is a shambles, however. The food is disgusting, the terminal in Waterloo is . . .'

She forced herself to look at him carefully as she listened to the horrors of the Eurostar. Pretend you're playing poker with him, she told herself. What kind of man is he? Does he bluff? Does he take risks? Or is he a rock? In superficial ways he was similar to her father: a tycoon, a creative businessman, a success story. Yet he didn't seem to enjoy himself as her father had. For Geoffrey Sands, making money was a kind of game; one he liked to play and loved to win, but he was also naturally funny and unabashedly vivacious. As Peter had said, he was expansive.

He didn't fidget, he didn't chuckle falsely, and he was at his best when entertaining others. Isabel remembered not only his energy but his zest. That's what she had missed the most when he'd left; his ability to pick up the pace in any situation. With Geoffrey Sands in the room, everyone was alert. When he left, they sagged. Isabel ran fast, she drove fast, but she couldn't carry his speed within her. She couldn't keep up with him. Her father would have finished this meeting in approximately two minutes. But then he wouldn't have needed to have the meeting in the first place. He never needed anyone else to organize his fun.

Paul Malcolm was wearing a dark blue velvet smoking jacket and a pale blue shirt. He kept stroking imaginary lint off the jacket, as if he couldn't bear not to be in constant touch with the velvet, as if the jacket were a favourite pet. As if he wished he could be in a room alone with it so he could give it his full attention. He's passionately attached to it, she thought. Why? Within a second, Isabel had answered her own question. She reached out, picked her champagne glass off the silver coaster on the table beside her and took a sip as she waited for Paul to finish his harangue.

'We have another theme for you, Paul,' David said as soon as Paul had ended his sad tale of trying to find a decent porter in the Gare du Nord. 'Noah's—'

'Paul – who would you have liked to have been, if you'd been born a woman? What famous woman would you like to be?' Isabel cut David off. She kept her gaze fixed on Malcolm, but she could feel David's eyes on her, she could sense his irritation.

'Interesting question.' Paul Malcolm pursed his lips. 'Let me ponder that for an instant. Actually, I know. I don't have to think, I know. Elizabeth Hurley.'

Isabel bit the inside of her cheek.

'Really? That's fascinating, Paul.'

'I've met her, of course, a few times. I find her charming.'

'I'm sure she is. And she has such amazing clothes, doesn't she?'

'She wears them well.'

'She wears them beautifully. Well, the reason I asked you that question is because we thought it would be wonderful, a truly fun theme, to come to your party dressed as the person of the opposite sex you'd most like to be. If we could know in advance who people had chosen to be, we could have huge photographs of them as decorations. It would be possible, then, to have a photographer take pictures of the real person with the dressed-up guest, if you follow me. In your case, it would be even better, I'd say, to have Elizabeth Hurley there. You and she could pose together; she might even come dressed as you. Don't you think that would be wonderful? You could be the only person there with the real person.'

Paul Malcolm stopped wriggling.

'I love it,' he said, clapping his hands together. Isabel was shocked by how plump those hands were on such an otherwise thin man. 'I adore it, Isabel. An inspired idea! And good psychology, if I may say so. How clever to save the *pièce de résistance* for the last, to make me think you were floundering when you had the perfect answer all along.'

'Yeah, well, I always check with aces.'

'Isabel?' David looked at her with incomprehension.

'Sorry,' she said, to both of them. 'It's an old poker expression my father always used. It slipped out somehow.'

How did Stryker know about the cross-dressing? And did he tell Peter? More importantly, why did he tell me? He wasn't trying to get Paul Malcolm back, he was trying to help us keep him. Why?

'Do you think your wife will like it?' she asked

'She'll be ecstatic.'

There it was again, that word ecstatic. Mrs Malcolm must be in a permanent state of ecstasy. Maybe she was taking E – she and Isabel's aunt in Berkshire. Isabel smiled at the memory of the scene Lily had conjured up. Soon she would tell Lily about her Saturday nights at the casino. The only problem would be that Lily would be begging Isabel to go back to the Empire and bring her along. Lily would be a craps player, Isabel decided. She'd love blowing on the dice and hurling them across the table. Except Lily would be so enthusiastic she'd most likely end up throwing them halfway across the room.

'Now that's settled, we can get down to the business of fine wine and good food,' Paul Malcolm chuckled. 'The reservation at Mark's Club is at seven-thirty. We can have another glass of champagne and head off. Julia is meeting us there.'

'Do you mind if I ask you something?'

'Isabel, my dear. Ask away.'

'What was Stryker McCabe's theme for your party?'

'Oh that—' Paul waved his hand, then brushed his jacket. 'He suggested *Some Like It Hot*.'

'As in the film?'

'Yes.'

'Ah,' Isabel nodded. 'I have to say, that's quite good.' Given the circumstances, she added silently.

'Yours is far superior. David? More champagne?'

'Yes, thank you,' he said. When she looked over to him, he gave her a thumbs up signal and she flashed one back. The crisis had been averted. He was back to normal; she could see the change in his eyes. Whatever had made him act so bizarrely was no longer in evidence. They were partners again. David was David.

Elizabeth Hurley? Isabel allowed herself a private smile. Oh God, I hope Paul Malcolm wears one of those safety pin dresses for this bash. It's almost too much fun to be true.

Mark's Club didn't intimidate her. Isabel had gone to plenty of stylish restaurants as a child and was not awed by the lush, exclusive atmosphere. She was interested to see Diana Ross and her husband at a table in the corner; she noted that Paul Malcolm waved to them and had a nod of acknowledgement in response, but she was perfectly at ease and had no desire to gawp at celebrities. The fact that David wasn't making much of an effort in the smalltalk stakes with Paul Malcolm didn't bother her either; she could do this bit of the business with both hands tied behind her back and a blindfold on. All she had to do was ask Paul Malcolm questions and listen with rapt attention to his long-winded, egotistical responses.

She hadn't envisioned her first dinner out with David in this manner, but it was exciting nonetheless to be sitting at a table with him, outside of the office, in the real world. Later, she hoped, they could go on somewhere else together, full of champagne and the pleasure of having done a good job. The prospect of that kept her happily listening to Paul and nodding away enthusiastically as her thoughts anticipated dessert, coffee, the bill paid and the real night commencing.

Paul was in the middle of an anecdote about a golf game he'd played with a Cabinet Minister when a woman appeared at their table, a woman dressed in black leather trousers, a man's white shirt and wearing remarkably green eyeshadow.

'Julia.' Paul stood up, gave her a quick kiss on the cheek and motioned to the chair beside him, facing David and Isabel. 'Sit down, darling. Julia – this is David Barton and this is Isabel Sands, our very own party people, from *Party Time*.'

Julia Malcolm took a step back.

'What happened to *Your Fantasy Team*?' she asked. 'I thought Stryker McCabe was in charge. I thought we were going to have dinner with him tonight.'

'It didn't work out.'

'Why not?'

'David and Isabel here came up with a better theme. You'll love it. We all dress up as the person we would be if we'd been born the opposite sex.'

'But I thought you'd signed a contract.'

'Sit down, darling. Contracts come and go. We want the best party, we're going to *get* the best party.'

Sitting down, Julia glanced at David, then away, back to Paul.

'I don't understand,' she said.

She's beautiful, Isabel thought, beautiful in an original, startling way. She dresses as if she wants to hide it, but it comes through, probably even more strongly because of that. I would have thought she had put that white streak in her hair, but she doesn't seem the type. It must be a strange freak of nature. When someone who looks like Julia, dresses in a plain white shirt, she makes every other woman feel overdressed and silly, as if they were trying too hard. My black silk blouse feels stuffy and old-fashioned in comparison.

'Julia, I'm going to the gents. You can have a little talk with Isabel and David here, get to know them.'

Julia Malcolm said nothing as Paul got up from the table. He winked at Isabel before he walked off, as if to give her encouragement.

'We were hoping you'd like the theme as much as Paul does,' Isabel said, diving in, looking Julia Malcolm straight in her deep green eyes, eyes which were so narrow Isabel at first had problems making out their colour. Now that she could see the green, she noticed it matched exactly the green of her eyeshadow.

'It's Paul's party.' Julia shrugged. 'It was his idea. I don't like parties. I think they're a waste of time, if you want to know the truth. What do you think – Mr Burton, is it? Do you think parties are the be-all and end-all of life?'

'Barton. Well, parties are my business,' David answered. Isabel was impressed by how even his tone was, how undisturbed. 'But I take your point. I can see why some people might think they're a waste of time. My wife feels the same way. Actually, I should say my soon to be ex-wife. I'm about to be a divorced man, as it happens. I had a long lunch with my wife today and we discussed the situation. I think we can tie things up relatively amicably.'

'David?' Isabel couldn't stop herself.

'Yes, Isabel?' he looked at her, smiling thinly.

She didn't know what to say next. He was definitely getting a divorce? But why say this now? Why hadn't he told her before? In the office, in the taxi? He'd been keeping it to himself and now he had to let it out in a *restaurant*? With Julia Malcolm sitting there, across from him, her eyes blinking furiously.

'Excuse me?' She leaned back in her chair, reached up and pushed her short hair off her forehead. 'Are you serious?'

177

'Yes.' He nodded. 'I know this may be an inappropriate place to announce an impending divorce, but . . .' He picked up his glass of wine, took a sip. 'I felt I should.'

Why? Why now? Isabel looked at him with blank amazement. What was he doing? This was a business dinner. Julia Malcolm must be shocked to hear a stranger suddenly tell her he was divorcing his wife. He had gone on tilt. She had to get him out of this restaurant, and soon. He needed to talk about it, obviously. But he should have waited until they were alone.

'Well, I suppose I should offer my consolations, or something.' Julia waved her hand in the air in a flustered gesture. 'I don't know what to say.'

'How was Paris?' David asked her.

What the hell? Was he drunk? He must be. From divorce to Paris in two seconds flat? I should take charge somehow, but I'm too shocked to speak myself.

'I went on a whim,' she said quietly. 'I needed to leave London. I had to be on my own. Sometimes I do silly things.' She smiled at David. 'I guess we all do. In the heat of the moment.'

Julia suddenly turned her face to Isabel, with an odd, abrupt snap.

'What about you, Isabella, do you do silly things ever? Do you make mistakes?'

'It's Isabel. Yes, I do, I'm afraid.'

'That's good.' Julia now smiled at her. 'That makes me feel a little better.'

I feel as if I'm in a play, but I don't know what my lines are or what part I'm supposed to be playing. Is David using Julia's presence in order to say things to me? Is he so shy he needs a third person present to tell me about his divorce? When we manage to get out of this place he'll let himself go and tell me everything. That's what we need, to sit down on our own. At the moment he's communicating with me through Julia as if she were a medium in a seance.

You don't need her, David, she said to herself. We don't need her. As soon as we leave, I'll make you understand we don't need anyone else.

Paul Malcolm reappeared and took his seat.

'I'm glad to see you all getting along,' he said. 'Have you decided you like their idea, Julia?'

'Yes, I have,' she answered.

'Who will you come as, which man would you like to be?' Isabel asked, putting the conversation back on the business track. They had to eat dinner, they had to get this over with. She'd like to drag David out now, but she couldn't offend him. Hurry up, she thought, watching Paul put butter on his bread in an infuriatingly slow motion. Hurry up and eat.

'Let's see.' Julia Malcolm looked as if she were concentrating hard on the answer, but there were no furrows on her forehead. 'Fred Astaire,' she said. 'I'd love to be able to dance like Fred Astaire.'

Isabel, hearing this, felt as if Julia had stolen something from her. Calm down, she told herself. Who cares? Let her pick Fred Astaire. It doesn't matter. All that matters is the fact that David is actually getting a divorce.

'Isn't that wonderful?' Paul Malcolm put his hand out and rested it on Julia's shoulder. 'How romantic. But you're already a wonderful dancer, darling. And I'm not bad myself. I have my moments on the dance floor too.'

'I suppose we all do. Have our moments, that is.' Julia reached up, took Paul's hand and squeezed it. 'Is the waiter going to have one of his moments soon, do you think? I'm famished.'

The evening, from that point on, turned into the Paul Malcolm Show. He snapped his fingers for the waiter and snapped to attention himself, telling stories of how he had accumulated his wealth, of how he had spent his wealth, of how he was planing to spend his wealth in the future. He didn't pause and no one interrupted him. They were an attentive, silent audience.

Eat faster, Isabel kept saying to herself as she watched Paul take an eternity between bites. How can you be a successful businessman when you're so bloody slow? Stop talking for a second and shovel that food into your mouth. I feel like force-feeding you myself. Just get it down and move on, you self-obsessed idiot. No one in the world eats as slowly as you do.

When they'd finished coffee and the bill finally arrived, Isabel felt like kissing the waiter. It was only ten-thirty, but it seemed like midnight. The process of getting their coats from the cloakroom was agonizing as well. The woman couldn't find Julia's denim jacket at first, Paul was wittering on about golf again, David was standing patiently, seemingly oblivious to the time. Restraining herself from going into the cloakroom and finding Julia's coat herself, Isabel clenched her teeth and hands and shifted from foot to foot as if she were on a boat in a storm.

'Ah, here it is,' the cloakroom girl announced. 'Sorry about that.' She handed Julia's jacket to her and Isabel made a beeline for the door. Luckily, the Malcolms' chauffeur-driven Lexus was right outside, waiting.

'So, David, Isabel. Fantastic idea, great evening,' Paul said as he climbed in. 'We'll be in touch.'

'Nice to have met you both,' Julia added. 'And it *is* a very clever idea. I wonder how you thought of it.' She climbed into the back seat and waved as they drove off.

'Thank God,' Isabel sighed. 'They're gone. I thought it would never end. I thought we'd be trapped in Mark's Club for the rest of our lives. I thought I'd died and gone to hell.'

'Isabel—' David stepped back. 'You didn't enjoy yourself?'

'Please—' She hugged her coat to her. 'It was torture. Paul Malcolm banging on about Paul Malcolm? I think the man is incapable of saying a sentence without the word "I" in it.'

'What did you think of Julia?'

'Honestly? I can't make her out. She's beautiful. She's unconventional. I don't know what I think of her. David – let's go somewhere, some place we can sit down and relax.'

'I—' He put his hand on her shoulder. 'I'd like that very much.' He squeezed it. 'But I don't think I should.'

'Why not? We need to talk, David. We should sit down together and talk. All these things – we have all these things to talk about.'

'You're shivering.' He pulled her to him and hugged her. 'It's been a very long day. And I had far too much to drink over the course of it. I think I've talked myself out. I'll find you a taxi and then get one myself.'

His coat smelled of burning leaves. Isabel burrowed into his chest, unwilling to let go or let him walk away from her now, willing him to change his mind.

'Listen,' he stepped back, disengaging himself from her. 'I'm exhausted, you must be as well.'

'No. I'm fine. I'm not tired at all.'

'There's a taxi.' He stepped out onto the street and flagged it down. 'Get some sleep, Isabel. That's what I need to do.'

Before she could protest, the taxi had pulled up in front of them and David had opened the back door. 'Here you go. And give Peter my love. Tell him I'll see him tomorrow.'

No, no. This can't be happening. You can't bundle me off like this. We have to be together. Somehow I have to stop you from going.

'David—' Isabel grabbed his elbow. 'I probably shouldn't tell you this, but Peter is in love – with Stryker McCabe. He's fairly desperate about him.'

'Peter's desperate about Stryker?' David surprised Isabel by laughing. 'Oh my God! Poor Peter. You know, he gets crushes all the time, I'm afraid. Once, when Peter was fifteen, some friend of our older cousin's came over to lunch and talked to him about Shakespeare's sonnets for approximately ten minutes. Peter fantasized about this man for the next ten years. I hope this doesn't last as long. I suspect it won't. Peter should be at least a little more down to earth these days. I'm assuming Stryker McCabe isn't gay.'

Right – it's working. I've got his attention. He'll want to talk about Peter and Stryker, he'll climb into the taxi with me. This night is not going to end now. I'm sorry if I used Peter for my own ends, but I had no choice.

'No. He's not gay. At least as far as I know. In fact, I—'

'Then Peter will get over it. Night, Isabel. See you tomorrow.' David put his hand on the small of her back, shoved her into the back seat and slammed the door.

But I was going to tell you about meeting Stryker, about our poker match. I would have told you about all that and then you would have told me about everything else and we would have stayed up all night and . . .

'He was in a hurry to see you off, wasn't he? So where are you going then?' the driver asked.

'He's in a rush, that's all,' Isabel said, before giving her address. How humiliating. David had humiliated her in front of a taxi driver. Who must think she was a leech David had been desperate to pluck off and get rid of. That's how it must have looked. And that's how it felt as well. She was someone he wanted to discard, not a woman he was in love with. How could she have been so self-deceiving as to imagine a romantic night ahead? He was as keen to get shot of her as she had been to see Paul Malcolm take the last sip of coffee.

Once, when Peter was fifteen, some friend of our older cousin's came over to lunch and talked to him about Shakespeare's sonnets for approximately ten minutes. Peter fantasized about this man for the next ten years.

Yes, and I have had a crush for fifteen years, so I win again, don't I? The longest-lasting crush known to man. The World Championship crush. What a title.

Who is the sucker, Isabel? Who, exactly, was the sucker at that table tonight?

Isabel rubbed her forehead. Then she placed it against the taxi window, hoping the glass would cool it down.

Stryker looked at the mess that was his desk and sighed. There had been too many calls, too much response generated by the *Tatler* piece. The magazine had hit the stands only that morning and already he had more parties on his plate than he knew how to deal with. On the one hand, that was fantastic, on the other, worrying.

He hadn't trained Belinda or the others well enough yet to delegate, he didn't have the contacts he needed in certain areas. This publicity had happened too quickly, before he'd scouted around enough. In Manhattan, he'd worked up from the bottom of the business; he knew the best wholesalers to approach, he could get the right discounts on everything he needed. When he'd come to London, he had given himself six months to find the people in the trade he needed to find; at the moment, though, he was using the wrong middlemen. Suppliers were already ripping him off. Now, with this rush on, they'd have him by the balls.

He needed help, that much he knew. But from where? He could hardly call Isabel and ask her, could he? No. Isabel was the competition. And Isabel had the perfect partnership with Mr David Barton. Fuck David Barton. The man was obviously a jerk. He might have a nice brother but that didn't mean he was nice himself, did it? No. The guy was an asshole. He and Paul Malcolm deserved each other.

Reaching into the right-hand drawer of his desk, Stryker pulled out a packet of Nurofen and gulped down two of them. These were the ninth and tenth Nurofens he'd had that day, but none of them seemed to make an impact on his nicotine-mixed-with-caffeine headache. All of his head hurt, not just the front or the back, but all of it. He wished he could remove it and replace it with a new one. There were six cans of Coca-Cola on his desk, sitting there in a row, none of them entirely finished. He'd gone through twenty Silk Cuts and another five espressos. At no stage of the day had he eaten. The phone hadn't stopped ringing and Stryker hadn't stopped talking. Talking, talking and talking some more.

Themes. Fantasies. Clothes. Foods. Drinks. Venues. He thought if he heard one more person suggest the Natural History Museum as a good place for a party, he would slam the telephone down, walk out of the office and go destroy a dinosaur. By four in the afternoon, he'd been so exhausted and so giddy, he'd found himself lapsing yet again into his old bad habit.

'Of course, if you're going to have a tennis tournament for your executives as part of this party, I *could* get John McEnroe to appear for a few hours and give pointers, but he has this problem with his right foot. He's grown a second big toe on it and he's not only embarrassed, but he has problems playing; his balance is all shot to hell.'

The executive making the call didn't make any comment about a second big toe. All he said was: 'Any other ideas for a well-known player?'

Then, only minutes later, Stryker found himself suggesting to a woman whose voice was making his headache even worse, that she have her husband's surprise fiftieth birthday party in the dark, entirely in the dark – no lights, no candles, no source of illumination.

'They do it all the time in Manhattan for fiftieth birthday parties,' he'd said. 'They have to because most of the guests have just had face-lifts and don't want to be seen in public. It's a really hot theme. No one knows what they are eating or who they're talking to or who they're dancing with. It's fantastic. All kinds of fun can be had. You have it in a field. Guests are lucky if they can find it. And it's even better when it rains. That gives the people who do manage to get there a team spirit.'

She thought it was a brilliant theme. Which meant that now he'd have to work out a way to make it happen.

Stryker considered taking another Nurofen, but decided he might OD if he did. When the telephone rang, he let the answering machine take it. This late at night it was bound to be Julia Malcolm, calling to blast him about cancelling out on her anniversary party.

'Yeah, Y, I tried calling you at home, but no luck. Where the hell—'

'Micky.' Stryker picked the receiver up and smiled for the first time that day since he'd left Peter at Picasso's. 'Sorry, it's been an unbelievable day here. The phone has been ringing non-stop and I'm about to crash out.'

'A lot of parties?'

'A whole bunch of parties. There was an article in a magazine about me. So everyone is suddenly deciding I'm the man to call.'

'I'm at the Empire. I was wondering where the fuck you were.'

'Well, now you know. I'm swamped. My head is killing me. I couldn't tell an ace from a two, so I decided I should stay away from the tables.'

'Wise move.'

'Mick, you don't happen to know someone in the wholesale flower trade, do you?'

'Sure.'

'You're kidding.'

'You think that's funny?'

'No, I mean it. I mean I need to find someone who knows people in the party trade, people who supply the party trade, that is.'

'Yeah. So?'

'Things like flowers, booze, tents – stuff like that. At a big discount.'

'Dead easy.'

'Mick.' Stryker picked up a pen from his desk, chewed on the end of it. 'I need kosher people. Nothing . . . nothing . . .'

'Off the back of a lorry?'

'What?'

'I keep forgetting you're a Yank. OK, kosher, you want kosher. Like I said, dead easy.'

'Tell me again – what do you do for a living?'

'I've told you. I fight.'

'Right.' Stryker rubbed his temples.

'You have some kind of problem with that?'

'No, no, of course not. I was just thinking, that's all. Maybe you could help me in your spare time, help me make some connections. I need it. I need help badly.'

'You want it? You've got it.'

'Really?'

'Yeah. I'll come by that office of yours tomorrow, you tell me what you need, I'll make some calls, maybe go see some people, some friends, and that's that. Sorted.'

'Bob's your uncle.' Stryker smiled.

'Listen, Y, Bob's your father if you want him to be. You deliver that Malcolm party to Iz?'

'Yup.' Stryker paused and lit another Silk Cut. 'She and her partner, David Barton, are an item, apparently. A romantic item. His brother told me that. He's gay.'

'Izzy's in love with a shirt-lifter?'

'No, no—' Stryker coughed. 'The brother's gay, not David. David and she are the perfect partners, it seems. She probably wanted to win that game for him. True love and all that shit.'

'I don't like the name David.'

'Neither do I.'

'David Gower. David Batty. David bloody Ginola. Never liked any of them.'

'I haven't *heard* of any of them. But I'm sure I wouldn't like them either.'

'Of course you wouldn't. You're a man of taste, Y. Discrimination or whatever. Even if you do blow up lousy balloons. So let me tell you something. And I want you to listen to this with both ears and all your brain. I went to Vegas for the World Series once, you know. And there's this journalist there interviewing all the big players – Amarillo Slim, Johnny Moss, you know, the big names in the game. This journalist asks them all what makes a good poker player and they all say the same thing.' Micky paused. 'Patience. You need to sit and fold hand after hand. You can't get bored. You can't get restless. You can't bet with shit hands just because shit hands are all you're getting.'

Stryker waited for Micky to say more, but he had evidently finished.

'I'm not sure I'm following you, Mick,' he said finally.

'Yeah, well, let me put it this way, then. You lit a cigarette a few seconds ago, right? Easy peasy. The thing fires up in one go. My cigar, now that takes a while to light, you know. But it's a better smoke.'

'I don't really like cigars, Mick.'

'I don't give a shit if you like them or not. That's not my point. My point is you've got to learn to light the fuckers.'

Stryker reached out and popped another Nurofen from its plastic shell.

'How'd it go with Paul Malcolm?' Peter asked as soon as Isabel came through the front door. He was sitting on the sofa reading an Agatha Christie book.

'Oh, wonderful. Fine. He's the slowest eater I've ever seen. He takes fifteen minutes to eat a pea.' She took her jacket off and threw it on a chair. 'And he wants to be Elizabeth Hurley. So I suppose all we have to do is find Hugh Grant. Or resurrect Versace. Or get him a contract with Estée Lauder.'

'Are you all right, Iz? You sound more than a little pissed off.'

'Do you want to hear something silly? An absurd story?'

'I love absurd stories,' he replied. 'Would you like something? Some coffee? Or wine?'

'No, thank you.' She collapsed on to the sofa beside him. 'This is my ghost story, Peter. It's called: "I can be foolish, too." You'll love it.'

'Izzy, what's going on? Has something dreadful happened?'

'What's going on? I'll tell you. I fell in love with your brother when I was fourteen years old. I met him at a wedding. I didn't see him again for fifteen years and when I did I realized I was still in love with him and always had been. *But*—' Isabel took a deep breath. She was staring at the floor, not looking at Peter as she spoke. 'But, he doesn't remember meeting me. He doesn't seem to have any recollection of our meeting. Isn't that absurd? The fact that I spend so long thinking about something the other person doesn't even remember? Isn't that silly?'

'The fact that he doesn't remember doesn't mean anything,' Peter said quickly. 'It certainly doesn't mean David's not in love with you now. Have you reminded him of it, Iz? Have you ever told him about that first meeting?'

'No. There are all sorts of things I haven't told David. Because

187

David doesn't seem to want to hear them. At least he doesn't seem to have any desire whatsoever to be alone with me. He slammed the taxi door on me tonight. He couldn't get away from me quickly enough. I give up, Peter. I've been wishing and hoping and waiting for David for so long and now it's time to give up. You have to know when to fold them, don't you? You have to realize when you've lost and be a good loser. I'm a bad loser. I'm a hopeless loser.'

'But you're not sure of David's feelings, are you? I told you before, he might be waiting for the right moment – after he's dealt with his abysmal marriage.'

'He *has* dealt with it. They're getting a divorce; it's settled. He told me tonight. We went out to dinner with the Malcolms and he announced it then, in the restaurant. God knows what the Malcolms thought. It was the oddest thing to do, Peter. Tell total strangers you're getting divorced.'

'His nerves must be shot. He's not thinking clearly. You should be pleased he's made the decision. You should be thrilled.'

'Oh, I would be. I *was*. But then he ran away; after dinner, he pushed me into a cab and went off on his own. I was on the verge of throwing myself at his feet to stop him. I'm afraid I told him about your feelings for Stryker. I *almost* told him how I won the party off Stryker.'

'Won what party off Stryker? What are you talking about?' Peter sat up straight.

'Oh, God, I've never told anyone before. I didn't mean to say that now. I'm all over the shop.'

Peter was staring at her, his brown eyes intense and curious. Isabel took a deep breath.

'I play poker. Every Saturday night, when I tell Lily I'm visiting my aunt, I play poker. Actually, I should say I *used* to play poker because I've stopped now, as of yesterday.

'Anyway, Stryker showed up last Saturday night in the casino I play in. And last night I challenged him to a poker match, to win the Malcolm party back. I won, I beat him. I'm sorry I didn't tell you all about this before, but it was too complicated given your feelings for him. It was a scheme I hatched which I wasn't sure would come off. I didn't say anything to him about you. I was careful not to mention your name. This was separate, this was business. Anyway, my plot did work, and I won. So I should be dancing in the streets, dancing till dawn. But what's the point without David? I don't even know where David went tonight. Did he go home? Is he staying in a hotel? He didn't tell me anything. It's as if I don't exist – you see – this *is* a ghost story. And I'm the ghost.'

'You go to a casino?' Peter leaned back against the sofa and closed his eyes. 'The same one . . . oh, I wish you hadn't told me that, Isabel. I can't tell you how much I wish you hadn't told me that.'

'I know, I know. You think I'm like my father. I'll die in Las Vegas or in some seedy casino off the Edgware Road. I'm an addict. Except I'm not. I'm stopping. I liked to play, that's all. I had fun playing. I was good at it. Is that so awful?'

'Anybody but you.' Shaking his head, his eyes still closed, Peter sighed and whispered: 'Wherefore art thou, Romeo?'

'It's not a curse on my family, Peter. Just because I'm a Sands doesn't mean I have to die gambling. I mean, I have it under control. And my father would have probably had a heart attack anyway. His heart was bursting out of his chest most of the time, he was thinking and living so hard and fast. I *want* to be more like him. He wouldn't be throwing himself at any woman's feet or harbouring a secret obsession for years. He'd get on with it, and if it didn't work out, it didn't work out. *He* was a good loser, not that he lost very often. Oh shit.' Isabel put her face in her hands. 'I hardly knew the man. Why am I talking as if I did?'

'It makes sense. Of course. It has nothing to do with that shallow as glass business, whatever that was. There was a good reason. But he didn't want to tell me. Jesus, I'm stupid.'

'Peter?' Isabel stared at him. 'What are you talking about?'

'Nothing.' He stood up. 'It's not anything you need to know about.' He frowned. 'It's something I just remembered. I was talking to myself. I'm sorry, Isabel. I have to go.'

189

'What do you mean, you have to go? You're staying here.'

'No, no, I can't. I must go. I have to get back to Antigua.'

'But you're not going back there until Saturday.'

'One of the pilots has come down with something. They need me back as soon as possible. In fact, I'm going to get my things from Gorgonzola's now and get out to the airport, stay in a motel. The flight is early in the morning. I was waiting for you to come back so I could say goodbye and thank you.'

He was talking so rapidly Isabel could barely keep up with what he was saying.

'Peter? You're not leaving now? Right this instant?'

'I have to, Isabel. Sorry.'

'But I wanted to talk. I thought we could talk about everything. David and me. You and Stryker. Everything. I thought we could help each other. I know I've been talking about myself and my own feelings since I came in, and I'm sorry. I've been selfish. This night has been too much for me. David saying he was divorcing, then running off like he did. Don't you run off too. Please stay.'

'I'm sorry, Isabel, but I can't stay. Duty calls.'

He had a panicked look in his eye, the look of someone caught in the act of committing a crime.

'You don't even have time for one glass of wine?'

'Honestly. I *must* leave. Now.'

He fled. He didn't kiss her, hug her, even look at her as he left, he simply bolted for the front door and disappeared into the night.

Does he have a horror of gamblers? Isabel asked herself. Does he think I'm a sinner? What can I have said to make him run out like that?

She drummed her fingertips against her lips, trying to arrange the chaos in her brain.

He's like David. They've both shut the door on me. Why? I thought we were friends. I even hoped he might convince me that I didn't have to give up on David. I thought Peter might explain that this was David's way, that everything would be fine if I waited a little more. But no. I seem to have been wrong on every count. I

190

wish Lily were here. Where is she? Is she searching for a tennis player or has she run away from me too? Is everyone important in my life destined to leave me?

Isabel felt the urge then, it crept up on her and tugged at her mind. She wanted to be sitting at a poker table, she wanted the safety of the Empire. She could go now. They'd still be playing. All she had to do was get into her car and drive the ten minutes it would take to get there and then she'd be there, sitting with Micky and Hermes. One more night – that wasn't so bad. Just one more night. Tomorrow she'd give up.

But Stryker would be there too. And if Stryker was there, it would ruin everything. She wouldn't be able to relax, to lose herself in the play. And she shouldn't go running to a casino when things went wrong in her life, either. That was the true sign of an addict, wasn't it? She had to give up poker and David, both at the same time. She had to get back some control and live without being dependent on either of them. She could work with David, yes, but she'd smother all her feelings. She'd step on them and crush them. Unless . . . unless he said or did something concrete, made it completely clear that he had feelings for her.

You're keeping the window open, aren't you, Isabel? Just like Peter was when he talked about that lunch with Stryker. Don't fool yourself into believing you're still not hoping, because you are.

Staring at her wine glass, Isabel bit on the knuckle of her thumb. She bit hard, hard enough to hurt. And then she stood up, went upstairs to her room, turned on the computer on a table in the corner. She clicked twice, moved the cursor, clicked twice again and sat back.

'Welcome to the World Series of Poker,' she heard the voice announce. 'Shuffle up and deal.'

Chapter Twelve

Looking back, Isabel knew she was tempted to blame it all on Stryker McCabe. Everything that had gone wrong could, if she thought about in a certain light, be linked directly to him. When she'd met him in February she'd been a reasonably happy woman, albeit one with improbable romantic hopes; now, at six in the morning on a warm June day, she was a depressed computer game addict, sitting at her keyboard, clicking 'Fold', 'Raise' or 'Deal' every couple of seconds.

Trying to banish Stryker from her thoughts, Isabel looked at her two new cards on the screen and clicked the 'Raise' box. A jack/king of diamonds was worth a two-thousand-dollar raise, definitely. She had reached the final day of the tournament and was guaranteed to win some money, but she wanted it all. She wanted the million dollar World Series prize to add to the thirteen million dollars she'd already accumulated. Isabel Sands, the queen of Computer Poker. If only the money were real. Then she could pump it into *Party Time*, and put Stryker McCabe out of business. Send him scuttling back to Manhattan.

One article. One article in *Tatler* had done it. How could that be? It wasn't fair. She and David had tried to stem the tide of clients flowing to *Your Fantasy Team*'s offices, but they hadn't managed. They were clinging onto the wreckage, a few parties here and there, but nothing big. Nothing like Stryker's parties. Every party in London seemed to have been organized by Stryker McCabe. He was getting as much publicity as his famous clients. Now *he* was famous. The only arrow missing from his quiver was the Malcolm party – tomorrow night's huge event.

Isabel knew, as she watched the other players on the screen fold, that she shouldn't be playing poker now; if she managed to wake up so early in the morning, she should be working on the Malcolms' party, all the last-minute details which were so crucial. But she didn't have the heart.

She couldn't bear to go into the office and see David's desperate face. And she knew he'd be there. He'd told her a few weeks ago that he came in at six in the mornings to get an early start and she'd been about to say she'd join him, but she was stopped by the distant look in his eyes, the unapproachable mask he'd put on, feature by feature, over the months. At first it had showed itself in his smile. From the day after they'd gone to dinner with the Malcolms at Mark's Club, David's smile had changed seemingly permanently into the one she'd seen briefly before; the slightly askew, slightly false and thin smile which excluded her. Isabel waited for his natural smile to reappear, but it didn't. Even when he laughed, his laugh didn't manage to move the configuration of his lips. He laughed through the smile. She didn't know how to talk to him when he smiled like that; she held back from any personal conversation and he seemed content to talk to her about business only.

David's distant manner was hardly Stryker's fault, she knew. When she forced herself to be rational, she remembered that she had vowed to give up her feelings for him the night he'd slammed the taxi door. And David had slammed that door, not Stryker. Yet she still felt Stryker was somehow involved in the chain of events which led to that evening and so somehow responsible. Her supposed renunciation of her dreams of David turned out to be as half-baked as her decision to give up poker. Yes, she had managed to stay away from the Empire or any other casino, but she spent almost all her free moments playing this computer game; it took up far more time, in fact, than her Saturday nights ever had. And yes, she had tried to smother her emotions for David, but she knew perfectly well she still harboured them. Instead of hanging around the office at the close of work, she'd leave immediately, but that was the extent of her adhesion to her resolution.

Yeah, great, Iz, she said to herself, watching as she raked in another pile of chips. You've done a brilliant job of kicking him out of your heart.

She knew David had moved from his house into a flat off Parson's Green; she knew the divorce was proceeding, she knew he was living on his own, but that's all she knew. She hadn't had to exercise any self-control by turning down offers for drinks or refusing to get involved in personal conversations. He'd done the job for her; he'd closed himself off. It was as if a confirmed smoker had resolved to quit and then found all the cigarettes in the world had been destroyed. Will-power didn't enter into the equation – there was no choice.

Somewhere around the middle of March, Isabel noticed, David began to rub the bridge of his nose. He didn't do it occasionally, he did it often. She could see why: there was perspiration on it. He'd wipe it or rub it and get rid of a tiny bead of sweat, but within ten minutes or so it would appear again. That was the time when it was becoming clear Stryker McCabe was making an outstanding success of *Your Fantasy Team*. Photographs of his parties were all over *Hello, OK!*, *Harpers* and, of course, *Tatler*. And in each caption, *Your Fantasy Team* was mentioned. Newspaper articles in colour supplements appeared with depressing regularity. Whenever Stryker appeared in a picture, he was dressed in black tie, with a glass of champagne in his hand and a woman at his side, always a different woman.

How does he do it? she wondered. When we organize parties, we don't get mentioned. Who is doing his PR? Asking around, Isabel learned he did it himself somehow. She couldn't fathom how he managed. He must have had contacts everywhere, in all the magazines and papers. But how? And how had he found suppliers Isabel had never known existed? Again, she had asked about where he found his flowers, where he bought his wine, but no one seemed to know the answers. All they could tell her was that he had some 'good connections'. Good connections? He'd organized one bash based on a theme of orchids. The flowers at that, she could see from the pictures, put Kew Gardens to shame.

'It was the perfect spring party,' one of the guests was quoted as saying. 'We all felt as if we were in an enchanted garden.'

Meanwhile, her spring had been anything but enchanted. Every weeknight she would get home from work depressed, and head straight for her computer. Every morning she'd wake up early and switch it on. Her wrist ached from clicking the mouse. At night she'd dream of being at the Empire again, sitting and trading jokes with Micky and Hermes. Stryker would occasionally make a guest appearance in these dreams and each time he did, she'd wake up with the knowledge that she had screamed at him in the dream, shouting for him to go back to where he came from and leave her in peace.

While David kept smiling his thin smiles, rubbing his nose and pretending nothing was going wrong, Isabel tried to talk to him about Stryker, make him understand that *Party Time* had to rise to the challenge of *Your Fantasy Team*.

'You told me yourself, Isabel,' he'd say in a bored, dismissive tone. 'Stryker McCabe is a flash in the pan. People will get tired of him and come back to us. We have to be patient, that's all.'

David's eyes had changed too. They rarely focused, but jumped around, resting on objects for a second and then taking off again like a bird on amphetamines. What was he thinking? That the business would fail? That he'd have to find a new career in his late thirties? How much was Jenny demanding in the divorce settlement? Isabel didn't know. She knew nothing.

There were times when she wanted to collar him, push him against a wall, rearrange his face into an expression she recognized from the past and then make him talk to her. Their business was in trouble, he was obviously suffering, and she had no information with which to work to make things better. He'd disappear from the office unexpectedly at odd times, he was often distracted when he was there, and although they managed to keep the show on the road and organize as many parties as they could get their hands on, she could sense an inevitable disaster looming.

We're treading water, she thought. And unless we do something positive and start swimming for shore, we'll drown.

With a worrying frequency, she had fantasies about firebombing the offices of *Your Fantasy Team*. At those times she thought she might be going slowly mad, a madness exacerbated by the fact that Lily had been away for the past month, doing a modelling shoot in Mauritius, leaving her too much time to play the poker computer game and much too much time alone.

But the Malcolm party could change everything, she said to herself as she rubbed her aching wrist. There would be heaps of publicity; important people who would want to give parties of their own would be there. *Party Time* could be flourishing again after it.

And then . . . and then she'd do it. She'd tell David she was going to leave unless he sat down with her and talked. She needed to know where they were heading, both professionally and personally. The forlorn hope that he had feelings for her had faded; at this point she had lowered her sights so much she knew she'd be reasonably content if he professed simple friendship. But she had to know at least that. Was she his business partner only? Did he have an iota of respect for her? Or was she disposable as far as he was concerned?

The offhand way he was treating her now left her feeling even more abandoned than she'd felt when her father left. David had left too, but he was still there, in the office every weekday.

I never thought it was possible before, she thought. I never thought I could be more lonely when I'm with him than when I'm without him, but I am.

Isabel looked at the hand the computer had dealt her. A pair of kings. One more hand. She'd play this one more hand. And then she'd quit for good.

'I don't see myself in a frock, Y,' Micky said. He was sitting where
he always sat when he came in to Stryker's office – on the floor, his
back to the wall, his legs stretched out. On his black t-shirt were
the words: "What if the hokey-cokey really *is* what it's all about?"

'You'll look fetching, Mick.'

'It's not our party, either. It's like we're gatecrashing on Izzy's do.
What's she going to think when she sees me?'

'I think she'll be pleased to see you. I'm sure she misses you.'

'So how'd you get the invites?'

'I have friends.' Stryker smiled.

'Mais, oui. Evidement.'

'What's with the French?' Stryker grabbed a baseball off the top
of his desk and tossed it to Micky, who caught it with one hand.

'Yeah, you think I don't have skills? I'm talking to these geezers
outside Paris, getting that foie gras shit sorted for the Frasier party.
I can speak the lingo. I went to school once upon a time, Y.'

'You never fail to amaze me, Mick.'

'Hey, I do my best. So when's the shirt-lifter showing up?'

'His name is Peter. And he's showing up soon.' Stryker looked at
his watch. 'In an hour or so.'

'I don't get it. Why are you getting him here? What's the
plan?'

'I'm not "getting" him here. He was coming anyway. He called
me and said he was flying in this weekend so I decided to get an
invitation for him to this party. The theme was his idea, after all.'

'You've got me all curious, Y. I mean, I figured you'd given up on
Izzy, seeing as how you're hurting her where it hurts – in the
pocket. You know and I know that *Party Time* has got to be
struggling these days. We're coining it and they're not. Izzy has to
be pissed off. At you. That is no fucking way to light a cigar –
taking her business away from her. And now what's the idea?
You're going to show up at this Malcolm party with me and the
shir . . . with me and Peter, who, if I remember right, is her partner's

brother, that David bloke she's keen on – and what? What's supposed to happen then?'

'I don't have any idea.'

'That's a brilliant plan. How'd you manage to come up with that one?'

'Do I have to have a plan?' Stryker frowned. 'Can't things happen spontaneously?'

'Like what things?'

'I'm not sure.'

'And you're not sure whether to go after Izzy or not, right? You don't know if she would even speak to you if you phone. You don't know what is happening with her and that partner of hers, all you know is she hasn't shown up at the Empire for months. You don't know whether you should throw in the towel or give it another go, and you don't know what she thinks about you getting all this business off her, but you're still doing the business anyway. Because if you turn down all these parties, she may turn you down anyway and then where are you? Is that how it's coming down?'

'Kind of.'

'You're not sure about anything, are you?'

'No.'

'Hey, Belinda,' Micky shouted out.

'Yes?' Belinda came to the doorway.

'Be a love and tell your boss here he's losing it.'

'Sorry?' Belinda looked nervously from Micky to Stryker.

'Tell him he has to get his shit together.'

Belinda hesitated.

'Go on, Belinda. He needs to hear it.'

'You have to get your—' She whispered the next words. 'Shit together.'

'You heard her, Y,' Micky smiled. 'So, you going to do that or what?'

'How about if I do what,' Stryker smiled.

'Ever heard of a sticky wicket?' Micky tossed the baseball back to Stryker. 'You should take up cricket, Y. You have to learn to catch without a glove.'

He rose from the floor then, with surprising agility, went over to Belinda, whispering something in her ear and then ushered her out of the office. Stryker heard Belinda giggle as they exited.

Micky was the find of the century. Without him, Stryker knew, he would never have done so well so quickly. Whatever needed doing, Micky did. As if by magic, he could find the right foie gras supplier in France, the right flower person in Holland, the right answer to all the problems Stryker would have otherwise been hard put to solve. There were often moments when he wanted to ask Micky what was happening with his supposed boxing career, how he could take all this time out to work for *Your Fantasy Team*, but he was afraid if he did ask, Micky might turn around and say, 'Yeah, you're right. I better get back to the gym. Now.'

He didn't come into the office every day, but he'd appear on Monday, Wednesday and Friday mornings, at nine-thirty on the dot, stroll into Stryker's office and say: 'What needs doing?' Stryker paid him, paid him very well, but Micky never asked for a contract or a permanent position. He floated in and out like his hero, Ali, Stryker thought. Float like a butterfly, sting like a bee. A few times, Stryker had sat and listened while Micky made a business call on his telephone. He'd perch on Stryker's desk, punch in a number and start a conversation with, 'Yeah, so Tom, how's the boy? Is he still doing like we did in the old days, or has he settled down? And your daughter? Is she still an old man's dream?'

The conversation would continue in this vein for ten minutes or so until Micky got to the point and asked Tom, or whoever was on the other end of the line, which 'geezer' was the person to talk to if 'I wanted to find like a camel' or if 'I wanted to get like three hundred footballs autographed by Alex Ferguson'.

Micky was a star. And Micky always delivered. He also delivered little enigmatic sayings such as 'You have to learn to catch without a glove' every time he had any protracted conversation with Stryker. I'm not sure what the hell he means half the time, Stryker thought. But I don't think he is, either.

Micky flirted and joked with the 'babes', and was perfectly comfortable in the *Your Fantasy Team* surroundings. Belinda seemed to be his favourite, but you never could tell with Micky. He might be playing a different game; paying attention to Belinda while actually angling for Laura's affections. Although he appeared to be straightforward, Micky always came in to a situation or a conversation at an angle. It was as if he were always searching for an opening; the exposed jaw he could clout with an unexpected right hook. And even though he now considered Micky a close friend, Stryker sometimes wondered what Micky thought of him; he knew there was affection there, and a degree of respect as well. How far that affection and respect went, he wasn't sure. But then, as Micky had said, Stryker McCabe wasn't sure about anything. Especially his feelings for Isabel.

He was a little ashamed of himself for still thinking about her. He'd done the right thing, managed it so she would get the Malcolm party, and that should have been the end of it. He shouldn't have gone to the Empire almost every Saturday night in case she showed up. And he should have accepted the fact that Isabel was in love with Barton. To sit and brood about her was demeaning and pathetic. So he had to stop. And he would stop. After this party. He'd see her one more time and then call it quits. He'd acted honourably, he'd helped her when he didn't need to, he'd behaved well. For one brief moment he'd been a saint, or as close to a saint as he was ever going to get.

When the parties had started to roll in, he knew he couldn't turn them down, even if that meant hurting her business. He could decide to throw a poker game, but he couldn't sacrifice his entire company on the unlikely chance she might come running to him full of gratitude. She wouldn't want his pity. Stryker knew she'd be mortified if she found out his intentions in that poker match. If she knew he was throwing even more parties her way, she'd be both mortified and, rightly, furious. Isabel was the type of woman who wanted to compete on an even playing field. Well, now she and *Party Time* were doing just that – and they were losing.

Paul Malcolm's party might help them, give them the boost they
needed at the right time. Stryker thought David and Isabel were
nuts to hold it in Syon House, but that was their call. It was a
boring call, to his mind; it didn't show enough creativity. Still, that
was their business, not his. Oddly enough, one of the best parties
he'd organized so far had started out as a joke – the party in total
darkness. For some reason, that idea had caught everyone's imagination. He'd had more publicity than he would have believed
possible. Apparently the Brits liked nothing better than to stumble
around in a field on a freezing cold night, trying to recognize each
other. One of the guests had said it reminded him of boarding
school after 'lights out'. Stryker wasn't sure exactly what he meant
by that, but, hey, if it worked, it worked.

'Hello, Stryker.'

Peter Barton, tanned as ever, was standing in the doorway of his
office, a suitcase in hand.

'Peter.' Stryker stood up, went over and shook his hand. 'Great
to see you – how was the flight?'

'We landed early – mega tail wind pushing the old crate. And
we were piloted by a female. I'm not sure what I think about
that.' Peter put his bag down. 'I know I should be the last person
to find that disconcerting, but I can't help myself. I wondered
whether she'd be putting on lipstick at the wrong moment, you
know?'

'Unfair.'

'I know, I know.'

'Peter, what do you say? Let's get out of here. I'm swamped with
work and if I stay I'll be taking calls the whole time. I think I need
a break.'

'Fine by me. Do you want to get some coffee?'

'I think I need a walk. I've discovered a park off the A4. We
could take a quick drive there and walk around in the sun. Do you
have the energy?'

'Absolutely. Let's go. Let's fly. But can you tell me something
first? Who was that man I passed on my way in? He was wearing

jeans and a black t-shirt with something about hokey-cokey written on it.'

'Micky. Micky Dawson. He does some work for us. Why?'

'No reason.' Peter picked up his bag. 'Curiosity, that's all.'

'He's a boxer.'

'Is he now?'

'And he's straight, Peter.'

'Of course he is.'

Nothing could go wrong. They'd worked on this party for four months. Everything was organized; everyone was happy. The venue was fine, the caterers were in place, the weather was set to be beautiful. Isabel sat in her office and tried to relax. There were no last-minute hitches, no problems. She should sit back and bask in the pleasure of knowing she'd done such a good job. Tomorrow night she'd see the fruits of her labours, she'd even be able to enjoy them herself. Isabel had been slightly surprised when Paul and Julia Malcolm invited her and David to attend; normally she didn't go to the parties she organized. It was nice of the Malcolms to include them; all she had to do now was figure out who she was going to go as. She couldn't be Fred Astaire, given that he was Julia's choice. Who was her second choice? Maybe John Travolta? It would be fun to dress up in *Saturday Night Fever* clothes. Fun and relatively easy. Or she could be the legendary poker player, Amarillo Slim, wearing a stetson and cowboy boots.

'David—' she called out to him as she saw him passing the door.

'Yes?' He stopped, and came in.

'How are you going to dress as Marlene Dietrich tomorrow night? What exactly are you going to wear?'

'I'm not going to dress as Dietrich,' he said, his eyes doing that nervous bird darting. 'Or rather I am, because Marlene Dietrich often used to dress in black tie, and I'm going in black tie.'

'Won't you be accused of being a spoilsport?' She tried to put a teasing tone in her voice.

'Probably. But I refuse to dress as a woman.'

'You could go as Gertrude Stein,' she suggested.

'I suppose that's an option.'

'David, the party is going to be wonderful. Everything is fine. You seem so anxious. Can I do anything to help?'

'I'm fine.'

Slam that door again, why don't you? she thought. It's not as if I'm not used to it by now. She pulled a piece of paper from the side of the desk to the middle and pretended to concentrate on it. 'I'm going to be in charge of setting up all the photographs of the famous people the guests are coming as tomorrow afternoon,' she said in her business voice. 'I suppose we'll leave ourselves out of the equation. Especially as you aren't going to get dressed up.'

'Makes sense. We have photographs of the whole lot, do we?'

'Of course. I organized all that ages ago.'

'Excuse me.' Tamsin, Isabel's assistant, came to the doorway. 'We've just had a fax from Paul Malcolm. Three new party guests.'

'Fucking hell—'

'Isabel.'

David looked at her as if he were her teacher and she was a foul-mouthed girl in kindergarten.

'I'm sorry, David, but I can't believe they're giving us three new people at this point.'

Tamsin handed the fax to Isabel. She took one look and said, 'Jesus Christ!'

'Isabel!'

'I'm sorry, I'm sorry. But this can't be right. It's some sort of joke.'

David took the fax out of her hand.

'Peter? What's Peter doing on this list?'

'Exactly, and look who else – Stryker McCabe and someone named Micky Dawson. Who the hell is Micky—' Isabel stopped, stunned.

'Peter told me he was coming for a visit, but he never said he was invited to the party.'

'Stryker and *Micky*?'

'Who's Micky, Isabel?' David raised his eyebrows.

'No one. I mean, no one important. How did Stryker McCabe get invited?'

'I have no idea, Isabel.'

The way David kept using her name when he spoke to her was making her even more jumpy.

'Stryker wouldn't be planning to sabotage the party, would he? No – I'm being paranoid.' Isabel answered her own question. 'He wouldn't do that.'

'How would you know? You don't know him, Isabel.'

'Why is Peter coming?' she asked, avoiding a lie. 'Have you spoken to him often since he left?'

'No.' David shook his head. 'He rang out of the blue the other day. Said he felt like a trip to London, that he missed England in June. That's the first I've spoken to him since he left.'

'I see.' At least Peter hadn't told David about her poker game with Stryker McCabe. She would have rung him in Antigua herself, but she was still hurt by the way he'd rushed off that night after her dinner with the Malcolms.

'Well then,' David waved the fax in the air. 'We'd better get working on these three new guests. Peter is coming as Amelia Earhart – you'll have to find a photo of her. Stryker McCabe has chosen Ivana Trump. Very funny. And this Micky person is Madonna. Madonna as in the singer, do you think, or as in the Virgin Mary?'

'The singer. Definitely.'

'Definitely? So you do know Micky Dawson?'

'I've met him, yes.'

'And—?'

'And he's a nice man.'

'Why so secretive, Isabel? You sound as if you're hiding something.'

I'm hiding something. That's a laugh.

'I haven't seen him for a long time. He's someone I used to know.'

'Oh.' David smiled his thin smile. 'An old flame?'

'No.' Crossing her arms, Isabel felt her foot jerk under the table. Why was he cross-examining her? Did he actually care whether she'd ever had an old flame? Doubtful. So why was he asking?

'I must find out one of these days. I must ask you about your past – what went on before you came here. Now it's back to work.'

I must water the flowers. I must take the rubbish out. One of these days I must remember to ask you something about yourself, to be polite, Isabel said to herself as she watched him walk out of her office. Yes, David, and one of these days we're going to have that celebration we've never had. The champagne and ice cream sandwiches you forgot about and then remembered and then forgot about again. One of these days is never going to arrive.

Stryker was surprised as he and Peter ambled through Osterley Park, to find himself suddenly ambushed by a feeling of homesickness. He had no history in London, no old friends with whom he could share memories. Most of the people he socialized with were acquaintances only, aside from Micky. And Micky, though fun to be with, was as foreign as some of the words he used in conversation. Stryker had picked up a few expressions as he went along, but he was learning a new language, and wasn't fluent yet. Only the day before he'd had to ask Micky what the hell 'Her indoors' meant. As soon as it was explained to him, it was obvious, but Stryker was uncomfortable not knowing the lingo straight away. He wished he could have one night with a bunch of Americans, sit back, chill out and discuss college football. Instead he spent his days and nights listening to stories of politicians whose names he often didn't recognize or soccer teams he didn't care about or people everyone else knew and he didn't.

'Do you ever get homesick in the West Indies?' he asked Peter as they did a circuit of a small lake.

'Homesick is a funny word, isn't it? If you're carsick or airsick it means you physically get sick in cars or planes, but when you're homesick, you're longing for home. Why is that, I wonder? Anyway, I get airsick in the same sense of the word as homesick. It doesn't matter where I am, if I'm not in the air, I'm not home.'

'Really?' Stryker could feel the warmth of the sun on his face, and a corresponding warmth for Peter Barton. Strangely, he'd had a short, sharp twinge of jealousy when Peter had asked him about Micky. If Peter was going to be in love with a heterosexual man, Stryker realized, to his embarrassment, he wanted it to be him.

Is this what women feel about men they like but aren't attracted to, men who are in love with them? Do they want to keep that love even if they can't return it? Is it vanity, this feeling? An ego running rampant?

'Home is where the heart is, Stryker.' Peter smiled. 'My heart lives in the clouds. How is your heart doing these days?'

'My heart?' Stryker grabbed his chest and pretended to stumble. 'It's killing me, Peter.'

'Come on—' Peter took him by the arm. 'Let's sit down on that bench there. You can tell me all about it and I'll give you some bad advice.'

When they reached the bench and sat down, Peter took off his omnipresent sunglasses and stared straight up at the sun.

'Are you looking for even more of a tan?' Stryker asked.

'I'm looking at flight paths.' Peter turned and faced Stryker. He put his arm around his shoulder, leaned in and kissed him on the lips.

Stryker stiffened almost immediately, broke off the kiss. 'Jesus, Peter – I told you before, I—'

'Oh, relax.' Peter laughed. 'That was a goodbye kiss. I was kissing my dream goodbye. I promised myself on the plane over I'd do that and now I've done it and you're a shit-awful kisser anyway, so that's a relief.'

'I am not.'

'Yes, you are.' Peter laughed again. 'That doesn't mean I don't have feelings for you still, but I know I have to do something else with those feelings, put them in a different place. Much as I'd like to spend my days pining for you like some tragic figure, I'm afraid I can't exist without sex. And I know you're pining for Isabel, anyway. I worked out who the mystery woman at the casino was just before I left in February. Poor Isabel, when she told me she went to that casino, I acted as if the house were on fire. I ran out as if my life depended on it and never went back. I didn't tell her about your passion, though. Remarkably enough, I kept that secret to myself for once. Perhaps I was trying to repress the awful truth.'

'I should have told you the woman was Isabel,' Stryker frowned. 'But it seemed a little too close to home at the time. I didn't know how you'd react. I'm sorry.'

'Don't be. It was a shock, but I managed to absorb it. After a while, that is.'

Peter put his face up to the sun again and sat without speaking for a few minutes. Unsure of what to say, Stryker kept silent as well, wondering if that kiss had been the same sensation as being kissed by a female he wasn't sexually attracted to. Yet no woman had ever taken the initiative and kissed him before he kissed her. So this was his first time to be the recipient rather than the giver. What is it like for a woman, he wondered, to wait for a kiss? And what is it like to get one when you don't want one, but when you don't want to offend the person kissing you either? Peter's kiss hadn't been awful, just surprising. His first reaction had been to pull away, so he couldn't tell what he would have felt like it if it had continued. But he wasn't going to ask Peter to kiss him again in order to find out.

'You do have beautiful teeth, you know.' Peter nudged him with his elbow. 'So stop frowning like that. You're probably a good kisser when you want to be.'

'My parents are both dentists.'

'Ah.' Peter nodded. 'That makes sense.'

'You're supposed to laugh when I say that.'

'Am I? Why on earth should I laugh?'

'You don't think that's funny? Having two dentists as parents?'

'Not particularly, no. I've heard funnier, Stryker. So what are they like? Do you get on with them?'

Stryker sat back on the bench and considered his response for a few seconds. And then he started to talk. He told Peter all about his parents and his childhood. Each time he'd try to make a joke or be cavalier about his memories, Peter would interrupt him and tell him to 'cut the bullshit' and tell the truth. Realizing he was telling someone the story for the first time in his life, he related his débâcle with Miss Fellowes. He gave his version of the events slowly and awkwardly, pausing often. He felt self-conscious, unable to look Peter in the eyes as he spoke. Yet he also had a sense of relief and the feeling, after he'd finished, that this story which had taken on such large proportions in his mind and heart was actually fairly trivial and banal.

'It was no big deal,' he said, as he ended with an account of his recurring Miss Fellowes nightmare. 'I don't know why I've told you about it. I'm sure everyone has some moment like that in their lives.'

'So that's where the "shallow as glass" statement comes in.' Peter nodded. 'Tell me something. Why did you believe Miss Fellows in the first place?'

'What do you mean?'

'I mean, she can say you're as shallow as glass, but why did it affect you so deeply? Why did it worry you so much?'

'Maybe I thought she was right.'

'But why?'

'I don't know.' Stryker stared at Peter. 'I've never asked myself that question.'

'You know, when I was eleven or so, I overheard my mother talking to a friend of hers on the telephone. She was discussing me, as it happens. She said: "It's dreadful. Peter has no personality to speak of." I ran up to my room and sobbed on my bed for a long time and then I sat up and I thought: no, she's wrong. I have a personality. It may not be one she likes particularly, or it may be one she's frightened of, but I have one.'

'Well, that's the difference between us. I must have been shallow or I wouldn't have listened to Miss Fellowes.'

'Stryker.'

'What?'

'If you'd been shallow, you wouldn't have cared so much about getting caught out. You wouldn't have minded. You would have loved your new-found popularity and forgotten all about that incident. Don't you see that?'

'I don't know.' He shook his head. 'Look what I do for a living. I give parties. I'm not exactly contributing to the well-being of the planet.'

'I'm not exactly contributing to the well-being of the planet by flying airplanes, either.' Peter reached into his pocket and pulled out a packet of cigarettes. 'But I don't torture myself on the subject.'

'I still make up lies too, sometimes. Off the wall stories.'

'That's terrible. Shocking. I'm appalled. Want one?'

Stryker nodded and Peter handed him a Benson and lit it for him.

'So, tell me, Stryker. What are you going to do about Isabel? Have you got over her yet, or is it ongoing unrequited love?'

'She's spoken for. By your brother.'

'And you're biting the bullet, sliver by sliver?'

'I guess so.'

'When I spoke to David the other day, he told me he was living on his own. Isabel doesn't seem to have moved in, despite the soon-to-be-finalized divorce. I would have thought they'd be to-gether now, but he didn't even mention her. When I brought up her name all he said was that she seemed fine and was working hard. "Seemed" struck me as an odd way of putting it if they're a couple. All in all, he was close-mouthed on the subject of his personal life, but then he always has been.'

'Maybe he has some kind of secret.'

'You're not suggesting—' Peter stopped, put his hand to his forehead and grimaced. 'You're not suggesting David's gay, too, are you?'

'No. I meant maybe he's close-mouthed for some other reason.'

'Phew.' Peter smiled. 'I don't think I'd fancy competing with my brother for lovers. But I can't think of any secret he could have. And I've known him for ever.'

209

'I guess I was hoping he had a secret. I was hoping something is wrong somewhere.'

'So that Isabel would fly to your arms?'

'I know. I'm being ridiculous.'

'From a purely selfish standpoint, I have to say, I hope she does fly to your arms.'

'Why?'

'Because Isabel likes me. She wouldn't be threatened by our friendship. Many women would. That's unfair on David, I know. But I said I was speaking selfishly. Perhaps I'm the one who is shallow as glass. I should go and seek Miss Fellowes out. See what judgement she passes on me.'

'Don't even think about it.' Stryker shuddered. 'Don't go there.'

'Can I go to your parents and get free dental work?'

'Absolutely. They'd love you.'

'Well—' Peter put his sunglasses back on and gazed up at the sky again. 'Life is certainly interesting. I *thought* David was in love with Isabel. I *knew* she was in love with him. I *found out* you are in love with her. And as for me, well, Antigua was a haven of peace after that trip of mine in February. I licked my wounds and did a fairly efficient job of glueing my heart back together. Now it seems your heart is in a mess, Isabel's *must* be, given that she and David don't seem to have gelled yet, and we don't know about David, do we? I can't wait for tomorrow night when all the players are back together on the same stage. It's going to be some party.'

Chapter Thirteen

Isabel looked at the outfit lying on her bed, waiting to be donned. In the end she'd opted to be Billy Smart, and before her was a top hat and a circus ringmaster's tailcoat, a white one, bedecked with garish rhinestones of every colour. She had chosen it because she thought it suited her profession; organizing parties was not so far from organizing a circus, she had decided. And she liked the heavy weight of the tailcoat. Over the past months, she'd shed almost half a stone and she felt as if she needed this protective layering to give her a feeling of substance.

Before she put it on, she wondered how the other Malcolm partygoers were feeling as they dressed. Were they excited? What were they expecting? The time spent getting ready, dressing up for a party, was a private time of high anticipation, often the best time of the entire night. Stryker McCabe had been clever to name his company *Your Fantasy Team*, she knew, but she also knew that fantasy was not the only element of a party, and it wasn't the key element either. If it had been viable to name a party company *We Guarantee Romance Tonight*, Isabel would have done just that, because romance, or the prospect of a romantic encounter, was at the heart of any truly successful party.

Occasionally Isabel found herself wondering why married people or firmly entrenched couples bothered to give parties. They could have fun, absolutely, but the excitement factor was a lot lower than at parties where a single man or woman could spot the person of his or her dreams across a crowded room. At that point the fantasy became real, and the party would last far longer than the time actually spent at it. Isabel's definition of the perfect party was one that started days before with fervid anticipation and lasted days after, with telephone calls full of news detailing what had gone on between whom.

Having fun at one's own party was difficult, she knew, and having fun at a party she had actually organized herself was going to be near impossible. She would spend her time checking that everything was as she had planned it and panicking if it wasn't. Tonight was not going to be a night of fantasy for her or for David. In fact, she couldn't wait for it to be over and done with.

Seeing Stryker and Micky would make things worse; she had no desire to set eyes on her nemesis, the Surfer Boy, and Micky must have reached the status of Stryker's best friend by now – how could he have been invited otherwise? Stryker had to have arranged it. The only potential bright spot on the horizon would be catching up with Peter again. She knew that as soon as she saw his face, she'd forgive him for leaving so abruptly that night; she'd forgive him for anything if he could make her laugh. With Lily away, she couldn't remember the last time she'd laughed out loud.

The week before, Isabel had received a letter from California – from her half-sister, an eighteen-year-old girl named Shane.

Dear Isabel

This might come as a surprise to you, but I thought I should get in touch. We are sisters, after all. I don't know how close you were to Dad. I felt like I was pretty close to him when I was growing up. And then he left and married someone else – when I was eight and a half. Do you think about him a lot? I do. The thing I remember most is him telling me never to lose my sense of humor. That was just before he left. I don't remember *having* a sense of humor. But I guess I did.

It's hard to have had a father like him, isn't it? I mean, I felt

as if he really concentrated on me for a while and then blew me off, you know? Like maybe he never wanted to deal with grown-up kids because he was a kid himself in a way? Does that make sense to you? I'd like to talk to you about this stuff. Is that possible? I'm feeling kind of lost. Like something's always missing – a piece of a puzzle. Do you think I could come over there and visit you? If you don't want me to, tell me, but I think it would be nice to get together. Let me know,
   Love, Shane.

Shane Sands was the first thought that ran through Isabel's mind. What a name for a girl. What had her father been thinking of? And then she re-read the letter, again and again. Should she see Shane? Yes, she knew she should, although she had no clue what she'd say and was dreading with an unspecified fear the talk they'd have. She hadn't considered the other children in her father's equation before, thinking only of herself and her own loss. By never getting in touch with her various half-siblings, Isabel knew she had effectively 'disappeared' them. If they didn't exist, neither did her father's life post-Isabel. Only she counted, she was his one and only child, the one he'd abandoned, the one he would eventually return to as if nothing had happened.

Now Shane was expressing emotions Isabel had kept to herself for years, forcing her to acknowledge that she and her father weren't the sole players in the Sands family drama. And Shane had had the nerve to write, a courage Isabel was aware she didn't possess herself. *Like maybe he never wanted to deal with grown-up kids because he was a kid himself in a way.*

Isabel had been stunned by that sentence, the possible truth of it that she hadn't considered herself. The fact that her father always looked so young may have made him think he *was* a perennial child. Like an ageing female movie star, he might have ranted against the passage of time, but instead of having face-lifts, he'd married younger and younger women and had more and more babies. Babies who, when they grew up, only reminded him yet again of his own age. At which point he would move on. Was it as simple as that? Isabel didn't know. What surprised her was the notion that she didn't like being part of a pattern.

When he'd left, she had taken it personally; she and her mother hadn't lived up to his expectations, they hadn't kept him entertained enough to stay. Between them, they'd forced him to slow down, to tread water.

Always in the back of her mind was the thought that she could learn how to make up for that failing. When he came back, she could play poker with him, she could have lively, grown-up conversations with him, she could keep him amused. But if the mere fact of her age was enough to make him head for the hills, nothing she could say or do would have made a difference. Not being able to make a difference should have made her feel better; instead it made her think of herself as one of a group – nobody special, no one unique, one in a long line of victims of a serial deserter. And if her father was a selfish, vain baby, she shouldn't pay attention to what he'd told her, all the things she remembered and treasured which he'd said.

But did his seemingly glaring faults render all his advice meaningless? Isabel thought of another line in Shane's letter, the one about her father telling her never to lose her sense of humour. That was precisely what she herself had done over the last four months. Except she hadn't lost it, she'd murdered it and buried it so deep she wondered whether she could ever retrieve it again. Her father might have been a bastard, but he had never been a woeful, self-pitying bastard; he had never behaved as she was behaving now, like a sulking, miserable teenager.

'Oh Dad,' she found herself saying out loud. 'You were the real ringmaster. You put on the show, you staged the circus and then you bowed out. But somehow it feels as if you're still in charge, still cracking the whip – because you've left us all, not only me, but, it would seem, all of your children, still guessing.'

Looking at the reply to Shane she hadn't posted yet, sitting on top of her computer, sealed and stamped, Isabel decided to take it with her to the Malcolm party and stop at the postbox on the way. She'd told Shane she'd be pleased to meet with her, she'd love to see her in London, whenever it was convenient for her to come. Why hadn't she sent it immediately? Because she knew that the minute she did, she'd accept finally what she hadn't been able to accept for years: her father really was dead, not just, as he had been for so long, missing.

Picking up the ringmaster's tailcoat and putting it on over her trousers, Isabel looked at herself in the mirror. 'It's party time,' she announced, again out loud. 'Get your act together, Izzy. It's your show now.' When she put on the top hat, she made a little bow. And then she burst out laughing.

'All right, OK, I'm chickening out,' Stryker laughed. 'I admit it. But look at that wig. I can't put it on, Mick. It's a monstrosity.'

'Isn't that the point?' Micky picked up the blonde beehive wig off the top of Stryker's living-room coffee table. 'You go to a party as Ivana Trump, you have to look like her.'

'Excuse me, but do you honestly think you look like Madonna? Black leather trousers, a blank tank top and a black leather vest? I don't think so. You look like you're auditioning to be a Hell's Angel.'

'Madonna is into leather, isn't she? Anyway, the reason I chose her is because I reckon I can wear anything I want. There's no point in being rich and famous unless you can wear whatever the hell you want. Look at you – you're in jeans and a t-shirt. You wanna tell me how that makes you Ivana Trump?'

'Ivana Trump is a great skier, Mick. This is what she'd be wearing skiing on a sunny day.'

'Oh yeah. That's what everyone thinks of when they picture her – Ivana on a ski slope in jeans. Exactly. You've got her down to a T, Y. Go on. Do it. Put on the wig.' He tossed it over to Stryker.

'No. Look—' Stryker picked up two chunky gold necklaces from the table and hung them around his neck. 'How about these? She's wearing them for après ski. Definitely Ivana. I am she.' He stood up, pirouetted, made a curtsey and sat back down. 'Where is The Donald? What hotel should I buy next?'

'You look more like Hermes than Ivana. And where are the earrings? Ivana would wear as much jewellery as possible, jewellery hanging from every available hanging space on her body.'

'I can't wear earrings.' Stryker frowned.

'You're gutless, you know that?'

'I don't see you wearing *any* jewellery, Mick. Or any make-up, come to think of it.'

'Madonna is into the natural look now, didn't you know?'

'Let's face it,' Stryker said, sighing. 'We're both gutless. Neither of us wants to look like a woman. Why is that? What's so threatening about dressing in drag?'

'It's not threatening.' Micky pulled a cigar out of his pocket. 'It's not something we want to do, that's all. I don't want to be a bird. Never have, never will. Christ – can you imagine having to wear those tights like they do?' Micky made a disgusted face. 'Or a bra? The only advantage to wearing a bra would be knowing how to unhook one quickly. I have a problem with that, you know. I've never worked it out right. I think my fingers are too fat. They make great fists, but that's about all they're good for.'

'I had a girlfriend once—'

'Oh yeah?' Micky interrupted. 'You actually had a girlfriend, Y? That's hard to believe.'

'I had a girlfriend and we were sitting around one day and her earrings were on the table – she'd taken them off, and I was playing with them, just fooling around – and I put them on. They were clip-on ones.' Stryker was surprised to feel himself begin to blush at the memory.

'She stared at me and her face went white. I thought she was going to be sick. I took them off. I think I had them on for a total of ten seconds, but after that she kept looking at me strangely. She'd stare at me and her face would get contorted and I could tell she couldn't forget whatever image she had of me when I had the earrings on, and that it wasn't a nice image. We broke up pretty quickly after that. In any event, I ran into her about a year later and we went for a drink and she told me, after a bottle or two, that suddenly, when I put on those earrings, I looked just like her college roommate, whom she had hated, and no matter how hard she tried she couldn't get that picture out of her mind. Every time she looked at me, she thought of her college roommate. Some girl named Sandy.'

'Sandy.' Micky tilted his chair back. 'Sounds cute. I can see you now – Sandy, with a little cheerleader's outfit and those earrings. Are you sure you don't want to put the wig on?'

'I don't think I would object to being born female,' Stryker said, ignoring Micky's teasing. 'I think it might be interesting. But that business with the earrings taught me a lesson. Women don't like to see men looking like women. That threatens *them*. I don't know any woman who'd be pleased to see her man having a facial, for example. Or putting his hair in those curler things they use. They're more freaked out by the feminine side of men than men are by the masculine side of women. Which is why I think this party is going to be difficult for a lot of the women there. I honestly don't believe they like to see their husbands wearing dresses. I'm not sure why that is.'

'Cave days, mate. You go back to the cave days and you think – well, maybe it would be all right to have two people out there hunting for meat, you know. The man and the woman together, it might not be such a good thing for the kids left alone back in the cave, but it's better for the species than having both people staying in the cave tending the fires and shampooing their hair. Someone has got to go out there and kill. If the bloke acts like the bird and doesn't go hunting and gathering or whatever the fuck it's called, you got a species that starves to death. End of story.'

Looking at Micky puffing away, Stryker was struck by the odd thought that if Isabel had fallen in love with another man, it should have been Micky, not David Barton. He might have been able to accept that notion; he could even picture Isabel and Micky together, talking poker hands and Micky's personal take on Darwinism, laughing together.

But that's only because you think you and Isabel are alike, he said to himself. And you don't have any time for David Barton, even though you've never met the man. Well, you'll meet him tonight. And then you'll find out why he's such a hot shot.

When the doorbell rang, Stryker whispered to Micky: 'Please, no shirt-lifter cracks, OK?' and went to answer it.

Peter was there, dressed in a flying jacket and camouflage trousers, with a scarf tightly knotted around his neck. On his head was an old-fashioned pilot's hat complete with flaps over the ears. Instead of his usual sunglasses, he had goggles on.

'Jesus, Peter,' Stryker laughed. 'You look like Rocky.'

'Sylvester Stallone? Never,' Peter said, coming in.

'No, Rocky the cartoon character. Rocky and Bullwinkle the Mose. Rocky was a squirrel, a flying squirrel, I guess, because he always dressed up like a pilot. Like you're dressed now. In any event, you look ridiculous. No one would guess you're Amelia Earhart.'

'Thank you so much. And I see what a big effort you've made in the dressing-up stakes. Ivana would sue if she saw you. You have not done her proud, Stryker. Jeans and a few necklaces? Fake gold at that? This is sad.'

'Hello.' Micky stood up. 'I'm Madonna.'

'Oh dear. I thought you were a woman dressed as Tom Jones, in which case you would have been a major success story. Madonna?' Peter shook his head. 'I'm afraid that's almost as lame as Stryker's get-up.'

'Peter, this is Micky Dawson. Micky, Peter Barton.'

They shook hands and Peter sat down.

'I think this party is going to be a disaster,' Peter announced. 'David isn't making a hint of an effort. He's going in black tie.'

Micky sat down as well, across from Peter. He picked up his glass of whisky and began to sing *It's My Party And I'll Cry If I Want To*.

'What is it with you and Sixties songs? You're stuck in a time-warp, Mick.' Stryker poured Peter a glass of white wine, handed it to him and said: 'I should warn you, Peter. Micky occasionally behaves bizarrely. He starts humming and singing Beach Boys songs, Herman's Hermits songs, all the oldies but goodies.'

'Yeah, I like those songs.' Micky shrugged. 'They say more than songs say these days. Think about it. *It's My Party* tells a whole story, see? This poor girl, it's her party and what happens? The bloke she likes gets off with another bird – right there at the party. So she cries. And she's saying: you'd cry too if it happened to you – which isn't what *I'd* do, I mean I wouldn't cry in front of people, you know, but I take her point. The bloke she fancies has given the other bird his *ring* even. Which comes as a blow to the party girl. She doesn't run away to her room and cry on her own, she does it right there at the party – breaks down in sobs. It's a Jerry Springer kind of psychodrama. With a great tune. You don't get that in songs these days.'

'Whoa,' Stryker smiled. 'That's heavy.'

'And that song *Leader of the Pack*? That's a classic. That's like Shakespearean tragedy, Y. She meets this guy at a candy store, right? And her parents disapprove and he's the leader of a pack of motorcycle geezers, but they're in love and they're going to go against the odds and make it work and then they have a fight I think or something goes wrong and he tears off on his bike and—'

'And she screams No, No, No!' Peter put in, leaning forward, clearly captivated.

'Exactly. She's screaming NO NO NO and he crashes and dies. You can't beat it. I mean what's the competition? Songs which go on and on saying "I'm So Horny"? Pathetic.' Micky sighed.

'Now I get it. Now I know why you've dressed in leather. You want to be the Leader of the Pack, don't you, Mick? That's *your* secret fantasy.'

'I *am* Leader of the Pack, Y. All that's missing is the pack. And the babe in the candy store.'

'Don't you just love *Tell Laura I Love Her*?' Peter tugged at his scarf.

'Tell Laura I love her,' Micky began to sing.

219

'Tell Laura I need her,' Peter joined in.

'Tell Laura not to—'

'Tell Laura to shut up,' Stryker cut in. 'I can't take this, you two.'

'You know there was a follow-up to *It's My Party*,' Peter commented, 'It was called—'

'*It's Judy's Turn To Cry*.' Micky cut in with a triumphant note in his voice. 'The party girl got him back off Judy. Johnny came back to her.'

'I can't remember.' Peter sat back and scratched his nose. 'Did she get the ring too?'

'I think so. It makes sense, dunnit? I mean the ring was important.'

'The ring was *crucial*,' Peter nodded.

'Enough. Please. I can't take any more. We should get going.' Stryker looked at his watch. 'We don't want to miss any of the action.'

'What action? A bunch of rich wankers in drag?'

'You may meet the love of your life tonight, Mick. You never know. This could be candy store time for you – a rich candy store.'

'Yeah, and with my luck, this love of my life will be married to some bloke with a title.'

'I can hear the lyrics now,' Peter said. 'I met her at a cross-dressing ball/she was married to an earl so tall/she went out in her Rolls for a ride/ended up on the other side/No! No! No!'

'We're out of here,' Stryker groaned. 'I mean it. Now.' He stood up.

'Stryker—'

Stryker started, surprised by the fact that Micky had called him by his name for the first time, instead of Y.

'Yes?'

'Put on the wig.'

'The wig?' Peter looked over at Stryker.

'He refuses to wear a wig,' Micky said. 'I think we should see what it looks like, don't you, Peter?'

'Absolutely. Go on, Stryker, put it on.'

'Will you stop it with the old song routines if I do?'

Peter and Micky exchanged a glance and nodded.

'All right.' Stryker picked up the wig and pulled it onto his head.

'Oh no!' Peter put his hands over his goggles.

'No! No! NO!' Micky laughed.

'Come on, guys. It's not that bad, is it?'

'Of course not, Y.' Micky bit his lip. 'It's not that bad. It's worse.'

'Peter?'

'Stryker, I'm sorry,' Peter grimaced. 'But—' He began to laugh.

'OK, OK.' Stryker tore the wig off and threw it on the floor.

'Someone should step on it and put it out of its misery,' Peter said.

'No, honestly, Y, it looks fantastic.' Micky tried but failed to smother his laughter. 'It looks fabulous. You'll be the belle of the ball.'

'There'll be no space on your dance card,' Peter added. 'The girls will be queuing up, they'll be—'

'Are you two through making fun of me?' Stryker kicked the wig into the corner of the room. 'Have you had enough of a laugh at my expense?'

'Hey—' Micky looked up at him with an angelic expression. 'Don't get all shirty. You know, you can cry if you want to.'

'Cry if you want to,' Peter sang.

'Cry if you want to,' Micky sang.

Stryker headed for the door.

Isabel had arranged to meet David at the office and go to Syon House together. Arriving five minutes early, she was surprised to see that David was already there, sitting at his desk, looking out of the window. He was dressed in black tie and looked, to Isabel, impossibly young, like a teenage boy about to go to a friend's eighteenth birthday party. She had stopped at the doorway of his office, taking him in, feeling a tenderness with a sad tinge, a tenderness which cut to her heart and made it wince.

221

'Hello,' she said quietly. He turned to her, seemed to study her closely, his eyes moving from her top hat to her black pump shoes, with an appraising but also surprisingly affectionate glance.

'Nice,' he said. 'Billy Smart?'

'Yes.' She stayed in the doorway.

'Isabel.' He waved her in. 'Come and sit down. Share the calm before the storm with me.'

She went over to the chair, pushed her coat-tails out of the way and sat down.

'It's an absurd business we're in, isn't it?' he asked. His head was to the side, his voice wistful.

'I suppose so. Yes, in a way it is. But no more absurd than a lot of other businesses.'

'That's true. Tell me again – tell me why you came to me, why you decided to go into party organizing.' He had leaned forward now, his elbows on the desk, his chin resting on the palm of his hand.

'Tell me, Isabel. I want to know,' he repeated. 'If I understand why you're doing this, I might have a better idea of why I am.'

'But you know why you went into party organizing. You talked about your photographs, you know, being able to spot what was wrong with them but not knowing how to fix it.'

'And knowing how to fix parties, yes.' He nodded. 'I know. But right now I can't help but wonder if that was just a line I used to myself. To explain my choice. It doesn't seem to me to be a job a grown-up man should be doing.'

'We're giving people a good time, David. Is that so awful?'

'No. I suppose not.' He looked away from her, then back. 'Is that why you're in it? To give people a good time?'

Isabel's eyes fell to the floor and then she closed them. She imagined herself on the edge of a diving board. Now was the time to jump, she knew. If she didn't jump now she was suddenly certain she never would. And she had nothing to lose, anyway. What was the worst that could happen? He wouldn't remember. By this time, she was beginning to think he'd only remember that wedding if he were put under hypnosis. His not remembering couldn't shock her now. Opening her eyes and looking up, back at David, she saw his gaze was fixed on her. His eyes hadn't wandered, he hadn't rubbed his nose, he was concentrating. On her.

'Someone told me once,' she began, and then stopped. She could feel herself backing away from the edge.

'Someone told you what, Isabel?'

Taking off her top hat, she placed it on the floor beside her. She ran her hand through her hair, then put it over her mouth, then forced herself to remove it.

'Someone told me when I was fourteen years old that I would make a great party-organizer. I was at a wedding. I was a bridesmaid, sitting on my own in a hideous dress, and this person came up to my table and he sat down and we started to talk. We talked about the wedding, what was wrong with it. The lighting was too bright, the tent was too stuffy, the—'

'Wait a second.' David stopped her, his hand up in the air. 'Hang on. A wedding. You were a bridesmaid? And someone told you the lights were too bright. And the tent was too stuffy. A wedding . . .' Now he closed his eyes. 'This person – he came to your table. There was something about – about canapés. The canapés were . . . the canapés were . . . I'm not sure. And you talked about—' he opened his eyes, stared straight at her, unblinking. His left hand went up to his forehead and started rubbing it. 'You talked about your parents getting divorced. Am I right, Isabel?'

She nodded. She didn't dare speak, thinking if she did it might break the spell somehow, stop him from remembering.

'You'd been crying under the table before that, hadn't you? He saw you, this person saw you dive under the table, disappear. And then he watched to see what the hell you were doing. For a long time. What was it? Ten minutes? It must have been – he couldn't work out what you were doing under there. And then you came back up and you were wiping away tears, buckets of them. Wiping so furiously . . .' David paused, drummed his fingers against his lips. 'Of course. That's right. He came over and sat down. Of course.

You told him your name. Isabel Sands. Oh, Isabel.' He looked at her with such sadness, Isabel felt tears begin to start up at the back of her eyes. 'And you never told me. You never reminded me. Why not?'

'I don't know,' she mumbled. The tears emerged, they were coming more quickly that she could brush them away with her hand. David stood up, came to the front of the desk, handed her his handkerchief and sat down on the desktop, a foot away from her.

'I forgot. How could I have forgotten? The girl broke my heart. I saw her crying and I felt as if she were carrying the weight of the world. But when I sat down she was trying so hard not to show it. Putting on a brave little face. Talking about canapés. And – wait . . . yes, that's when I told you about my sad efforts to be a professional photographer. That was you, Isabel? You remembered it all? Really?'

'Yes.'

'But why didn't you—? And you—' He reached out, grabbed her hand. 'You remembered everything. You came to see me. How many years later?'

'Fifteen.' Isabel wiped her eyes and then smiled. 'Sorry. I don't know why I'm crying. There's nothing sad about it.'

'It's sad you didn't tell me.' He returned her smile. 'I should have remembered, though. I should have remembered your name. I can see you now in that dress.' His hand squeezed hers. 'You looked so miserable in it. You looked as if you wanted to run away.'

'I did. I did want to run away. Until you came. Until you rescued me.'

'You were lovely, Isabel. A lovely, sad teenager.'

'I couldn't have been lovely.' She tried to laugh, but couldn't manage it. 'Not in that dress.'

'So.' He leaned back. 'I was the knight on the white charger?'

'That's how I saw it.'

'You saw me as the knight. How ironic.'

'Why?'

'Oh, I don't know.' His eyes suddenly darted again, going around

224

the room at speed, finally resting on the window. Isabel had the same cold feeling she'd had when she'd seen Stryker's pair of sixes, a chill that went through her and left her shivering. David was disappearing again, just when she thought he'd come back.

'I like the image, I guess,' he continued. 'I would like to be a knight. I haven't seemed to manage it very well in my life so far, that's all. Except, it would seem, on one occasion when I didn't even know I was being one.'

'David—' She tugged his hand, literally pulled him back to focus on her. 'It still counts. You don't know how important that evening was for me. I never forgot it. It stayed with me, all those years.'

'We danced, didn't we?'

'Yes.'

'And then I left.'

'I wanted you to stay.'

'You should have told me, Isabel.'

'I didn't know what to say. I was fourteen.'

'And you found me again, all those years later. It's unbelievable. But why not tell me? It's been months, almost a year since you first came in. Why wait until now?'

'I told you, I don't know why.' Isabel tried to look away from his searching stare, but couldn't manage. 'No, that's not the truth. I do know why. I wanted you to remember on your own. Without me telling you. I hoped that meeting had made some sort of impact on you as well, but then I knew it hadn't and it seemed silly. *I* seemed silly.'

'Silly because? . . .' David kept staring at her, a full-on wondering, curious stare, until his eyes began to reflect a knowledge which must have taken all that time to reach his brain. She could sense him processing his thoughts, going from knowledge to a hesitating decision-making process. When he finally blinked, she knew the decision had been made. But she had no idea what that decision was.

'Silly because you had a crush on me?'

'It was more than a crush, David.' She paused. Go on, she told

herself. You're in the water now. You've landed safely. Don't tread
– swim.

'I had more than a crush. I *have* more than a crush.'

'Oh.'

He hadn't relaxed his grip on her hand. She saw his shoulders
straighten, she watched him take a deep breath.

'More than a crush. You're saying you—?'

Isabel waited for him to finish the question, but he wouldn't.

'I'm saying—'

If you wait all this time to say something, when the times comes
why is it so impossible to actually say the words themselves? Hadn't
she said enough? Why was he forcing her to come out with more?
It was as though Micky were in front of her, demanding that she
show her cards. 'On their backs, Iz. Let's see what you've got.'

'I'm saying it's a *lot* more than a crush.' Her free hand came up
to her mouth and she bit her knuckle.

'Well—' he cocked his head; his eyes narrowed. He inhaled
audibly. 'Well—' he exhaled, cocked his head to the other side, all
the while staring at her.

Say something, she wanted to scream. Do something. Don't
make me wait like this. I've put everything on the table. It's your
turn.

'Well, what do you suggest we do about this then, Isabel Sands?
What are we going to do about this thing that's a lot more than a
crush?'

The way he spoke, his teasing tone, made her heart explode in a
smile. But Isabel kept very still.

'What do *you* think we should do?' she asked, careful to use his
same bantering voice in response.

'I don't know what you should do, but I think I should do this.'
He leaned over, kissed her lightly on the lips.

Her smile went from her heart to her face as she waited for him
to kiss her again, a proper kiss. Instead he resumed his original
position and folded his arms across his chest.

'I've been an idiot, haven't I?' he asked. 'For not taking this on board, so to speak. Your feelings for me.'

'Well, I tried not to be too blatant about it,' she replied, knowing she shouldn't feel put off by the way he had expressed himself, but feeling so nonetheless. What had she expected? That he'd tell her he'd had the same feelings all along as well? Not exactly, but she didn't relish being in the position she was in, exposed as the woman who had been carrying a torch for fifteen years. And she still wasn't sure what his response was, how much his thoughts matched hers.

'You weren't blatant. I didn't mean to suggest you were. We've been a team, Isabel. And I've been preoccupied. I haven't been paying attention. I relied on you as a partner and I didn't stop to think—' He rubbed his nose. 'I should have been more attuned to you, that's what I'm trying to say. You should have been able to tell me about the wedding a long time ago. I've been elsewhere, really. In a different world.'

What was he saying? Was he telling her he had feelings for her or not? Isabel felt as if he had his fist tightly closed around her heart, but she didn't know whether it was trying to smother it or trying to hug it.

'You've been going through a difficult time, David.'

'Yes, I have. But that's over now. I know it is. All over. It has to be.' He reached out again and cupped her chin in his hand, then released it. 'Will you dance with me again tonight, Isabel? Would you do me the honour?'

'Of course I will. I'd love to.'

'I need you.' He said it so quietly Isabel wasn't sure whether she'd imagined it. 'We can salvage something out of this wreckage. Can't we?'

'Wreckage?'

'My—' He waved an arm to the side. 'My life to date. That wreckage. We can make it all come good. You can set me straight, keep me sane, keep me from screwing up.'

A deal had been done, a hand had been played, a romance had begun – or had it? Isabel still wasn't sure exactly what was going on.

227

David had given her a quick, almost negligible kiss, and asked her to dance; those actions in themselves didn't amount to much, but then he was talking about their future as if they had one together. He hadn't professed love, but he'd said he needed her. They'd taken huge, giant steps, but they didn't seem to have moved forward, at least not in any way which she could comprehend. If he'd kissed her passionately, or even if he'd smiled shyly and blushed, she would have had more of a clue as to how he felt. What did he mean by her keeping him sane? Was she supposed to do that as a friend or a lover?

'I'm not sure I understand, David. Are you saying—'

'Your hair was different then,' he interrupted. 'It was longer, wasn't it?'

'Yes.' Isabel felt her hand go involuntarily to her head.

'And the dress – it was some Laura Ashley dress, wasn't it?'

'Yes.'

'I remember now.' David beamed. 'I remember it all. You looked so alone, sitting there at the table. So vulnerable. I spotted you and then I saw you do that dive under the tablecloth and I was asking myself: what is that girl up to? Has she dropped something? I remember – yes – I remember noticing you at the wedding itself. How uncomfortable you looked walking down the aisle. And I thought: who *is* she? And why have they made her wear that ghastly dress? You stood out from everyone else there, Isabel. There was something special about you, something *different*. How could I have forgotten? I can't believe I forgot that night.'

'You noticed me before the reception?'

'Of course. You made an impression on me straight away.'

I *was memorable*, Isabel thought. I *was memorable*.

'Have I changed much, David? I mean, aside from my hair?'

'No. Not at all. You're exactly the same. God—' He slapped the top of the desk. 'I can't tell you how glad I am you've told me all this. It makes all the difference in the world. We can go on from that night, we can forget all the years in between and we can go on as if nothing had happened to intervene. Except this time I won't leave the party, Isabel. This time I'm staying – with you.'

He kissed her forehead then and stood up.

'Let's go. It's time to dance again. We'll set the place on fire.'

Wait a minute. This has gone too quickly, all of it. I feel as if he has spun me around the dance floor so much I'm dizzy. Has this actually happened, what I think has happened? Are we together now? Then why kiss me on the forehead as if I were a two-year-old? Is he the one waiting now? Waiting until after the party to make his move? The party . . . oh shit – the party. Stryker McCabe. He'll be there. What if he meets David? What if he talks about our poker game?

'David—' she clenched her fists. 'I should tell you something before we go. I have to be totally honest with you. I play poker at the weekends – that is, I used to play poker. I don't any more. Anyway, I played poker against Stryker McCabe. I won the Malcolm party from him. That's why he dropped out, that's why Paul came back to us. I beat Stryker McCabe in a poker game.'

'Amazing.' David smiled. 'You beat him in a poker game?'

'Yes.'

He's smiling. He doesn't mind. I was so worried and he doesn't seem fazed in the least.

'Stryker McCabe didn't cheat?'

'No – no, he was a good sport actually, when he lost. He behaved surprisingly well. I'm a little nervous about seeing him tonight, though. I feel as if I cheated somehow.'

'Did you cheat?'

'No, I didn't.'

'Well, then. That seems fair enough to me. To tell you the truth, I don't give a toss about this party. How we got it back, how we lost it in the first place. Of course I want it to be a success. It has to be a success. We need a success badly. But—' he shrugged. 'I will be very pleased when it's over.'

'You're not horrified that I play poker?'

'Why would I be?'

'I don't know.' Isabel squirmed slightly in her chair. 'Remember when Peter said he thought I must be a gambler and you acted as if that was a ridiculous notion?'

'Well, I never thought you gambled, but it's over now, isn't it? You say you've stopped. Both of us are putting all sorts of things behind us, Isabel. That's the point. The future is the point. Isn't it?'

'Yes,' she said. 'You're right. The future is what's important.'

Our future together or the future in general?

'Come on then.' He held out his hand, she took it and he pulled her up from the chair. 'It's party time.'

'Party time,' she mumbled, feeling as if she'd pay a lot of money not to go to a party. She was both nervous and listless. All this time of waiting and now she felt a profound sense of anti-climax. David was still David and she was still Isabel. He may have been talking about the future, but it was a future which wasn't going to differ wildly from the past. She shouldn't have allowed herself to get her hopes up. He didn't love her, he didn't want to make love to her. If he had felt passion, he would have kissed her passionately by now. He might dance with her, but that was all that was going to happen tonight. She'd tried to read more into his words than had been there, reverting to her old habits. Isabel reached down and retrieved her top hat from the floor.

'Messy,' David said as he put his hand on the small of her back. 'The canapés were too messy, weren't they?'

'You remember that bit?'

'We're carrying on from that evening, Isabel. That conversation only just happened. Of course I remember.'

'In that case I'm fourteen years old,' she smiled wanly.

He swung her round so that she was facing him, as if they were going to start to dance. And then he leaned into her and whispered in her ear.

'Fourteen? You're a minor then. That could get me into a lot of trouble later on, couldn't it? Do you think it's worth the risk?'

Isabel felt it travel through her, that whisper. It sped around her entire body as the meaning of the words reached her brain. All this time, she thought. All this time and it was worth every minute of the wait for those two words: later on.

'Definitely worth the risk,' she stood on her tiptoes and whispered back. 'You can't lose.'

Chapter Fourteen

Fireworks were always good, Stryker thought, watching the air exploding above him. They were a colourful, exciting touch, especially on such a balmy summer's night. The Malcolms had struck lucky with the weather; the day had been hot and cloudless, the evening presented a perfect, star-studded sky, with the crescent moon giving an impression of a woman lying back luxuriantly in a deck chair. Guests stood on the terrace outside, their faces looking up expectantly, glowing. Some of that glow was childlike enthusiasm at the display, Stryker could see, and some of it was probably as a result of champagne and wine. Whatever the mixture, they were definitely enjoying themselves. And their commitment to the cross-dressing theme was impressive.

Stryker's gaze panned the crowd, checking out the men in their dresses and skirts and felt embarrassed for wimping out himself. Some of these costumes were a sight to see: to his right stood a dead ringer for Elizabeth Taylor, his arm around a woman who had dressed as Gandhi. Margaret Thatcher was joined up with Groucho Marx, Scary Spice with Winston Churchill, Yoko Ono beside George Clooney. And Paul Malcolm had outdone himself as Elizabeth Hurley. He had a dark wig, a short black sheath dress with neckline plunging to his belly button, heavy black eye make-up and stiletto heels. How he managed to walk on those, Stryker couldn't figure out, but he was sashaying across the terrace, a deliriously happy camper.

Julia Malcolm made, Stryker had to admit, a wonderful Fred Astaire. She hadn't done the obvious and dressed in a top hat, white tie and tails; she was wearing a pair of white duck trousers with a man's striped tie for a belt, a white shirt and a cravat, with her hair slicked back. Looking loose-limbed and casually chic, she seemed as if she might break into a tap dance at any second.

The party was a success, there was no doubt about it. Isabel – and Stryker was sure Isabel, not David, was responsible for this because he would like to think he would have thought of it himself – had decorated Syon House with life-size portraits of the people whom the guests had dressed as. And she had made these photographic portraits 3-D.

Wandering through the hall on his way to the terrace, Stryker had smiled to see John F. Kennedy sitting in a chair in the corner with Marilyn Monroe on his lap. There were cleverly fashioned cardboard cut-outs of celebrities throughout the house and in the marquee extension, all of them in some form of witty pose.

Good for your, Isabel, Stryker had said to himself. You deserve this party. The food at the sit-down dinner had also been fabulous; quails' eggs for starters and then delicious salmon with butterfly prawns and grilled vegetables. He would have enjoyed the dinner more if he hadn't been so busy looking over at Isabel and David, sitting at a table so far away he could barely make them out.

Sandwiched between a woman who told him she had come dressed as someone he'd never heard of – Grant Mitchell – and another one who had, disturbingly, chosen to be Joseph Stalin, he kept craning his neck to catch a sight of them.

As he listened to the history of the Queen Vic pub and the Mitchell brothers, he would get the occasional glimpse of Isabel and David whispering to each other. Not once did he see either of them talk to the person on his or her other side. Bad manners, Izzy, he said to himself. Or are you so in love manners don't matter? And this doesn't look like business talk to me. It looks like you've just had an afternoon in bed together.

233

'So then Grant had an affair with Tiffany's mother,' the woman on his right was saying. Stryker forced himself to look away from Isabel and tune back into the conversation.

'This was after Phil had an affair with Grant's wife?' he asked.

'Exactly. Sharon. Phil had an affair with Sharon and then Grant had a one-night stand with Michelle, Sharon's best friend.'

'You Mitchells sure get around,' he remarked, and the woman, who was wearing a white bathing cap to make her appear bald, laughed uproariously. Stryker saw Micky, across the round table from him, throw a few punches in the air. The woman on Micky's left – Elvis Presley – was obviously enthralled by this macho display.

'You just watch,' Micky had remarked in the car on the way to the party. 'These upper crust women love rough trade. They won't be able to keep their hands off me. They'll be fighting to get a piece of my body.'

'My goggles are steaming up,' Peter said, putting his head out the window. 'I won't be able to watch your amorous conquests if I don't get rid of them. Can we stop for a drink in a pub before we get there? I'm dying of thirst.'

The three of them received odd looks when they entered the Black Lion pub by the Thames, but Micky's imposing physical presence stopped anyone from making a crack at their expense. Stryker drank water while the other two downed two rounds of vodka and tonics. By the time they rolled up to park at Syon House, they were late and had to go straight into dinner in the marquee.

As Stryker was told the next episode in Grant Mitchell's complicated life, he glanced at Peter, who was sitting on the other side of Joseph Stalin. An American Indian was on his left, probably Sitting Bull. Peter had taken off the goggles and loosened his scarf. Stryker heard him say: 'How fascinating, I've always been compelled by the plight of native Americans. I spend nights thinking about it. Tell me more about how persecuted the tribes have been. But first – is there any possibility of getting more firewater at this table?'

When dinner was over and the guest went outside to view the fireworks, Stryker saw Micky and Elvis move away from the crowd and head straight into the dark, towards the treeline. Peter was at the far end of the terrace, ensconced in conversation with a man who had to get the prize for the most outrageous costume of all. He was wearing a blonde wig, the hair of which reached to his thighs, and, seemingly, nothing else whatsoever. Stryker wondered whether this Lady Godiva had flesh-coloured Y-fronts or was brave enough to do without them.

Good for Peter, he thought. He has escaped Stalin and Sitting Bull and hasn't wasted any time honing in on the guests with a sense of humour. And I've got a good idea what Micky and Elvis are up to under cover of darkness.

Isabel and David Barton were nowhere to be seen. Stryker leaned against the wall of the house and lit a cigarette.

'Who are you supposed to be, Mr McCabe?'

He hadn't seen Julia Malcolm approach. She was standing a few feet away from him, her back to the wall as well.

'Ivana Trump.'

'You're not very convincing.'

'I know.'

A firework in the shape of a red heart broke out in the sky above them. The guests burst into applause. Julia Malcolm didn't join them.

'Are you enjoying your anniversary party, Mrs Malcolm?'

'Not particularly. I'm not a party person. Paul is enjoying himself though. That's what counts.'

'I heard Elizabeth Hurley was supposed to come but couldn't make it at the last minute. That's a shame.'

'We'll live.'

'No doubt you will,' Stryker smiled. He was surprised to see Julia smile back, a natural, almost sweet smile. I keep forgetting how young she is, he thought.

'Why did you bow out? Why did you give up this party?' she asked.

'I didn't give it up, I lost it – in a poker game.'

'A poker game?' For the first time he saw true curiosity on her face. 'A poker game with who?'

'Whom. Sorry, I have a friend who always corrects me on that. A poker game with Isabel Sands.'

'Isabel.' Julia Malcolm nodded. 'I see. Isabel seems to be multi-talented.'

'She has done a great job on this party.'

'She certainly has. Where is she, by the way? Do you know?'

'I think she must be somewhere with David Barton.'

'Of course. I saw them during dinner. They looked quite the couple.'

'I guess that's what they are.'

'Stryker?' Julia shifted her position, put one shoulder against the wall and a hand on her hip. 'Would you do me a favour later?'

'If I can.'

'Would you dance with me?'

'Hey,' he grinned. 'I can't pass up the opportunity of dancing with Fred Astaire, can I?'

'Absolutely not. Now I have to go back to the action. You know Fiona is looking for you. She's very upset. She persuaded me to get you and your two friends invited and she hasn't seen you all evening. She thought she'd be at your table for dinner but I switched her at the last minute.'

'Why?'

'I thought you deserved Grant Mitchell.' Julia smiled and walked away.

Isabel could hear the whistle of the fireworks outside, but she wasn't the least unhappy to be missing them. She and David had stayed in the marquee after dinner, the only two not to have moved. As waiters cleared up around them, they sat together, oblivious.

It's all coming true. All my fantasies, all my dreams, are now reality, she thought, studying David as he poured her and then himself another cup of coffee. We've talked about the wedding for hours, going over every single detail. I'm not even bothered how the party is going. All I want is to sit here and talk the night to sleep, to tell David everything.

'I'll introduce you to Micky,' she said, stirring a spoonful of sugar into her coffee. 'Micky Dawson. Remember you asked me if he was an old flame? I'll tell you about my old flames at some point, but Micky isn't one of them. He's a friend. I haven't seen him yet but I know he's here tonight. Stryker must have managed to get him invited somehow. They've bonded, those two. But you'll like him, I know. He's the one I miss the most, now that I've stopped going to the Empire. Micky's special.'

'I like the sound of Hermes, the one with the toupee,' David commented. 'You should take me there sometime, Isabel. I'd like to see the place. You make it sound fascinating.'

'Really?'

'Yes. Sounds as if it's full of interesting characters.'

'They're not exactly characters. They're people.'

'But that's how you described them in the car on the way here. Remember? It was the first thing you said when you began to tell me about the place. You said there were some remarkable characters there.'

'Did I?' Isabel frowned. 'Yes, I suppose I did.' I was surprised that you weren't more curious, that you didn't even ask how I met Stryker in the first place and how I arranged to play the game with him. So maybe I exaggerated a bit when I talked about the Empire – to get your attention. Did I really call them characters?

'If I said that,' she continued, 'I didn't mean to make it seem as if I was different from them. I'm a character too. I'm one of them, or I was. That's the point about poker – it's a great equalizer, in all sorts of ways. The men don't care what I look like, or—'

'I find that hard to believe,' David cut in.

'No, it's true. They don't. I don't, I mean I didn't go there to get picked up. That doesn't happen. All the men care about is the cards, the game. That's all anyone there cares about – winning.

What you do for a living, what you look like, how old or young you are has nothing to do with anything. You're equal. It's a level playing field.'

'And the fact that you're a woman – that didn't give you any advantage?'

'Maybe at the beginning, but only because men make assumptions at the beginning. They think women can be bluffed more easily, for example. But as soon as you show them you know what you're doing, well, sex doesn't enter into it.'

'You must have loved beating men at their own game.' David smiled.

'No, that's not it either. There are other female players. I enjoyed beating *anyone*. I enjoyed the game itself. There are so many things going on at the same time. Working out how everyone plays, the psychology of each person at the table; whether someone always bluffs or never bluffs, you know—'

'I'm afraid I don't.' David reached over and took her hand in his. 'It's not a game that interests me. In the end it's luck, it's no different from any other form of betting. It's like the Lottery and I've never bought a Lottery ticket in my life, nor do I plan to. But that doesn't mean I wouldn't like to see this place, see the atmosphere there and try to understand why you were so involved in it. Although, of course, I'm sure it has something to do with your father and his reckless gambling.'

'He wasn't reckless,' Isabel protested. 'He knew what he was doing. Yes, he lost a lot at the tables, but then he had a lot to lose. It was his money, he made it, he should be able to spend it in whatever way he wanted to.'

'And die in the process?'

'A lot of people would say that's not such a bad way to die.'

'Well, that's hardly the point. I would be concerned if I thought you'd inherited that reckless streak, but I know you haven't. You were getting something out of your system with this poker business, that's all. I'm sure an analyst would say you were battling with the ghost of your father or some such thing. But now you have me—'

David squeezed her hand. 'Come to your rescue. Only this time you were *at* the tables instead of underneath one.'

'Right,' she said quietly, thinking: is this our first fight? No, it's a misunderstanding, that's all. How would he be able to comprehend what the game itself means to me? If he suddenly turned to me and said he was a secret bowls player, I might not be able to empathize either. What I have to do is forget about poker entirely. No more computer World Series games. It's time I went cold turkey. Anyway, by the time this night is over, I'll have other pursuits to keep me occupied, a different kind of game to play.

Stryker prowled. The fireworks had ended with two huge bursts of light forming the initials J and P in red and green. Romance at its height, he thought as he wandered amongst the two hundred or so guests who seemed reluctant to leave the terrace. They milled around, chatting and smoking, as if they were waiting for another round of entertainment to set fire to the sky above them. He spotted a few celebrities he recognized, some of whom, like him, hadn't done much in the dressing-up stakes. A photographer was also present, snapping away with a permanent scowl on his face.

Why is he so pissed off? Stryker wondered, staying on the move. At least he's getting paid for being here, recording the rich at play. Whereas all I'm doing is wandering aimlessly for nothing. Why did I make Fiona invite me to this bash? I've been avoiding her all night, which is hardly a nice thing to do, and I'm spending my time silently criticizing a bunch of people I don't know and don't really want to meet. I should be working the scene, drumming up business for myself, but right now parties strike me as a dumb way to spend a lot of money in a short space of time. You get dressed up, you get drunk and you go home. What's so fun about that? Normally I'd be right in there with them, partying till I dropped. But not tonight. I look ridiculous in these jeans and necklaces. I'm not in the spirit. I wish I hadn't come. So why did I weasel my way in here?

To get another look at Isabel, the circus ringmaster. And who am I? Not Ivana Trump. I'm one of the tigers in the cages, itching to get out and bare my fangs. At whom? David Barton? That would make me popular. It would do a lot for my reputation. I challenge David Barton to a duel at dawn in the grounds of Syon House. With a *Hello* photographer on the scene, recording it all for next week's issue. American party man goes wild and fights rival! Inside pictures plus a twelve-page spread on Jane Seymour's new Hollywood home.

Well, Stryker, time to get it over and done with. Go see Isabel and say goodbye to your little fantasy. You won't kiss her the way Peter kissed you, but you can see her and wrap the package up and send it into outer space. Mentally kiss it goodbye.

'Hello there.' Peter came up from behind Isabel and planted a huge kiss on both her cheeks. 'Greetings from the long-lost pilot. What are you two doing here? Why weren't you out watching the display?'

'We missed it?' David asked.

'It's over. Finito. I've come to find my cigarettes. I left them behind and Lady Godiva wants one.'

'Does she now?' Isabel laughed. 'And what is Lady Godiva like?'

'Gorgeous.' Peter pulled out a chair and sat down on Isabel's left. 'So gorgeous I think I should play hard to get for a few minutes here and make him wait.'

'Could Lady Godiva possibly be—'

'Gay? You better believe it, bro. Gay and gorgeous both. It's my lucky night.'

'Mine too.' David put his arm around Isabel's shoulder.

'Ah ha!' Peter rocked back in his chair. 'Is this what I think it is? Do I see a romance blossoming in front of me? Am I in the presence of young love?'

Isabel blushed. David squeezed her shoulder.

'You might say that, Peter. Young is an apposite word. You might not think it, but Isabel is all of fourteen years old.'

'You certainly *look* fourteen, Izzy. You look like a waif in that tailcoat – it swamps you. So, fireworks all round. Isn't this fabulous?

Should we toast? I see that bottle of champagne sitting there isn't empty.'

'I'm so pleased to see you, Peter.' Isabel took the bottle and poured him a glass. 'It feels like ages since you were here. And I'm pleased you've survived that earthquake. You have, haven't you? It's over now, isn't it?'

'In a manner of speaking. I didn't have much choice, did I?' Peter said, his voice suddenly serious. 'It wasn't easy at all. There are times when I still . . . anyway, let's forget about all that. Let's drink a toast. I'm hurt that you've stolen her away from me, David. But I guess a sex change was out of the question. Too expensive, was it, Iz?'

'Too long a waiting list.'

Peter laughed and clinked his glass against Isabel's, then David's. 'Cheers. When are you taking her home to meet our wonderful mother, David?'

'Not for a while. A long while.'

'Wise.' Taking a sip of champagne, he focused on Isabel. 'So. The battle is over, it would appear. And I'll have to wait to see whether the next object of devotion can get her mind around a heterosexual man being friends with a homosexual one.'

'What are you talking about?'

'Nothing, Izzy,' Peter waved his hand in the air dismissively. 'I'm tipsy. No, I'm drunk. I should get back to Lady Godiva.' He finished his glass in one gulp. 'Before I say something I shouldn't.'

'Say what?' Isabel pressed.

'Where's Lily? I'd like to see here while I'm in town.'

'She's in Mauritius. She's due back soon, though. I'm not sure exactly when.'

'Well, give her my love.' Peter stood up. 'If she were here we could have tripped the light fantastic tonight. Wowed the assembled multitude with our carefully honed and polished routine. So—' he put his hand on David's shoulder. 'Will I see you later on? If I'm unfortunate enough not to be sleeping elsewhere, that is?'

'I—' David looked at Isabel. 'No, I don't think you will be seeing me tonight. I think *I'll* be sleeping elsewhere.'

'Young sex.' Peter grinned. 'But remember. You two must remember – keep away from motorbikes.'

'What's he on about?' David turned to Isabel as Peter walked away.

'I haven't a clue.'

'Look, the band is about to start up. And here we are, sitting at a table on our own.' David took her hand in his. 'History repeats itself. Shall we dance, Isabel?'

'I think Paul and Julia are going to dance together first. There they are now—' Isabel pointed to the dance floor at the far end of the marquee. 'What a bizarre couple they make. How is he going to manage in those heels, do you think? This will be worth watching.'

'I'll be back,' David said, standing up. 'Don't leave. I'll be back.'

'You can't stay for a second and watch?' Isabel looked up at him. 'Watch Fred and the gorgeous, pouting Miss Hurley do their thing?'

'No.' David was moving away as he said this. 'That's a sight I can miss. Don't move. Promise me you won't move.'

'I promise.'

'Hello, Isabel,' Stryker sat down in the chair David had vacated ten seconds earlier. 'Nice party.'

'Thank you, Stryker. I feel badly about—'

'Don't. All's fair in poker and parties. I'm about to go dance with Julia Malcolm. But right now she's otherwise engaged. Paul looks ravishing, don't you think? Oh – look, he's fallen over.'

Isabel looked and saw Paul on his bottom on the dance floor. Julia was standing over him, helping him up. When he got to his feet, she pulled him off the floor and towards a table. Isabel tried to stop herself from laughing, but didn't succeed.

'Paul Malcolm flat on his ass. I hope someone got a picture of that.' Stryker laughed too. 'He's a nice piece of work, isn't he? All that money and all he wants to do is be Elizabeth Hurley. I wonder how Julia copes.'

242

'Julia Malcolm seems pretty competent at coping to me. I suspect she could cope with anything.'

'She likes you too,' Stryker grinned.

'I didn't meant to be bitchy.'

'No, no, of course not.'

Stryker's grin didn't budge. Isabel wanted to leave the table, get away from him, but she had promised David she'd stay there.

'Hey, the gang's all here.' Micky appeared, waving a bottle of champagne. 'Whose deal is it anyway?' He sat down on the other side of Isabel. 'And what are the stakes this time?'

'Micky.' Isabel kissed him on both cheeks. 'I'm so glad to see you. How are you?'

'Let me put it this way, Izzy. I was sitting beside Elvis at dinner and then Elvis and me went for a little walk in the woods, and all I can tell you is that underneath that Elvis disguise is Monica Lewinsky.'

'Micky.' Isabel put her hand over her eyes. 'You're outrageous.'

Stryker sat back in his chair. 'Jesus, Mick. They *do* like rough trade. Where is she now?'

'She's had enough of rough trade for one night, I reckon. She's off hobnobbing with some bloke who looks like Roger Moore. I can't work out if he's Roger Moore or not. This party is confusing me. I passed by Peter on the way in here and he had his tongue down Lady Godiva's throat, so I reckon Lady Godiva is gay, but what's the kick for two guys who are gay to be dressed as girls and have a lesbian scene, 'cos isn't that like your old girlfriend seeing you in the earrings and thinking you were like Sandy or is it different, 'cos . . .? Oh, sod it, I'm pissed. And I need some more champagne so's I can get more pissed.' He reached out for the bottle and took a swig from it.

Isabel spotted David walking towards them. This was not the opportune moment for David to meet Micky, she knew; and she didn't like the idea of Stryker being there either. David, faced with Butch Cassidy and a drunken Sundance Kid, might have a seriously negative first impression.

'Mr McCabe—' David went up to Stryker, his hand outstretched. 'It's a pleasure to meet you finally. Needless to say—' he glanced over at Isabel. 'I've heard a lot about you.'

Standing up and shaking David's hand, Stryker said: 'Stryker. And it's good to meet you, too. I think I may have stolen your seat here.'

'No, no. Sit down. I'll sit beside – it's Micky, isn't it? Micky Dawson?' He went to Micky's side and shook his hand as well. 'David Barton. Isabel has told me all about your casino life. It sounds fascinating.'

'Yeah.' Micky struggled to his feet, then collapsed back in his chair as David sat down on his left. 'It's fascinating all right.'

'Isabel described your friend Hermes. The toupée must be something to see – the toupee and the necklace. I'd like to meet him, too.'

'Yeah.' Micky frowned. '*Très amusant*. We're a *très amusant* little group at the Empire. And you don't have to pay even to meet us. Just walk in and there we are. On display.'

'I didn't mean—'

'Ah, fuck it, I know.' Micky interrupted, waving his hand in the air. 'Inadvertent patronizing that was, wasn't it?'

'Micky—' Isabel put her hand on his arm. 'Do you think you should get some fresh air? Or should I get you a cup of coffee?'

'I don't need nothin', Izzy. Ta very much.'

'Isabel tells me you're a boxer,' David said, in a placating tone. 'Do you find it difficult. I mean at your age and—'

'Where'd you come up with the idea of the photographs, David?' Stryker interrupted. 'They work really well. I especially liked the one of JFK and—'

'You have a problem with me being a fighter?' Micky turned his back on Isabel and faced David square on. 'You don't think I'm in shape? Is that it?'

'No, no—' David shook his head. 'I didn't mean that.'

'Marilyn Monroe,' Stryker continued. 'The way she's sitting in his lap – that's fantastic.

244

'It is, isn't it?' Isabel said quickly. This was fast turning into a disaster. Whatever David said now was going to spur Micky on to a higher point of rage. Isabel knew from nights at the casino that Micky could take an instant dislike to someone for no apparent reason. If the object of his scorn then tried to get into his good graces, Micky would head full steam into outright contempt. Ninety-nine per cent of the time, Isabel thought she understood why Micky turned on people; she prided herself on being able to see what it was that had set him off, and ninety-nine per cent of the time she silently empathized with him. But that was the casino; those were people who were show-offs or idiotic players. David didn't deserve Micky's wrath. He was *trying* to be friendly. Micky should have understood that. Was he jealous, she wondered? Could that be why he'd reacted in this way? No, she decided; *she* wasn't an issue, alcohol was. The drink made him aggressive. Aware that Stryker was trying to bail David out, she felt, for one instant, profoundly grateful to him, but that feeling reminded her of how well he'd taken his poker defeat at her hands; it took her back to that dreadful behaviour she wanted to forget, when she'd lost control of herself, when she'd acted like a spoiled, ill-tempered brat. She wanted Micky and Stryker to leave; everything would be fine if she and David could be alone together again. They were wrecking a perfect night.

'Hey, Mick, let's go.' Stryker stood up, as if he had heard her thoughts. 'Help me find Julia Malcolm. I said I'd dance with her.'

'You're dancing with Julia?' David asked.

'You have a problem with that too?' Micky glared at him.

'Come on.' Stryker took Micky by the elbow, physically lifted him up. Isabel was reminded of Julia Malcolm lifting Paul off the dance floor. 'I need your help.'

'Yeah, OK.' Micky turned to Isabel. 'See you later, Izzy. Get rid of this wanker here and we can have some fun.'

Isabel dropped her head in her hands. A few seconds later, when she looked up, she saw that Micky and Stryker had gone.

'I don't think your friend likes me,' David stated matter-of-factly.

'He's drunk. He's not usually like that, David. He's usually a sweetheart. Well, not exactly a sweetheart, but a lovely man.'

'I'll take your word for it.'

'Sorry.'

'No problem. I don't have a problem with it, Isabel. Your friend is wrong, you know. I don't have a problem with him being a boxer, I don't have a problem with *anything*. Not tonight.'

Stryker half-dragged Micky outside and sat him on the wall at the edge of the terrace. He pulled a cigarette out, lit it, handed it to Micky, then lit one for himself.

'The man's a wanker, Y. Upper-class twit of the century. Classless society. That's a laugh. Take a look around this place. Classless society, my ass.'

'You thought I was a wanker when you first met me. I was Surfer Boy, remember? Anyway, you don't have to fight the class struggle with David Barton.'

'Izzy shouldn't be with that wanker. She should be with you – you know that. I know that. The only person who doesn't know that is her.'

'Well, her ignorance of that blindingly obviously fact is blindingly obvious. Listen, I know I've lost Izzy, but I never had her in the first place, so it's not a tragedy.' Stryker smiled. 'It's not a Sixties pop song.'

'I hate these things.' Micky ground his cigarette out on the gravel beneath him. 'Where's a cigar when you need one? I should get going, Y. I don't belong here. Neither do you.'

'No,' Stryker nodded. 'You're right. I don't.'

I wanted to see her one more time, that's all. I wanted to see her and get her out of my system, but it hasn't worked. I'm tired and I'm way too sober and I don't know what I'm doing here.

'Guess who?'

Stryker turned around when he heard the voice, and saw Elvis crouching behind Micky, her hands over his eyes, blindfolding him.

'Monica,' Stryker whispered in Micky's ear.

'Elvis! You're back from the dead!' Micky leaped up, turned around, enveloped her in a bear hug.

So much for the class struggle, Stryker thought.

'Are you ready to rock?' Elvis gyrated his/her hips.

'You bet,' Micky gyrated back.

Boy am I going to give him a hard time about this tomorrow. I can't wait, Stryker said to himself, watching them head off to the dance floor. He was planning to stay and smoke his cigarette in peace, but he saw a figure approaching him from the side of the terrace, a person who he guessed was supposed to be Rudolph Valentino and who looked suspiciously like Fiona. Getting up and brushing off his jeans, Stryker stepped on his cigarette, then went back into the house as quickly as he could. Halfway to the marquee, he bumped into Julia Malcolm coming in the opposite direction.

'Julia,' he cried with heartfelt relief. 'Time for that dance.'

'I was going to get some air,' she said.

'No, no, I'm footloose, I'm fancy free. Let's go for it. Let's rock.'

As he propelled her to the dance floor, he wondered when he could leave the party and where Peter was. Would Micky and Peter find their own way home or were they counting on him for a lift? He wanted out. He wanted to leave and goo home and brood on his own. Failing that, he wanted to dance his socks off.

The band was playing *Simply The Best*. The Tina Turner look-alike and soundalike lead singer was, Stryker was not surprised to see, on closer inspection, a man. Stryker took Julia in his arms in the old-fashioned style, his right arm around her back, his left hand holding hers.

'My God, you can dance, Mr McCabe,' she said after a few steps across the floor. 'I didn't think Americans could dance.'

'We can walk too,' he smiled. 'Sometimes we can even talk. Not often, but sometimes.'

He was beginning to like Julia Malcolm, and he knew he was right on the verge of having fun. Then he spotted Isabel, being spun around by David Barton. She was so obviously in her element, so clearly having the time of her life, he stopped in the middle of a step and managed to tread on Julia's foot.

'Ouch.'

'Sorry. I lost my concentration.'

'At least you didn't fall down.'

Tina Turner stepped back from the microphone as the song ended and one of the back-up singers took her place.

'Who's this?' Stryker asked Julia.

'I don't know. Whoever it is has very strange lips.'

When she began to sing *I Can't Get No Satisfaction*, they looked at each other and laughed.

'I should have guessed,' she said.

'Do you want to sit this one out?'

Julia Malcolm surveyed the dance floor quickly, then shook her head.

'No, let's keep going.'

Stryker obliged by starting off on an incredibly fast foxtrot.

'Where'd you learn to dance?'

'My parents. They're dentists. They're also *habituées* of the Arthur Murray dance studio. They made sure I flossed three times a day and learned how to do the cha-cha-cha at some point in between. Dentistry and dancing – I grew up having them both drilled into me, so to speak.'

'My mother made me go to dancing lessons when I was three. I don't know anyone my age except me who dances like this. Stryker—' Julia leaned back, away from him. 'Could you do me one more favour?'

'Shoot.'

'Could you cut in on David Barton?'

'You want to dance with David? I'm not good enough? You've wounded me, Julia. My parents would be grief-stricken.'

'I want to thank him for organizing the party and this seems a good time. It's no reflection on your dancing skills.'

'All right,' Stryker shrugged. Isabel wasn't going to appreciate

248

this, he knew. She'd hardly like being torn from the arms of her beloved and deposited in his own. I can always say I was only obeying orders, he thought. Following the wishes of my hostess. Manoeuvring Julia and himself over to the spot where David and Isabel were dancing, Stryker tapped David on the shoulder.

'Can I borrow Isabel for a minute?'

David stopped, stared at Julia, then let go of Isabel.

'All right,' he said. He took Julia's hand in his and put a noticeably stiff arm around her. They moved off, and Stryker went to take Isabel's hand. *I Can't Get No Satisfaction* segued into one of the Rolling Stones' slower songs.

'Come on,' he said. Let's show them. Let's waltz.'

'Waltz?'

'That's what I said.'

'I don't know how to waltz.'

'Follow me. Pretend I'm Arthur Murray.'

'Who's Arthur Murray?'

'Isabel Sands. Your education is lacking. You're like me that first night at the Empire. Except you won't lose any money learning. Just let me lead you, all right?'

'All right,' Isabel murmured.

He took her in his arms, he held her in such a way that she couldn't not follow his steps and he set off. Waltzing to the Rolling Stones was easier than he'd thought it would be, and while he danced he forgot everything and concentrated on letting his body go with the beat. A waltz is as good as catching a touchdown pass, he thought. Dancing is a sport. She can move, too. She can follow me. It's like a sport and it's like sex. The world dissolves around you and you're aware only of your bodies and how they fit and what magic they can make.

When the song ended, Stryker smiled down at Isabel.

'See? It's a piece of cake.'

'You're very good,' she said. The frown accompanying this statement made his smile broaden.

'What, Iz? I cease never to amaze you? Is that it?'

'No, no, that's not it.' She shifted uneasily from foot to foot. 'I mean, I don't know. I never pictured you waltzing. But then I never pictured myself waltzing. I'm surprised at myself too. Or how you managed to make it easy, I guess. I don't know.'

The next tune began. Another female dressed as a man had stepped up to the microphone and was singing the Beatles song, *I Don't Want to Spoil the Party*.

'OK, here we go again,' Stryker said. 'Bop 'till you drop.'

'Sorry, Stryker, I don't feel like dancing any more at the moment. I have to go to the loo, actually.'

He could see a blush rise and spread over her face.

'Fine with me,' he replied.

I don't want to dance with you either, sweetheart. You don't have to make up an excuse to get away from me. I'll be happy to leave you alone. He turned his back and strode off.

The party's over. I was out of my mind to fall for her in the first place. OK, it's impossible, OK, she isn't attracted to me. I get it. These things happen. You can't always fall for the people who fall for you. But, shit – you don't have to treat them like dirt. At least I was civil to Peter when he was in the throes of his crush. I didn't brush him off so brutally. I acted like a grown-up and we became friends. She's been childish from the start. What the hell did I see in her anyway? She's shallow—. Stryker stopped on that word and straightened his shoulders. Dancing with me is like taking the bone test. She wants to get out of it, so she makes a lame excuse about going to the loo. And I get all enraged and pissed off. That's amazingly grown up of me, isn't it? I should get a medal for outstanding maturity.

Shit, I should have told Miss Fellowes I had to go to the loo, not basketball practice. Then she would have said, 'Loo? What's that?' and I could have stood there in the hallway and gone on a riff about this cute little country called England where they have Kings and Queens and loos and motorways and all these weird words like 'crikey' and . . .

'Hey, Y, what's happening? What planet are you visiting?' Micky was at his side, clapping him on the shoulder. 'Come sit down with me. Elvis has buggered off to go with her own crowd again. She's had enough of the boy from the wrong side of town.' Micky seated himself at a table on the edge of the dance floor and pointed to the chair beside him.

'Sit, for fuck's sake. Aha, look who I see – the shirt-lifter. Come over here, Peter,' he called out and beckoned. 'The Third Musketeer. Can't you take off that fucking helmet now? You look like a rabbit.'

'Excuse me?' Peter said when he sat down. 'I look fantastic. At least that's what Lady Godiva tells me.'

'Where is she, I mean *he*, now?' Stryker asked.

'He's gone – he has a modelling shoot early tomorrow. Or that's what he said, anyway. Now that I think about it, who models on Sundays? I suppose I've been left in the lurch yet again. I'd take myself to a nunnery but I'm not sure about those clothes.'

'Where's Izzy got to? Is she still with that wanker?'

'Are you referring to my brother, Micky?' Peter raised his chin.

'Izzy's gone to the ladies,' Stryker said. Why am I always in the middle of a fight? And how am I going to stop this one getting out of hand?

'Listen. What's that old song? I've been trying to remember it all night. You two would know. It's something about a plane crash. The guy is waiting at the airport for his girlfriend, who is flying in, when he hears an announcement—'

'*Ebony Eyes*,' Micky and Peter said simultaneously.

'Can you remember the lyrics?' Stryker silently congratulated himself.

'Yes, of course.' Peter looked at Stryker as though he'd asked the stupidest question in the world. 'The Everly Brothers. It starts—' Peter stopped, his mouth half-open.

'Go on – you do the first bit, I'll do the next,' Micky nudged Peter, but Peter wasn't listening. Peter was looking at the dance floor.

Stryker swivelled halfway around in his chair to see what Peter was staring at.

251

'What's the big deal, you two?' Micky asked. 'What's going on there? Some striptease? I wanna see that.' He turned and looked. 'I don't get it. That brother of yours is dancing with that woman in the white trousers, the one with that weird white streak in her hair. Is that what you're looking at?'

'Where's Isabel?' Peter asked, turning back to the room, his eyes searching.

'It's OK,' Stryker said quietly, not taking his eyes off the dance floor. 'She's not here.'

'Oh. *Now* I get it. I see.' Micky nodded. 'They got something going there, don't they? But, hey, don't get all worked up. It's just a dance.'

'You don't know David,' Peter frowned. 'You wouldn't say that if you knew David.'

Stryker sat back and lit a cigarette.

Chapter Fifteen

David was where she'd so often imagined him to be; sitting on her sofa, his head back, his eyes closed. Isabel put the glass of wine down on the table in front of him, then sat down herself, her legs folded underneath her. She'd taken off her tailcoat and top hat as soon as they'd come through the door, and he'd removed his shoes.

'Thank you,' he said, opening his eyes. 'But I shouldn't have any more wine. I've had quite enough as it is.'

'Are you exhausted?'

'I'm tired, yes. Aren't you?'

'Yes. But I'm happy tired. The party was fabulous. The whole thing went like clockwork, didn't it?'

'What happened to your friend Micky? He disappeared without saying goodbye. Was that on my account, do you think? I don't know what I said to upset him so much.'

'He can get touchy sometimes. It's not your fault. I saw him leave when I was coming back from the loo, actually. He and Peter and Stryker left together. They were probably heading off to a club.'

'I don't understand why Peter went so potty over Stryker McCabe, why everyone seems to go so potty over him. This supposed charisma of his eludes me.'

'That's just as well,' Isabel smiled. 'Anyway, let's not talk about Stryker.'

With an abruptness Isabel was unprepared for, David pulled her head towards his and kissed her. His teeth and hers clashed so soundly she felt as if she'd been teeth-butted and drew back, covering her mouth.

'Sorry,' he said. 'That wasn't the way I meant for that to go.'

'No, I'm sorry – I wasn't expecting you to – I should have been – I don't—' Isabel ran out of words and stopped, embarrassed. Picking up her glass of wine, she took a sip and surreptitiously ran her tongue over her stunned teeth.

'Come on—' He took her hand and pulled himself and her up off the sofa. 'Where's your bedroom, Isabel? Lead on.'

Lead on? Is this a military exercise? Why does he look so pained and so put upon? He looks as if we had to get out of our bunker and charge the enemy, as if there's no choice and we have to get it over with, do the frightening deed as quickly as possible.

No, he's embarrassed, that's all. We both are – shy and self-conscious, especially after that disastrous kiss. Once we get upstairs, we'll be fine. We'll be able to relax.

She followed his order and led him up the stairs and into her bedroom.

Do I turn on the light or leave if off? I feel like I actually am a teenager, as if I've never gone to bed with a man before. I'll leave it off.

David peeled all his clothes off with incredible speed and leaped under the duvet.

'Here,' he patted the pillow. 'Your turn, Isabel.'

She wasn't sure quite what to do next. Should she undress as he had, or keep her underwear on, or what? This was yet another leap of faith and she knew she had to make it quickly, not stand as she was, staring at him, trying to make out his features in the dark. If she did take all her clothes off, should she try to do it in a seductive manner? Feeling a crazed desire to turn on the computer and play poker, she mentally slapped herself back into the real world, and undressed as if he and she were the only two competitors in a 'get your gear off' race. As soon as she finished, she climbed into bed but didn't snuggle up to him; she couldn't, not yet. She was far too nervously aware of her own naked body and what he'd think of it.

'Come here, Isabel.' He pulled her to him and she felt his cool skin against hers. He didn't attempt to kiss her again; instead he immediately rolled on top of her and began to make love. Once more, his abruptness took her off balance and she felt unsure of how to react. Whenever she had envisioned this moment, she had imagined it as ineffably tender. There would be a slow build-up, a gentle process of coming together which would allow them to discover each other. What was happening at the moment wasn't physically unenjoyable, but it was emotionally unconnected. They weren't moving together in any identifiable rhythm as they had been on the dance floor. David's love-making had a desperate quality to it, as if he were trying to obliterate himself and her both as he pounded away.

It's the first time, she kept saying to herself as this went on. The first time is always difficult. Neither of us knows what the other likes or wants. Maybe he's right in getting it over with straight away, without any preliminaries. There'll be plenty of time for foreplay and exploration later. After this is finished we can settle down comfortably.

One second after climaxing, he rolled back to his former position and put his elbow up and over his eyes.

'That was very nice, Isabel. Thank you,' he said.

'You're welcome, David,' she replied.

What is this – a tea party? I know I've always loved how polite he is, but isn't this kind of behaviour actually rude, even though he thanked me? Shouldn't he take a little more notice of what I'm doing here? Shouldn't he kiss me?

'I'm exhausted, I'm afraid. Completely done in. What is it? Four o'clock in the morning?'

'Give or take a few minutes, yes. You should get some sleep.'

'So should you.' He removed his elbow and gave her a kiss on the cheek. 'We've both had an eventful day. And night.'

'Right.'

'Goodnight, Isabel.'

'Goodnight.'

She watched him turn over on his side, facing away from her. This has happened to me before, she thought, looking at his neck and shoulders. I've cried after sex once or twice before, when it's been a mistake. There is no sadder feeling than being in bed with someone after a physical act which should have brought you closer together but which in reality drives you further apart. But it can't be the same now. We're both tired, that's all. It's all happened too quickly. We need more time to make the transition from friends and partners to lovers; the party was distracting, we had too much to drink. The wretched kiss started things off badly.

I'll make any and every excuse in the book for him and for me. One of them must be the right one. I have what I want now, what I've dreamed about for years. So what if he turned his back to me? The point is he's here, in my bed. I shouldn't be crying – I should be smiling. Sex isn't everything. Besides, we'll sort it out in time.

Isabel closed her eyes and saw herself and David on the dance floor in the marquee. That had been perfect. If the whole night had been as perfect as that . . . but then Stryker McCabe had cut in and her waltz with him had been perfect as well, which made no sense at all. He shouldn't have been able to dance like that or to make her dance like that with him. She had yielded to him, for a few moments she'd even forgotten who he was. Closing her eyes, she had felt as if she were with David, but when she opened them again and saw Stryker's grin, she'd been embarrassed and upset. Although she couldn't say exactly how he'd done it, he'd managed to make her feel foolish yet again. And a bad sport when she'd refused to continue dancing.

From the moment she'd turned Stryker down, the perfection of the evening had become more and more flawed. David, when she returned from the loo, suggested that they mingle with the guests, and the rest of the night and early morning passed by in meaningless chatter with partygoers. He didn't ask her to dance again. The mood had slipped, and they were back to doing business together.

Stryker McCabe shouldn't have cut in, Isabel thought. Stryker McCabe should have left them alone. Why didn't he? No one cuts in at dances any more. It was an old-fashioned custom. She was surprised someone like Stryker even knew it existed.

He'd looked so ridiculous in those jeans and necklaces. If he wasn't going to dress up, he should have done as David did and wear black tie. But no, not Surfer Boy, the waltzing whiz. Where had he learned to dance like that? What the hell was she doing asking herself questions about him when David was lying asleep beside her?

Reaching out tentatively, Isabel put her hand on the back of David's neck. He didn't stir, and she moved closer, kissing his shoulder.

You don't have to do a thing, she thought. Just lie there and I'll look at you. I could spend the next three days looking at your back and still be happy.

We've won, David, she whispered. Now all we have to do is rake in the chips.

Stryker had been sick for what seemed like hours. He lay in bed, hoping that it would end soon, wondering whether a cup of tea would make him feel better or set the nausea off again.

What an end to a miserable night, he thought. What a way to end a party. It serves me right for going in the first place. I should have steered clear – it wasn't my party, it was Isabel's, Isabel's and David's. Paul's and Julia's. Julia . . . Stryker closed his eyes. It fit, that was the problem. The pieces of the puzzle all fit perfectly. Why had Julia come to his office in the first place? Not because she had heard such great things about *Your Fantasy Team*, but because she must have been pissed off at David Barton for some reason. Maybe he'd promised her something he then didn't deliver on. He might have broken a covert date. Who knew? What was clear was that they had a history, those two. A man and a woman didn't dance the way they were dancing without sexual knowledge of each other. Stryker had seen enough couples dancing over the years to read the signs – and Peter had read them too.

'Are you going to say something to Isabel, Stryker?' Peter had asked on the ride back. Micky was passed out, snoring loudly in the back seat.

'No.'

'Do you think I should?'

'No.' Stryker shifted into third and kept his eyes on the road. 'It's none of our business.'

'You don't think she's entitled to know?' From his tone of voice, Stryker could hear that Peter had sobered up quickly.

'Why? Your brother and Julia – whatever was going on may be over – that may have been a dance for old times' sake. One last goodbye. How do we know what went on between them or what is going on between them?'

'But I *do* know David. I've never seen his face look quite like that. If it is in the past, it most certainly is in the recent past.'

'It's still their business, not ours.'

'But he may be taking up with Izzy on the rebound.'

'Peter, leave it alone. Izzy can take care of herself, David can take care of himself. What we saw back there – it's not relevant.'

Peter was quiet then and Stryker drove on, listening to Micky snore. By the time he'd dropped them both off at their respective flats and driven himself back to Chelsea, his stomach was beginning to cramp badly. Within seconds of getting inside his front door, he was in the bathroom, throwing up.

There's a kind of clarity after a night like this, he thought. I'm so weak and exhausted and empty I'm almost floating above myself. I understand now part of the reason I was so besotted with Izzy. I thought she might be the catalyst to make me change my life. I drifted into the party business because I was good at it and because I had made such a good job of screwing up everything else in my life. I didn't give myself any options, I was frightened to do anything else in case I failed. Parties are easy, parties are formulaic.

You feed off other people's dreams and ideas of a great time. You give people what they want – a service industry made up of one-off events.

You want to be Zorro for the night? You got it. You want to be Elizabeth Hurley – fine. You don't want to be anyone in particular, you just want to get drunk and dance – Stryker's your Uncle. I wave the wand and make magic happen.

If you're busy enough giving other people what they want, you don't have to think about what you want yourself.

And gradually, without being aware you're doing it, you get used to the idea that you're not going to get to be you. You can be Stryker McCabe, party-giver, the successful man around town who is always pictured with a glass of champagne in his hand. But you're not going to be the Stryker McCabe you see yourself as – the one who has more to offer, the one who is not about parties only but who has a whole unspecified, unlimited wonderful future in front of him. You come to terms with the fact the future has arrived already and it's never going to be a hell of a lot different from the past. You get up in the morning, you do your job, you try to do it well, and then you go to bed.

Everyone has his or her own fantasy – that they themselves will be special, will make a big impact, that other people will want to come to parties dressed as them. When they give up on that dream, they make the adjustments life requires. They settle down and find as much happiness as they can within the limits age and circumstances have forced them to recognize.

Changing cities, swapping countries, is one way of staving off that moment of recognition, but nothing I have done here is different from what I did in New York. There are different faces and different places, but the bottom line is the same. Or it was the same – until Izzy came into my life. Isabel – sharp, funny, poker-playing Isabel, the girl who can do backflips. I didn't know how she was going to change my life, but I was sure she would. She made me want her to see me the way I would want to see myself. I wanted her to be proud of me, I thought together we could defy the odds and find something in ourselves that we knew was there, but couldn't get to without each other's help.

Isabel Sands.

Stryker got out of bed, went to the kitchen and switched on the kettle.

Looks like I'll have to do it without you, Izzy. And that's a crying shame. But I'm sure as hell going to have some fun along the way.

'Wake up! I'm back! And I've brought some amazing spices from Mauritius!' Lily bounded through the door and jumped on the end of Isabel's bed. 'Oh my God – sorry. Who's that?' She pointed to David, who woke up as soon as Lily landed on his feet and was struggling with the duvet, pulling it up over his chest.

'David. Lily – this is David Barton; David, this is Lily Carroll.' Isabel grabbed her side of the duvet and covered her top as she sat up.

'We meet, finally we meet.' Lily put her hand out and shook David's. 'Sorry about squashing your feet.'

'No problem,' David replied. 'It's nice to meet you.'

'Mauritius was fabulous. You wouldn't believe who I saw there – Quincy – as in Quincy, that guy who cuts up dead bodies and solves crimes on TV. He was staying at the same hotel. I kept hoping there'd be a murder so I could help him solve it, even though I know he's only an actor and it's not the same, is it? But it would have been fun to try. So have you two had wanton sex? Do you need time to recover? Should I leave you in peace or go fetch you some coffee?'

David, Isabel could see, was nonplussed. He squirmed beneath the duvet and grimaced.

'Coffee would be wonderful, Lily,' Isabel said.

'Right – coming up. Croissants? Chocolates? Spices? Anything else?'

'Just coffee.'

'Iz – you sly dog. You should have told me he'd be here.'

'I didn't know he'd be here, Lily. And I didn't know when you were coming back, either.'

'I know, I should have rung. Anyway, I'll be right back. Feel free to talk about me.'

'We will,' Isabel laughed.

'This is embarrassing,' David commented when she'd gone. 'Doesn't she have any sense of privacy? Does she always talk like that?' He climbed out of bed and began to put on his clothes. 'God,' he said, looking at his watch. 'It's nine o'clock already?'

'Lily's naturally friendly,' Isabel apologized. 'Sorry.'

All her expectations of a relaxed morning making love vanished, and she rushed to put on a pair of sweat pants and t-shirt, self-conscious of her nudity in the daylight. By the time Lily returned with the coffee, Isabel and David were sitting on the bed, dressed.

'This is like a pyjama party, isn't it?' Lily said, handing out the mugs. 'A black tie pyjama party. What a great idea. There was no need to get dressed, though. I'll be going to bed myself soon, to sleep off the jet lag.'

'I'm glad you had such a good time, Lil.'

'Beach, ocean, TV star – what more could a girl ask for? A younger, more hunky TV star, I suppose. Anyway—' She sat back down on the end of the bed, her legs crossed beneath her. 'Obviously a lot has happened in my absence. You look a little like Peter, you know?' Lily narrowed her eyes and stared at David. 'Except you look older.'

'I *am* older.'

'Peter's in town,' Isabel said. 'He sends his love.'

'We should ring him up and get him over here. I heard a fantastic new ghost story last week. Maybe he has something else in his wardrobe I covet. Which reminds me – what happened to Stryker? Has he succumbed to Peter's charms?'

'No.' Isabel shook her head and took a sip of her coffee. 'But Peter seems to have recovered.'

'Really?' I thought he'd stay forever obsessed. I want to see that guy, you know. See what the deal is. Why he's so hot. What's that top hat doing on the chair over there? Oh shit. I remember now. Last night must have been the Malcolm party. How was it?'

'Great,' Isabel smiled.

David was looking at Isabel's computer, focusing on it as if it were a television and his favourite show was on.

'You know, on the plane I was leafing through some magazines and there in *OK!* was a photo of Paul and Julia Malcolm. Julia was dressed in this fabulous miniskirt and her hair was in a punk style and I thought: wow, she has all this money, she's married this rich tycoon and she looks seriously trendy, not like some woman who haunts Bond Street, more like someone on *Top of the Pops*. I liked her style.'

'She came dressed as Fred Astaire last night,' Isabel said. 'And she did look good, I have to admit.'

'What's she doing with that old codger? Do you think it's worth it for the money? Do you think I should go out and try to snag Richard Branson? Or is he married already? Yes, he is, isn't he? So I better not. No married men for – oops, wrong thing to say. Anyway, can you imagine having to sleep with Paul Malcolm? It would be like having sex with an old praying mantis. It can't be worth it.'

'Julia Malcolm had a difficult childhood.' David finally turned his attention from the computer to Lily, but he was speaking in an irritated tone.

'She did?' Isabel turned to him. 'How do you know that?'

'I talked to her a little last night. She had a difficult childhood and Paul Malcolm saved her from it. He was like a father to her. She was grateful to him.'

'Haven't I seen that movie somewhere?' Lily asked. 'Was it *Annie*? Did Little Orphan Annie have to marry Daddy Warbucks and have disgusting sex with him or did he adopt her?'

'I should be making my move homewards,' David announced.

'David?' Isabel couldn't stop herself from sounding both surprised and disappointed. Was he going to leave straight away? Why rush off on a Sunday morning? Was he regretting last night?

'No, no – stay,' Lily put in quickly. 'I'm going to my room now.

You two should—' She was interrupted by the sound of the doorbell. 'Who the hell is that? You stay here. It might be a Jehovah's Witness. I love those people. I love asking them whether they'd have a blood transfusion if they were at death's door. They always say they wouldn't, but I don't believe them. Then I tell them I'm a vampire and we get into really good discussions. Anyway, I'll run down and find out.' Lily scampered out of the room and down the stairs.

'You've got company,' David said, standing up. 'I'll be off.'

Don't push him. Let him do what he wants. If you say anything, you'll sound as desperate as you feel.

'I'll ring later.' He kissed her on the forehead. 'When I'm compos mentis. I'm not at my best in the mornings.'

'You guys,' Lily called up to them. 'Guess who's here? Peter. He's come to join the party.'

'Peter?' David's eyebrows raised. 'What's he doing here?'

'Who knows?' Isabel mumbled as she followed David down the stairs. What was she supposed to make of his behaviour? Was it as simple as being a bad morning person or was there more to it? He seemed to be wilfully ignoring her, heading off on his own to see Peter without waiting for her, dying to get out of the door and back to his flat as quickly as possible. It reminded her of the way he had undressed the night before; he had an agenda, he wanted to get on with it and what she thought or felt didn't enter into his plans. The messages he'd sent over the past twenty-four hours were so mixed she needed a code breaker to sort them out.

'I'm afraid you two have a small problem,' Peter said when David and Isabel arrived in the front room. He was dressed in a pair of bright yellow shorts and a white t-shirt, his sunglasses, as ever, perched on top of his head. 'I hate to be the bearer of bad tidings at this particular point in time, but I thought I should tell you what's going on.'

'What's going on, then?' David asked.

'Why don't we all sit down?' Isabel said. 'Would you like some coffee, Peter?'

'No, thank you, Iz.' He pulled up two chairs from the table at the back of the room, offered one to Lily and then sat down on the other himself. Isabel sat down on the sofa and David joined her, but a couple of feet away.

'So what's going on, Peter?' David repeated.

'I had a telephone call from Julia Malcolm this morning. She rang to talk to you, but of course you weren't there. So she told me to tell you that various partygoers have been sick – sick all night, apparently. I think some of those prawns must have been off – that's the only explanation. She seemed a little upset not to be able to talk to you personally. She asked me where you were.'

'What did you say?'

'I said I didn't know.' Peter's eyes narrowed as he stared at David.

'Oh.' David looked away from his brother and, sitting forward, turned to Isabel. 'The prawns were off? No, that's impossible. We used the same caterers we've used thousands of times. We've never had a problem before.'

'No, we never have.'

'Well, you do now,' Peter sighed. 'There are too many people involved for it to be a bug of some sort. It has to have been the food. I would have rung you, but I felt I should tell you both in person.'

'We weren't sick.' Isabel looked from David to Peter. 'We ate the prawns too and we weren't sick.'

'It must have been a batch of prawns, not all of them.'

'Are they going to sue?' Lily asked.

'Sue?' Isabel rocked back. 'They wouldn't sue.'

'They could, Iz. Food poisoning. It's bad news.'

'But it's not our fault. Who would they sue? The caterers?'

'Listen, people,' Peter stated. 'Julia said no one is going to sue. We discussed that. She said they were pissed off but no one has been seriously affected. No one is in hospital – at least as far as she knows.'

'How many people are we talking about?' David queried.

'Ten, so far. There may be more.'

'Word's going to spread like wildfire.' David looked up at the ceiling. 'It will be known as the food poisoning party. Given by *Party Time*. We're stuffed. Whatever credibility we had is gone now.'

'No—' Isabel reached over and grabbed his arm. 'No, David. It's not all over. Everyone will remember what a good time they had, they won't blame us. They'll know it's not our fault.'

'I don't think so, Isabel,' David said very slowly.

No one spoke. Isabel tightened her grip on David's arm.

'We'll work this out. It will be fine, I promise.'

'How will we work it out?' David rolled his eyes. 'How? What? Will you play another poker match with Stryker McCabe to salvage our reputation? How's that going to work, Isabel? You know, I wouldn't be surprised—' He paused, drummed his fingers against his lips. 'I wouldn't be at all surprised if McCabe hadn't arranged this somehow.'

'You think Stryker poisoned people to keep on top?' Peter sat bolt upright. 'David, I can't believe you said that. Stryker *gave* this party to you. Why would he sabotage you after he'd given it to you?'

'He didn't give it to us,' Isabel protested. 'I won it, Peter.'

'No you didn't.'

'I did, I won it. You didn't see, you weren't there.'

'No, I wasn't, but Micky was. And he told me about it last night, he told me Stryker threw that poker game because he thought you were so desperate to win, that you needed it more than he did.'

'That's bullshit.' Isabel let go of David's arm and stood up. 'He didn't throw the game, he was about to win. He *should* have won, he had the better hand. I was lucky to beat him.'

'Iz, I don't know anything about poker, but that's what Micky said. He said Stryker thought you had an amazing hand at the end so he bet against you and he lost. On purpose, or "not inadvertently", as Micky put it, in a surprisingly coherent way given his semi-comatose state last night.'

'Why would Stryker do that?'

'Because—' Peter stopped. 'As I said before, because he thought you needed it more than he did.'

'I hardly think Stryker McCabe is such a selfless person,' David commented. 'That doesn't strike me as convincing.'

'No. You're the only good one, aren't you, David? You've always been perfectly behaved, haven't you? It pisses the hell out of me, you know. I love you, but this holier than thou stance of yours I've lived with all my life drives me mad. David's the good one. David's the polite one, David does all the right things. Well, maybe this time someone else has acted honourably for a change and you just can't bear to believe it.' Peter bit his lip and then turned his eyes away from David and down to the floor. 'I'm sorry, but it's too much. Trying to blame Stryker for this.'

'He threw the game?' Isabel sat back down heavily.

'That's what Micky said,' Peter replied. 'He also told me that Julia Malcolm came to Stryker and asked him to take the party away from you two. That was supposed to be a secret apparently, but you know what I'm like with secrets.'

'Why would Julia Malcolm do that?'

'I don't know, Iz. David—' Peter turned to his brother. 'Do you know, by any chance?'

'Why would I know? You've said some very harsh words, Peter. If you want to discuss our childhoods and our respective reputations, or assumed reputations, I think we should discuss them alone, not with an audience in attendance.' David stood up. 'I think we should go back to my flat now. Right now.'

'What are we going to do about people being sick?' Isabel looked up at David. 'Don't go now, David. Stay, and we can sort it out somehow.'

'There's nothing to sort out, Isabel. There's not a thing we can do. Send the afflicted flowers? That might be a gesture, but it's a gesture which admits culpability. I suppose we could sue the caterers ourselves, but the legal fees would be grotesque and our reputation wouldn't be enhanced either. I think we should consider—' He paused. 'We'll talk about it all later. Right now, Peter and I should leave. Come on, Peter.' He walked over to where Peter was sitting and pulled him up. 'We're going.'

'I'm sorry, Izzy, Lily.' Peter waved his hands in the air. 'I didn't mean to turn this into a family squabble. I wanted to help—' Before he could finish, David had dragged him off and out the door with a force which frightened Isabel. They looked like such an absurd pair, David dressed in black tie, Peter in his shorts. As she watched them, she wondered what their relationship had been like as they grew up. Did Peter really resent David for being a goody-goody, or had he overreacted because of David's attack on Stryker? How many childhood memories were about to be dredged up in David's flat? She wished she could be there with them; if she could listen to them, she might get more of a sense of what made David react in the ways he did.

'I wouldn't give that man any prizes for being polite,' Lily said.

Isabel had almost forgotten Lily was there. She'd been unnaturally quiet, sitting on her chair, observing the goings-on, but not, for once in her life, interrupting.

'He's stressed out, Lily. You heard. We're in big trouble.'

'Izzy—' Lily sat perfectly still. 'I know you're going to hate me for saying this, but I have to. You're making a huge mistake.'

'You don't understand.'

'I know what I've seen. I've seen a man who was lying beside you in bed but who doesn't touch you once, OK? And I see a man who is so jumpy he can't be happy about anything. The guy is about to explode with unhappiness, but not because of those people getting sick. He was unhappy when I walked in to your room, he was even more unhappy when he walked out of this house without so much as saying goodbye to you – or me, for that matter. He's in another world, Iz. You're not in that world with him. I don't care what he's like between the sheets. Although I doubt he—'

'Stop, Lily. I mean it. You don't understand. You'll like David when you get to know him. Today was the worst possible time to meet him. I'm going to lose *my* temper if you go on like this.'

'I'm not going to do it, Iz.' Lily pulled her leg up and put her chin on her knee. 'I'm not going to sit around here and watch you waste your time on David Barton. It's painful, it's more painful than you can imagine, watching you throw yourself away on a lost cause. You know how people send out signals? Well, you have to read those signals early on in a relationship. Once, when I was with Jack, and I was sick, feeling rotten with the flu, he couldn't give a toss. He'd planned to have a night of passion and he was going to have it whether I felt like death or not. I didn't pay attention to the signal which was waving in front of my face like a giant flag. I pretended it didn't mean anything. As if. Now you're doing the same thing and I can't stand seeing it. David waved approximately five hundred flags this morning, in the space of – what? An hour? And all those flags were saying one thing: get me out of here. I don't want to be here. This is not the woman who makes my heart do Olympic gymnastics. He may be a perfectly nice man, but as far as you're concerned—'

'I'm going to bed, Lily.' Isabel stood up and headed for the stairs.

When she reached her room, she climbed into the side of the bed David had vacated and stretched out, pulling the duvet over her head.

It had all collapsed, in no time at all. Everything had cratered. The party was now a disaster instead of a success, David and Peter were at war, Lily was saying awful things, and she was left alone in bed on the morning she should have been having slow, wonderful sex with the man she loved. How much worse could it get? Well, *Party Time* could go out of business, for one. And then what? What would they do then?

Your Nightmare Team, Isabel said to herself. We should rename our company *Your Nightmare Team.* 'Pick us to organize your party, everyone. You won't regret it. David Barton and Isabel Sands will give you a party you'll literally die for.'

'Stryker, it's Fiona. Where were you last night? I looked everywhere for you.'

'I was there, Fiona.' Stryker held the telephone an inch away from his ear; Fiona's voice was piercing.

'Well, you weren't very polite. You didn't try to find me, did you?'

'Fiona, I apologize. I've been sick to my stomach all night. I'm not feeling very well.'

'You too?'

'What do you mean, me too?'

'I mean a bunch of guests have been ill all night. Lucy Payne and Deborah Medway and a few others I've heard of. Apparently some of the prawns were off.'

'Oh shit,' Stryker frowned.

'You should be pleased, Stryker. I'd say this puts your rivals in a very bad spot indeed. I doubt anyone will hire them now.'

'It's not their fault. The caterers must have screwed up.'

'Well, it may not be their fault technically, but I certainly wouldn't use them myself and I don't know anyone else who would either. Shouldn't they have had a food tester or something? To sample it before?'

'What? Like the person in the Middle Ages who ate the king's food to test for poison?'

'Yes, exactly.'

'I think that custom is a little out of date, Fiona.'

'Well, it shouldn't be, should it?'

'Fiona, you've caught me at a bad time. I have to hang up now.'

'Stryker – I can come over. I can minister to you.'

'No, no, you wouldn't want to, really. It could be contagious.'

'Contagious? I didn't have any prawns.'

'That's not the point. You know, some things can be contagious if you smell them. For example, people who have allergies to nuts get sick if there is a nut within a hundred yards of them. So if you come within a hundred yards of me you'll get sick, like I am.'

'I don't follow you, Stryker. You're not a nut.'

'Oh, but I am. Gotta run, Fiona. Pip pip and hurrah and everything.'

He hung up, walked slowly to his kitchen and poured his lukewarm cup of tea into the sink.

Prawns. Of all the stupid things to happen at a party.

OK, Stryker. Get off your sickbed and get into action. You've made your decision. You made it at five o'clock this morning. Now you have to act on it. And this has made it even easier. Now's the perfect time to move in for the kill.

Chapter Sixteen

'Izzy – wake up. There's someone downstairs to see you.'

'David?' Isabel struggled to surface from the dream she'd been having. David and she had been dancing, on a roof; he had been dressed as Ginger Rogers and was having a hard time moving skilfully in his heels. 'Is David here?'

'No, not David, Iz. Someone else.'

'I don't want to see anyone else.' She buried her head in the pillow. 'What time is it?'

'Noon. Come on. You can't sulk in your room until David deigns to show up again. Come downstairs.' Lily's voice was fierce. 'Now.'

She lifted her head slightly.

'Who is it?'

'Stryker McCabe.'

'What the hell does he want? I don't want to see him.'

'All right, Iz. I'm going to do a David on you. I'm going to drag you out of bed the way he dragged Peter out of the house this morning. And I'm bigger and stronger than you. You're not a rude person. You have a visitor. He knows you're here. You can't refuse to see him. Come on. Get a move on.'

'OK, fine. You don't have to manhandle me. I'll come down.' Isabel stretched and then rubbed her face. 'But I'm not going to brush my hair or change out of my sweats. I'm going down looking like this. I don't care what Stryker McCabe thinks.'

'Well, if you don't, I do. I care about the way *I* look. Lily McCabe. It has a certain ring to it, don't you think?' Lily picked Isabel's brush off her dressing table and swept it through her hair. 'I'm coming with you. I want to hear what this vision has to say for himself. I love his accent, by the way. Don't you?'

Isabel rolled her eyes, pulled herself out of bed with an immense effort and trudged out of the room. As she went downstairs, she could feel Lily one step behind her.

'Stryker,' she said wearily when she reached the bottom and saw him standing in the front room, his arms crossed. For an instant she regretted not changing; he looked very smart in his khaki trousers and dark green t-shirt, a fact which made her competitive instinct kick in. He was already at an advantage and he hadn't even opened his mouth.

'What are you doing here? Why am I bothering to ask? You've heard about the Party Poisoners. You've come to gloat.'

'Hello, Isabel. Listen, I have a good idea. I'll open my mouth very wide, and that will make it even easier for you to jump down my throat.' He grinned. Isabel frowned.

'I'm sorry. I'm always apologizing to you, aren't I?' Yawning, she thought about going to sit down, but decided against it. Whatever Stryker wanted to say he could say standing up. If she didn't make a move, he wouldn't either. They could have a Mexican stand-off.

'So, have you come to challenge me to a poker match? Another one you'll supposedly lose on purpose?'

'I don't know what you've heard, Isabel,' Stryker spoke very slowly. 'But I have no intention of throwing our next poker match. And yes, that's exactly why I'm here. I've come to challenge you.'

'Fantastic. What are the stakes this time? My house? My car? My business? My life?'

'Whatever you want.'

'Would you like something to drink, Stryker?' Lily asked, stepping out from behind Isabel.

'No, no thank you, Lily. It was nice of you to offer, though.'

'You two are on a first-name basis already?'

Stop it. You're like some bitch on a soap opera. Every word is spiked and barbed. Stop taking your frustrations out on Stryker. Is he serious about a poker game or is this some sort of joke?

'Did Margaret Thatcher abduct you while I was gone, Iz? Did you go back to work at Dickins & Jones? What's going on with you?'

'I'm sorry, Lily.' Isabel put up her hand. 'I just woke up. I'm not functioning properly. Would you like to sit down, Stryker? I didn't mean to be rude.'

'I'm fine. I'm not staying. I came to challenge you, as I said. I wanted to deliver the challenge in person, so I looked you up in the phone book.' Stryker rubbed his stomach then took a step forward. 'A one on one game. Head to head, like before. Only the stakes are slightly different. You write down on a piece of paper what you want from me if you win, I write down what I want from you if I do. Neither of us knows what the stakes are until the game is over.'

'So . . .' Isabel stared at him, trying to work out what he was doing. What could he want from her? Was it business? Would he take all of *Party Time*'s clients if he won? He was already beating them. Did he need to demolish them as well?

'So . . . the sky's the limit, is that what you're saying?'

'Yup,' he grinned again. 'That's it, Isabel. The sky's the limit.'

'And you're not going to throw the game because you feel sorry for me? Don't bother to deny it. That's what Micky told Peter last night.'

'Well, think about that for a second. If it is true, if I did try to throw the last game, and if I decide to throw this one, what can you lose? Nothing. You win whatever you choose to win, whatever you put on that piece of paper. As I said, I have no intention of throwing this game, but even if I did, I don't see why you wouldn't take me on.'

'It's the principle.'

Was this a dream, had she segued from dancing with David dressed as Ginger to talking to Stryker about poker? It might make dream sense, this conversation; it definitely didn't seem real.

'Oh, Isabel.' Stryker stepped back a pace. 'You're all cross with me. Why's that? Don't you think you can beat me?'

'I prefer to play with someone I trust. Someone who wouldn't cheat in any way, even if that cheating is to my advantage.'

'Sounds like an excuse to me. Sounds like you're scared. What do you think, Lily? Do you think she should play poker with me?'

'I'll play if she doesn't,' Lily smiled. 'Any game you like.'

'Hang on—' Isabel went to the sofa and sat down. 'I'm imagining this, aren't I? I'm imagining all of this. It's some twisted version of my going to the casino to challenge you, only it's Lily instead of Micky and we're here instead of there, and I have to make myself wake up, that all.'

'Izzy,' Lily came beside her and put her arm around her. 'You're awake. I promise. Here—'

'Ouch! Jesus, Lily, you didn't have to pinch me.' She rubbed her arm. 'That hurt.'

'But now you know you're awake, right?'

'Oh, thanks.'

'Isabel—' Stryker hadn't moved. 'This can be like a duel. You can bring a second with you. Bring Lily or David or whomever you want. They can keep an eye on me, make sure I'm not up to anything fishy, OK?'

'Go on, Iz.' Lily nudged her in the side. 'Be a sport. I want to see you play.'

'What do you want, Stryker? I mean really? Why are you challenging me?'

'Maybe I want to beat you.' Stryker tilted his head, raised his eyebrows.

'Maverick – that's it!' Lily exclaimed. 'That's what your mother should have named you. I mean Stryker's good, but Maverick, think of it. Maverick McCabe. Unbeatable. I don't think you *can* beat him, Iz. I think maybe you shouldn't play.'

'He's not unbeatable,' Isabel said softly. I can beat him. I will beat him. But what will my stake be? What do I want from him? I know exactly what I want. Now that my brain is functioning I know what I want from Stryker McCabe and I know I can get it. He wants to beat me – it's his ego. He wants to prove something to himself and I'm the lucky recipient of his macho pride. He didn't throw the game on purpose last time. He told Micky that to make himself look better. And now he wants to get back at the woman who thrashed him.

'You're on, Stryker,' she said. 'When do you want to play?'

'Tonight, at Micky's. Eight o'clock.'

'This is fabulous.' Lily made a strange movement that looked like a sitting hop. 'This is like the showdown at the OK Corral. Or what's that film? *High Noon*.' She looked at her watch. 'Perfect timing. I love Grace Kelly. I never liked those swimsuits though. They were a big disappointment.'

'What swimsuits?' Stryker stared at her. 'Did someone go swimming in *High Noon*?'

'Princess Stephanie's swimsuit line, am I right, Lil?' Isabel allowed herself a smile. The powerless feeling she'd had from the moment she'd exchanged that awkward kiss with David the night before evaporated instantaneously. Playing poker with Stryker was like going home to your old bed, the one you slept in as a child. It was comfortable, easy, familiar. She knew how he played and she knew how to beat him. This wasn't having sex with a man you'd never had sex with before, this wasn't trying to decide whether to take off your clothes in the dark or the light or how to take them off or what to do after you had taken them off or trying so hard to please someone when you had no clue what he was thinking. This was going to be easy, a breeze. She'd grind Stryker into the dust. And then step on him.

'You're right about Stephanie.' Lily put her arm around her. 'You know, I missed you, Iz. No one in Mauritius knew what I was talking about half the time. I don't know what their problem was.'

'Weird people, those dudes in Mauritius.' Stryker smiled.

'Stop, you two, please.' Isabel put her hands up to her temples. 'This *has* to be a dream. There's no way it isn't a dream.'

'Well, it's time for me to leave your dream,' Stryker bowed. 'Bye,

275

Lily – I hope I see you tonight, when Iz finally wakes up. And Isabel, may the best dreamer win.'

He pulled a cigarette from behind his ear and walked out.

'Hang on a second,' Isabel said to Lily after Stryker had exited. 'I told David I'd never play again. I told David I'd stopped. How can I do this tonight? What was I thinking?'

'Maybe you can stop thinking about David for one tiny second. Izzy, this is exciting. This is something else. What are you going to play for? What are you going to write on the piece of paper?'

'I can't do it, Lily. What if Stryker wants *Party Time?* What if that's what his stake is and by some fluke he wins? I can't possibly do this. I was mad. I was half awake. I have to ring Stryker when he gets back and cancel.'

'You can't. You agreed. You can't back out now. Besides, Stryker will probably bet a night of passion, like in *Indecent Proposal.* He looks a little like Robert Redford. And a little like Paul Newman, too. Actually he looks a little like every good-looking male movie star. And he fancies you like crazy. God, this is so romantic.' Lily sighed.

'He wouldn't do that, would he? He wouldn't demand sex? That's almost criminal. That's impossible. I wouldn't, I'd never agree to that – I don't care what happens.'

'In for a penny, in for a pound. Of flesh—' Lily bared her teeth in a manic smile.

'This is not funny. I can't believe you're joking about this.'

'Oh, chill out, will you? He's a gentleman, Izzy. Can't you see who is the real gentleman here? You bang on about David opening doors and shit, but Stryker's the guy with the heart, don't you see that?'

'No. And I don't see how you see that either.'

'Listen, I'm a better detective than Jessica Fletcher. I've worked out why Stryker McCabe lost that poker game to you before. *He's* in love with you. Remember Peter told us Stryker had fallen in love with some woman? Well, that woman was you. Is you. Why else would he lose the Malcolm party on purpose? There's no other good reason, you know that. It's obvious. And he'll lose again tonight. That's his plan. I can see right through him. He'll throw the game again and you'll get what you want – which must be something to do with *Party Time*, right? He heard about the bad prawns and he's come to rescue you. Sacrifice himself at the altar of love. See?' Lily spread her hands, palms up. 'Easy peasy. It's sorted. Why can't I meet someone like that? That's what I want to know. No wonder Peter was crazy about him.'

'That doesn't make sense.' Isabel shook her head. 'Even if you're right, which I don't believe for a second, why not just come over and ask me what I want from him and give it to me? Why go through a charade of a game he'll then throw?'

'To make it look legitimate, dummy.' Lily grinned. 'So you won't think you owe him anything. It's beautiful. Perfect.'

'It's ludicrous.' No one could be absurd enough to play for affection as a stake, no one could be that emotionally retarded, Isabel told herself. No, he wasn't in love with her, he wanted something. But what?

'You'll play him, won't you? Come on, Izzy. You have to do it. I have to watch. I'll kill you if you bottle out now. Ever since you told me you played poker instead of going to that old bag in Berkshire, I've been dying to watch. And now I get the chance. This is real life drama. What am I going to wear tonight? I can't wait.'

Biting the knuckle on her thumb, Isabel sat back and tried to go through the pros and cons rationally. If she beat Stryker, she could ask for whatever she wanted. But if he beat her, who knew what he'd demand? How good was he? She'd been lucky to win the last game. Would she need luck to win this one?

'I think I have to talk to David about all this.'

'Iz—' Lily groaned.

'No, I do. If David thinks it's all right to play, then I will. I'm going to get dressed now and ring him, then I'll go and see him. I'll leave it up to him.'

'But you'll ring me if you're going to play, won't you?'

'Of course.'

'Because I have to see this. This is crucial viewing. I'd even miss the ten o'clock showing of *Frasier* on Paramount for it.'

'Lily, that's a huge sacrifice.'

'I know.' Lily nodded. 'Especially since I've only seen this episode twice before. It's the one where Niles and Daphne go out dancing together and snog. So what happens when you get cards of all the same colour. Is that good or bad?'

David's flat off Parson's Green was small and untidy, littered with clothes, books, magazines, glasses and ashtrays which Peter must have used. Isabel took a quick look around and tried not to show her surprise. At work, David was invariably neat. He didn't seem to mind her seeing the mess, though; when he cleared the sofa and motioned for her to sit down, he did so without any apologies.

'Where's Peter?' she asked.

'He's gone out to get some cigarettes and coffee. We've had a long talk. I think we understand each other better now.'

'That's good.' Isabel shifted in her seat. 'I don't know about siblings. I didn't have any, except my half-brother and sisters and I've only met them once. But I'm about to meet one of my half-sisters again. She's coming over from California to see me. Sibling relationships are complicated, I guess.' Talk about wittering on. God, I sound so feeble.

'They are, yes.' David sat down beside her. 'You said you had something important to talk to me about.'

'I do.' She found herself plucking distractedly at the cushion on her side. 'I do. David – what's happening between us? That's not what I came to talk about, actually, but I need to know. You ran out this morning without saying goodbye. You didn't ring. I don't know what's going on in your mind. I feel silly sitting here like a nervous guest. I feel as if we're strangers all of a sudden.'

'No.' He took her hand. 'We're not strangers. I've been going through a difficult time lately, that's all. It's no excuse, I know. I'm confused at the moment, that's all.'

'Confused about what?'

'What I'm going to do with the rest of my life. I don't know whether to continue on with *Party Time* or not. Although that decision seems to have been taken out of my hands anyway by a bad batch of prawns. I don't see how we're going to continue the business, Isabel. Everyone will go to *Your Fantasy Team* now. Everyone. I should be thinking of a new career, but what would that be? I know what I *should* do but I don't see how I can do it.'

'What should you do?'

'I should take up photography again.'

'That's what you want?'

'Isabel, it may be what I want, but I may not be capable of succeeding in doing it. Nothing's simple, is it? I thought, last night, that I'd solved all my problems – that you and I – well, it's all gone haywire now, hasn't it? How can I contemplate the future without a means of making a living in it? The prawns have done for us.' He smiled wanly.

'Not necessarily.' She put her hand up to his cheek. 'We can have a future, David. *Party Time* isn't dead yet.'

'It's on a life support machine. What I wanted, what I was planning, was to make enough money with *Party Time*, after the Malcolm party re-launched us, to be successful enough to be able to try out photography again. I could go back and give it one more try, see if I gave it up too easily.'

'Listen, David. It's all still possible. Stryker McCabe came over to my house a while ago. He challenged me to another poker match – any stake I want. If I play, if I win, I can fix everything. We won't have any problems with *Party Time*.'

'Hold on, Isabel. You'd play for the *company*? Is that what you're saying? You'd what? Bet him for *Your Fantasy Team*?'

'I'd make sure he wasn't competition any more,' Isabel said.

'How exactly?'

'I'll show you when I've won. We both write our stake down on a piece of paper beforehand. I'll show you what I've written when I've won. It's fair, David. What I'm asking him to do on that bit of paper is perfectly fair.'

'We have other competitors, too. Are you going to play poker with all of them?' David began to rub his wrist with his thumb.

'They're not serious competitors, you know that. Stryker is our only serious competitor.'

'You told me you'd stopped gambling.'

'I have. This is one game – one game only. And when I win, that will be the end.'

'What if you lose? What will Stryker McCabe want? He'll want to destroy us the way we want to destroy him. What if you lose?'

What if I lose? I won't lose. I have to show David I'm a winner. I *am* better than Stryker McCabe. I don't need luck.

'I'm better than Stryker, David. I've been playing longer. I know more.'

'I don't know.' David looked as if he were digging a hole in his wrist. 'What if he cheats? I know Peter defends him to the hilt and I understand what's behind that, a misbegotten passion, Peter's most bizarre choice of fixation to date, but look at McCabe's track record. The pheasant shoot, and that fox hunt he put on later. Remember? Remember the rumour we heard that he paid off the terrier man? How do you know he isn't going to mark the cards somehow? I'm still dubious about those bad prawns, you know. I think he might have had a hand in that.'

'I can bring my own cards, new decks I've bought today, all wrapped. If he won't play with those, we'll know. But I don't think Stryker would cheat on this. And I don't think he was responsible for the prawns. I don't understand the man, but I don't think he's evil. More . . .' Isabel pondered. 'More playful. Those tricks of his don't really hurt anyone. Not that I approve of them, but they're clever ways to give people what they want.'

'Bribing someone to bag foxes? You call that clever?'

'I don't want to argue about that.' Isabel pushed her hand through her hair. 'I want to know if you think I should play him. Tell me what you think – honestly.'

'Honestly? I'm not sure. It goes against my better judgement. But as I explained to Peter, I haven't always been the good little boy he apparently has always thought I was. I've done some things I'm not proud of. And playing poker pales in comparison, if I think about it. I'm trying so hard to start over, Isabel, to make a clean sweep of my life. Get rid of the parts that were, well, painful. One day soon I'll tell you about the mistakes I've made.'

'You can tell me now.'

'No,' he patted her hand. 'Not now. Later, when we don't have all this confusion. When I can explain it all properly. I'm not sure I can now. I wouldn't know where to begin. I need some time. You understand, don't you?'

Sometimes . . . Isabel thought. The way he pats or kisses me on the head makes me feel like his dog. I wish he'd be demonstrative in a different way.

'I understand. As long as you do tell me.'

'I will, I promise. As to this game, well – are you absolutely sure you can win?'

Show off. Go on. If ever there was a time to show off, this is it.

'Almost absolutely. As absolutely sure as possible. I've won a lot of tournaments, and in tournaments you always play head to head at the end. When you win a tournament at the Empire, you get your name put up on a board and—'

'We are in desperate straits,' David cut her off. 'If *Party Time* could be in a good financial position, if your winning meant that we could get back on top and stay there, then I guess . . . I don't know. Poker? I don't know what I think.' He shook his head slowly. 'Now I'm even more confused.'

'Desperate straits call for desperate measures, David.'

'I suppose they do. And as long as those measures don't hurt anyone else—'

'They're reasonable measure to take. Stryker said that you can be there. You can come as my second, that's how he put it. And Lily wants to come too. We're playing at Micky's flat.'

'Oh, that will be interesting.' David suddenly laughed. 'Maybe I should bring along Peter as well, for back-up. Micky is such a big fan of mine he might take a swing at me when he has nothing better to do.'

'It's so nice to hear you laugh.'

'Well, it's nice to be able to laugh for a change.' He leaned over and kissed her on the tip of her nose, then drew back. 'God—' He put his hand to his head. 'Would you look at this mess? I have to clean it up, don't I?' Standing up, he surveyed the room and sighed.

'Now?'

'If I don't do it now, it will languish and nasty things will start to sprout.'

'I'll help.'

'You will? You're an angel of mercy, Isabel. Sent by the gods. I'll get some bin liners from the kitchen.'

If you're not going to have sex, clean up. That would make a good t-shirt slogan.

Isabel picked a half-empty glass of orange juice off the floor and followed David into the kitchen.

'What are you up to, Y? What's this all about?'

'A poker game. Simple.'

'Yeah, dead simple. What are you playing for?'

'Hey, Mick. That's for me to know and for you to find out – when I've won.'

'You're pretty cocky.'

'I need to win this. I'm going to win this.'

'Izzy's out of practice. You've got a shot at it, I suppose. But what do you want from her? You're not going to . . . no, you wouldn't do that – would you?'

'Now what would you be thinking of, Mick?'

'I'm thinking you might ask for something you shouldn't. Do you get my drift?'

'Sex? You think I'd play for sex?'

'Would you?'

'Well, you'll have to wait and see, won't you? Meanwhile, you want me to help you set the table up?'

'Stryker.' Micky scratched his head. 'I'm serious. What's going on here? What's the agenda?'

'I'm doing what I should have done the first time I met you.'

'Which is?'

'Which is—' Stryker grinned. 'Keeping my cards close to my chest.'

Chapter Seventeen

Lily and Peter were in Micky's sitting room, chatting away, a background noise Isabel found soothing. David, on the other hand, was hovering above her seat, watching, like some bird of prey. She wished he'd go and join the others and let her get on with playing in peace. What she didn't need was a backseat driver who knew nothing about the game inhaling loudly with every bet she made, exhaling with evident relief when she raked in chips, sighing when she lost them. He was more nervous than she was and, although she understood his angst, it was distracting her. Peter and Lily watched as well when the play began, but after fifteen minutes Peter had announced he had no clue what was going on and headed for the sitting room, Lily close behind him.

'David,' she finally turned around and said. 'Why don't you go and talk to Lily and Peter? Or get something to eat. Micky has some ham and turkey slices. Make yourself a sandwich.'

'I'm not hungry,' he replied in a petulant voice Isabel had never heard him use before.

'She wants you to get lost, mate,' Micky announced. 'You watching like this is putting her off. It's putting me off too, if you want to know the truth. We don't need cheerleaders here, not unless they're from Texas and wear skirts.'

'You want me to go into the other room?'

'It would be easier,' Isabel said. 'I'm not used to having someone behind me like this.'

'But I want to watch.'

'Give it a rest, will you?' Micky rolled his eyes. 'We'll tell you when the time comes for spectators.'

It's as if I was having a baby, Isabel thought. And the father is banished to the waiting room until delivery time. She looked at Stryker, who was coolly unconcerned by this conversation. He had been maddeningly nonchalant from the moment she, David, Peter and Lily had arrived, welcoming them as if this were his own flat, helping to get drinks, giving Peter a hug and Lily a kiss on both cheeks. Although he was still dressed in his khakis and green t-shirt, he seemed fresh and remarkably clean. She had chosen to put on black jeans and a long-sleeved white Diesel cotton shirt. The sleeves were rolled up past her elbows, and the shirt hung out over her jeans. In her jeans pocket, at the back, was a St Christopher medal her father had given her for her sixth birthday. Before leaving for the game, she'd ransacked her dressing table for something that might bring her luck and decided that would be the charm. On the way to the game she'd also, to David and Lily and Peter's puzzlement, insisted that they drive to Micky's via the King's Road. She didn't tell them she needed to wave at her newsagent's shop, and when they passed it she did so surreptitiously.

'Why are we taking this detour?' Lily had asked, from her position in the back seat, beside Peter.

'No reason,' Isabel had replied.

'Then why are you insisting we come this way?'

'The traffic is better.'

'Iz? Are you mad? This is so far out of the way we could have detoured via China.'

Isabel stayed silent and waited for Lily to segue into another topic, which she did in the next breath.

Within ten minutes of arriving at Micky's, she and Stryker had sat down to play with the new packs of cards she'd bought. And within five minutes of the start, Isabel knew her hunch had been

285

right and Lily's wrong. Stryker wasn't intending to throw this match. He was playing conservatively and carefully, taking his time with each bet, never betting any huge amounts, folding often. As before, he didn't indulge in small talk, nor did Micky, nor did she. They played hand after hand in silence, Micky's cigar smoke wafting over the table. Occasionally Stryker would light up a cigarette to add to the dense atmosphere, but all the windows in Micky's flat were open and Isabel found that she liked the smells anyway; they reminded her of the Empire.

As soon as David wandered away from the table, she could feel her shoulders relax and her neck loosen up. She was back where she belonged. It didn't matter whom she was playing against or for what stake. It should have mattered, she knew. She should have been a bundle of nerves, considering that she didn't know what she'd lose if she did lose, but she was revelling in the feeling of having human competition again, not the damn computer.

They'd been playing for an hour and neither she nor Stryker had made much of a dent on the other's chips. Isabel guessed Stryker was a little ahead at the moment, but not much. She was happy with her own play, pleased that the months away from the tables hadn't seemed to have affected her abilities.

'Five-minute break,' Micky said, after Isabel had won a small pot. He stood up, stretched. 'I need some coffee. This hangover of mine won't go away.'

'Looks like it's going to be a duel to the death, Iz,' Stryker commented, rubbing the back of his neck. 'Where's your piece of paper with your stake?'

'I gave it to Micky when I came in.'

'I gave mine to him too,' he smiled. 'It's going to be interesting, isn't it?' He stood up and followed Micky into the kitchen. Isabel went to join Peter, Lily and David in the sitting room.

'How's it going?' Lily was lying on the sofa, her feet on Peter's lap. 'Are you slaughtering him or is he slaughtering you?'

'Neither, we're pretty much even,' she answered.

'We'd watch, but there's not much point, seeing as neither of us knows anything about the game. So I'm doing something risky myself – I'm trying to set up a match between Peter and my brother.' She poked Peter in the stomach with her toe. 'A love match, not a poker match. He claims he doesn't want to be set up with someone, but I know better, don't I?'

'A blind date?' Peter sighed. 'If I wanted a blind date, I'd poke my eyes out.'

David, slumped in the chair in the corner, looked up at Isabel.

'I was wrong about this game,' he said. 'It's not right, Isabel. You shouldn't be doing this.'

'A little late now, isn't it, David?' Lily frowned at him. 'They're in the middle of it.'

'It's not right,' he muttered. 'It's all about luck. Luck shouldn't decide anyone's future.'

'Luck usually does decide people's future,' Peter stated. 'Cheer up, David.'

'Yeah, David.' Micky had appeared beside Isabel, a mug of coffee in his hand. 'Cheer up. You were happy enough last night, dancing with the rich hostess lady in the white trousers. Or is happy not the apposite word?'

'Apposite?'

'Yeah, apposite, David. You know the word, don't you? Don't they teach you vocabulary at Eton?'

'I didn't go to Eton.' David glared at Micky.

'So where'd you go?'

'Harrow.'

'I didn't catch that. Say again?'

'Harrow.'

'Makes a fuck of a lot of difference, don't it?'

'I'm not going to apologize to you for the school I went to.'

'Guys, guys—' Stryker stood at the entrance of the sitting room, a Coca-Cola can in his hand. 'We have a game to play, remember? You two can discuss schools another time.' He took a swig of Coke. 'You know, I went to Warwick High School. Our motto was: Fly like an eagle or gobble like a turkey.'

287

'I'd like a scalp massage for Christmas.' Lily lifted her head and looked around the room. 'Anyone, feel free to give me one.'

'What's she talking about?' Micky turned to Isabel. 'Why's she talking about Christmas in June?'

'Don't worry,' Isabel managed to smile. 'Lily has a language of her own.'

What did Micky mean? What was *he* talking about when he said David had been happy dancing with the rich woman in white trousers? That was Julia Malcolm, it must be, but what did Micky mean by 'happy wasn't the apposite word?' What *was* the apposite word? And why had Micky brought it up in the first place? Why did he dislike David so much? Was it to do with class? Micky had played poker with people who went to public school before. He'd rib them, but he didn't attack them the way he attacked David. Why was he picking on David so unremittingly?

'I get it. Turkeys made her think of Christmas. Christmas made her think of presents. Lily, you make total sense to me.' Stryker began to walk back to the card table. 'Anyway, let's go. As Hermes would say, it's time to shut up and deal.'

Isabel gave David a questioning look, then followed Stryker to the table. Don't let it bother you, she told herself. Whatever Micky was on about, it's not important. The game is important. Concentrate.

Micky shuffled and dealt; shuffled and dealt, and within five minutes Isabel was back into the rhythm of the game, blocking out any extraneous thoughts. When she next glanced at her watch, another hour had passed. She was a little ahead of Stryker, but there still wasn't much in it. He was playing well and so was she. Once or twice she had got away with a bluff, but so, she suspected, had he.

'How long is this going to go on for?' David had come up to the table without her noticing his arrival. He was standing with his hands in his pockets; his eyes went from Isabel's pile of chips to Stryker's. 'Is there a time limit? We're all exhausted from the party. This can't go on for ever, can it?'

'It goes on as long as it takes,' Isabel replied. 'You don't have to stay, David. You can go out and come back later if you want.'

'No.' He shook his head. 'I'm staying.'

He retreated to the sitting room and the game continued. The more they played, the more Isabel found that she was enjoying herself. At times she would admire a bet of Stryker's and nod her head in a gesture of respect. At others she could sense that she was playing above herself, making moves she wouldn't normally make, but ones which paid off.

I don't want this to end, she realized as she watched Micky shuffle. When this ends I have to go back to real life, where I don't know the rules and everything is messy and confusing. As long as this continues I can feel safe and secure. How can that be? Gambling is about risk, not safety, but the risks in gambling are known risks. There are set parameters. When you push your chips out onto the table you don't have to put your heart out there with them.

'Could we take another quick break, please?' Stryker asked, sitting back in his chair. 'I need another Coke. I'm feeling a little dehydrated. Five minutes?'

'Five minutes.' Micky stood up. 'My hands are tired from all the shuffling. I need a break too.'

Stryker rose and made his way to the kitchen, Micky went off in the direction of his loo, and Isabel, when she walked into the sitting room, smiled to see Peter and Lily and David all fast asleep in their respective seats. Lily still had her feet on Peter's lap, but she'd turned onto her side. Peter's head was resting against the wall behind the sofa, his legs stretched out on the table in front. David was scrunched up in his corner chair.

'I think I could do with a Coke too,' Isabel said as she entered the kitchen. 'Could you grab me one, please?'

'Certainly.' Opening the fridge door, Stryker bent down to get one, then swayed slightly as he straightened.

'Are you all right? You look pale all of a sudden.'

'I had a not so hot night,' he said, handing her the can. 'Not much sleep.'

'You didn't—? Oh no, you didn't have a bad prawn too, did you?'

'I did, yes.'

'I'm sorry. God – what a disaster.'

'It's not your fault.' Stryker leaned against the kitchen counter. 'Shit happens, as they say. The caterers screwed up. You're not responsible.'

Would I like him if we had met in different circumstances, if we weren't competitors? Isabel asked herself. What was it my stepfather said to me all those years ago? I remember. He said, in his French accent: 'Isabel, you don't have to dislike me. I think you might even like me if I weren't marrying your mother. I'm not trying to take your father's place, I'm only hoping we could be friends. Don't you think we would be friends, if we'd met at, say, a party?'

He was right, she knew. And subsequently they had developed a decent, amicable relationship.

'I feel as if I am responsible.' Isabel took a sip of Coke. 'Stryker – can I ask you something?'

'Shoot.'

'Why is Micky being so aggressive to David?'

'Well,' Stryker hoisted himself up on the counter. 'A couple of reasons, if you want my opinion. First, he's protective of you, like an older brother almost. So anyone he sees you with would have a hard time. I don't know if he has sisters, but I'd bet if he does they'd have the same kind of problems, probably a lot worse. Secondly, David's from another world, you know. I mean as far as Micky is concerned. Schools, accent, all that crap – it counts sometimes. You've got a foot in both camps and you're at ease in both. It doesn't seem like you're slumming when you go to the Empire. It's not like that woman last night, Elvis, getting off on the rough trade aspect. You're for real in both worlds. Not many people can pull that off.'

'You seem to be able to.'

'I'm American.' Stryker threw back his shoulders and saluted. 'I'm different by definition. So I don't push any buttons, you know.

I can get away with anything because I'm not part of the system. If I say something stupid at the Empire, they all say – oh, that's the Yank. We know Yanks are idiots. If I say something stupid with a group like that group at the party last night, they say exactly the same thing. I'm not a threat. David opens his mouth and Micky immediately has a reaction. Upper-class guy, maybe with inherited money – the whole nine yards. Maybe if David could play poker it would be different. Poker's a great leveller.'

'Poker and death and—' Isabel hesitated.

'Sex,' Stryker finished her sentence. 'That's the problem with the party business.'

'I don't think I'm following you.'

'What? I'm talking like Lily? Geez – it's contagious.' Stryker smiled. 'What I mean is, who do we give parties for? Rich people. Those are the only people we deal with every day, all day. Champagne, caviare, expensive clothes, upmarket parties. I know it sounds sappy, but that kids' party, the one I blew up balloons at? That was the most fun I've seen people have at a party for – well, ever since I was a kid myself.

'But that idea I had of giving a kids' party for adults doesn't work. Not because it's been done, like you said, but because it's fake. You can't recreate that kind of magic. Something's lost in the translation. Have you noticed how much rich people like money? The more they have, the more they like it. It's all they think about. Money's great, I have nothing against it. But money's not fun.'

'What is fun?' Isabel sat down on one of the chairs at the kitchen table. She watched Stryker, saw how his face reflected the workings of his mind. His eyes were thoughtful, his mouth was intent, his cheekbones suddenly sharper.

'Fun is being unconscious. I don't mean drunk or stoned or drugged to the eyeballs, I mean being so involved in something you're not thinking about what you're doing, you're hardly aware of what's going on. You know when you get swept up in a great conversation and it turns out you've been talking for hours when you thought you'd been talking for ten minutes? Or when you're having such a good time dancing you almost don't need the music? Or you're playing a sport or a game and you're so involved in the beauty of it, the spirit, that you don't really care who wins? That kind of fun . . . the kind of fun you have when you're having sex that's so great you feel like you're in a whole new universe, a universe that's made up of two bodies and two bodies only.'

A whole new universe? Isabel felt her foot twitch and hoped Stryker hadn't noticed. Two bodies in a whole new universe? I've never felt that way. Is something wrong with me? What makes him feel that way? How do you get to feel that way?

'That's what I mean by being unconscious.' Stryker picked up his Coke can and took a long sip. 'Losing yourself in the beauty of a greater force than your own individuality. Whoa – did I say that?' He grinned, slapped the bottom of his palm against his forehead. 'At any rate, that's my kind of party, Isabel. Those kids I blew up balloons for, when they were attacking me and throwing ketchup at me, they were caught up in some amazing spirit of fun. They lost themselves in it. No booze, no fucking social game-playing. Just fun.'

'Do you think people can have fun on their own, or do they need other people to have fun with?' Isabel leaned forward in her chair.

'Time's up!' Micky yelled. 'Get back in here, you two.'

'I guess we'll have to wait to discuss that philosophical question.' Stryker leaped from the counter. 'We've been called back to the battle.'

'Stryker—' Isabel stopped. She wanted to thank him, but she was aware she didn't know what she wanted to thank him for.

'Yes?' He stood a few feet away from her.

'Nothing. Never mind.' She rose from her chair. 'Back to the battle.'

The next two hands were non-eventful, but on the third, Isabel looked down at the cards she'd been dealt and saw a queen and jack of hearts. It was her turn to start off the betting, and she pushed a reasonable amount of chips into the pile; not too many, but enough to signal she was holding a good hand. Stryker called her bet and

Micky discarded the top cad and dealt three face-up in the middle of the table – a jack of clubs, a queen of spades and a ten of hearts. Those cards gave her the top two pairs, plus a chance at filling either a flush or a straight.

Isabel thought before betting. She thought of the piece of paper now in Micky's possession, what she had written as her stake for this game. For the first time since she'd written down her bet, she thought about the impact her winning would have on Stryker. It was too much, what she was asking him to do if he lost; way too much. No matter how much difficulty he'd caused in her life, she shouldn't have made the stake so big. But what could she do about it now? Throw the game herself? Somehow steal the piece of paper back from Micky and eat it?

'What's happening?'

David had emerged from the sitting room. He was looking weary and frightened and out of place.

'They're in the middle of a hand. It's Izzy's bet,' Micky replied.

At least Micky hadn't bitten David's head off this time, Isabel thought. Poor David, who had to watch, spectate on a game he knew nothing about, one which could have a major effect on his future. Not only did he look tired, he looked old. *He* should have some fun, she thought. Why am I worried about Stryker McCabe when David is so unhappy? I'm the one who put David in this position. If I hadn't won the Malcolm party back from Stryker, there wouldn't have been this business with the prawns. I've put him here, I'm the one who got him in this mess, I have to get him out of it. I told him I'd win the game and I'm holding the hand which might just do that.

Pushing half of the chips she had into the middle, Isabel then reached into the back pocket of her jeans and took hold of the St Christopher medal. Stryker didn't hesitate. He said, 'Raise, all in,' and thrust the whole lot of chips towards the pile.

Doing a quick calculation, Isabel realized that if she called his raise, she'd have only enough chips left to ante up for the next deal. This would be, effectively, the deciding hand.

293

What could Stryker have? A pair of aces, kings? It was possible he had paired jacks or queens in his hand, giving him three of a kind, but that was less likely, seeing as how she had a jack and a queen herself. The odds were against it. Or he might have a straight. But her two top pair was a very good hand indeed. The question was: was it good enough?

Look at him. Read him. Figure it out, Isabel. You should know him well enough by now. You've played with him, one on one, for hours. Study his face.

She stared at him, unashamedly. He was doing a good job of keeping a poker face, but she saw something nonetheless, a look. A look which came right at her, hit her full on and then disappeared. In that split second, though, as she felt its impact, she knew what the look meant. It was a look of sheer affection. No, it was more than that. It was a look of love. They way he'd spoken to her in the kitchen, the way he'd waltzed with her the night before; he'd been giving signals, signals she had refused to see. He must have told Peter about Paul Malcolm's cross-dressing fetish, he may well have been intent on throwing the game last time. He was in love. Isabel recognized the look because she could sense that her eyes had the same sad and fervent shine behind them when she looked at David.

She knew then that Stryker was throwing this game too; if she called him, she'd win. Lily had been right after all. He was giving it to her, yet again, only this time she was aware of his sacrifice.

Could she do it? Could she live with herself if she took advantage of his feelings for her?

Why not use any advantage I have? A casino knows the odds are in its favour in blackjack and roulette and the other house games, and the casino owners don't say: 'No, no one should play these games, it's not right.' It's up to the punters – if they want to lose their money, that's their business. All's fair in love and war and gambling. If I see a man on tilt at the poker table, do I sit back and stop playing or do I go in for the kill with the rest of the players and take everything he's got? I've played against men drunk out of their minds and cleaned up. I didn't feel any qualms about that. Why am

I suddenly thinking about scruples? Poker is about money, it's about winning, it's not about moral ethics. I don't owe Stryker anything. I haven't led him on in any way. We're competitors. And I want to beat him. Of course I want to beat him fair and square, but if he's dead set on losing, that's his problem, isn't it?

'Iz,' Micky said quietly. 'Are you going to call?'

She glanced up at David; his shoulders were sagging, he looked twenty years older than he had two minutes before.

'Izzy?' Micky tapped the table.

She closed her eyes and pictured Stryker on the first night she'd seen him, the vision he'd presented of health and energy, his self-confident, easy grin. Then she saw David, sitting at the table at the wedding, staring at her with his brown, unblinking eyes. She remembered the feel of the back of his neck the night before, how soft his skin had been. That image immediately melted into photographs of Stryker at parties, standing with his glass of champagne, always with a beautiful woman at his side.

Stryker might think he's in love with me, she thought. But that's only because I haven't succumbed to his charm. It's only because I'm a challenge. If I returned his affection, he'd lose all interest. Everything comes easy to Stryker McCabe. Women, business, life. I can't let him affect me now.

When she opened her eyes, she kept them focused on her chips. She watched her hands reach out and gather the necessary amount to call him, she observed them taking those chips and sweeping them into the centre of the table.

'I call,' she heard herself say.

'OK.' Micky rubbed his hands together. 'We've got a pot. Tell the spectators it's showdown time.'

'Excuse me?' David took a step back, as if he'd been punched. 'Is this the deciding hand?'

'It may well be,' Isabel said softly. 'Lily and Peter might want to watch.'

I feel as if I'm taking part in a public execution, she thought. But who is being killed? And am I the one pulling the trigger?

Stryker pulled a cigarette out of the packet at his side and lit it. Isabel couldn't bring herself to look him in the eyes. Did he suspect what he would be sacrificing for her? Did he know how drastic a choice he was making?

Calm down, Isabel. He might still win, however bad his cards are. He could have a dreadful hand, a six/three off suit, for example, but if two more sixes came up in the next two cards, he'd win. He could be trying to lose and end up the victor nonetheless. She shouldn't feel guilty in that case, not really. He wasn't in control, neither of them was. The turn of the cards would decide their fate.

'Whoa, is this the big moment?' Lily came in, rubbing her eyes. 'Will you talk me through it, Micky? I can see those three cards on the table there but I don't know what they mean.' Peter followed in behind her and Micky began to explain to Peter, David and Lily exactly what the situation was, as if he were an MC on a game show.

'Stryker has gone all in, he's bet all his chips. If he loses, he's out. Isabel has a few chips left, but not many. If she loses, she has enough to ante for the next hand, but that's all.

'Now – we've got a jack of spades, a queen of clubs and a ten of hearts showing. There are two more cards to come. Stryker and Isabel make the best five-card hand out of the two cards they're holding plus the five cards in the middle.'

'But then they have seven cards,' Lily said.

'They take the best five out of the seven.' Micky sighed. 'It's complicated if you don't know the game, but that's how it works. They can use one or both cards from their hands, along with any of the five on the table, OK? There can't be any more betting because Stryker has gone all in, so now he and Isabel have to show their cards. On their backs, you two, then I'll read the hands for our crowd here.'

Isabel turned over her queen and jack of hearts.

'Right – Izzy has the two top pairs, queens and jacks, plus a shot at a flush with the hearts. And a possible straight, too. Y – go on, show us what you've got.'

Taking a deep drag of his Silk Cut, Stryker flicked over his cards.

'A pair of jacks.' Micky's eyebrows raised. 'He's got three of a kind. Which means he's winning at the moment.'

Oh my God. Isabel felt her head reel. I read it all wrong. How could I have? How could I have possibly thought he was in love with me?

She looked down at her queen and jack, then up at David. His eyes were lifted to the ceiling; he looked as if he were praying. She silently willed him to look at her, but he didn't respond. Instead he said, 'I can't watch this,' turned and walked back into the sitting room.

'Iz.' Peter came and put his hand on her shoulder. 'Are you all right?'

'I'm fine,' she said. No, I'm not. I'm hurt. Some vain, selfish bit of me wanted Stryker to be in love with me. I liked the idea. Why? Power? The thought that someone could care enough about me to sacrifice something big on my behalf? Was that so thrilling? Yes. Yes, it was.

'It's not over yet, Peter.' Stryker doesn't love you and he doesn't love me either. I'd like to see how he behaves when he is in love. Does he talk the way he talked to me in the kitchen? Does he dance the way he danced with me? Does he . . .? Hang on, Isabel. You're still playing a game. Stop thinking about emotions. Emotions are what got you into this ridiculous situation.

'Right. Now I burn a card—' Micky took the top card of the deck and discarded it. 'And now I deal another.' Isabel saw an ace of hearts appear. 'Ace of hearts. That doesn't help Stryker, but it helps Iz – a lot. If the next card is a heart, she hits her flush. If it's a king of any suit, she fills her straight. And if it's a king of hearts, she's done something most of us only dream about – hit a royal straight flush. The only other way she wins this pot is if the next card is a queen. Then she'd have a full house of queens over jacks, which would beat Y's full house of jacks over queens. So that's what she's praying for – a queen of any suit, a king of any suit or any heart. Stryker would like another ace or another ten but he's also fine if none of Izzy's cards come up.'

'Say that again?' Lily asked.

As Micky repeated what he'd said, Stryker was puffing away silently, intent on the cards on the table.

'So, I discard now – that's called burning a card, Lily.'

'Why?'

'Fucked if I know.' Micky smiled up at her. 'And now – the river. Fucked if I know why the last card is called the river, either.' Micky put the last card on the table. 'A two of clubs – no help to anyone. Which means Stryker wins. Rake em in, Y.'

Leaning forward and gathering all the chips, Stryker pulled them towards him. He didn't look at Isabel; he concentrated on piling his chips neatly in front of him.

'Sorry I couldn't help you, Iz. Couldn't deliver the goods this time to get you out of the hole.'

'It's OK, Micky.' Isabel forced the corners of her mouth to move upwards. 'You can't bail me out in every game.'

What the hell was I doing? That's twice I've played badly against him, made a huge mistake. I would have never made that bet on the computer or at the Empire. What does he do, how does he manage to trip me up? What is it about him that makes me lose my sanity? I was crazy to take this bet, but even crazier to play that hand. Thank God David's in the sitting room. If I looked at him now, I'd burst into uncontrollable sobs.

'Iz.' Lily put her hand on Isabel's other shoulder, squeezing hard. 'It's going to be all right. You've got a little left. And even if you lose it all, I'm sure it's going to be all right. Stryker wouldn't make you do anything horrible, would you, Stryker?'

Peter and Lily, standing on either side of her, grabbing her shoulders, made Isabel feel suddenly preternaturally calm. It doesn't matter, she said to herself. What matters is the way I behave now. What matters is not losing my self-respect. I lost the game but I can keep a hold of myself. I have to.

'Sorry. What did you say, Lily?' Stryker glanced up from arranging his chips.

'I said you wouldn't make Iz do anything horrible.'

'Depends what you define as horrible,' Stryker shrugged.

'Next hand.' Micky finished shuffling, put the deck out for Stryker to cut, then dealt. 'Iz has gone all in on this with her ante – and before you ask, Lily, we have to have antes and keep raising them all the time or the game would go on for days, not hours. Iz is all in, I've now dealt the cards, so she and Stryker turn their hands over again.'

Isabel looked briefly at her cards before showing a four of diamonds and two of spades. For some reason she knew even before the hand was dealt that she wouldn't stage a dramatic comeback and snatch victory from the jaws of defeat. Seeing those two hopeless cards only confirmed her prediction. Stryker's hand consisted of an ace of spades and three of hearts. Within five seconds, Micky had dealt the five cards which ended all of Isabel's hopes. A king of spades, a ten of diamonds, a jack of clubs, a nine of clubs and a six of spades.

'OK, that's it,' Micky announced. 'Stryker wins with an ace high. The fat lady has sung. Time to find out exactly what Y has won.'

'David,' Peter called out. 'I think you'd better get in here.'

'It's over, isn't it?' He appeared, rubbing the bridge of his nose. 'Isabel, you've lost, haven't you?'

I'm not going to cry. I'm not going to fall apart. If I don't look at David, I can keep a grip on myself. Maybe Stryker will ask for something simple, something easy. Yes? Like what? A backflip? A ticket for a West End play? Dream on, Isabel.

'Yes,' she said, staring at the table. 'I'm sorry, David.'

Micky reached into his shirt pocket and pulled out two folded pieces of paper. He unfolded them both, read them and frowned.

'Yeah. All right. Here is what Stryker wants: *Party Time* has to give *Your Fantasy Team* the next ten big parties it has on its books. Parties of over a hundred people. But no charity events. That's the stake. Shit, Y—' He swung his head to the left. 'That's brutal. I mean, that's a lot to ask, innit?'

'It's the bet,' Stryker replied.

'She's on the ropes anyway, and you're hitting hard.' Micky shook his head. 'That's not like you. What's the point?'

'He won.' Isabel's voice was calm. 'He can ask whatever he wants to ask.'

'This is ridiculous,' David exclaimed. 'You don't have to go along with this, Isabel. We don't have to give Stryker McCabe a goddamn thing.'

'What was her bet?' Stryker leaned forward in his chair. 'What was her stake?'

'She doesn't have to say – she lost.' Micky had a mean edge to his voice.

'Go ahead, Micky, tell him. Or I will—' Isabel stood up, stared across the table at Stryker. 'I wanted you to leave London. I wanted you to go back to the States. My bet was just as brutal.' She turned to Micky. 'Actually, more so.'

'This whole thing is ludicrous. Ridiculous. We're not going to give up any parties. It was a mistake, I said so. Gambling is illegal.' David straightened his back. 'Isabel didn't know what she was doing.'

'I knew, David.' She went over to where he was standing and put her hand on his shoulder. 'It's a bet. I honour my bets.'

'I would not have allowed it the other way, either. If you had won there is no way I would have forced Stryker to leave the country. The whole thing is preposterous, I realize that. I was tired, I wasn't thinking straight when you came to see me. I was desperate. It's not on—' He looked over to Peter. 'You see that, don't you, Peter? You can't think this makes any sense whatsoever, no matter who won or lost. It's inhuman.'

'I don't know, David. I sympathize, obviously. I didn't think—' He glanced at Stryker quickly. 'I would never have thought Stryker would make that sort of demand. Frankly, I'm a little stunned.'

'Join the crew,' Micky muttered.

'He's joking,' Lily announced, sitting down on the chair Isabel had vacated. 'You're joking, Stryker, aren't you?'

'No.' Stryker remained in his chair. He looked at each person in the room in turn. 'I'm serious.'

'What the fuck, Y? We've got enough parties on our hands as it is. Why take Izzy's? We'll be up to the eyeballs and beyond.'

'We?' Isabel asked. 'What do you mean, *we*? Are you working with Stryker, Micky?'

'Yeah.' Micky's head dropped slightly. 'I do some things here and there.'

'What sort of things?' she pressed. What work could Micky do? What did he know about parties?

'Actually, I wanted to talk to you about that, Mick.' Stryker stood up as well. 'I won't be needing your help any more.'

'What?' Micky looked as if he'd been knocked out in the first round. 'What're you talking about, you don't need me?'

'Sorry—' Stryker glanced at his watch. 'That's just the way it's coming down. You've been great, but I'm sure you've got other things to do anyway. Listen, I'm beat. I've got to get out of here. Isabel—' He walked over to where she was standing with David. 'Obviously it's up to you whether you want to honour this bet or not. If you do, I know you can find a way to turn over to me the ten parties as described. David, I'm sorry you feel so upset about all this. It's only a game, after all. So, 'bye, everyone. I'm out of here.' He grinned. Stryker McCabe grinned at each person in the room, then turned and walked out the front door.

'Fucking hell.' Micky looked at Isabel. 'Do you believe that? Do you believe it?'

'I don't believe it.' Peter shook his head. 'That wasn't Stryker. That was some clone. He looks like Stryker, but he isn't Stryker.'

'You wish,' Lily said. 'And I thought he was a hero. Maverick. His mother should never have had him, much less named him.'

'What are you going to do, Iz?' Micky asked.

Now she wasn't looking at an accident on the side of the road; she was involved in one herself, yet she felt as if it was happening to someone else. Was she in a state of shock, was that why she felt so unfazed by this débâcle? What was capturing her thoughts was the idea that Micky was working for Stryker. That seemed, strangely, more important than the fact that she'd lost such a huge bet. That and the fact that David didn't want her to honour it. He could say he would have felt the same way if she'd won, but was that the truth? Who was trying to cheat now? Not Stryker McCabe – David Barton.

'I lost, I pay up,' she stated. 'I have no choice.'

'Yes you do,' David protested.

'I'm not going to cheat, David.'

'You wouldn't be cheating. The *game* was a cheat. He fattened you up like—'

'Don't say it,' Isabel interrupted. 'He played fair. This had no similarity to a pheasant shoot. Micky—' She left David's side and went over to him. 'What were you doing for Stryker?'

'A little bit of this, a little of that. I know some people, Iz. They're good with flowers and booze and all that kind of shit.'

'Well—' Isabel smiled. 'You seem to have been let go from that job. How about working for us?'

'Isabel – *what* us?' David threw his hands up in the air. 'What are you on about? If you insist on holding to this agreement, and we lose our next ten parties, what "us" is there? We were in trouble enough as it was.'

'We'll survive. I overreacted. We both did. The prawns won't kill us. Some people might be a little wary, that's all, but one batch of bad prawns won't do us in, not if we work hard enough.'

'How are we supposed to survive giving ten parties to Stryker McCabe?'

'We'll figure it out.'

'You make it sound so simple. You know it's not.'

'No, you're wrong, David. I do know it's not simple. I also know we can do it. If we want to, that is.'

'I'm with you, Izzy. I'll help you, no problem.'

'Thanks, Micky.'

'I'm going to cry,' Peter sniffed. 'You're a prince, Micky. But I still don't believe it. I mean, Stryker. I can't think how he could act this way.'

'You're still in love, that's your problem, Peter. I'm going to introduce you to my brother tomorrow. I can't bear it if you keep carrying a torch for that creep. What I can't believe is that I was taken in by him too. I'm usually a great judge of people. My first instincts are always right.'

'Lily – I have one word for you,' Isabel said.

'What's that?'

'Jack.'

'Oh shit. OK, fair cop.'

'Who's Jack?' Micky asked.

'Have you got a couple of bottles of wine?'

'Yeah.'

'Well, open them and start pouring. I'll tell you all about him.' Lily crossed her arms and stretched her legs out.

'How about if we go out somewhere instead?'

'Whatever.'

Now *I* can't believe it Isabel thought. Micky and Lily? No. Not possible. It can't be possible.

'Can I come with you?' Peter asked.

'Of course,' Micky replied. 'Only we ain't going to any gay place.'

'That's fine by me. I'm giving up sex anyway. It's too much trouble. My heart can't take this constant clear air turbulence. Are you coming, Iz? David?'

'No, thanks.' Isabel looked over at David. 'We have some things to sort out.'

'Right,' David nodded. 'We should get going now, in fact.'

After giving Lily, Peter and Micky a hug and kisses goodbye, and telling Micky she'd ring him in the morning, Isabel left with David. They didn't speak as they waited for the lift. As soon as it arrived and she had pushed the ground floor button, Isabel turned to him.

'Do you now you can make a lift go down faster by jumping up and down in it as it goes?'

David didn't say a word.

Chapter Eighteen

While David drove his grey Audi down the Edgware Road, Isabel sat with her head resting against the window. As soon as she'd stepped out of Micky's block of flats, she had felt exhaustion slam into her body as if it were an articulated lorry. She didn't want to argue with David about the poker game or the business or anything at all. The thought that he might take her home, carry her up to her room and rub her back as she lay in bed was an unlikely notion, she knew, but she had it nonetheless. David was busy drumming his fingers against the steering wheel. She closed her eyes and tried to turn that noise into the sound of steel drums playing on a moonlit night on a beach in the West Indies.

I should have asked Peter to fly me to Antigua, she thought. That was my mistake. I should have played poker against Peter with a flight to paradise as the stake. No way would I have lost then.

'What's so funny?' David asked.

'What do you mean?'

'You just laughed. I wanted to know what was funny.'

'I laughed? I'm sorry. I'm so tired I don't know what I'm doing.'

'That's my point, Isabel. You didn't know what you were doing when you played. I didn't know what I was doing when I let you play. Therefore the bet is null and void.'

Isabel kept her mouth shut. After some sleep, he'd understand she had to deliver on Stryker's bet. He was a gentleman. One of the things which had always struck her about him was his manners. He wouldn't renege; he was as tired as she was, that was all.

How many times have I added those words to a sentence when I think of David? she asked herself. He's having problems, that's all. He's worried, that's all; he doesn't remember, that's all; he's tired, that's all.

'David?' With an immense effort, she sat up, grabbed the seat belt she hadn't had the energy to put on before, and hoisted it over her. 'What was Micky talking about? When he said that about you and Julia dancing together? What did he mean?'

'I don't know.'

'You said you talked to Julia about her difficult childhood. Was that when you were dancing with her?'

'No.'

'So when did you talk about her childhood with her? You were with me the entire night, except when you danced with her, when I went to the loo.'

'Is this a cross-examination, Isabel?'

'It's a simple question. Why are you sounding so defensive?'

In one swift move, David pulled the car over to the side of the road and switched off the engine and the lights.

'David. What are you doing? Why are we stopping? We're in a bus lane.'

'I'll put the emergency lights on.' David pushed a button. His lights began to blink on and off.

'David? What's going on?' She unhooked the seat belt she'd just fastened. 'Why have you pulled over?'

'I had an affair with Julia Malcolm.'

'What?'

'I had an affair with Julia. It's over now. It started in January. Paul rang to talk to me about the party one Friday in early January. And then Julia rang later. You'd gone by then, I was alone in the office. Julia and I met up for a drink, to discuss the party. And all hell broke loose. That's the only way I can think of to say it. I've been waiting for the right moment to tell you, and I suppose this is as good as any.'

Julia Malcolm? No – he was making it up. He was getting back at her for losing the poker game, taking perverse revenge. He couldn't have had an affair with Julia. He didn't know her. They met for the first time at that dinner, at that dinner at Mark's Club, when he'd told them he was getting a div . . .

The same rush of adrenaline she used to get as soon as she walked into the casino hit her. Think, she told herself. Think. Why would he announce his divorce in front of a stranger? Unless that stranger was anything but a stranger.

'Isabel – say something. This is very difficult for me. I don't know how to explain.'

Julia Malcolm? Rich, bizarre, beautiful Julia Malcolm? Since January? And I had no idea.

'Isabel?'

She opened her mouth to say something but ended up shaking her head and remaining mute. What could she say? She was too stunned, too confused.

'It's over, Isabel. It ended last week. The whole thing was mad from the start, anyway. It never made any sense. It was far too explosive, too emotional. We couldn't have sustained it. We were acting like lunatics, the entire time. Having rows, making up, having rows. She thought I shouldn't be in the party business, she—'

'Why not?' Isabel asked dully. 'Does she think parties aren't fun?'

'No, no. She thinks parties aren't serious.'

'I see.'

'Isabel – what's on your mind? Talk to me. You feel as if you were a million miles away from me, not sitting beside me.' He reached over and took her hand. 'This doesn't change anything between us.'

'She thought you should go back to photography? Is that what made you think of it? Was it her suggestion?'

Concentrating on the details made it possible for Isabel to push away the terrible images she was having of Julia and David together in bed, together on the dance floor, together full stop.

'Yes. She thinks organizing parties is . . . is beneath me.' David frowned. 'And although I don't agree exactly, I see that she has a point, that I should have tried harder to do what I wanted to do in life.'

'That make sense.' Isabel took her hand away from David's. 'And you divorced Jenny because of Julia?'

'No, absolutely not. My marriage to Jenny had been a bad one for years. Julia might have played a small part, but she wasn't the root cause of my divorce.'

'Right.'

'You sound as if you're a doctor taking notes on my medical history. You sound so matter of fact.'

'I'm trying to keep things straight, David.' Isabel surprised herself by her own calm voice, her rational thought process. But she knew that this no-nonsense attitude was saving her psyche; if she couldn't be calm, she'd go completely crazy. She stared through the windscreen, concentrating on keeping herself on track, at the same time knowing that track was inexorably leading to a black hole.

'So . . . let's see . . . A: you tell me you've had an affair with Julia; B: that it ended only last week; C: that she wants you to be a photographer, which is what you want as well; D: you and Julia had lots of rows. I would guess when you and Julia had one of these rows, she went to Stryker McCabe to give him the party, to get revenge on you. Is that correct?'

David put his hands on the steering wheel at the quarter to three position and straightened in his seat.

'She thought I was lying when I said I was going to divorce Jenny. She didn't believe I'd actually do it. Yes, we had a row. She flew off to Paris.'

'And then she came back. And you saw her at dinner. Which is when you informed her that you actually were getting a divorce. You couldn't wait, could you? You couldn't wait until you could be alone with her. You had to tell her immediately.'

'I thought—'

'She must have been amazed to see us sitting there that night. She must have wondered what the hell was going on, why Stryker wasn't there after she'd made sure he had the party. I'm not even going to bother to ask why she would have an anniversary party while all this was going on with you. Or why you couldn't tell me what was happening, why you felt it necessary to lie to me, and let me sit there like a stooge, like a sucker, while you two doubtless played footsie underneath the table.'

'Isabel—'

'No wonder you didn't want to have a drink with me afterwards. Did you rush home and phone her?'

'I needed to speak to her, and—'

'How did you do that without Paul knowing? Oh, don't bother telling me. I don't care.' Isabel closed her eyes. 'You didn't tell me about her because I wasn't involved, was I? I wasn't a part of your emotional life. I was your business partner. Why should I know? Besides, I might blab. Maybe you knew how I felt about you and knew I'd be jealous, and so you were worried I'd make trouble.'

'That's not fair, Isabel. And it's not true. I didn't tell you because I knew you'd disapprove of what I was doing, and I disapproved of what I was doing so much myself, I couldn't stand to hear you say what I was already thinking.'

'A secret.' She opened her eyes. 'We all have secrets. What did Julia say that night? She said we all made mistakes. She's certainly right about that one. The only thing I don't understand is why you're not with her now. What was the latest big row, David? What happened last week?'

'She doesn't understand me, Isabel.' Releasing his grip on the steering wheel, he turned to her. 'We don't understand each other. She thought she would divorce Paul and that I would leave *Party Time* and we would then happily live off his alimony money. How could I live off Paul Malcolm's money? I can't do that. *You* know I couldn't do that. When I told her I couldn't, she said I was silly and stupid. I left. It was over. That dance we had last night – I hadn't planned it. I wanted to avoid her. But she asked Stryker McCabe to cut in. The dance was a goodbye.'

Isabel could hear the emergency lights flashing, she could see the lights come on and go off, come on and go off. It was mesmeric, the clicking sound and the flashing. She couldn't think. All she could do was watch the lights.

'You saved me, Isabel.' David unhooked his seat belt and grabbed her hand again. 'When you told me how you felt, I realized how foolish I'd been. There you were, all the time, the person I *should* have been paying attention to, not some unhappy, complicated young girl who can't live without money. You showed me what love is all about: it's about innocence and patience and friendship.'

'And passion?' Isabel kept her face averted from his as she asked this.

'Passion isn't the point. The point is to have a real base, which is what you and I have. Julia was – well, our relationship was a fantasy. It was mad, what we had, as I said. It wasn't real. When I told you I'd done bad things, this is what I was talking about. And now it's over. Like your poker playing. That's why I should never have let you play tonight. We have to put the past behind us, all the things that screwed us up.'

'You know – I thought Stryker was going to give me the game tonight because he was in love with me.' Isabel emitted a strangled laugh. 'That turned out to be a joke, didn't it? Almost as big a joke as thinking you were in love with me.'

'But I am.'

'Oh, *please*. You have a sentimental feeling for a fourteen-year-old girl who idolized you. You were flattered by my persistence, my dogged persistence. You liked the image of it, that's all. You liked the idea of rescuing me that night at the wedding, because what you really want to do is rescue Julia from the clutches of Paul. Only Julia wants to be rescued and keep the money as well. So she's not exactly a maiden in distress. Well, neither am I, David. I'm *not* fourteen years old any more. And innocent? I don't think so. If I'd won that game tonight, I would have banished Stryker McCabe from London. That's not innocent, is it? And there I was spending months sitting and waiting, hoping your marriage would fall apart and you'd finally notice me. Actually, if I'm honest, I probably would have had an affair with you whether your marriage was falling apart or not. I'd say that puts me in the guilty category. Neither of us deserves a white knight, not Julia and not me.'

'But don't you see?' David reached out with his other hand and cupped her chin in it. 'I told you. I've made mistakes too. I'm not innocent, either. Far from it. But I do have limits. For Julia to think I'd take Paul's money means she doesn't know me, she doesn't love me. She doesn't understand who I am.'

'You think I know you? I don't have a clue. I would never in a million years have thought you'd be involved with Julia Malcolm. Not in a million years. And I have no idea what you would have done if I'd won that game. Would you have let me enforce my bet? Would you let me chase Stryker out of London so you could make enough money to show Julia you didn't need hers? Is that what would have happened? We'd take all *Your Fantasy Team*'s business and make so much money you could take time off and be a successful photographer and then go back to Julia on your own terms?

'Or would you have been principled, if I'd won? Would you have insisted that the bet didn't stand? You see I don't know any more. I know nothing. I know a man who sat down at a table with me for ten minutes, fifteen years ago. Who danced with me once when I was a teenager. That's the basis on which I fell in love. That's hardly knowledge.'

'But you know me now, you know me very well. You know I wouldn't have let Stryker leave. I couldn't do that.'

'Really?' She shook her head. 'But you could let me sit there and believe you'd never met Julia Malcolm, you could allow me to worry about the Malcolm party when you knew that as soon as you told Julia you were getting a divorce, she'd give it back to us? You could help plan an anniversary party for the man whose wife you were sleeping with?'

'Don't.' David groaned. 'I hate myself enough as it is.'

'And you don't know me, either. We're two people who worked well together, we gave good parties.' Isabel inhaled, held her breath for a long time, then exhaled in a rush. 'Besides—' She paused. 'Besides, David. Where are the ice cream sandwiches and champagne? Where the fuck are they?'

'What?'

'I'm going.' She opened the car door. 'Go back to Julia. Make up, have the passionate sex you couldn't bring yourself to have with me and then row again. I don't want to be kissed on the top of my head or patted like a dog or spend my time helping you clean up your flat so you can put off that terrible moment when we might have to be intimate. That's not what I want.'

'Isabel—'

'Watch out – there's a bus coming.' She slammed the door shut, and ran behind the bus as it pulled up. She didn't jump on, but crossed the road instead, at a run. I'm still fast, she thought as she ran towards Baker Street. He can't catch me even if he tries. Which he won't do because he doesn't want to catch me, any more than I want to be caught. Julia Malcolm. When was David last in bed with Julia Malcolm? And what was it like? Not like last night. Not like it was with me. I bet he didn't turn his back on Julia Malcolm.

She slowed down, caught her breath and walked as decorously as she could into the foyer at the Empire. Showing her membership card, she then walked downstairs to the gaming rooms. She headed straight for the cashier and wrote out a cheque for a thousand pounds. When she got the money, she traded it in for chips. Isabel didn't even look in the direction of the poker tables, but walked directly to a roulette wheel. There wasn't much of a crowd, only four or five punters. For ten minutes or so she stood and watched the wheel make its spins.

It's beautiful in its own way, she thought. The red and the black. What did Dad bet on before he dropped dead? Was he playing the numbers or the colours or odds and evens? The colours, I reckon. Black. That would be – what's the word – apposite?

Micky saw them dancing. Micky knows. No wonder he was giving David shit. Micky is the only man I can trust.

Reaching out, she placed her thousand pounds on black. The croupier spinning the wheel gave her a quick, interested look before doing his job. As she watched it spin, she thought of David's emergency lights, the flashing red. *Black*, she whispered, putting her hand into her back pocket and taking the St Christopher medal out. *It has to be black.*

The ball bobbled, it shimmied across the wheel, it danced, and then it landed on 22 – black. Isabel left her two thousand pounds on black for the next spin. This time she rubbed the St Christopher medal as she observed the wheel.

I've had my heart attack already, she thought. *This is the intensive care unit. This is what it feels like not to feel a thing.*

Once again, the ball chose to land on a black number – 12. She had won three thousand pounds in the space of two roulette spins. Taking all her chips, she then placed them on a number – 14.

I'm fourteen years old. I'm going to win. I'm going to win something no one can take away from me.

'Izzy?'

Spinning around, she saw Hermes at her shoulder. 'Izzy, what are you doing here? Playing this mug's game?'

'Wait, Hermes, wait. Look—' She pointed to the ball as it spun. 'I'm lucky tonight. I'm going to hit my number. 14. I have four thousand pounds riding on this. Watch.'

Hermes stared at the wheel in action. Isabel put the medal up against her shirt, close to her heart, and held her breath.

'Bloody hell! Hermes cried, as he saw the ball jiggle and then settle between the grooves marking out 14. 'Izzy. I don't fucking believe it! That's 135,000 pounds you've just won!'

Isabel burst into tears.

'Um, Stryker. You have a fax.'

'Sit down, Belinda. Read it to me, please.'

'OK.' Belinda sat down, tossed her head back.

He looked so happy, she thought. Like he'd met someone special the night before. Who met anyone on a Sunday night? Nothing ever happened on Sundays. Even the television was boring on Sundays.

'It says: "To Stryker McCabe, In accordance with our agreement, I have telephoned Mary Jenkins re the party she is holding on 15 July to tell her *Party Time* is unable to organize it for her and suggest she give her business to you instead. Mrs Jenkins will be ringing you shortly. You will see that this meets your requirements in that it is the first upcoming party *Party Time* was contracted for, which is also a large party without being a charity event. I cannot transfer the three reasonably large parties we have scheduled before that date because I feel strongly it would not be fair to those clients to pull out on such short notice. I trust you will understand my thinking on this.

I am working through our list now and will proceed in the same manner with others of that nature which are scheduled in the second half of July and onwards. Unfortunately, as it stands now, I can see only five parties which meet your standards. The others on our books are either medium sized – i.e. fifty to one hundred people attending, or charity events. The only way I can fulfill our agreement, therefore, is to decline any offers of that size when they are made in the future and suggest your company as the alternative until we reach the figure of ten. Does this seem reasonable to you? Isabel Sands." '

Belinda wrinkled her nose and made an unidentifiable noise.

'Yes, Belinda?'

'Sorry. I don't understand. Is this a joke?'

'No.' The telephone on Stryker's desk rang and he picked up the receiver. 'Yes, Laura, put Mrs Jenkins through, please.' Swinging his legs up on his desk, Stryker leaned back in his chair and smiled at Belinda. 'Stryker McCabe . . . Good morning, Mrs Jenkins.' He kept smiling as he listened. 'Terrific. *Your Fantasy Team* would love to help. I'm sorry *Party Time* had to drop out, but these things happen, don't they? 15 July. I know it's relatively short notice, but that's fine. Don't worry. We can handle it. Can you fill me in on what's required?' Stryker reached out and picked the baseball off the top of his desk, throwing it up and catching it with one hand as he cradled the receiver against his ear. 'That sounds great, Mrs Jenkins. No problem. And going the vegetarian route is easy. More and more people are doing that these days . . .' He arched his eyebrows and rolled his eyes. 'Of course, no, it's not a fad, I understand. It's very serious. Of course. Animals are people too.' Belinda smiled when he winked at her. 'Leave it to me. Your birthday party will be a huge success. It will be unforgettable. Don't worry. I'll call you this afternoon and let you know how we're proceeding. The Museum of Natural History? What an original idea. Great. Sit back and relax. I'll be speaking to you soon.'

'OK.' He hung up and took his feet off the desk. 'We have to start bopping, Belinda. Get this party into gear. It's Mrs Jenkins' fortieth birthday, sit-down dinner for two hundred, black tie, blah, blah, blah. Piece of cake.'

'But our schedule is so crowded in July.'

'Hey—' Stryker put the baseball down on the desk and threw his hands up in the air. 'What are we here for, Belinda?'

'Sorry?'

'What's our role on this planet?'

'Our role?'

'Survival of the fittest. Charles Darwin. We have mutated. *Your Fantasy Team*'s genes have mutated in such a way as to be able to handle more parties than anyone else could conceive of handling. We have the rogue party gene.' He laughed. Belinda stared at him as the laugh intensified. What was he on about? He was laughing like a madman, like some wild person. Had he taken drugs last night?

'Mrs Jenkins wants vegetarian food at this party. Isn't that perfect? It couldn't be more perfect. I couldn't ask for anything more.' He was laughing so much, he doubled over.

Cocaine – he might be on cocaine. She'd heard that people on cocaine couldn't stop talking. Maybe they couldn't stop laughing either. What was so funny about vegetarian food? This was sort of scary. She wished he'd stop laughing.

'Tell me, Belinda. What's the weak link here? What's the weak link in a vegetarian party?' Now tears were rolling down his face.

'I think I should get back to my desk. I can hear the telephones.'

'Bells to be rung, songs to be sung!' Stryker stood up, grabbed a pen, wrote something quickly on a piece of paper. 'I'll tell you what the weak link is. The weak link is—' He waved the piece of paper in the air. 'Meat!' With that one word he exploded into laughter again.

Standing up, Belinda backed away from him. He approached her. She thought of turning and running out of the room, but couldn't do it. She was rooted to the spot.

'Could you fax this to Isabel Sands, please?' Handing her the paper, he went back to his desk. At least he'd finally stopped laughing.

'Um. Micky isn't here yet, Stryker. I meant to tell you, Micky is late. Should I ring him and find out if he's all right?'

Micky would sort everything out, she knew. As soon as Micky arrived, Stryker would get back to normal.

'Micky isn't coming in any more.' He grinned. 'Micky is fine, though. Don't worry about Micky.'

'I . . . what's? . . . is something wrong? I mean, Micky is brilliant, isn't he? How come he—'

'Fax that for me, please.' Stryker sat down. 'Now.'

'Um. OK.' Belinda exited and headed straight for Laura's desk. 'You wouldn't believe what just happened in there,' she whispered. 'He's gone mad. He's laughing like a hyena. He says Micky isn't coming back. He's on about genes or something. I think he's on drugs, like maybe cocaine, I think.'

'Coke?' Laura's eyes brightened. 'I've always wanted to try that.'

'You're all mad.' Belinda shook her head and began to think very seriously about quitting. She didn't want any part of an office of druggies. Her father would die if they got raided and put in jail. And how could she explain she wasn't a part of it? He'd never believe her. He always said there was no smoke without fire. She looked down at the piece of paper in her hand.

'To Isabel Sands,' Stryker had written in a scrawl. 'It's a deal.'

Micky was sitting on the floor, leaning against the back wall of her office. As he spoke, he'd occasionally reach out and touch his toes, then straighten again.

'It's easy,' he was saying. 'The people I know are loyal to me, right? I tell them who and when and where and what. They don't care who I'm working for.'

'These people, they're—'

'Legit.' he smiled. 'Yeah, Iz. Stryker was worried about that too.'

'OK.' She rose from her chair, went over and sat down beside him on the floor. 'But it's going to be difficult here for a while, Micky. We're giving six big parties away and even after that we've got four more we owe Stryker. I'm not sure how to handle that.'

'Simple. Someone offers you a big party? You tell them you're too busy, yeah? You'd love to take them on, but you're full up. Make like you're operating from a position of strength, not weakness. Like you're holding aces.'

'Mmm.' Isabel nodded. 'Micky, you're a hero, you know? I don't know what I would have done today if you hadn't come in. I'm trying to keep on top of things, but whenever I stop to think – well, it all gets on top of me.'

'You got to hang on, Iz.'

'I know.'

You Just Keep Me Hanging On. Isabel could hear the music. She could picture David on the dance floor, but as soon as she did, she saw Julia Malcolm in his arms.

'Listen—' Micky gave her an affectionate cuff on the arm. 'I'm a big bear, Iz. And big bears are good at certain things. That's why I came in here bright and early. I can help you out. I want to help. I'm as pissed as you are at Surfer Boy. He used me and I don't like that one bit. You and I can get our own back. We can beat him at his own game if we put our minds to it.'

'It's not only Stryker—' Isabel hung her head. 'There are other things as well.'

'Like the wanker? He's been getting off with the rich lady? I figured. You gotta learn to stay away from the wankers.'

'David's not a wanker, Micky.'

'Yeah, and the Pope's not a pro-lifer.' He paused. 'Never mind. Your luck's changing, like you told me. That roulette win – shit. I wish I'd been there.'

'So do I.'

After she burst into tears, collapsing in Hermes' arms, Isabel had pulled herself together, collected her winnings in the form of a cheque and then fled the Empire, grabbing the first taxi home. She'd gone straight to her bed and cried and cried and cried some more. She'd wept through two pillowcases before she'd finished. And then she'd passed out with exhaustion. When she woke up, for one brief second she couldn't remember what had happened the night before, and, for that second only, she was happy. As soon as she recalled her conversation with David, she pulled the duvet over her head and cried again. The only reason she stopped and forced herself to get dressed and go to the office was because she knew she had to start the long, difficult job of delivering her debt to Stryker McCabe.

Within minutes of Isabel's arrival at the office, Tamsin had come in to inform her that David had rung, saying he wouldn't be in, that he was taking an unscheduled holiday and would be away for two weeks. This news came as a relief to Isabel. She'd been dreading the moment he arrived, not knowing what she would or could say to him. The more she thought about it, the more she knew there was nothing to say. He was a stranger to her; a man who had shared her bed and her body for one night. A man who was clearly besotted with another woman. The way he had talked about Julia was all the proof she needed. His voice, whenever he used her name, was full of longing, of – Isabel stopped on the next word she was thinking – yearning. David was yearning for Julia as she had yearned for him, as Peter had yearned for Stryker. Julia, he had said, was his fantasy. Which made Isabel herself his – what? His second choice. You could win a poker game without holding the best cards, but you couldn't win a relationship that way; you couldn't bluff passion.

To give him credit, he hadn't tried very hard to fool her. His efforts in bed had been perfunctory; if she hadn't been so besotted herself, she would have realized after that first kiss that his mind and heart were elsewhere. The entire exercise had been a charade. It was as if they'd come dressed up as lovers to a romantic-theme party which ended as soon as the clothes came off.

Do I love him? Isabel asked herself. Or did I convince myself I did because of the past? And am I jealous and angry and hurt now, or am I convincing myself of that as well? I had so much at stake in this relationship. It seemed so important that he be the person I end up with, since he was the first man who affected my emotions so strongly, other than my father.

I'm the one who fattened up the pheasant for the cage. I wanted him to fall in love with me; it didn't matter much to me whether he wanted the same. I was so intent on getting what I wanted I invested in his company, I did everything humanly possible to make my dream come true, to win. I would have paid off thousands of terrier men to bag my fox. Only I didn't understand: you can fatten up the pheasants and put them in cages and you can bribe terrier men, you can set everything in motion for success, but you can't guarantee it. Those Americans might have failed to shoot any of the birds or kill the fox in the end. Stryker could have done everything in his power and still ended up with a failure.

I've seen enough parties that didn't work, ones which had all the ingredients for fun, but never took off. The buzz never happened, they never got off the ground. The spark which ignites a party was, somehow, inexplicably missing. And those parties are not unlike the sex David and I had. Something was missing. Something simple like real desire.

Micky had been doing his toe-touching exercise as Isabel's

thoughts had occupied her. He seemed to know that she needed time to think without speaking and she was full of gratitude for his silence.

'Micky? Have you ever been in love?'

He touched his toes again and came back to the sitting position. 'Nah.'

'Really? Never?'

'Nah.'

'Do you think that's because you haven't met the right woman?'

'No such thing as the right woman. You just gotta decide how wrong you're going to go. Like how much you'll put up with, you know? I'm not ready for that yet. Don't get me wrong – it works both ways. I'm not a prize myself. Someone's gonna have to put up with a fuck of a lot if she takes me on.'

'I bet deep down you're a hopeless romantic, Micky.'

'What'd you win last night? A hundred and thirty-five grand, wasn't it? You want to stake the whole lot on that bet?' Micky smiled. ' 'Cos I can't lose, Izzy. Not on that one. And there's a shitload of things I could spend that money on.'

'Starting with?'

'Starting with—' Micky touched his toes. 'A suite at the Mirage in Vegas. Complete with a couple of birds who look like Pamela Anderson and who don't give a toss about romance. Who have no problem whatsoever with test drives.'

Chapter Nineteen

Isabel drove out of the short-term car park at Terminal Four and made her way onto the A30. Turning on the radio, she tuned in to Capital Gold and found herself listening to a song called *He's A Rebel*. Over the past month, Micky had tried to convince her that the old songs were the best songs and she was just about beginning to believe him. When she joined in on the chorus herself, she wished Micky could be there to see her. He'd tease her, she knew, and that thought made her smile. As far as she was concerned, Micky could tease her mercifully for ever. Micky could do whatever he wanted. He'd worked furiously for her, he'd put his heart and soul into *Party Time* from the moment he'd walked in the door four weeks before. Isabel was starting to think that they might triumph after all. Maybe they wouldn't have as much business as Stryker for a good long while, but they'd give him a run for his money. Micky was determined to win, and so was she.

Concentrating on work had made it easier to cope with her tangled emotions on the subject of David Barton. At times she thought she despised him, at others she thought she didn't care about him at all. He'd hurt her, definitely, but she was self-aware enough to know she'd played a large part in that particular disaster. At least he hadn't come back to the office yet, and as far as Isabel could make out, he wasn't going to for a long time, if ever.

He'd written her an e-mail, which she'd received on the

Wednesday after the Malcolm party weekend, an e-mail which was full of apologies for having 'taken advantage' of her and also for having 'no stomach' for the party business.

'I'm deciding what to do with my life at the moment, Isabel, and that decision may take some time. I realize now why you ran away from me and I think you were right to do so. I was wrong to lead you on. I seem to have been wrong about too many things to list. I hope you can forgive me and that some day we can be friends again, if not business partners. I will sort out all the financial complications when I know exactly what my plans are.'

She hadn't heard from him since, but she wasn't anxious to. Julia Malcolm, she guessed, was still in the picture. No doubt she and Paul would be divorced soon; Isabel felt instinctively sure of it. What she hoped now was that she could work out a way to buy David out of *Party Time*. If he wanted to buy her out with Julia's money, well, she'd have to start up another company of her own. Still, the odds were that Julia, hating parties as she did, would make sure David never had anything to do with them again. Which was fine by Isabel. Perhaps she and David could be 'friends' some time in the future, but she couldn't quite envision the prospect.

A sadness accompanied the end of her dreams about David; she missed harbouring those dreams in the same way as she missed believing in the magical powers of that first building her father had told her to make a wish on. They'd both let her down. In both cases, she knew, she'd made impossible wishes, but she felt some nostalgia for an innocence lost. Why couldn't people she loved live for ever? Why couldn't the man of her childhood dreams turn out to be the man whom she loved and who loved her as an adult? Lost innocence and dead dreams weren't going to kill her, but they weren't something she liked being reminded of, either. If David Barton married the ex-Mrs Malcolm, she wasn't going to rush to see the wedding pictures in *Hello*.

Turning left off the A30, Isabel headed for the M4. Being on her own felt a little odd after the week she'd spent with her half-sister. She'd given Shane a huge hug as she saw her off at Heathrow and promised to e-mail her as soon as she got home. Shane's arrival in London had been awkward at first. How could Isabel treat her as a sister or a friend when she didn't know her? They had a father in common, but that was about all, and Shane's mission, to find out more about Geoffrey Sands, only reminded Isabel of how little she knew her father herself. She had as many unanswered questions, although more concrete memories. Together they tried to dissect their father and come up with a man who would satisfy both of their psyches, but after a couple of nights ploughing through memories, they gave up and relaxed.

'There's all this stuff we'll never know,' Shane had said over a bottle of wine. 'I mean, my Mom never figured out why he split on her either – she said she thought they were happy as hell. Sounds like it was the same for your Mom too. And it's not like we can ask Dad. We can make up all these reasons, like him being a kid, but we'll never know. So maybe it's like we should let the mystery be. Or is that too Californian?'

Isabel had laughed then and Shane had joined in, and in that one moment of laughter they crossed into a comfort zone.

'So, Iz, have we bonded?' she'd said at the airport. 'Are we like sisters or what now?'

'I think we definitely qualify as siblings,' Isabel had replied.

'Well, what if I find the others too? How many have we got out there? Five? Six? I mean there are all these children who haven't met up. Should I be in charge of getting Dad's random family together?'

'That's a scary thought.'

'You're not kidding. Maybe I should quit while I'm ahead. There's that one, whatshisname? In Oregon? Jake? That's it. He's like five years old. I don't think he's ready for us.'

'I don't think we're ready for him.' Isabel smiled. 'He's the only boy. He might be just like Dad.'

'Freaky. He's probably in Vegas right now. The youngest person ever to keel over at the roulette tables. In his high chair.'

'You have a seriously sick sense of humour, Shane.'

'I know. Don't you love it?'

Shane had reminded Isabel of her father in strange, unexpected ways. Her voice when she laughed, the way she walked with her toes pointed out, her habit of bouncing a little whenever she was saying something serious; all these mannerisms sparked off memories in Isabel, but none of that recognition pained her. Instead she felt increasingly at ease and safe with her half-sister.

It's like going back in time, she thought. But without the bad bits.

The night before, she'd told Shane the entire story of David and her life in the past months. Shane had listened and nodded and occasionally interrupted to ask a pertinent question.

'Most of us are luckier than you,' she'd commented when Isabel had finished with a description of David's e-mail. 'It's like we all have crushes when we're kids. I had a crush on Michael Jackson, which I haven't told anyone about in my life, thank God, except you now. But it was such a big crush I think if I had met him when I was older, it would take me for ever to realize he wasn't *my* Michael Jackson, you know. You get so illusioned that disillusionment takes a long time to break through all that. Even now, I hear him sing *Ben* and I practically weep. You should never have to meet your hero.'

'You should keep him wrapped up in your own private, secret box?'

'Something like that. Like I said before: let the mystery be. But I can say it again 'cause I'm going back to new-age California tomorrow. And, Iz, one more thing. I noticed something while you were telling me all this. You talked a lot about David and all that wedding stuff, but you talked just as much if not more about this guy Stryker. I don't mean to be a back seat shrink or anything, but that seems pretty interesting to me.'

'I did? I talked about Stryker as much as David?'

'More. And there's something in the whole story I don't understand. It doesn't make sense.'

'What?'

'That bet of his, the one he won. What's in it for him? Oh, I know, he gets some more parties, but the way you described it to me, he was getting enough parties anyway. And why get rid of the man who worked for him? You're saying he's totally excellent at helping you, so why did Stryker dump him? Stryker had no need to bury your company, so why make that bet? Everyone thought he was charismatic, now everyone thinks he's a creep. It doesn't make sense.'

'Not everyone thinks he's a creep, I'm sure.'

'Yeah, but you do. And so does that other guy, whatshisname – Micky. And David's brother, too. He blew off everyone in one move. Why?'

'I don't know. Actually, I've been wondering about that too. But I can't work it out, I can't understand what his motives are.'

And I still can't work it out, Isabel thought, as Talgarth Road turned into Cromwell Road. Why take ten parties? If he wanted to ruin us, he could have asked for them all. His stake could have been *Party Time*'s entire business. And why rule out charity parties? The organizers collect a fee for those in almost every case. As Shane had said, it didn't make sense. Whatever Stryker's driving mechanism was, Isabel didn't believe it was rank avarice. She could remember his good-humoured expression when he accepted her first challenge, his good-natured attitude when he lost that game. He didn't wear ostentatious clothes; he didn't brag about his fancy car or how much money he had. When he'd talked about being tired of rich people's parties that night in Micky's kitchen, she would bet her life he'd been sincere.

Had Peter been so off-track when he'd fallen for him? Had Lily's first instincts about him been warped as well? And Micky. Micky wasn't normally someone who could be so comprehensively conned. What was Stryker up to? He was doing a fairly good job of presenting himself as a devious, manipulative man, Isabel knew. Micky and Peter and Lily were all disappointed in him; not only disappointed but also angry. He was the bad little boy who'd let them all down. But every time Isabel thought of him, she saw him sitting on Micky's kitchen counter and that image didn't match with the hard-hearted business mogul.

That's what made her think about him so often, and must have made her unconsciously talk about him to Shane so much. She couldn't banish that conversation in the kitchen from her brain, or the time before it, when they'd played against each other in such an enjoyable way. They'd been equals, having fun. How had she described him to David that night? She'd said he was 'playful'. If pressed, she knew she'd be tempted, despite everything, to admit that she wished she could sit down and talk with him again, find out exactly what was going through his mind and why he'd acted in the way he had. She couldn't quite bring herself to believe he was out to destroy her business or to hurt her in any way.

But then she'd been wrong about David, so she knew all too well she could be wrong about anything and anyone. Stryker was most probably revelling in his victory and never once thinking of his effect on her. The glimpses of affection for her she thought she'd caught in his eyes and heard in his tone of voice must have been mirages, as unreal as her dreams of David had been.

David's face reappeared briefly before her as she signalled a left-hand turn, and then vanished. Was it as simple as Shane had said – should you never meet your hero? Or never meet your hero *again*? Maybe when that woman had come into the Dickins & Jones office wearing the Laura Ashley dress, Isabel had read the sign wrong. She wasn't meant to call David, she was supposed to realize that she herself had moved on. She wasn't the teenager in the horrid dress any more, she was beyond those days and that wedding. Or maybe she should stop thinking about all this sign business and all her superstitions and get real.

As soon as she walked through her front door, Lily grabbed her and dragged her over to the telephone.

'I just woke up,' she said. 'And I came down and there were tons of messages. Listen—' she pushed the play button on the machine. 'You're not going to believe this? Did Shane get off all right?'

'Fine.' Isabel stood and listened while the first message played.

'Isabel, it's Tamsin. Have you heard yet? Well, in case you

haven't, let me be the first to tell you. You know Mrs Jenkins' fortieth birthday party? On Saturday night? One of those we gave to Stryker McCabe? He mucked up, he seriously mucked up. It was a vegetarian party. Mrs Jenkins *hates* meat, but guess what they served for dinner? Fillet steak! Isn't that fantastic? She's livid, apparently. Absolutely fuming. OK – see you tomorrow morning. Have a happy Sunday – you should now. I certainly am.'

'The next three all say the same thing. Three people called to tell you about the steak. Do you want to hear them?'

'No.' Isabel stared at the phone. 'No. I think I need to sit down. Steak? What's he doing?'

'He fucked up.' Lily began to dance. 'The great Stryker McCabe fucked up in a major way.'

'It's not like him.'

'Who cares?'

Lily danced over to the sofa and plopped down on it. Isabel joined her.

'He's toast – no, he's burnt meat. He's barbecued.'

'The caterers must have been at fault. Stryker wouldn't have made that big a mistake.'

'Like I said, who cares whose fault it is? His reputation will take a dive.'

'Maybe a little dive.' Isabel rubbed her forehead. 'It's so strange.'

'Run with it, Iz. Knife him with it. The bastard deserves it.'

'Right,' Isabel murmured. The phone rang and Lily sprang up and rushed to it. 'More news of the *Titanic* crashing,' she panted. 'I'm so happy . . . Izzy?' she called out after a few seconds. 'It's Micky. He wants to speak to you. You two can have a good gloat together. Can I go upstairs and join in on the extension? No, wait, I have to put on my make-up first. My mother told me never talk on a telephone without make-up on. It gets you into bad habits and pretty soon you'll be going out to dinner without it on and then you're doomed.'

Isabel went into the kitchen and picked up the receiver.

'Micky,' she said. 'How are you?'

'Yeah, fine. You've heard, huh? About the vegetarian meat party?'

'I've heard.'

'What do you think?'

'I think it's really odd, Micky.'

'How odd?'

'Very. Stryker doesn't make mistakes like that. And it's not like a bad batch of prawns, it's an entire menu gone wrong. On a night when the menu is crucial.'

'There's probably some explanation for it.'

'I suppose so.'

'It helps us.'

'Yes.' Isabel wrapped the phone wire around her wrist. 'When's his next big party, do you know?'

'I'm ahead of you, Iz. I checked already. I have it on file on my computer – all Stryker's gigs. It's tomorrow night. A bash some minor telly celeb is giving. You know, one of those blokes who used to be on *Blue Peter* and has now reached the big heights and stars in panto.'

'Is there a theme?'

'Yeah, old classic films. Like *Casablanca* and whatnot. Come dressed as Humphrey Bogart or one of them. But not in drag, no transvestite stuff. Boring.'

'OK.' She nodded. 'See you tomorrow, Micky.'

'Hard to believe Y screwing up like that.'

'Mmm.' Isabel realized that was the first time Micky had called Stryker 'Y' since Stryker had walked out of his flat. After she'd said goodbye and hung up, she went upstairs, into Lily's room.

'Lil, put some eye make-up on, too. Let's go out for brunch and have a ton of Bloody Marys and get pissed.'

'Isabel,' Lily turned, with a blusher brush midway to her cheek. 'You're inspired sometimes, you know that? And after we've finished getting pissed, let's go check out the windows at Dickins & Jones. I'd call that the perfect Sunday entertainment.'

'Have you got in touch with Stryker, Peter?'

'No. I thought of ringing him, but I never got around to it.'

'So you're over him completely?' She was sitting in her office, rubbing the eraser of a pencil against the side of her head to try to ease her hangover. The consequences of a Sunday morning and early afternoon drinking spree should have ebbed by Monday evening, but she was still feeling the pain.

'Oh, I have a sneaking affection for him, I'll admit. But I don't like what he did to you, that bet of his. Which leads me to say I don't like what David did to you either, Isabel. He's my brother though, you know, so it's complicated. I should have rung you when it all happened, in June, but I felt torn. My loyalties are all over the shop.'

'Don't worry, honestly, Peter. I'm all right.'

'I hope so. I have to say, I'm so glad to be out of London. It's far too confusing there. I thought Stryker was in love with you, and then he did that awful thing. And David – oh, God,' Peter sighed. 'People are unreliable. They're all passengers without tickets.'

'You thought Stryker was in love with me?'

'Yes. You were the mystery woman, the one he fell in love with at first sight. That's why I ran off that night. You told me about going to the casino, and I realized you were Stryker's object of desire. I wasn't ready then to deal with it. It was too painful. Anyway, I must have been wrong. It must have been some other woman at the casino. He'd hardly make that bet with you if he were enamoured.'

'No.' Isabel rubbed harder with the eraser. Another woman at the casino? Who? There weren't any other women at the table the first night, and who else at the Empire would Stryker have fallen for? Not Louise, unless he liked eighty-year-olds, not . . . she shook her head, remembering she was in the middle of a conversation.

'But then he *told* me he had a thing for you. Before the Malcolm party. Oh, I don't know,' Peter sighed. 'It's beyond me, this whole business.'

'It's beyond me, too.' Isabel threw the pencil down and dragged her hand over her face. What was going on? Had Stryker been in love with her and then changed his mind? But why? What had she done wrong?

No, stop it, she told herself. Stop thinking about Stryker McCabe.

'You should have taken up Lily's offer to meet her brother, Peter. He's lovely.'

'I'm sure. And Lady Godiva was lovely too. For approximately ten seconds. I'll stick to having emotional attachments to planes. And maybe the occasional cabin crew member. But why are you asking about Stryker now? Is something up? Something I should know about?'

'No. Not exactly. He messed up a party. I'm curious, that's all. He made a major mistake. I was wondering if you were in contact with him.'

'No. Sad but true.'

'I heard Julia Malcolm is going to get a divorce soon.'

'You've heard? God, word travels fast. I only found that out a few days ago. David told me they're going to get married as soon as it comes through and that he's trying to convince her not to ask for any alimony, but he's having a struggle. Oops – that was a secret, I think.'

Some bluffs do pay off, Isabel thought. And now I know my instinct was right.

'I won't tell anyone, I promise.'

'Are you positive you're OK, Iz?'

'I'm fine. I'm busy working. Very hard. It's going well, actually. Despite the odds.'

'Good for you. When I come to London again can I see you and Lily? Or is this another Romeo and Juliet warring families tragedy? Am I banned because I'm a Barton?'

'Peter, I miss you. Lily does too. We'd both be really upset if you didn't see us.'

'Has she found a tennis player yet?'

'No, for a second I thought she and Micky might start up

something, but then he refused to watch Wimbledon with her and that was the end.'

'Romance,' Peter sighed dramatically. 'It's awful, isn't it? Uh oh. I have to fly – literally. I'll ring you soon, Iz. We have to keep in touch.'

'Fly carefully, Peter.'

'I always do. Goodbye, Iz, and lots of love. Remember, if I've recovered from my earthquake, you can recover from yours, too.'

David and Julia, Isabel thought after she'd hung up. David and Julia are getting married. Will they have a church wedding? Some people do, even though it's their second time around. Maybe I can be bridesmaid.

She smiled then and, as she did, felt something click in her brain. She felt her shoulders relax in a way they hadn't since she'd walked into the *Party Time* offices for the first time over a year ago. All that time she'd been tense, nervous, stressed out, and all that time she'd been unaware of the extent of her state of anxiety.

Switching on her e-mail, she typed a message to Shane: Hope your flight was fine, and I'll write at length later, but I just wanted to tell you we are definitely sisters. I have as sick a sense of humour as you do. Don't you love it? Iz.

It was seven o'clock. She put on her linen jacket, locked up the offices and walked home. On the way she tried but failed to make a decision. Should she go and check it out? Drive to Stryker's party and see what was going on? She knew where it was being held, in the Kew Observatory. That was only a twenty-minute drive and she could easily stay in the car park, observing, pretending she was picking up one of the waitressing staff. But why go? What was she expecting? It would be far more sensible to stay at home and relax. If something odd was going to happen at the party, she'd hear about it the next day.

Reaching Roland Gardens, she let herself into the house and forced herself to find a book to read. Lily was out. She could take a long bath and then read in bed. There was no point in going to Kew Observatory, none at all. The kind of feeling she was having about this party was the same as a superstition, and she'd managed to banish her superstitious reflexes. She never waved at the news-agent's on the King's Road any more, she'd put the St Christopher medal back in the bottom of her drawer, she'd stopped thinking about signs altogether. This premonition she had about the party tonight was silly. Stryker had made one mistake. He wasn't going to make another.

And he wasn't in love with her, definitely not. Peter had misheard or misunderstood. Stryker wasn't in love with her and she had no feelings for him either. She wasn't a romantic sap any more and she wasn't about to get caught up in another fantastical scenario just because of one stupid conversation and one dance. She'd done it once before. Once was enough for a lifetime.

She was lying in her bed reading, about to drop off, when the phone rang.

'Iz, do me a favour, will you?'

'Anything, Micky.'

'Come with me to the party tonight. Y's do at the Kew place. I need to be there.'

'Why?'

'Dunno. It's just a feeling I have.'

'I have the same feeling. I thought of going too, but I told myself it was stupid.'

'Well, we're stupid together then. Look, I'll come over to your place now and pick you up, all right?'

'What? A test drive?'

'Yeah, Iz, right. We're going to have sex in the back of my car in the car park 'cos I'm such a hopeless romantic. Get dressed, if you aren't already, OK?'

'OK.'

They were in the car park talking bad beats in poker hands when it happened. People began to pour out of the Observatory, running out as if the place were on fire.

'Shit. What's going on?' Micky got out of his car. So did Isabel. They sprinted together towards the building.

'Look—' Isabel grabbed Micky's shoulder. 'They're soaking. All of them. They're drenched.'

People were rushing past them, shaking water off themselves, swearing.

'What's going on in there?' Isabel stopped a woman in a white satin dress with a white boa. 'Why's everyone wet?'

'Damn.' The woman reached down, took off her shoe and tipped water out of it. 'I don't know. The band started playing *Singing in the Rain*. And suddenly it was like fire hydrants were let off, water shooting out at everyone from everywhere. If this is Simon's idea of a party, he's taking more drugs than I thought he was.'

Isabel turned to Micky. Micky began to laugh.

'Fucking Y,' he said, shaking his head. '*Singing in the Rain*. You gotta hand it to him.'

'Come on, let's go back to the car.'

'He's doing it on purpose, isn't he?' she asked Micky when they were both back in their car seats.

'Not inadvertent.' Micky smiled. 'The bastard. I should have known.'

'But why? If he wants to give us business, why not just throw the poker game we had? He did it once, he could have done it again.'

'And have to leave town when you won? Listen, Iz, the guy is clever, all right? He knew you wanted him out, he guessed your stake would be something like it was. But he doesn't want it to be on your head – you understand? You win that game and you make him go and you're always going to be thinking you were a bitch – you know? Or a coward who couldn't take the competition. This way he's master of his own destiny. And you're not responsible. It's his choice to screw up, and on a great scale. What I don't get is *why* he's choosing to go kamikaze. Why's he gone on self-destruct?'

'He told me, that night of the second game, in your kitchen, he said he didn't think parties were fun. That he spent too much time dealing with rich people who never really had fun.'

'Yeah?'

'Maybe he wants to get out of the business. Like David, but for different reasons. But why sack you, Micky? Why not let you in on it?'

'My guess? He wanted me to help you and that was the simplest way of doing it. I wouldn't have left him, Iz. And, you know, if he hadn't acted like such a bastard that night, I would have tried to stop him from doing all this crazy shit. I would have tried to talk him out of it and make him do something more sensible. Get him off tilt. But he makes like he's a bad guy by taking all those parties off you and he knows that's going to get both of us working our socks off to get even with him. He's making us compete, he's giving us a reason to compete like crazy. He's our target, right? He's the one to beat. He's made us focus – you know? Meanwhile, he's planning to blow himself up and waiting for the right opportunity to do just that.

'I love it!' Micky pounded the dashboard. 'I love it! Turning the hoses on them. Making all these drips drip. Serving steak to veggies.'

'So that's why he wouldn't take any charity parties.' Isabel started to drum her fingers against her lips, then stopped abruptly. 'He's crazy. Micky, you know that? What's he going to do? He'll run *Your Fantasy Team* into the ground. Then what?'

'Who knows? Y can do anything he wants. Shit, he must have had fun planning this.'

'Fun,' Isabel mused. 'And he's having it all by himself.'

'Maybe so, but he's not on his own in his head. He's crazy about you, Iz. He always has been. He'd do anything for you, including giving you that Malcolm party, although I gotta say he did a lousy job of throwing that game. But he's got better at throwing things since then. He throws me to you. And he gives *Party Time* the chance to clean up all the parties now. People will run away from *Your Fantasy Team* as fast as their cheque books can take them.'

'He's done it all for me?'

'No, Iz, he's done it for Tony Blair.' Micky snorted.

'I don't want him to ruin his company for me.'

'He wouldn't do that. What I'm saying is that as long as he's decided to throw in the towel, he wants to do it in a way that helps you out at the same time.' Micky turned his gaze to Isabel and narrowed his eyes. 'Why don't you want him to ruin his company? Don't tell me you're worried about his well-being?'

'That's not allowed?' Isabel turned away and stared out of the car window. 'I'm not allowed to care?'

'How much do you care?'

'I don't know.'

'I think you do know, Iz. I think I was right at the very beginning. I think you're going to break my ailing heart and go off with Surfer Boy.' He paused, hummed a few bars, and then sang: 'Well, it's been building up inside of me for, oh, I don't know how long.'

'What? What's that song?'

'*Don't Worry, Baby.* The Beach Boys. You know, there's a song for every occasion, an oldies song, that is.'

'I'm sure.' Isabel smiled.

The cars around them all began to fill up with partygoers. Isabel looked over at the Observatory, squinted up at the stars and then turned back to Micky.

'You miss him, don't you, Micky? You thought something was fishy all along, too, but you didn't know what it was either. Both of us suspected deep down that that bet of his wasn't what it seemed. We didn't allow ourselves to believe it in case we were wrong.'

'And now we know for sure. So what happens next? Do we sit back and watch him screw up some more?'

'I don't think so.'

'What do we do? Tell him we're on to him? And then what?'

'Well.' Isabel paused. 'I think this calls for some action. Something stylish. Something different.'

'Uh oh.'

'Are you up for some fun and games, Micky?'

'You're making me nervous, Iz.'

'Good.'

Chapter Twenty

'Ed, Table Twelve, you're wanted on the phone.'

'Ed—' Hermes nudged Stryker. 'You've got a call.'

'A call?'

'That's what Matthew just said. Heads up, Eddy. You're not paying attention.'

'Sorry.' Stryker stood up. 'Save my place. I'll be back.'

'You'd better be. We all want a chance to take a few of those chips you've got piled up there so neatly off of you.'

'I'll be back.'

Stryker made his way to the back of the room and Matthew handed him the telephone.

'Hello,' he said.

'McCabe,' Micky's voice barked. 'I'm in the bar upstairs. I want to talk to you.'

'Mick, if you're going to give me shit, I—'

'Just get your ass up here.' Micky hung up.

When Stryker reached the bar, he saw Micky sitting at a table, nursing a beer and smoking a cigar.

He went and sat down beside him. 'So. What's the deal?'

'I'm here to challenge you.' Micky sat back and motioned to the bar. Stryker saw Isabel get up from a stool and approach them. 'We're here to challenge you.'

'Oh, Jesus. Not another head to head.' Stryker sighed. 'Not

again, Mick. We've done it. It's finished. Hello, Isabel.' He stood up. 'I'm sorry, but I can't play you again.'

'It's not exactly a head to head, Stryker.' Isabel sat down. She pulled out a deck of cards from her bag and fanned them out in front of her. 'Pick a card.'

'What?' Stryker stared at her. 'What is this?' He sat down. 'What are you two up to?'

'Pick a card, Y.'

Stryker turned his stare to Micky.

'Is this some kind of joke?'

'Pick a card,' Isabel repeated.

'All right, all right, I'll pick a card.' Stryker reached out and grabbed one from the middle of the pack.

'Look at it,' Micky ordered.

Obeying him, Stryker saw, from the corner of his eye, Isabel quickly tilt the pack up and take a glance at the deck, at the card preceding the one he'd just chosen.

'You looked, Isabel,' he said. 'I saw you look at the deck just then.'

'Now put the card back in the deck.' Micky puffed on his cigar.

'Not unless she shuffles the deck, Mick. This is a set-up.'

'Put it back where she tells you to put it back, OK?' Micky glowered.

'OK, OK, but this is a cheat and I know it is. Whatever you're trying to win off me, I'm not paying.' Stryker put his three of diamonds back in the pack, on top of the card he'd seen Isabel look at.

She's wearing the same clothes she was wearing that night she came here and challenged me the first time, he thought. What's going on here? What are they trying to pull? What are they trying to prove?

'Now—' Isabel paused dramatically. 'Here we go.' She began to turn over the cards in the pack, one by one. As she did so, Stryker reached into his pocket, pulled out his cigarettes and lit one.

'This is really, really stupid,' he said.

She kept turning over the cards. Stryker watched as she turned over the three of diamonds and then kept on turning. He reached up and scratched his head. She'd gone by his card. But she must know what it was. Why had she gone right by it? Isabel stopped. She visibly pondered. And then she spoke.

'The next card I turn over is going to be your card, Stryker.'

'You know it's not, Isabel. This is ridiculous.'

'I bet you it is.'

'God. What are you two on? All right – tell me – what do you want to bet?'

'That's for us to know and for you to find out.' Micky smiled.

'I'm supposed to bet blind? Not knowing what I lose if I lose?'

'You've done it before,' Isabel said. 'We both have.'

'Look.' Stryker leaned forward. 'I don't know what this is all about. All I know is that you know the next card in the pack is not my card unless you've fixed the deck and there are two of my cards in it.'

'We haven't fixed any deck, Y. Trust me.'

'Oh yeah. Definitely. I trust you.'

'Are you going to play or not?'

'Why should I?'

'Because—' Isabel smiled. 'It's fun.'

'Yeah, it's fun,' Micky echoed.

'Fine.' Stryker put his hands up, palms forward. 'Fine. You want to lose, you can lose. But I'm telling you right now, I'm not betting anything. When I win, I'll ask for a drink – that's it. Understood?'

'Whatever.' Micky shrugged.

'All right, go ahead, Isabel, turn over the next card, which will not be mine, and I'll have a gin and tonic, please.'

Reaching into the pile of cards she'd already turned over, Isabel found the three of diamonds and flipped it.

'There—' She pointed to it. 'Your card.'

'But you already turned it over before.'

'So? I turned it over again,' Isabel laughed. 'I said the next card I turned over would be yours. That's yours. We win!'

337

'I don't believe this.' Stryker shook his head. 'What a load of . . .
OK, all right. What do you want? You want me to leave London,
you want me to get out of town? Fine, I'll get out of town.'

'Good.' Micky reached into his pocket. ' 'Cos that's exactly what
we want, Y. Here—' he tossed a plane ticket onto the table. 'Here's
your ticket.'

'You're *paying* for me to leave? You've got my ticket already?
Jesus!' Stryker sat back. 'You two really hate me, don't you?'

'And here's mine—' Isabel opened her bag, pulled out a ticket
and threw it down next to the other.

'And mine,' Micky said, placing a third beside the other two.

Stryker stared at the tickets in the middle of the table, then
picked one up gingerly.

'Los Angeles. Connecting flight to Las Vegas. Las Vegas?' He
looked up at Micky, then Isabel. 'Las Vegas?'

'You got a problem with Vegas?'

Stryker put his head in his hands. 'I need a drink.'

Micky waved to the bartender and shouted, 'Gin and tonic over
here, please.'

'That's a kid's card trick, Y. I'm amazed you didn't know it.'

'I didn't do card tricks when I was a kid – I flossed,' Stryker
replied.

'So, this is the deal. We leave tomorrow. Three days, three
nights, staying at the Mirage.'

'Uh huh.' He lifted his head from his hands.

'Iz here won a shitload at the roulette table a month back and
she put most of it in the kitty of *Party Time*, but she kept some in
reserve – enough for a spree for the three of us in the gaming capital
of the world.'

'The three of us in Las Vegas?' The gin and tonic arrived and, as
he took a long drink, Stryker eyed Micky and Isabel. 'OK. What's
the catch? When we get there you strip me and take all my clothes
and money and leave me in the desert?'

'It's an idea.' Micky turned to Isabel. 'Why didn't we think of
that?'

'Stupid.' Isabel put an imaginary gun to her temple and fired. 'Dumb.'

'What's going on? Come on, tell me. What's the story? What is this? What do you want – I mean really want?'

'What do we really, really want? Y, you should have come to the Malcolm party as a Spice Girl.' Micky patted Stryker on the arm. 'Look, we're hurt, that's all. There you are having all the fun serving meat to vegetarians and raining on that idiot TV guy's parade and you left us out of it. There we were giving kosher parties and busting our balls – sorry, Iz – you're an honorary bloke in my head. Anyway, how come Stryker gets to have all the fun? That's what we asked ourselves. Unfair. So we figured that Laura and Belinda and the girls can fuck up your next parties however you've planned to fuck them up—' Micky paused to finish his beer. 'And Tamsin can handle the *Party Time* end of things, so – presto! Magic. Viva Las Vegas!'

'I didn't fuck—'

'Oh leave off, or I'll knock your head off. We know what you're up to, Y. Don't bluff two bluffers.' Micky nudged Isabel. 'Tell him to leave off, Izzy.'

'Leave off, Stryker.'

'OK, I'll leave off.' Stryker took a puff on his cigarette and, as he exhaled, he smiled. 'You're for real on this, aren't you?'

'You bet.'

'Isabel—' Stryker turned to her. 'What about you? I mean, what does David think of this?'

'David's not at the table.'

Stryker turned back to Micky with a puzzled expression.

'She means David isn't playing, Y. David has folded his cards and left the room. He ain't in the game any more.'

'Ah.' Stryker switched his gaze again and studied Isabel, then stubbed out his cigarette.

'You don't look entirely heartbroken.'

'That might be because I'm not.'

'Ah.'

'So are you in, Y?'

Stryker sat forward. He dragged one of the tickets from the middle of the table towards him and lifted it a fraction of an inch. Staring at it for a few seconds, he then let it drop.

'I'm in,' he said.

Isabel found him sitting at the bar, smoking a cigarette. She pulled herself up on the stool next to his.

'Why did you leave?' she asked. 'You were hitting some fantastic cards.'

'I don't know.' Stryker pushed his hand through his blond hair. 'I didn't feel like playing any more. We're going back tomorrow night. I have to think about that I'm doing. Whether I pack up, come back here to the States, what I do if I do come back, all these—' he lowered his voice and whispered dramatically. 'Life questions. Would you like something to drink, by the way? That's another crucial life question.'

'Maybe later. Are you really thinking of moving back? To New York?'

'Who knows? But it feels good, being back. At least I understand the language.' He smiled.

'What about *Your Fantasy Team?*'

'Well—' Stryker pushed an ice cube down into his gin and tonic and watched it pop up again. 'I'm not sure. I've been thinking about that. I like making fantasies come true. The parties I liked the best? They were the ones where I played a little fast and loose. Where my fellow countrymen were amazed at their pheasant-shooting abilities or fox-hunting success. In cases like that, I helped make a dream come true. I didn't just get the right champagne. So, and don't laugh when I say this, please, Iz. I was thinking I might shift my line of work.'

'To what?'

'You know that organization, I'm not sure what it's called, something like Make A Wish? The one that helps sick kids go to Disneyland or meet their favourite football star? I was thinking my skills, as such, could be useful to organizations like that.'

'You're serious?'

'I asked you not to laugh.'

'I'm not laughing, Stryker.'

'Look, I'm not trying to be a hero or anything. I need to make a living. But instead of helping businessmen shoot pheasants, I could help sick kids meet Micky Mouse. I was just thinking about it, that's all. But I don't know if I'd like to do it because I'd like to do it or because it makes me seem more serious. That's the problem. I'm not sure what my motives are.'

'Does it matter?'

'Doesn't it? If I want to do something worthwhile because it makes me sound good, doesn't that also make me a fake?'

'Don't you think everyone who does something to help others gets at least a tiny little feeling of self-satisfaction at the same time? Does that mean they shouldn't do it?'

'I don't know. That's one of those questions you talk about all night at college, or so I've heard. I was too busy giving parties at college to discuss philosophy.'

'We're back to philosophy again. Remember our philosophical discussion on the nature of fun at Micky's? We never got a chance to finish it. I've been thinking about that a lot, about some of the things you said then. Anyway, I think Las Vegas is the perfect place to be philosophical in.'

'It is, indeed.' Stryker nodded. 'I think it has something to do with all these slot machines. I'm sure they hold the key to the meaning of life in some way, but I haven't figured it out yet. So what are *your* philosophical thoughts here in the Mecca of profundity?'

'Mine? Well, I've been wondering whether I'm a gambling addict or whether I simply like to play poker. At the moment I can't seem to decide. When I stopped going to the Empire, I played poker constantly on the computer. And that makes me think I'm hooked. But then I don't *feel* like an addict. I don't see myself losing my house or ending up a broke, desperate woman forced into a life of crime to keep up her habit. Still, when I think about those games with you, how big the stakes were, how I was trying to get rid of you and make you move out of London, I don't know. That seems fairly excessive behaviour to me at the moment. More than excessive. Completely out of control, actually.'

'We were both involved. We both liked the challenge, I guess.'

'We were outrageous.'

'I know.' Stryker nudged her with his elbow. 'Don't you think that's kind of great?'

Isabel asked the bartender for a beer before she answered.

'I think we were both mad, in different ways. I don't know if that's great or unbelievably silly.'

'For what it's worth, Izzy, I don't think you're an addict. You like to compete, you like this particular sport and it happens to involve betting. But you also have a life outside of it. Friends and a job and all that serious stuff. Poker is your fun.'

'When I thought I'd lost to you that first time we played head to head, it didn't feel like fun.'

'No.' Stryker shrugged. 'I could see that.'

'I was a bad sport then, wasn't I?'

'You were a little freaked out.'

Taking a sip of the beer which had just been put down in front of her, Isabel tilted her head.

'I thought I had to win for David's sake. Little did I know the party was going to be ours anyway. Did Julia Malcolm tell you why she wanted you to have it instead of us?'

'No. She said she had heard about *Your Fantasy Team* from a friend of hers or something. I didn't really care at that point why she came to see me. I was glad she had, that's all. But it looks like I was used in the game she was playing. As Hermes would say, I was a mug.'

'Not as much of a mug as I was.'

'I'm sorry. I mean I'm sorry about the way things worked out. Julia and . . .' Stryker's voice tapered off.

'Julia and David. You can say it. I won't dissolve in a heap. We're having a philosophical discussion, remember? I can talk about it philosophically now. You know, I had no idea what was going on, I didn't read the people properly. And I'd always thought I was so good at that, reading people, working out quickly what kind of a person someone was. But it looks like the only place I could do that was at a poker table, and even there I made mistakes. I never thought David was someone who'd have an affair with a woman like Julia, but then I had this picture of David in my mind which I more or less superimposed on the real David. And I had another picture of you. And that picture doesn't fit either.'

'No?'

'Stryker—' Isabel laughed. 'Are you fishing for compliments by any chance?'

'God, no.'

'Then why are you blushing?'

'Where's Mick?' He shifted in his seat and looked to the entrance of the bar. 'Where's he gone?'

'He's probably out chasing Baywatch babes or else bluffing with a nine/three off suit. Stryker—'

'Have you ever talked to him about his boxing career?'

'Do you mean have I ever challenged him about it? Asked if it was real? No. Have you?'

'No. Are you ever going to?'

'No. Are you?'

'No. I think we're wise not to.' Stryker pushed his ice cube again. 'It's his business.'

'Exactly.' Isabel nodded. 'Sometimes I think he works for MI5 or MI6.'

'You're kidding?'

'That's *my* fantasy.'

'It's a great one. I love it.'

'You know,' she leaned back, studying his face. 'You're grinning in exactly the same way you grinned when you first came into the Empire.'

'When you phoned me to tell me the guy was cheating.'

'Yes.'

343

'Why'd you do that? Why did you let me know what was happening?'

'It seemed the right thing to do.'

'You felt sorry for me, didn't you?'

'No, I thought you were a cocky idiot.'

'Oh.' He finished his gin and tonic and stared at the bottom of the glass.

'Aren't you going to ask me what I think of you now?'

'Isabel?'

'Yes?'

'Are you making fun of me?'

'Would I do that?'

'Yeah.' Stryker reached back and rubbed his neck. 'You might. I don't know. I can't figure you out. Is something going on here? I mean, between us? It feels like during this trip you might have, I mean, we might have . . . oh shit. Am I being an idiot again?'

'He's a rebel and he never, never does what he should,' Isabel sang.

'Whoa.' Stryker shook his head as if he were trying to clear it. 'Where did that come from? Is that one of Micky's old favourites?'

'It's my favourite.'

'Right. OK. Are you . . .? I mean, have you had a lot to drink or something?'

'Or something,' Isabel smiled. 'You know, I don't think you should worry about your motives, Stryker. Everyone has motives. You'd be good at making children's dreams come true. That's what's important, that you'd be good at it.'

'Easier than making grown-up dreams come true, right?'

'I don't know.' Isabel twirled on her barstool. 'Making anyone's dream come true is fairly difficult.'

'So what's *your* dream now, Iz?'

'Oh, I'm fairly grounded in reality these days.' She took another sip of beer and then wiped her mouth with the back of her hand.

'No dreams at all?'

'Maybe one.' She picked up her beer, finished it in a long swig

344

and got off the stool. 'Unconsciousness.'

'OK, I get the picture.' Stryker rose as well. 'Philosophy class is over. Time to get some sleep. I *am* being an idiot. Looks like sometimes I read things wrong too.'

Stryker paid the bill and they walked together to the bank of elevators.

'You know,' Isabel looked up at him with a pensive expression as they stood waiting. 'I haven't beaten you since that hand in the Empire, the first night you were there. You threw, or you tried to throw, the first head to head game we had, so it doesn't count, and you won the next one. If you bow out of *Your Fantasy Team*, I won't get a chance to compete with you in the business arena either. I'm going to miss that.'

'You're going to miss having me as Public Enemy Number One?' Stryker frowned.

A ping sounded and the elevator door opened in front of them.

'So,' Stryker said, stepping in after Isabel. 'Up to our beautiful Las Vegas hotel rooms. Do you have a view in yours?'

'I have a fantastic view of the television set.'

Stryker pulled out his key from his jacket pocket and hit the button for the twelfth floor.

'I hate these plastic keys,' he said. 'A fact which I'm sure must be of huge interest to you.'

Isabel reached out, pushed the '28' button and said: 'Raise.'

'Raise?'

'Raise. I raise you sixteen floors, Stryker.'

'What happens if I call?'

'Now you *are* being an idiot.'

The door opened on the twelfth floor. Stryker took a step towards it, then stopped.

'An idiot?' He put his hand out to keep the door from closing. 'You know I'm going to re-raise when we get there, Izzy.'

'Fine by me, Ed.'

He took his hand away and the door closed.

Isabel grinned.